DAMAGED GOODS

Helen Black was brought up in a mining town in West Yorkshire. She moved to London in her twenties and trained to be a commercial lawyer. On qualification she shifted lanes and has practised criminal and family law for over ten years. She specialises in representing children in the care system. She now lives in Bedfordshire with her husband and young children.

For further information on Helen Black, visit her website at www.hblack.co.uk.

HELEN BLACK

Damaged Goods

AVON

AVON
A division of HarperCollins*Publishers*
77–85 Fulham Palace Road,
London W6 8JB

www.harpercollins.co.uk

This paperback original 2012

3

First published in Great Britain by
HarperCollins*Publishers* 2008

Copyright © Helen Black 2008

Helen Black asserts the moral right to
be identified as the author of this work

A catalogue record for this book is
available from the British Library

ISBN-13: 978-0-00-750280-6

Set in Minion by Palimpsest Book Production Limited,
Falkirk, Stirlingshire

Printed and bound in Great Britain by
Clays Ltd, St Ives plc

MIX
Paper from
responsible sources
FSC® C007454

It's a truism but true nonetheless that books are not the work of one person. So I'd like to thank the following for their help along the way.

First call must be to the Buckman Gang – Peter, Rosie and Jessica who plucked my tatty script out of the slush pile and were prepared to give it and me a chance.

Then, of course, everyone at HarperCollins for taking a punt on a first timer – particularly Max and Kesh for their humour and patience.

Thanks to Peter Marshall for friendship through the years and for advice on criminal procedure.

A big shout out to the members of HUG especially David Stacey and Michael Crawshaw – without your honest tongue lashings and generous encouragement I wouldn't have finished this book.

Thanks is also due to the BW Mums whose ability to laugh at themselves made *Damaged Goods* much funnier than I could have done on my own.

Finally I owe a huge debt of gratitude to my family. My Dad for giving me my love of books. My Mum for assuming I would never be ordinary. My children for reminding me every day how lucky I am.

Then there's Andrew. Husband, best friend. When I mentioned I might like to write a book you didn't laugh. You bought me a lap top.

To Andrew

There are over 60,000 children being 'looked after' by the state in the UK.

One third of the homeless in this country were raised in care.

Sixty per cent of young offenders in this country have been through the care system.

Dear Mum,

I can't believe you did this to us. You always said that no matter how bad it got we'd have each other.

You said we'd always be together.

We did everything we had to.

I even kept my mouth shut when I knew I shouldn't.

And what was it all for? You've thrown us away like rubbish so that's how they treat us. We've been split up and I'm not even allowed to see the babies.

I can't tell you how much I hate you for what you've done, and if I ever see you again I'll cut you to pieces.

Kelsey

PROLOGUE

Grace worried the kitchen surface with the corner of a J-cloth, trying once again to remove a mark made years before by a hot spoon. The phone call had unnerved her and her hands shook. She bent over the cooker and lit another cigarette on the gas ring, hoping it would calm her. It didn't. What she needed was a hit. A £10 bag would do, just enough to put her in a better place, just enough to allow her to explain things properly. To make herself clear. Just one hit to get through this.

She checked her watch. Five past eight. That should give her ten minutes, enough time to race downstairs to the dealer on the ground floor. He charged over the odds but what could you do?

The tap on the door was soft but Grace jumped all the same. No time to get the brown now, this was one conversation she would have to do straight.

She took a last deep drag on the cigarette and answered the door. 'Oh, it's you.'

'Who were you expecting?'

Grace shrugged.

Outside, a dog scratched and barked.

'Get out of it,' Grace yelled.

'It's probably hungry.'

'Aren't they all,' said Grace, and turned on her heels. 'Shut it behind you, it's fucking freezing.'

'Hardly. Are you clucking?'

Grace rubbed her arms, their skin barely able to support the scars that ran like the rungs of a ladder from shoulder to wrist. 'Not really.'

'I thought you'd be back on the gear.'

'Sorry to disappoint you.'

'I don't really care one way or the other.'

Grace sighed and picked up her cigarettes. When this was over she'd have that hit, get completely out of it. She clamped a cigarette between her lips and turned to the cooker. In one sweeping and familiar action she bent over the front gas ring, one hand holding back her hair, the other reaching for the ignition. But before her finger pressed the button she felt the back of her head explode.

Grace was confused. Had she finally got her hit? Funny, she couldn't remember cooking up. She anticipated the melting sensation that the drugs would bring when they moved through her bloodstream.

Instead, the back of her neck felt warm and wet. As dazed as she was, she knew it was blood.

'Why did you . . . '

There was another explosion and everything went black.

CHAPTER ONE

Monday, 7 September

Lilly Valentine thumped the photocopier. 'Stupid piece of shit.'

'You'll break that.'

She yanked at the tray where her document was stuck.

Her boss floated to Lilly's side. 'I said you'll . . . '

'It's already sodding broken.'

Rupinder's deft fingers removed the tray in a tinkle of bangles and dislodged the offending piece of paper. 'You're late,' she said.

'I operate on Indian standard time,' Lilly said. 'As you're so fond of telling me.'

Rupinder opened the front door. 'Which is fine in Delhi . . . '

Lilly struggled outside, balancing three files, a mobile phone and her bag. She tossed her head to move the curtain of curls that had fallen into her eyes.

Rupinder shook her head and tucked the loose tendrils behind Lilly's ears. ' . . . but this is Hertfordshire.'

Lilly winked at her boss and stumbled towards her car.

She sped through Harpenden towards Luton. Bespoke shoe shops and upmarket gastro pubs soon gave way to pawnbrokers and kebab shops. The women on the streets no longer carried designer handbags and all-white floral arrangements, instead they pushed double buggies laden with bumper packs of nappies. Further still into the sprawling housing estates of Ring Farm and windows were boarded, overgrown gardens housed old sofas, and cars stood on bricks.

Eventually she pulled into a cul-de-sac overshadowed on three sides by granite tower blocks. Even on glorious days like today, at the height of a summer stretching into autumn, scarcely any sunlight fed through and The Bushes Residential Unit for Young People existed in permanent gloom.

Lilly parked in the shadows and pulled out the relevant file from the pile stacked beside her on the passenger seat.

BRAND, K. – CARE PROCEEDINGS

Kelsey Brand, eldest of four girls. Their mother, a heroin addict who funded her habit by prostitution, and was unable or unwilling to clean up, had finally given up the distracting charade of parenting and placed all four girls in care.

So far so familiar.

Lilly reached for some chocolate. She'd sworn to restrain herself to a bar a day, two in dire emergencies, in an attempt to stop the slide from sexy size twelve to pleasantly plump. As she bit into her first Twix of the day she smoothed her hands over her hips. Still the right side of curvy. Just.

She skimmed the pages in search of the ETF. Every case had one. An especially awful aspect that lawyers like Lilly looked for. Something to set their client apart, to prevent them from becoming '*just another kid in care*'. Something to remind the professionals that although they dealt with these stories every day of the week they weren't commonplace.

She found it on the last page – her search made easier by the lack of detailed notes – and it was tremendous. An all-singing, all-dancing *Extra Tragedy Factor*. Kelsey Brand, at fourteen years of age, had tried to kill herself by drinking a bottle of bleach.

Lilly closed her eyes and swallowed the chocolate. It stuck in her throat with a peppery sting as she tried not to imagine how Domestos might taste. She pictured herself instead as a corporate lawyer in a smart office overlooking St Paul's Cathedral in the heart of the city. Dressed in a black Armani suit, which fitted snugly but not tightly over her hips, she crossed a plant-filled atrium, her high heels clicking on the marble floor. Tap, tap, tap.

The heels dissolved as Lilly focused on the doughy twelve-year-old who was rapping day-glo talons against the car window.

'You on drugs?'

Lilly ignored her and got out.

'Got any fags?'

'Not for you,' answered Lilly.

The girl spat on the ground, inches from Lilly's feet.

7

Lilly appraised her with practised cool and nodded at the silver boob tube which threatened to release a small pair of spotty breasts. 'Been auditioning for a porn movie, Charlene?'

'You've got a big mouth.'

'All the better to eat you with, my dear.'

When Lilly got to the door she tossed a packet of Marlboro Lights to the girl.

'You ain't so tough,' Charlene said.

'Wanna bet?'

Lilly stepped inside the unit. It was buzzing. Most of its residents had just returned from their 'morning education session', along with all the pupils that had been excluded from every school in the area. Nearly all the kids in The Bushes went there for a couple of hours a day – if they learned anything it was a bonus. Lilly, who had represented at least half of the young people in The Bushes, was greeted with waves and requests for cash or cigarettes.

'Who're you here for, Miss?'

'Kelsey Brand,' said Lilly.

'Nutter,' came the chorus, and several boys pretended to drink from imaginary bottles.

'Enough of that.'

'She's well weird,' a boy in a baseball cap shouted, his left eye quivering in its socket.

Lilly rubbed his shoulder in long strokes to soothe away both the twitch and the habitual beatings he had suffered at the hands of an alcoholic stepfather, now serving life for setting the boy's mother on fire while she fed their six-week-old baby.

'We're all weird here, Jermaine, it's why we get on so well.'

Despite her bravado Lilly felt trepidation as she passed along the corridor to room twelve. Self-abusers didn't usually threaten Lilly's equanimity. Headbangers, cutters, anorexics, Lilly had worked with them all, but drinking bleach was so extreme. The girl must have been in the depths of wretchedness to punish herself like that.

The last kid in room twelve had been Irina, the daughter of a deported asylum-seeker. Attractive and well-educated, she had been easy to place with a middle-class foster family. Lilly fingered the soapstone pin she wore at the back of her lapel. It was smooth and cool to the touch. Irina had given it to Lilly on the final day of the court hearing when she learned she was not being sent back to a village torn apart by civil war.

Would the present occupant be so lucky? There was nothing to be done about Kelsey's family. If the mother didn't want her kids then no one could force her to take them back. Getting her out of The Bushes and fostered would be the next best thing, but placements for those fond of cleaning fluid were hard to come by. Lilly would give it her best shot but the question was whether her client would have the stomach for the road ahead.

Lilly knocked three times and waited. She gave the girl sufficient time to hide any contraband and let herself in.

'Hi there. I'm Lilly Valentine.'

The girl sat on her bed and hugged her knees. Her chin was tucked into her chest and her lank hair, the colour of pee, fell like a greasy mask, obscuring Kelsey's face. Her frame was so slight she reminded Lilly of a small bird hiding under her wing.

Lilly smiled and gestured to the bare walls. 'I love what you've done to the place.'

No reaction.

Lilly softened her tone. 'Can I sit down?'

The nod was almost imperceptible but Lilly caught it and sat on the bed next to her client.

'I'm sure someone's told you that social services have applied for a Care Order because your mum can't look after you.'

Kelsey retracted further. It was as if she were trying to implode.

'When we go to court it's my job to tell the judge what you want,' Lilly said.

Kelsey didn't move.

'I have to at least know that you understand what's happening to you,' said Lilly. 'If you can't face going to court that's fine. We can just write it all down in a statement.'

She reached towards her client, slid her fingers under Kelsey's chin and gently lifted her face.

What Lilly saw made her reel. The bleach had burnt off most of the skin from Kelsey's lips and chin and revealed a red-brown layer like days-old meat. Lilly flinched, but forced her gaze to remain on the child's damaged face.

'I can do all the talking, Kelsey.' She swallowed hard. 'But you have to tell me what to say.'

As her eyes locked with Kelsey's, Lilly flinched again. In fifteen years of practice she was unable to remember the last time she had seen such utter hopelessness.

'Speak to me, please.'

The noise when it came was somewhere between a choke and a sob. A strangled sound from the depths of Kelsey's throat. Lilly's heart beat loud in her chest as she realised her client could not speak.

Lilly shut the door to room twelve and hurried towards the kitchen to make coffee. She could still taste the cold void in Kelsey's eyes and needed to warm her mouth. Her chest was pounding as she filled the kettle. How the hell was she going to help Kelsey?

She opened the catering-sized tin of instant granules that sat on the otherwise empty and clean work surface. Presumably it was too big to fit in any of the cupboards. When she opened one she couldn't help but smile. The mugs, although a ragtag band of misfits, stood to military attention. When Lilly removed one, the space it left jarred to such an extent that even Lilly was moved to rearrange the others. In this place of chaos and ripped lives order was paramount; the comfort it gave immeasurable.

Lilly smiled again. It was going to be a hard case but she'd find a way. She always did.

Behind her someone was eating a bowl of cereal. The crunching was deafening. Lilly turned and saw Charlene, Rice Krispies dotting her pubescent cleavage.

'Don't you want some milk on those?' Lilly asked.

'I'm a vegan,' answered Charlene.

'What?'

'It means I don't eat animal products.'

'I know what it means.'

Crunch, crunch.

'I didn't know you were into animal rights,' said Lilly.

'I'm not. I just like to piss 'em off.'

Lilly chuckled and crossed the hall to the cramped and untidy manager's office, where a middle-aged black woman was hunched in front of a computer. She was typing laboriously with two fingers.

'You're too old for this crap, Miriam,' the woman said to herself.

'And I thought you were only twenty-one,' said Lilly.

Miriam looked up and smiled. 'How'd you get along with Chatty Cathy?'

'Laugh a minute,' said Lilly.

'Get anything out of her?' Miriam asked.

'A bit tricky considering she can't speak.'

Lilly collapsed in the chair next to Miriam. 'To be honest I don't know how I'm going to do this.'

'She can write stuff down.'

'I can think of easier ways to work,' said Lilly.

Miriam shrugged. 'No one said this job was easy.'

'True,' said Lilly. 'Anyway, I don't want to push too hard too soon.'

The approval in Miriam's smile forced Lilly to add, 'But I'll have to at some stage.'

Miriam's smile was intact but the approval had gone. Or at least that was how it seemed to Lilly. 'She needs time. She hasn't come to terms with what's happening to her yet.'

'Angry?' Lilly asked.

'More shocked.'

'Hasn't this been on the cards?'

'No.' Miriam reached for Lilly's mug and took a sip. 'They weren't exactly the Waltons, but not the Wests either.'

'Physical abuse? Neglect?'

Miriam gulped loudly. 'Nothing to interest the *Daily Mail*. Kids fed, clean, went to school mostly. Social worker says it was a watching brief.'

Lilly retrieved her drink and scowled at the bitter dregs. 'It must have been the gear.'

'You'd think so, but Kelsey's adamant her mum had been clean for nearly three months. It doesn't add up.'

Lilly had been in this game long enough to know that logic and reason didn't often play a part in her clients' lives. 'Who knows what goes through someone's mind the day they give their children away.'

'Yes, baby, come to Daddy.'

The girl didn't move or even register his words.

He raised his voice, his expression firm but cajoling. 'Pretty baby, come over here.'

Her heavy lids flickered but she remained on the sofa, unable to focus. Although his smile was fixed, the man's impatience grew visibly and he patted the space on the sofa next to him.

'I'm waiting,' he said, though he clearly had no intention of doing so any longer and pulled the girl to him.

He pressed his lips to her ear and sang her name. 'Tilly, Tilly, Tilly.'

She didn't answer, didn't even blink.

He removed her grubby underwear, fumbling on

the frayed lace, and turned her around to front the camera. He stroked the pale contours of her torso, starting at the hip and snaking upwards. Her breasts were not yet developed, just tiny buds.

'You are so beautiful,' he cooed.

The girl parted her lips.

'Tell Daddy what you want him to do.'

The lips parted again and the girl exhaled audibly.

When the man spoke again there was an edge to his voice. 'Tell Daddy what you like.'

The lips opened yet again and for a second it looked as if the girl might speak. The man held his breath, his anticipation palpable. Instead, a drop of saliva escaped from the girl's mouth and dribbled down her chin.

'This is hopeless,' spat one of the two men watching the video. 'She's drugged out of her mind.'

The young man opposite snapped off the television.

'I need to see some sense of her wanting it,' the older man said. 'Or not wanting it, if you get my drift.'

His attempt at inclusion sickened the younger man, and he shuddered. 'This ain't what I'm into.' He gestured to the stack of cassettes beside him. 'This stuff is just my product, Mr Barrows. Money in the bank, understand?'

'I do, but you understand this: your "*product*" is not satisfactory, and if you think I will buy inferior goods you really don't know me.'

Oh I know you. I know you better than you think.

'I've got some more I know you're gonna like. How about I drop them round tomorrow.'

A spark shone in Barrows' eyes. 'Young?'

'Very.'

CHAPTER TWO

Tuesday, 8 September

Lilly sniffed at the milk, which was two days past its sell-by date, and poured it over some cereal.

'What's that?' asked Sam.

'Special K.'

He turned the empty packet around in his hands as if it were the latest must-have electro gadget. 'Can I have some?'

'There's only enough for me.'

'Please.'

Lilly kissed the crown of her son's head. 'Frankly, I don't think you need to lose weight.'

Five minutes later Lilly picked at some Shreddies while Sam polished off the bowl of Special K.

'What time is it?' Lilly asked.

Sam squinted at his new watch.

'Put your glasses on,' said Lilly.

Sam sighed and rummaged through his pockets. Lilly was about to point out how much better it would be to keep them in their case when she saw her own pair lying lens down on the draining board.

'Bart is pointing to eight and Homer's nearly on six.'

'Shit!'

'That's a bad word,' said Sam.

'Thank you, Mary Whitehouse.'

'Who?'

Lilly scrambled across the kitchen to the cupboard above the fridge to shove the cereal boxes back inside. 'Never mind. We're late, get your shoes on.' In her hurry she tripped over the Lego fortress set up last night, banged her elbow against the fridge and scattered Shreddies across the tiled floor.

'Uh oh.'

'Hurry!' Lilly yelled, and crunched her way to the door.

The school grounds were deserted, devoid of the usual melee of babbling mums vying for a place to park. Had everyone been and gone? Surely they weren't that late? As she wondered, Lilly cast around for a plausible explanation to appease Mrs Thomas, the omnipotent Head of House, and checked the time on her mobile. Five past eight.

'Five past eight? You said it was . . . '

She looked at Sam.

'Just joking.'

At 8.45 a.m. Lilly left the school grounds and drove towards the village of Little Markham. She yawned and decided to go back home for a cup of tea. She had an appointment with Kelsey at ten so there was time to spare, even enough to call for a paper, but as she entered the newsagent's her mobile rang. Lilly checked the number of the caller and her heart sank.

The voice at the other end chirped like one of the budgies Lilly's nan used to keep. Sammy, Davis and Junior had spent their days pecking Trill and making a high-pitched racket. It was so grating that Nan used to put a gingham cover over the cage in the afternoon to fool the noisy buggers into going to sleep.

'Hi, it's me,' said David. Lilly wished she could put a cover over her ex-husband.

'Is it about tonight?'

'Yeah. Cara's just surprised me with tickets to the opera,' he said.

Lilly counted to ten. 'It's your evening to see Sam.'

'I know. She must have totally forgotten.'

Of course she did. After all, it must be such a stretch to keep track of her manicures and facials, how could she be expected to remember trivia?

'I'm supposed to be seeing a client,' said Lilly.

'Can't you get a sitter?'

'I could, but Sam wants to see his father.'

'You know I'll make it up to him,' said David.

Lilly couldn't be bothered to argue.

'I'll get him a programme,' David said.

'*La Traviata*, I'm sure he'll be chuffed.'

Lilly paid for three chocolate bars and stalked out of the shop. The assistant waved the newspaper she'd left on the counter but Lilly was too distracted to notice. As he put it back on the rack he shook his head at the headline:

PROSTITUTE BUTCHERED.
POLICE SUSPECT SERIAL KILLER.

People today were out of control, he thought.

'I think I have low self-esteem. Sometimes, when I'm in a room full of people I feel unable to speak. I think they won't want to listen to anything I've got to say. Do you understand, Doctor?'

William Barrows nodded but he wasn't listening either. He had no interest in her stupid problems. He couldn't even look at her directly without feeling ill. Her gnarled hands and wrinkled skin repulsed him.

As she droned on he fantasised about hurting her, ripping her apart and causing inexplicable pain. Sometimes he couldn't contain his fury, but today he internalised it, hid it deep within his core.

As soon as his patient left, Barrows threw open a window to rid his office of her smell. Piss, sweat and halitosis. Even with the air-conditioning on full blast the stench of her decaying body made him gag.

He looked outside to the street below where the nasty little black man was waiting. He wouldn't come in until he had to, his distaste of Barrows was too acute. Let the fool bake in the sun.

Barrows left the window, sat at his computer and made a swift exit from the site he had last visited. 'Modern psychiatry in practice' held little interest. Instead he went to his favourites in the hope of something fresh, but nothing new had been posted since yesterday.

Barrows drummed his fingers. There was insufficient time for what he really wanted, but could he resist? Self-denial had never been a virtue.

He wandered over to the cabinet beside the television and video recorder. He opened the doors and ran his forefinger along the meticulous rows of video cassettes. Each in exact line with its neighbours, each with its title printed neatly on the side. He let his hand hover over *'Girl Sucking Thumb'* but moved on to *'Nervous Redhead'*.

Decisions, decisions. At last he smiled and selected *'Shy Princess'*.

He always named the films after his co-stars.

Max waited outside the building. He pulled down a baseball cap to shield his eyes from the hard sun and lit a joint. The weed was good, but he yearned for something stronger.

A woman emerged from the clinic, presumably one of Barrows' patients. Her clothes were smart and her hair shone. She certainly didn't look mad, but you never could tell. Max guessed she was about twenty-five.

When he could put it off no longer, Max flicked the roach into the gutter and made his way inside.

It was a game. Barrows always waited until he was sure Max had seen what was playing before he turned off the video.

Max knew his discomfort amused Barrows. He pretended not to see the young girl on the screen, her tiara glittering, her vagina exposed, but his flinch gave him away.

He handed two 'audition tapes' to Barrows, together

with a handful of photographs. If Barrows liked one of the girls he would instruct Max to set the wheels in motion for a film session, and Barrows would pay handsomely.

The money was everything to Max, the only way out of this shit-hole of a life. For as long as he could remember he'd been trying to save up enough to leave the estate, to put distance between himself and the filth he saw all around him. Thieving, dealing, pimping, he'd done the lot, still did if an opportunity came his way. But this stuff, the kids and Barrows, made good money, more than the rest put together. It was his ticket to freedom. Of course, he still squirmed when Barrows played the tapes and ran his fingers over the Polaroids, and he still felt relief for those girls Barrows rejected. But business was business.

'I wasn't sure I should come. Maybe we should both be keeping our heads down,' said Max.

Barrows was dismissive. 'The woman's dead. Problem solved.'

He discarded the first tape within seconds, but the second retained his attention. His top lip trembled in appreciation of the girl larking about on a swing, nervously pulling at her silver boob tube.

Max wanted to smash every bone in Barrows' body, but contented himself with smashing the man's arrogance.

'Grace may be dead, but the daughter ain't.'

Satisfied with Barrows' reaction, he left.

Max sat in his car. He'd enjoyed the look on that sicko's

face. He knew full well that Kelsey would never grass, but Barrows didn't. The switch of power felt good, and yet it was not enough to expel the inevitable dread he felt as he anticipated the introduction of another child into Barrows' world.

As a child himself, Max had known he was dirty and unworthy of anyone's love. And as the years wore on, the layers of filth increased, until they were all that held him together.

He placed a small rock of crack cocaine into a pipe, put the flame of his lighter to it and inhaled as deeply as he could. The smoke rushed through him, minty cool yet white hot. It cleansed him from the inside out and peeled away the layers to reveal the man beneath. A pure man. A fearless man. A man without blood on his hands.

He bared his teeth at the world around him and laughed out loud. 'You can't touch me.'

All too soon the effects lessened and the dirt began to seep back into him until his pores were clogged and the layers had re-established themselves. He bit down hard on his bottom lip to recover some feeling, and pulled out his mobile phone to send a text to the girl in the video. After all, she was no angel, she knew the score, so no harm done.

Anyway, this was his last one. Barrows didn't know it yet but he was going to pay double for the girl in the boob tube, and Max would have enough money to get the hell out of here.

Lilly laughed to herself when she arrived outside The

Bushes. The scene was a classic. Kids milled in and out of the unit, beside themselves with excitement. Others leaned out of their bedroom windows and shouted to those below.

Surprisingly, Miriam stood apart from the throng. Perhaps she had decided to let the furore run its course. A risky tactic given how easily and regularly things got out of hand. The presence of Jack McNally's squad car confirmed Lilly's suspicions that something had really kicked off.

'Trouble in paradise?' she asked Miriam.

Miriam didn't smile. 'Kelsey's mum is dead.'

'Shit.'

'You need to talk to Jack.'

'Has he told you what happened?' asked Lilly.

'Not much, just that the police want to speak to Kelsey.'

Miriam placed her hand in the small of Lilly's back and steered her towards the building. 'You need to get moving.'

Lilly eyed her friend. Where was the fire? 'I'm not sure what I can do except hold the poor kid's hand.'

'Bugger that. She needs a solicitor and preferably one with her head screwed on.'

Miriam's tone worried Lilly. The beloved and almost soporific calm had vanished, and in its place was something Lilly didn't recognise, at least not in Miriam.

'Is Kelsey all right?' Lilly asked.

'Wake up, girl, they're saying she did it. The police think Kelsey murdered her mum.'

* * *

22

Lilly was always pleased to see Jack. Among the myriad professionals she worked with in child protection he could be relied upon to let common sense prevail and, like her, see the funny side of things.

They'd met on Christmas Eve, five or maybe six years ago, when Jack nicked one of her clients for stealing three tins of Roses from Woolies. The kid had denied it even when Jack played the CCTV footage showing the tiny figure tottering out of the door, his mountain of chocolate swaying precariously, his Santa hat askew.

As Lilly began to fear ever leaving the station, Jack had sent the kid packing with a telling off and a fiver.

Since then their paths had crossed so often they felt like old friends.

It didn't hurt that he looked so good either. Tall and thin with the dress sense of Boris Johnson wasn't every woman's dream, but Jack's thick dark hair, perfect skin and soulful eyes did it for Lilly. A mild flirtation with a handsome man eased the endless hours waiting in courtrooms. Harmless, yet highly effective.

He greeted her warmly, but they both understood that the gravity of the situation made their usual banter inappropriate.

'What's the story, Jack?' she asked.

Jack slouched in the door frame, his battered leather jacket thrown over his left shoulder, the collar hooked under his thumb. 'We need a word with Kelsey.'

Lilly smiled. If anyone could play things down it was Jack. The Irish melody of his voice lent itself to a light mood.

'No can do. She swallowed a bottle of bleach and her mouth is burnt to shit, she won't be able to speak for a few weeks.'

'She can write her answers,' he reasoned.

'Is that any way to conduct an interview with a traumatised fourteen-year-old kid?' she asked.

Jack sighed. He'd obviously anticipated this line of attack. 'Not my call, Lilly.'

When he said her name it sounded like a song and she had to fight the urge to plant a kiss squarely on his lips.

'Don't talk rubbish. You've got enough clout at the nick to stop some smart arse in CID from hounding children,' she said.

'This is a murder investigation, Lilly, no one's interested in my opinion,' he replied.

It was Lilly's turn to sigh, and Jack seemed to take this as confirmation that she knew it was futile to argue.

'This whole thing will be less painful if you cooperate,' he said, his eyes shining not with triumph but with relief at Lilly's apparent acquiescence.

She pushed past him and went inside. 'Bullshit.'

Lilly opened the bedroom door. Kelsey was sitting in exactly the same position Lilly had left her almost twenty-four hours earlier. It was if the child hadn't moved. Lilly felt again the enormity of the situation. How can you represent a kid who can't tell you anything? Avoidance tactics were her best bet.

'Kelsey, this is Jack McNally. He's a copper.' Lilly flashed a charming smile. 'He wants to ask you some questions.'

Jack returned the smile. His voice was low and deliberate. 'That's right. I'll drive you to the station myself.'

'So you'll need to get a psychiatrist,' Lilly said.

'What?'

Lilly shrugged as if her proposal were obvious. 'There must be a question mark over Kelsey's stability and whether she's able to sit through an interview.'

'On what basis do you say that?' he asked.

'Oh, I don't know – perhaps because Kelsey drank a bottle of bleach a couple of days ago and she's just been told her mother's been murdered.'

Jack stiffened. 'Are you saying you won't allow an interview to take place until she's been certified fit?'

'Not at all. You know as well as I do that I can't stop you doing anything. I'd just be surprised if an experienced child protection officer like yourself would speak to a juvenile before assuring himself that to do so wouldn't be harmful.'

'A few questions aren't going to hurt,' he said.

'Are you sure?'

Lilly glanced at the miserable creature sat at the end of her bed. Her head was buried in her chest, the crown, thick with dandruff, the only thing visible. Jack had walked right into this one.

'Has she said or done anything to lead you to believe that now is a good time, Jack?'

'I'll call the Gov.'

Ten minutes later, Lilly stirred a coffee and placed it in front of Jack. 'What did he say?'

'We can't get a psychiatrist today.'

Lilly already knew that the official police shrink was in court giving evidence on one of her other cases and that his assistant was sitting one of her final exams.

Jack gave a half-smile. 'We managed an educational psychologist.'

'Totally inappropriate,' Lilly said.

'Figured you'd say that and told the DI to send him home.'

Lilly couldn't resist a smile but could see Jack's patience was wearing thin.

'This isn't a game, Lilly,' he said.

'No shit.'

He fixed her with a hostile glare. 'Grace was found in her flat by another prostitute hoping to borrow some money. The poor girl's still in shock.'

'Cause of death?' Lilly asked.

'Her head had been smashed and her body was covered in knife wounds,' he said.

'There goes my OD theory.'

Jack drew himself up. Lilly's attempts at humour were patently annoying him. He rummaged in his bag, pulled out the scene-of-crime photos and slapped them onto the table between them.

'Whoever did this is dangerous.'

It was Lilly's turn to be annoyed. The attempt to get her on side was a parlour trick.

'Goodness, Officer, now you've shown me what a monster my client is I'll advise her to confess.'

'No one's looking for a confession,' he said.

'Of course you are, Jack. You've got no evidence.'

'What makes you say that?'

26

'If you'd anything strong to say Kelsey did that,' Lilly gestured to the photographs, 'none of us would be sitting here. The DI would have nicked her himself and the first I'd have heard about it was when she got her phone call from the station.'

'You're a cynic,' he said.

'I'm a realist,' she replied. 'Kelsey's a suspect for no other reason than she's family and has a motive. The fact that the DI sent you tells me the interview is important. Softly softly catchy monkey. If Kelsey squeals there's to be no room for me to object because you'll need to rely on it.'

Jack's shoulders drooped as the truth of what she was saying hit him. His naivety reminded Lilly that he was one of the good guys.

'You should use your influence to put an end to this,' she said.

'Like I said, it isn't my case.'

Lilly stared out of the window into the darkness surrounding The Bushes and wondered if the world beyond was still sizzling. Jack was right, this wouldn't be the end of it. The police had their hooks into Kelsey and would keep picking until something began to unravel. It would be virtually impossible to find a foster placement for Kelsey with this hanging over her.

Lilly was exhausted and on the brink of a killer headache. She pulled a plastic bottle of warm water from her bag. Sam would be starving when she collected him but cooking was not an option. It was strictly fish and chips after a day like today.

Miriam's voice pervaded the unit. Her lilting accent had returned, the anxiety of earlier banished, for now at least. Didn't the woman ever get tired of it all? Lilly would ask her one day, but not today.

'Miriam, I need fifteen quid,' came a familiar yell.

Lilly poked her head around the door. Jermaine stood on the stairs, his arms wrapped around him in his best gansta pose, glowering down at Miriam.

'I'm not deaf, Jermaine,' said Miriam.

'I need fifteen quid,' the boy repeated, almost as loudly.

'For what?' Miriam asked.

'A haircut.'

Miriam pushed a stray braid behind her ear and laughed. 'You must think I'm mad.'

'Why?' Jermaine shouted.

Miriam reached up, knocked off his hat and revealed his number-one cut. Jermaine kissed his teeth and disappeared.

'Kelsey okay?' asked Lilly.

'The poor kid's shattered. I don't know why the hell they think she killed her mum.'

Lilly shrugged. 'Most murders are by family members. Kelsey must have been pretty mad when her mum dumped her in here, so that gives her a motive.'

'That's not much to go on,' Miriam said.

'Which is why Jack's buggered off,' Lilly replied.

Miriam stepped out of her battered sandals and lowered herself into the chair next to Lilly. 'Kelsey didn't do it.'

Lilly passed over her bottle. 'Who else has a motive?'

'Come on, that lifestyle is dangerous,' said Miriam

between sips. 'Working girls get beaten all the time.'

'Yet according to Kelsey her mum was clean, so why would she even be with a punter?' said Lilly.

'Old habits die hard.'

Lilly conceded the point. 'True, and maybe some misogynist did bash her head in cos she wouldn't take it up the trap door, but why mutilate the body?'

Miriam raised her eyebrows. They both knew people got their kicks in the strangest ways. Most of the kids in The Bushes could testify to that.

The inhabitants of southern England had communally declared it too hot to cook and the fish and chip shop was full. Its owners bellowed at each other in Turkish, throwing their arms around them like Basil Fawlty on acid. Their young assistant fried the cod, his face glistening with sweat and hot fat, and ignored both his employers and the customers.

Eventually, a parcel of food was unceremoniously dumped onto the counter. Lilly's Auntie Val, who had run the Castle Wall Fish Palace for thirty-six years and knew every regular order by heart, would have turned in her grave.

The wrapping paper steamed and smelled of vinegar.

'What do you think we got today, big man?' asked Lilly.

Sam giggled in anticipation. It was like a Christmas present, you never knew what was inside until you opened it. The poor service annoyed Lilly but Sam lapped it up.

'Did you ask for a sausage?' he asked.

'Three times, my love,' Lilly replied.

'So it's probably a fish cake.'

Lilly's mobile rang. She ruffled her son's hair and checked the caller ID.

'Hi Jack. Sorry if I seemed a smart arse today, just doing what I thought was right.'

'Me too,' said Jack. 'Which is why I'm giving you a heads-up on this.'

Lilly left the correct money on the counter and scooped the greasy packet into the crook of her arm. 'Go on.'

'On the night Grace was murdered a neighbour saw Kelsey entering the flat on two separate occasions. She can also vouch that no one else visited that night.'

CHAPTER THREE

Wednesday, 9 September

It was the same as always. The girl covered her ears to drown out the noise. Life on site was never quiet. Sure, she shared a caravan with her ma, da and four baby brothers, so a moment's peace was a rare thing indeed, but this was different. The screaming and cursing into the darkness was unbearable.

She squeezed her eyes shut and turned in her bunk, her hand brushing the smooth stone of the wall. She flinched from the cold of it. The hardness of it. The suffocating density of it.

Rochene had been born in a caravan, had lived in one all her life, and until two weeks ago she had never before spent the night in a building.

When Lilly woke she too was touching the wall beside her bed. She shook the dream from her head and tried to get back to sleep. It always stopped in the same place, as if willing Lilly to play out the rest.

Not tonight. Lilly simply couldn't bear it.

Instead she threw off the sheets to the intolerable heat of the night and went downstairs to raid the fridge.

* * *

Lilly was in a rush. She needed to be at Ring Farm in twenty minutes. Given that she hadn't yet finished the school drop-off she was becoming increasingly agitated. She threw Sam's wellies into his boot locker and wondered why he needed them when it hadn't rained a drop for five weeks.

She stuffed a cap into his kitbag. 'That's not a regulation hat, is it?'

Sam responded with a sideways smile. 'It is for the England squad.'

She kissed his head. 'Smart arse.'

'That's a bad word,' he chided, wagging a finger.

Lilly laughed and ushered him into his classroom.

Then, on the verge of escape, she heard the nasal tones of one of the other mothers.

'What are you doing tomorrow, Lilly?'

She turned and saw the perfect smile of Penny Van Huysan. Was the woman having an affair with her dentist?

'The other mums are meeting for coffee,' Penny continued.

Had she not been so exhausted from her sleepless night, Lilly would have thought on her feet. Work, chiropodist, smear test. Anything.

'I think I'm free.'

Oh God, coffee with the Manor Park mums. Dante's third circle of hell.

Lilly parked outside the Spar. Although it was a good walk to where she needed to be, the shop was busy and her car stood less chance of being stolen. The

Clayhill Estate was one of the roughest in Ring Farm, awash with addicts and dealers. The crime rates were high and the employment figures low. Grace Brand had lived there with her kids for fourteen years.

Lilly wrinkled her nose at the smell of urine in the stairwell and made her way up to the third floor. The lights were smashed and the gloom coupled with the stench made a depressing cocktail.

A woman answered the door instantly. She was in her mid-seventies, sporting a frizzy perm and a scowl.

Lilly held out her hand. 'Mrs Mitchell? I'm Lilly Valentine. Sorry I'm late.'

The old woman smoothed down her house coat with arthritic fingers and frowned, no doubt offended by a younger generation who managed their lives so inexcusably badly that they couldn't make important appointments on time.

Lilly let her hand drop and followed Mrs Mitchell through the hallway to a stuffy sitting room with shelves full of china animals dressed in Victorian clothes. A tabby cat smiled out from the brim of her blue bonnet, the ribbons held in place by two paws.

Despite the weather every window was closed, and a man sat in the corner, a blanket over his knees, staring into space. A cuckoo clock sounded from another room and the man's lips began to move gently and soundlessly.

Mrs Mitchell gave her husband a contemptuous nod. 'Don't mind him, he's away with the fairies.'

The old man didn't look over but continued his silent monologue.

Lilly plumped for a no-nonsense approach and dived straight in. 'Can I ask you about Monday night, Mrs Mitchell?'

'That's why you're here, isn't it,' the old woman snapped.

Lilly remained polite. 'I've seen the statement you gave to the police and you say you saw Kelsey Brand going into their flat on the night Grace was killed.'

Mrs Mitchell sniffed. 'That's right, I saw her twice.'

'Are you sure?' asked Lilly.

Mrs Mitchell flashed an angry look. 'Of course I'm sure. The first time was around eight o'clock. I know that cos *EastEnders* had just started. The second time was about half an hour later.'

Lilly kept her smile glued in place. 'Maybe it wasn't Kelsey.'

Mrs Mitchell tightened her moue until she reminded Lilly of the pickled walnuts her nan had always loved. 'I may be old but I'm not daft. I know what I saw.'

Lilly cocked her head to one side and tried a different tack. 'Maybe you weren't paying much attention, maybe you were busy.'

The old lady shot a withering look at her husband. 'Doing what?'

A witness who was a prisoner in her own home. Great.

'Did you know Grace?' asked Lilly.

'Didn't want to.'

Lilly kept her tone light. 'How about Kelsey?'

'She used to go to the shops for me when she was little. Skinny thing, well, they all were,' said Mrs Mitchell, almost pleasantly, then, as if remembering

34

herself, she added, 'Of course the change started coming back short so I didn't ask no more.'

It was plain to Lilly that this witness had no intention of describing the Brands with anything less than poison. Their tragic end had clearly failed to temper her views.

'Did many people visit the flat?'

'Not since the social took her kids. Before that it was like Piccadilly bleeding Circus, men arriving at all times of the day and night. Clients, I suppose you'd call them. And more girls.'

'You mean prostitutes,' said Lilly.

Mrs Mitchell sniffed in disgust. 'Vile, the lot of them. Came for drugs, I suppose.'

Lilly was surprised. 'Was Grace selling drugs?'

'Not her, the darkie that was there all the time. Max, he calls himself.'

'A boyfriend?' asked Lilly.

Mrs Mitchell shrugged. 'I've heard him say he's an entre-whatsit.'

'Entrepreneur,' Lilly suggested.

'I know what he is,' Mrs Mitchell replied. She leaned in closer to make her point. 'This used to be a decent place to live before that lot moved in.'

Lilly gladly closed the door to number 62. The pungent smell in the walkway was an open meadow compared to the bitter hole behind her. She passed along to number 58, the Brands' flat, and paused at the police tape. She peered into the kitchen window and saw the room inside was modestly furnished but clean and tidy.

'Can I help you, Miss?'

Lilly could feel Jack standing behind her, close enough for her to smell the ancient leather of his jacket. 'Thanks for coming,' she said.

He gave a small chuckle. 'I suppose you want to go in.'

It wasn't a question and he was already unlocking the door.

Inside, the flat had the same layout as number 62, but Grace's home seemed much less claustrophobic. The hall was painted in a soft pastel shade and cotton curtains let in plenty of light. The carpet was worn but neat, unusual for a junkie.

Although Grace had sent the girls' belongings with them into care, the place remained full of evidence of their existence. A painting of a fairy was tacked to the fridge, her wand held aloft like a glittery spear. There were photographs of all four girls fixed to the walls with Blu-Tack, their edges curling inwards, the images, like the family, imploding. The shelf by the sink was empty apart from a lone spider plant, gently dying in the fierce sunlight, its pot incongruously colourful and inscribed with the words 'World's best Mum'.

Lilly rubbed the dry leaves between her thumb and forefinger, feeling the papery disintegration. 'Whoever did this must have had a reason.'

Jack gave Lilly a charming smile. 'Yeah. Her ma abandoned her and she got stuck in a children's home.'

Lilly smiled back. 'Have you considered that maybe she didn't do it?'

'Have you considered that maybe she did?'

36

Lilly didn't answer, instead she peered down the hall, her gaze following the trail of dark stains from the kitchen to the bedroom door.

'Is that where it happened?' she asked.

'She received the head wounds in here then got dragged down there.'

They skirted the walls as they passed along the hall and entered the room where Grace had been mutilated.

Lilly took in the scene, her breath shallow. The heavy velvet curtains were drawn, perhaps in deference to the deceased or perhaps they had been like that all along. Whatever the reason, the room was cast in a grey light and the noise of the world beyond was muffled.

Apart from the bed the only other stick of furniture was a single white wardrobe. Lilly opened the door and fingered the sparse contents. A few T-shirts and flimsy shirts small enough to fit Sam. A pair of black jeans, faded at the knee, and a plastic mini skirt. Lilly felt so solemn she made the sign of the cross, a meaningless affectation from her childhood, like saluting magpies.

She didn't want to but she knew she couldn't avoid looking at the bed. The sheets and mattress had been removed for forensic examination but Grace's blood had soaked right down to the base.

Without thinking, Lilly put her hand out to touch the black shape, using the same instinct that a wet-paint sign will arouse.

'Tell me about a face round here called Max,' she said.

Jack gently pushed her hand away before she made contact. 'If we're talking about the same person, he's hardly a face. Max Hardy, drug dealer, pimp, purveyor of porno films. Low-level stuff.'

'Had any dealings with him?' asked Lilly.

Jack shrugged. 'Loads. I've known him since his time at The Bushes.'

Lilly widened her eyes. 'The res unit?'

He applied a gentle pressure to the small of her back and eased her towards the door. 'In those days it was called The Bushberry Home for Disturbed Children.'

Lilly paused to let this information sink in, before allowing Jack to manoeuvre her out of the house entirely.

'I can't believe you knew him back then,' she said.

'I can't believe I've been doing this job for so bloody long,' he said. 'Twenty years and change.'

'And every day a joy.'

'A life sentence would have been shorter. What an eejit, eh?'

'A saint more like.' Lilly patted his arm. 'Anyway, this Max sounds like a nasty piece of work.'

Jack couldn't and didn't argue.

'Let's assume Grace worked for him and that he controls his girls in the usual way,' Lilly continued.

Jack closed the door and fixed a fresh piece of police tape around the frame. 'Fist and needle.'

'Exactly. So what if one of his girls gets clean, how can he make sure she keeps working for him?' asked Lilly.

'His charming repartee.'

Lilly worked through her thoughts to their logical conclusion. 'When that doesn't work he resorts to what he knows best.'

'He's no previous for violence,' said Jack.

Lilly gave a dismissive wave. 'No one's ever reported him.'

She wondered if this could be the lead she was looking for. She needed to get Jack interested and get him to do some digging. And do some herself.

'Is this why you asked me to meet you here?' asked Jack.

'Naturally. Did you have something else in mind?'

'Maybe a drink?'

She eyed his cheeky grin. 'Are you inviting me on a date?'

'I thought asking for a shag might seem a bit forward.'

William Barrows watched his wife reapply her makeup in readiness for her meeting. The process fascinated and appalled him in equal measure. He often wondered why she bothered to wear any since it made her look neither younger nor prettier, which was presumably her aim. It seemed to him that, as with any old building, the façade remained more or less the same after a paint job and any cement used to cover cracks was too obvious to fool anyone. If anything it drew attention to the flaws. He longed to dig his fingers into her cheeks and peel the painted flesh from the bone.

Sometimes he entertained himself by playing games with her and suggested a little more rouge or a darker shade of lipstick. It amused him that she was so ready to leave the house like a geisha girl. But today was for a different kind of game entirely.

'I read in the local rag that one of your constituents was murdered, darling,' he said.

Hermione continued to apply dark pencil around her eyelid. 'Mmm.'

'You don't seem very interested.'

She turned to her husband, pencil still poised. 'She was a drug addict living on the Clayhill Estate. I don't think *anyone* is interested.'

The estates in the Ring Farm area of Luton had the lowest voter turnout in her constituency, so Hermione Barrows, MP for Luton West, like her predecessors, expended little energy courting the support of their residents. She went back to her reflection.

'You could push the issue, make it gather some speed,' Barrows said.

'Why would I?'

He felt his impatience begin to rise. 'To raise your profile, darling.'

She snapped her head around. He had her attention now.

'Like you say, no one's interested, so anyone making some noise will have a clear field.'

Barrows watched her hungry smile emerge. She needed recognition and publicity as much as he needed the hobby. Well, almost.

'What angle could I use?' she asked.

He pretended to think about it. 'I hear the police think her daughter did it, but they're not pursuing it. Probably worried what the papers will make of it all.'

'What do you mean?' she asked.

He sighed at her incomprehension. She rarely grasped anything quickly and he often had to repeat and explain things as if she were retarded.

'Social services and the police should have done something about this family years ago. They sat back and let a heroin-addicted prostitute keep vulnerable children. Can you imagine the life they've had?'

Hermione nodded, but Barrows knew it was well beyond her wit to empathise with anyone who didn't drive a BMW.

He pressed on. 'Those children will be damaged beyond repair. I should imagine the eldest was driven to killing her mother in sheer desperation.'

'So what's the point of pursuing it? What's in it for . . .' Hermione stopped short.

Barrows prepared to deliver the clincher. 'Whatever the rights and wrongs of the situation, the child is dangerous, she shouldn't be allowed to wander the streets.' He paused for emphasis. 'The voters in Luton are already terrified of the young people from the estates and they'll be very glad that someone is taking it seriously.'

He saw ambition light her face. 'Tough on crime. Yes, they love that,' she said.

'And when the press turn on social services you'll be right in the middle of it,' he added. 'Everyone will want to know your opinion on the matter.'

Hermione looked faintly puzzled and Barrows berated himself for over-egging the pudding. He need not have worried.

'You really should go into politics, darling, you're even better at it than I am,' she said with a self-deprecating giggle.

Of course I am. It's hardly rocket science. Any fool can

be a politician. But I don't need the spotlight to validate myself. My longing is for something else. Something less complex.

After much negotiation with Lilly as to how late was too late on a school night, Sam was finally asleep.

Lilly made a vast bowlful of pasta, doused it in olive oil infused with chilli, poured a generous glass of wine and settled down to do some work.

She spread her case papers across the kitchen table and took a mouthful of food, savouring the spicy zing of the oil as it touched her tongue. If not Kelsey, then who had killed Grace? Could it have been Max, the man Mrs Mitchell had identified as a drug dealer? It seemed more likely than a child, even Jack had admitted that. She knew from experience that the police would keep pursuing Kelsey until they had another suspect. She just had to make Jack see that Max was the one who murdered Grace.

Lilly smiled to herself at the thought of him. They'd enjoyed their drink together, even if Lilly had spent most of the time haranguing him about this case.

'Do you ever let up?' he'd said.

'Not often,' Lilly replied. 'Anyhow, I bet you take your work home with you.'

'Only the handcuffs,' he said.

They'd laughed a lot, like they always did, finding humour in the darkest places.

'Name your all-time worst witness,' he'd asked.

'The man who was so pissed he fell asleep.'

42

Jack threw his head back in glee.

'I thought at one point the old sod was dead . . . Or how about the bloke who barricaded himself in his flat with the kids,' she said. 'And the armed police had to break down the door.'

Jack snorted on his beer. 'And when you asked him if the children had been frightened by the helicopters, he said no, they thought it was better than the telly.'

It was easy with Jack. Easier than Lilly could remember with anyone else since David had left, and Lilly found herself wishing she could spend more time with him. Something had changed. Maybe it was Jack, maybe it was Lilly, or maybe the time was just right, but she knew that she wanted to be more than friends.

If he felt the same then she ought to do something about it. But how was she to gauge his feelings on the matter?

'If you haven't got a crystal ball, better ask the question,' her mother had always said, but Lilly hadn't inherited her bottle – or her years in the south had worn it away.

'They're all soft down there,' her dad used to say.

Trust him. The silly sod had never been further than Skegness.

She took a gulp of wine and looked at some photographs of the Brand family. They had been taken by a social worker on a trip to the beach only weeks before Grace put the girls in care. The trip was funded by Sunny Days, a charity set up to help children like these escape the estates, if only for a day.

None of the girls had ever seen the sea before, and

one photograph showed them playing in the waves with excitement and abandon.

Lilly thought of her own early holidays in a caravan on the east coast. Sometimes they took Nan, who snored like a drill and the whole tin can would rattle. In the distance the fog horn at Robin Hood's Bay would sound and the donkeys in the next field would start braying for their food around five. Dad would throw open the door, the pee bucket swinging from his arm. 'There's nothing like a rest at the seaside.'

Lilly laughed and picked up the next picture. All four girls with their mother, sitting on a wall, eating ice cream. Kelsey, Gemma, Sophie and Scarlet. Peas in a pod. The same mousy hair covering most of their faces, the same tight mouths revealing chipped teeth. Grace at the end, squinting into the sun.

Kelsey seemed different in the picture, somehow lighter than she was now. Lilly wouldn't have described her face as happy but the despair wasn't there.

Lilly chased the last strand of spaghetti around her plate and picked up a housing transfer refusal. She placed it on top of the others and counted them. Five. In the past year Grace had made five applications to the council to move and had kept all five letters of refusal.

There was even a letter from Grace's MP thanking her for attending the surgery but apologising that she was unable to help as Grace had rent arrears, and it was local authority policy not to move anyone until all rent payments were up-to-date.

Lilly was puzzled. Junkies rarely pursued anything so persistently, except their drug of choice. To make and actually keep an appointment with an MP was unheard of.

Chocolate called. Lilly opened the fridge and fingered the small mountain of Kit-Kats, Snickers, Picnics and other bars she kept, as though it were pornography, on the top shelf.

David had found her love affair with such confectionery downmarket. He described it as *'cheap chocolate'* and encouraged her towards the dark, Belgian or Swiss varieties. Lilly had pointed out that Roald Dahl had shared her passion and he was a genius. And anyway, she couldn't care less about the percentage of cocoa solids, she'd always been crap at maths.

Now David was gone she could do what she liked. Apparently Cara didn't eat chocolate at all, it played havoc with her chakras.

Lilly took a bar and read the list of ingredients. Sugar, hydrogenated fat, emulsifier and salt. 'Delicious,' she said, and turned her mind once again to the housing applications.

Had Grace been trying to escape from her life of drugs and prostitution or was she trying to escape from Max? She'd suggested the latter proposition to Jack and hoped he could nudge the powers-that-be away from Kelsey towards Max.

The main obstacle, of course, was Mrs Mitchell. She may be poisonous but Lilly doubted she would have made the whole thing up, which meant Kelsey was undoubtedly at the flats the night Grace was killed. She swallowed the remaining chocolate whole and dialled Miriam's number.

'Kelsey was there the night her mother was killed.'

'You're sure?' Miriam asked.

Lilly thumbed the police statement, leaving brown smudges that she tried to scrape away with her nail. 'She was seen by one of the neighbours.'

'That doesn't mean she killed Grace,' said Miriam.

'No, but it does mean she might have seen who did,' Lilly replied.

'You know what else it means.'

Lilly did. She closed her eyes and pictured a fourteen-year-old watching while her mother's dead body was cut to ribbons.

She arranged to meet Miriam the following evening and went back to the case papers. The idea of Kelsey as a witness to the murder was horrible, but better than the alternative. Maybe when Kelsey was less traumatised she'd be able to help the police, and with some therapy there might still be some hope of a foster placement for her. Somewhere she could feel safe and rebuild her life. Things didn't have to turn out badly.

Feeling positive, Lilly placed the papers back into their file one by one. Suddenly her eyes widened and she gasped at the remaining document on the table. The handwriting was poor and the grammar worse but there was no mistaking what it was. Lilly was reading a letter written by Kelsey to her mother, threatening to cut her into pieces.

CHAPTER FOUR

Thursday, 10 September

The next morning Lilly dressed in a navy blue wool suit. The sun was shining and Lilly was hot but she had a meeting with the pathologist at eleven and needed to boost her confidence. Experience had taught her that looking the part helped her to feel the part.

She had given up even trying to sleep at 4 a.m. and had instead paced the kitchen, alternately drinking red wine and rereading Kelsey's letter.

She looked every bit as terrible as she felt and the suit was already starting to itch.

She scraped back her hair from her face and secured it in a tight knot at the nape of her neck.

'I like your hair better the other way, Mummy,' said Sam.

'I like a lot of things I don't get,' Lilly snapped.

'I only meant you look prettier with it loose.'

Lilly turned to apologise but Sam had already gone outside and was standing by the car.

The drive to school was torture. Lilly tried to make the peace but her attempts were rebuffed.

'I'm sorry I was grumpy, big man, but I'm very tired,' said Lilly.

Sam refused to face her. 'You're always tired.'

'I'm working very hard at the moment, trying to help a little girl whose mummy died.'

Sam's expression said it all. He didn't care about the girl or any of the other children his mother was always talking about, and he didn't want to share her with them.

'Nothing will ever be as important to me as you. You know that, don't you?' Lilly said.

Sam chose not to answer and collected his bags together to get out of the car.

'Maybe I could leave early tonight and we could do something nice. How about a movie?'

Sam reached for the handle before the car had even come to a stop. 'Last time your phone rang three times, and when the man behind told you to turn it off you had fallen asleep.'

'What do you want me to do, Sam?'

He said nothing but watched Penny Van Huysan approach the car, her linen shift complementing a healthy tan and an athletic figure. Was the woman having an affair with her tennis coach?

At last he turned to Lilly. 'I want you to be like the other mums.'

Penny waved. 'You haven't forgotten coffee this morning, have you?'

Lilly looked at Sam's forlorn expression.

'Of course not,' she said.

* * *

Hermione Barrows chooses her outfit with care. A black jacket, sharply tailored and begging to be taken seriously, over the crispest of white shirts. She has been taught from a young age that appearance matters. Her mother had almost bankrupted her father with her endless shopping trips for clothes and her demands for bigger cars and holidays in far-flung islands where they would all be bored senseless.

When it became clear Hermione wouldn't have children her mother didn't ask why, didn't actually care, but advised her to give the impression she'd at least tried.

'Say you love kids but it wasn't meant to be,' she said. 'People don't trust women who don't like babies.'

Yes, Hermione's mother would have made a fantastic campaign manager.

Hermione drapes a silk scarf around her neckline to soften the edges and pick up the aqua flecks in her eyes. The clothes say everything she wants to project. She's a tough politician but at the same time human. A no-nonsense woman of the people.

The previous evening, at a local party meeting, she had given a rousing speech on law and order and called for the police to investigate the death of Kelsey's mother. William is right, this is an opportunity she can't afford to miss.

'We cannot allow lawlessness to take over the streets of this constituency,' she'd announced. 'The police must take all crimes seriously, no matter how insignificant the victim seems, and this includes Grace Brand.'

A local reporter had recorded every word and

Hermione had been overjoyed to receive invitations to speak on both the local radio and television stations. If both run the story and include her involvement her profile will demand serious attention, maybe from the national press.

She pulls on kitten-heeled slingbacks and struts downstairs. In the hallway, William is on the telephone. He smiles up at her and she remembers to smile back. He places his palm over the handset. 'It's for you.'

'Direct it to Nancy, darling, my media need me,' she says with a laugh. Nancy Donaldson will have to tear herself away from the nail bar today. Hermione's parliamentary assistant is going to have an unusually busy day.

'It is Nancy. She's had a call from central office,' William says.

Hermione snatches the telephone from him. Today is going to be a very good day.

The table was laden with croissants, pastries and preserves, but Lilly noticed that she was the only one actually eating. A cursory glance at the other women who sipped their black coffees told her that she alone weighed more than nine stone. She helped herself to butter and smiled at them. No doubt they didn't have raging hangovers to quell.

'Have you gone part-time?' asked Luella Wignall, the mother of Cecily, who Sam always referred to as 'Onion Face'.

Lilly assumed Luella was smiling but it was so difficult to tell. Whatever her facial expression, Luella's mouth always turned down at the ends like a cross between Cherie Blair and the Joker from Batman.

'Afraid not, but my first meeting's not until eleven, so here I am,' Lilly said.

'And we're all very glad to see you,' said Penny Van Huysan.

'Where do you have to be at eleven?' asked Luella without interest.

'Path lab,' said Lilly. 'I mean, pathology lab.'

Luella was aghast. 'You mean where they cut up the dead bodies!'

'Not exactly. They do perform the autopsies there but they do all sorts of other forensic tests as well. It's not like in *CSI*,' said Lilly.

Luella's eyes were wide with horror. 'You won't see any dead bodies, surely?

'No. I'm not allowed in the actual lab, to avoid contamination, I suppose, but I'm meeting one of the pathologists to talk about one of his reports,' Lilly said.

'How exciting,' giggled Penny.

Lilly shook her head. It amazed her how other people saw her job. 'Not really. The reports are turgid but I'm hoping he can clear a few things up on one of my cases.'

'What's it about?' asked Penny, her tone somewhere between the Secret Seven and Dan Dare.

Lilly put down her croissant. 'I represent the eldest child of a woman who was murdered on the Clayhill Estate.'

'The prostitute!' said Penny.

Lilly was surprised that the women seemed to know who she was talking about. She'd assumed their contact

51

with the outside world stopped at the hairdresser's; maybe she'd been too hasty in her analysis of them. David had always said the chip on her shoulder was so big it was a wonder she didn't lean to one side.

'I suppose we, the taxpayer, will have to keep the girl living in the lap of luxury from now on,' said Luella.

Lilly pushed away her plate, her appetite gone. She warned herself not to react. These were the mothers of her son's friends, she'd come along today because he wanted her to fit in, not pick fights.

'It will cost thousands to keep her and she doesn't have to contribute a penny. Not a penny,' said Luella.

Don't do it, Lilly. Don't do it.

'I wish someone would give me some free money,' said Luella, whose husband had just become a tax exile in Dublin.

Lilly couldn't stop herself. 'She's fourteen, Luella, are you suggesting she fend for herself?'

Luella reddened.

'Have you ever been inside a children's home?' Lilly asked.

Luella shook her head.

'Then what makes you think it's the lap of luxury?'

Luella shrugged. 'You see things in the papers.'

Lilly was caught between amazement and exasperation. 'Can I suggest you don't believe everything you read.'

Yes, the chip was heavy, but it was perfectly balanced by the weight of other people's prejudice which she carried on the other side.

* * *

Jack finished a can of Coke and crunched it in his fist. Not a healthy breakfast, he conceded, but the only other choice in his fridge had been the leftovers of last night's chicken korma.

He was looking forward to seeing Lilly and although the path lab was not the most romantic place for a date, even by his low standards, he felt pleasurably nervous.

That morning he'd intended to make a bit of an effort and iron his shirt, but when he'd pulled out the old Phillips steamer he remembered he'd used the plug for his radio alarm and there wasn't time for a regraft. Still, he'd had a wash and combed his hair.

He waited for Lilly in the foyer, skulking in the shadows. From the outside the lab looked like any other government building, three storeys high, dull red bricks, an identical plastic blind at each window. Inside was grey and eerily noiseless, the sound of footfall muffled by nylon carpet tiles. Jack hated it and had no intention of going in alone. He would have waited in the street but for the overwhelming brightness of the day.

When she finally arrived, Jack was surprised to see Lilly's unruly hair raked back. He didn't like it at all, not because it didn't suit her but because he loved the mass of waves that usually tumbled around her face.

'Sorry I'm late, I had a coffee morning,' she said.

He winked. 'Top priority, eh?'

'What would you know about my priorities?' she barked.

Jack took a deep breath. Lilly's mood was as severe as her hair.

They moved through the building to a waiting area. Dr Cheney was already there, rocking on his heels and glancing at his watch. He was a tall man with hair almost as wild as Lilly's, a haystack that slipped past his shoulders, tucked behind his ears to reveal a shooting gallery of piercings. On his nose were perched black glasses, the standard issue of the NHS in the Seventies. Jack couldn't easily picture him poring over photographs of blood-splatter patterns or checking particles of dust under a microscope, but knew that this was precisely how Cheney spent his time.

Jack had first met Cheney five years ago at a leaving party for a mutual acquaintance who had been promoted to the Drug Squad. They had argued over a technician called Debbie, who they both claimed had given them the eye and for whom they had both bought a rum and Coke. When she finally left with her lips wrapped around a recently divorced dog-handler from Essex, Jack and Cheney went on a bender that finished the following lunchtime in a twenty-four-hour café next to King's Cross. They'd been friends ever since.

The doctor pulled off latex gloves. A tribal tattoo encircled his left wrist. 'Officer McNally, Ms Valentine. How can I help you?'

It was usual for the police officer to explain their visit, but Lilly was obviously in no mood for niceties.

'I represent Kelsey Brand, the daughter of Grace Brand. The court is in the process of deciding whether a Care Order should be made.'

'Judging by the condition of her mother I think that's inevitable, Ms Valentine,' the doctor said.

One of the things Jack liked about Cheney was his sense of humour. Dark, irreverent, like his own.

Lilly smiled politely. 'I'll be frank, Doctor Cheney, her mother's death is the least of my client's worries. If the police have their way she'll be locked away until she's too old to have children of her own, presuming she survives prison at all. They think Kelsey murdered her mother.'

'That's not entirely true,' said Jack.

Lilly's eyes flashed. 'Bullshit. You're not investigating anyone else.'

Dr Cheney coughed. Jack knew he would be amused by the scuffle, only too happy to see his friend snubbed, particularly by an attractive member of the opposite sex.

'And you want to head them off at the pass,' said the doctor.

'Yes. I need them to drop this nonsense so I can get the poor kid into a decent foster placement. If you have any information in advance of the autopsy report I'd appreciate it,' Lilly said.

'How about confirmation that a fourteen-year-old couldn't have committed this crime,' said Cheney.

Jack was irritated to notice that, despite herself, Lilly's shoulders relaxed and a smile played at the corners of her mouth. 'That would be great, but anything at all would do.'

The doctor laughed and flopped into a chair. Lilly and Jack followed suit.

'As you know, the cause of death was a trauma to the base of the skull.' Cheney touched the hairline at the nape of his neck. 'It was made by a blunt instrument, and by my estimation there were two blows, both hard, both clean.'

'What about the knife wounds?' asked Jack, determined not to be excluded from the discussion, which was in danger of becoming a cosy chat á deux.

Cheney answered Jack's question but kept his eyes firmly on Lilly. 'They're extensive but not deep, without the blow to the head I doubt any would have proved fatal. In any event, they're all post mortem.'

'Is it possible that the killer didn't know she was dead and simply continued the attack?' asked Lilly, lifting her knotted hair and rubbing the pale skin of her own neck, an action so unintentionally sensual it mesmerised both men.

Cheney recovered first and spread his palms. 'Anything's possible.'

Jack forced the doctor's attention from Lilly. 'But you don't think it happened that way.'

Cheney paused, but Jack knew it would not be in hesitation. His shambolic appearance belied a precise mind and he was a man who measured his words with care. When his answer came it was emphatic.

'No. The victim would have fallen to the floor almost immediately after she was struck. Even if the killer didn't realise she was dead he must have known she was unconscious when he began cutting her. There would have been no reaction.'

'Maybe he was in a frenzy and couldn't stop,' said Lilly.

'As I said, anything's possible, but the person who

inflicted the knife wounds wasn't out of control. He wasn't slashing or stabbing wildly, he moved the body, laid it on the bed and began his task in a careful manner.' Cheney drew lines in the air with his forefinger. 'The wounds are virtually all the same length and depth, and most are evenly spaced.'

'They're all on the torso,' said Jack unnecessarily.

Cheney smirked, clearly aware of his friend's efforts to redirect both his words and his gaze. 'Yes. Nothing on the face or neck. Our assailant wanted to make his point but he didn't want to rip her apart. There's a degree of respect shown that's intriguing.'

Now they were getting somewhere. 'Maybe the killer knew Grace, had feelings for her,' said Jack.

'That's highly probable. There was no sign of a forced entry or a struggle and there are no defensive injuries. It seems she let the killer in, suspecting nothing,' said Cheney.

Lilly shook her head. 'Isn't it just as likely the killer was a punter? She was expecting him, she lets him in, he gives her the money, she turns round to count it, and bam.'

'Why cut her up?' asked Jack.

'Who knows what people get off on? Some like shagging dogs, some like being whipped. Men are a curious breed, maybe some like cutting people up,' said Lilly.

Dr Cheney considered this for a moment. 'That would be a good theory, except the body has no evidence of any sexual activity, nor were any traces of semen found at the scene.'

Lilly snapped open the top button of her suit and

57

scratched her throat, leaving vicious welts. Jack resisted the temptation to move her hand.

'Surely we're looking at a man? From a purely practical point of view he'd need to be strong enough to kill her outright and then move the body,' said Lilly.

'The blow to the head could have been caused by anyone strong enough to swing a pan or a hammer, male or female. It's the density of the weapon that proved fatal,' said Cheney, 'and I'm afraid the deceased weighed only six and a half stone when she died.'

'Junkies don't eat much,' said Jack.

Cheney nodded. 'Anyone could have dragged the body out of the kitchen.'

'Even a fourteen-year-old girl,' said Jack.

Lilly jumped to her feet and shook Cheney's hand. 'Bloody marvellous.'

Then she left without giving Jack so much as a sideways glance.

Cheney reached for his gloves and chuckled. 'If you were hoping for your leg over, Jack, I think you can forget it.'

'Don't I know it.'

At 7 p.m. Miriam arrived at the Batfield Arms to meet Lilly. She bought two gin and tonics at the bar and made for their usual table.

Lilly gratefully accepted the drink. It was her fourth. She took a long gulp and pushed the letter across the table.

'This is a copy so I'm assuming you have the original.'

Miriam shook her head slowly. 'It was sent to Kelsey's mum at her request.'

'You took a copy for your records and sent one to me with the other documents relating to her time in care,' said Lilly.

Miriam nodded. 'Standard procedure.'

'Has anyone else seen it?'

'No.'

Lilly put her forehead on the sticky table. Part of her had hoped social services, the police and the pope himself had already seen it.

'It doesn't mean she did it,' Miriam said.

'No, it doesn't, but it's material evidence that points in her general direction.'

'I think it's just a bit of ranting from a distraught child.'

Lilly banged her head repeatedly against the hard wood of the table. 'Of course you do, Miriam, which is why you're so brilliant at what you do. You see the good in all these lousy kids no matter what they've done.'

A look of deep sadness followed by quiet resignation fell across Miriam's face. 'Someone has to.'

'But not me. I have to remain objective. I went to see the pathologist today and there's no good reason why Kelsey couldn't have done it. In fact, it's likely there was a close bond between murderer and victim. I have to imagine what other people will make of that, coupled with a letter that looks like a bloody confession,' said Lilly.

'Do they have to see it?' asked Miriam.

Lilly sighed. 'It might not be down to me. The police might find the original.'

'This is a murder investigation, the police will have been through everything in the flat. My guess is the mother destroyed it.'

They sat in silence. Lilly knew that Miriam had destroyed her copy as well. She drained her glass and accepted that the ultimate decision did indeed lie with her.

'I would never ask you to do anything wrong, Lilly, but you know what this would mean,' Miriam said.

Lilly squeezed her eyes shut and imagined the aftermath of disclosing this piece of evidence. The police would have enough to pursue Kelsey. With Mrs Mitchell's statement they might even secure a conviction. A child locked away with adult criminals. It was a pressure some kids couldn't bear.

'My duty to the court in care proceedings overrides everything else. If information comes my way that may affect the child's wellbeing then I must disclose it. It's then a matter for the judge whether or not the evidence is passed to the police.'

'But you have a different duty in criminal proceedings,' Miriam pointed out.

'The client's confidentiality is paramount in those cases. I'm not obliged to assist the prosecution in any way. I certainly shouldn't actively help them build their case,' said Lilly.

'That's a pretty heavy conflict,' said Miriam.

Tears stung Lilly's eyes. 'At the moment this is a care case so I ought to show the letter to the judge . . . '

'But,' said Miriam.

'But I get the feeling it won't be long before the police make their involvement official.'

'Arrest her?' asked Miriam.

'Bound to,' said Lilly. 'And I wouldn't want to make matters worse by waving around a letter they'll just use against her.'

She had no idea what to do.

Finally she sniffed and said, more to herself than to Miriam, 'Maybe the police will find out who killed Grace before I have to decide.'

CHAPTER FIVE

Friday, 11 September

Lilly arrived at The Bushes at 10 a.m. with the sun already soaring high and clear. After the discomfort of the previous day she'd dressed in a T-shirt, but when she got out of the car she rubbed her arms as the chill of the shadows greeted her.

Her plan was to find out what her client knew. Although the law made it clear that the child's welfare was paramount, Lilly wasn't about to abet a serial killer. Some straight talking was called for. She checked herself. Kelsey, of course, couldn't talk.

In Lilly's bag were a paper and pen. Not great, but it would have to do.

Lilly looked down at the photograph. It was a police mugshot taken a year before Grace's death, when she was picked up in a sweep of the red-light district. The mother of four had been twenty-nine when she died but looked nearer to forty. Her face was thin with eyes buried deep in their sockets, her skin pulled taut over her cheekbones. She had spots and wrinkles, the remarkable combination a result of long-term abuse, both physical and emotional. Her name was Grace, but never had a person been so misnamed.

Lilly wondered whether the poor soul had ever been truly happy.

She thought of the photograph taken by the sea, of the picture pinned to the fridge. It didn't need a detective to realise the only thing of any worth in Grace's life had been her family.

She pushed the photo towards Kelsey, who sat in silence at the other side of her bed, a notepad and pen beside her. All Lilly's harsh thoughts subsided. This was a child, and a traumatised one at that.

'Tell me about your mum.'

Kelsey shrugged and began to pick the scabs around her mouth, lifting the edges with the nail of her little finger.

'Okay, tell me about your sisters. Were you close? Did you fight?' Lilly asked.

Kelsey couldn't smile because of the scabs but a light danced in her eyes. It was the first Lilly had ever seen there and it answered both questions.

'Big families are like that. My brothers used to beat me up every afternoon so they could watch their programmes on the telly,' said Lilly, who was an only child.

Kelsey's nod was emphatic.

'I bet you used to let the little ones get their own way in the end.'

Again, the twinkle in her eyes was fleeting but it was there.

'Did you have to help out a lot?'

Kelsey put out her hand and rocked it to and fro.

'I suppose everyone had to chip in?'

The girl nodded.

Now for the hard one. 'Someone killed your mum, Kelsey, and the police think it was you.' Lilly swallowed. 'Did you kill her?'

Kelsey shook her head very slowly. Lilly watched intently for any sign of deceit.

'So who did?'

Kelsey looked down and went back to the scabs.

'How about a punter, did they ever come to the flat?' Lilly asked.

The girl held up her hand and seesawed it again. *Sometimes.*

'Were they ever strangers?'

Kelsey frowned and shook her head vigorously.

'So the only punters allowed at the flat were regulars – and the others, where did she service them?'

Kelsey picked up the pen and scribbled the word *message.*

'Message?' Lilly shook her head. 'I don't understand.'

Kelsey put down her pen and stroked her arms and legs.

'You mean massage! Your mum saw clients at a massage parlour,' said Lilly.

Kelsey nodded.

'Do you know which one?'

Kelsey spread her arms wide.

'Lots of different ones.'

64

Lilly wasn't surprised. Working girls often spread themselves thinly.

'Now tell me about Max,' said Lilly. 'Was he your mum's pimp?'

A single but firm shake of the head. A definite no.

'What then? A friend?'

Kelsey shrugged.

God, this was hard going, but Lilly tried not to show it.

'How did they meet?'

Lilly was shocked when Kelsey pointed to the floor and to the walls.

'Here! Grace knew Max when he lived here?'

Kelsey nodded.

'Did she visit him here?'

Kelsey looked puzzled and shook her head.

Lilly tried to grasp where she'd gone wrong. 'Not here. Your mum didn't visit Max here.'

Kelsey knitted her brow. She was adamant. Grace had not visited Max in The Bushes. She picked up the photograph of her dead mother and pointed to the bed.

'I don't understand,' said Lilly. 'Write it down for me.'

When Kelsey finished scribbling Lilly almost shouted out.

Mum was in care as well.

Grace had lived here too. She and Max went back years and had stayed in touch all that time. Could this be the close relationship Dr Cheney had described?

'Was he ever violent to your mum?'

Kelsey nodded then shook her head. Her eyes were bright with tears as if the truth were unfathomable.

Lilly wanted to shake Kelsey. Couldn't the kid see how important this was? But one glance at Kelsey told Lilly she didn't see that at all. She had lost her mum and everything else was of no consequence.

Lilly leaned over and gently moved Kelsey's hand from her mouth, which had started to bleed.

'I am truly sorry about your mum. It must be the worst thing that has ever happened to you.'

Kelsey held Lilly's gaze then picked up the notebook again.

The worst thing was when we got split up.

Charlene scrambled through the contents of her rucksack to locate her phone. Another text had come through, the fourth in so many days. When she had received the first she thought he was taking the piss but she had been wrong, he meant what he was saying. She reread all four and glowed. Apart from him, no one had ever said she was special.

Max parked his car across from the market. He wound down his window and waited for the girl to arrive.

He'd sent numerous texts but it wasn't a prearranged meeting. Most of the kids from The Bushes headed down here at lunchtime to mooch around the stalls and eat chips from white polystyrene trays.

He and Grace had done it themselves, laughing hysterically, arms linked, sharing their food if they were skint, which they were more often than not. If

Gracie's dad had had any luck on the horses he'd send her some cash and she'd treat them both to a battered sausage and chips. Since Grace could never manage more than a few mouthfuls before handing on her tray, Max would end up with a lunch fit for a sumo wrestler.

'You've got hollow legs,' she'd tease, trying to pinch the skin around his ribs.

Max had often wondered why Grace didn't live with her dad, since he obviously loved his daughter enough to share his good fortune, even if he was a bit handy with his fists.

'It's better this way, for him and me,' she'd say. 'And I couldn't leave you on your lonesome, could I?'

Max dragged himself from his memories and ordered himself not to think about her. Grace was dead. Grace was gone. And anyway, the bitch had betrayed him, just like everyone else.

He turned his thoughts to Charlene. If she turned up he'd grab her while he had the chance, if not he'd try again tomorrow. It was a total pain but he couldn't risk meeting her at the unit. Not with Kelsey there. He didn't think he could face her, not now.

Several residents got off the bus and made straight for Big Lynne's burger van. Most looked over at Max and admired his gleaming BMW. He'd have been just the same at their age, impressed by the bling of a luxury car, not noticing it was nine years old and worth about a grand.

He watched them larking around throwing chips at each other. Charlene wasn't with them. Maybe she hadn't come. He waited until they'd finished their lunch and set off to the arcades.

He'd been hanging about for nearly an hour and was itching for a toot. He was about to give it up and head back to the estate to score when he saw her. She was on her own, as usual, fingering a rack of cheap trousers, the sort that hung too low on the hips. Crap like that would cost a fiver at the most so he got out of his car and approached, intending to buy them for her.

Unaware that she was being watched by Max or anyone else, the girl slipped the trousers into her bag. As she turned to leave, the burly stallholder, a cigarette dangling from the corner of his mouth, caught her by the arm and a scuffle ensued.

Charlene struggled to get away and clawed at the man until her false nails began to snap off one by one, sounding like popcorn in a hot pan. She screamed that she was being attacked, but the stallholder clung on, his cigarette in place, one eye closed against the plume of smoke. A crowd began to gather, amused by the spectacle, glad for a reason to put down their shopping bags on such a warm day. They pointed and tittered; even Big Lynne put down her spatula and leaned her not inconsiderable girth over her greasy counter to see what the fuss was about. She gave a fleshy thumbs-up to her fellow market worker who seemed to have the situation under control until the girl gave her captor a swift kick in the groin.

'Ooh,' cried the audience as one.

In an effort to protect himself the stallholder let go of the girl's arm and she instantly fled, unchallenged by the shoppers until another man caught her around the waist.

'Jack Mc-fucking-Nally,' she shouted.

'Charlene Clarke,' he answered.

At the sight of the policeman Max cursed and slunk back to his car.

Hermione stirs her coffee but doesn't drink it. She already feels giddy with power and caffeine might send her over the edge.

When central office had suggested she request a meeting with the Chief Superintendent she had not shared their confidence that he would have any interest in hearing her views, but less than twenty-four hours later here they are in his office. The inner sanctum.

She wishes she had someone to tell, to share in the excitement. She is forty-six and doesn't have a friend. She has never had a friend. Colleagues yes, associates plenty, acquaintances by the truckload, but no special friend.

Even at boarding school, forced to spend twenty-four hours a day with the same set of girls, she didn't forge any firm bonds. She wasn't bullied nor deliberately excluded, just overlooked. In the dorm the other pupils would share her tuck and copy her prep, but she was never invited to birthday teas or slumber parties. During the school holidays the others often visited one another but Hermione was never asked. She supposes she should have done the inviting, but home was always fraught, with her father's ceaseless moans about money and her mother's demands that he get a better job.

Hermione recalls one summer when her mother had told every guest passing through that her daughter had been all-round winner at sports day with a special commendation for gymnastics. When the vicar had implored the singularly un-athletic Hermione to strut her stuff she'd been forced to perform a ludicrously cack-handed cartwheel.

'Actually,' said her mother to the embarrassed assembly, 'Hermione has sprained her wrist, but she's too polite to say.'

For the remainder of August her mother had suggested Hermione might like to sport a bandage.

Hermione sighs. She would have loved to share today's good fortune with her mother. Still, she has William.

The policeman smiles politely. 'You've been somewhat critical of the police in recent days, Mrs Barrows, and I'm wondering where you're going with it and whether you've considered how damaging your comments could prove.'

She gives him credit for his efforts to backfoot her, but William had predicted this tactic and warned against any platitudes on her part. 'Stay on the offensive, darling.'

'My comments reflect the views of my constituents, the people you and I serve. Your failure to act upon those views is damaging the police, not my rhetoric,' she says.

He steeples his fingers and taps his nose. She simply

waits, her smile sanguine. She has outwitted more complex characters than him before. She has kept her cool in situations more difficult than this.

'Does central office know you intend to pursue this issue?' he asks.

'Of course. But you already know that,' she answers.

He feigns innocence. 'How could I?'

Time for them both to lay their cards on the table.

'Your press office called mine this morning. If I was skiing off-piste they would have whipped me back in line and we wouldn't be having this meeting. Since I have party backing you are obliged to take me seriously.'

'What's your next move?' he asks.

'Interviews with the press in the next hour,' she replies. 'Tell me you intend to investigate the girl and what I say will be more palatable.'

'She's not fit to be interviewed at present,' he says.

'Then we've nothing to discuss.' She stands up and smooths her jacket from collar to hem. When she reaches the door, she turns. 'This is a huge mistake.'

When he is sure she has left he picks up his phone.

'Get me Jack McNally.'

Miriam did something she hated and shut the door to her office. A closed door meant she was off limits, too busy to speak, and when people had no one to speak to bad things happened.

'Did she do it?' she said.

Lilly shrugged. 'She says not.'

'Do you believe her?'

'What the hell do I know, Miriam, I'm not a shrink.'

Miriam watched her friend and colleague run her fingers through her hair. She knew how seriously Lilly took her job and could see how tortured she was feeling. She also knew from the fatigue etched around Lilly's eyes that old memories, and bad ones at that, were forcing their way into this mess.

'Go home and get some rest.'

Why bother saying it when she knew Lilly couldn't do that. Despite what her friend thought Miriam *had* kept a copy of Kelsey's letter and was bound by no professional rules on disclosure. She could hand it over to Jack and put Lilly out of her misery. Let the authorities decide what should happen to Kelsey. It seemed such a sensible course of action, and yet she would never do it.

Miriam had her own set of rules that she had adhered to since the death of her son, and they had kept her going so far. To break them now would be a betrayal, not only to Kelsey but to the life that Miriam had created. People admired her unerring commitment to the children in her care, but she was not self-deluded and accepted that without it she would be just another grieving mother, and she was not strong enough to face that prospect. She felt for Lilly, but Miriam had her own ghosts to keep at bay. By protecting vulnerable children she protected herself. What did shrinks call it? Transference? Repression?

She put her hand over Lilly's and was thinking about what to say when the door opened and Jack poked his head in.

'Is this a hot girl moment or can anyone join in?'

The tension was broken and Miriam was glad to see Lilly laugh.

'What can I do for you, Jack?' asked Miriam.

He pulled Charlene into view. 'I caught this one on the rob.'

The girl pulled at her dirty boob tube. 'I didn't do nothing.'

'Those trousers just fell into your bag, I suppose,' he said.

'It's a fit-up.' Charlene pointed a stubby finger in his face. 'You planted them on me.'

Jack pushed her hand away. 'You watch too many films.'

'Go to the television room, Charlene, I'll speak to you in a moment,' Miriam said.

Charlene bristled with indignation, but sloped off all the same.

Miriam was glad to be on well-trodden ground. It felt firm beneath her feet. 'What happened, Jack?'

'She tried to steal a pair of trousers from the market. Got caught,' he replied.

'Damn. The stupid girl's still on a caution from last time.'

Jack waved his hand. 'Don't worry, I squared it with the stallholder. He's not pressing charges.'

'You're a saint, McNally,' said Miriam.

He glanced at Lilly. 'Not everyone thinks so.'

Miriam caught the look that passed between them but couldn't decode it. 'Let's read her the riot act.'

Charlene was alone in the television room, the other children not yet back from the market.

'You lot wanna see this,' she laughed.

On the television was their MP, Hermione Barrows, her face contorted into something she no doubt called sincerity.

'From your comments it would seem you believe Grace Brand's daughter was responsible for her death,' said the *Look East* reporter.

'I am not party to the evidence in this case and have no idea whether there is anything to substantiate that. It isn't my job to say who is innocent and who is guilty. However, it is my job to speak out if I believe the police are not investigating fully.'

Hermione paused and looked directly into the camera. 'If the police have reason to believe that Grace Brand's daughter was involved then she should be arrested and charged. If she is guilty then she should be punished. It is time to stop making excuses and make the streets of Britain safer for everyone.'

'For fuck's sake,' said Lilly, and walked out.

Jack and Miriam watched the programme to the end. Spurred by the MP's comments, the great and the good came out of the woodwork to lend their support, and a spokeswoman for the regional constabulary confirmed that the murder was still very much the subject of an investigation. Finally, the reporter reminded the viewers of other murders committed by children, including Mary Bell and the killers of young Jamie Bulger.

When she heard the sound of the others arriving, Charlene sprinted off to spread the word.

'It doesn't look good,' said Miriam.

'No,' answered Jack with a sniff.

'Lilly's going to take a lot of heat.'

Jack shrugged.

'What's with you two?' Miriam asked.

'Dunno.'

Miriam patted his shoulder. 'You've crossed swords before.'

Finally she noticed Jack's hangdog eyes and the teenage pout. How had she missed it? Had she been afraid of intimacy for so long that she had failed to detect the sexual tension between Lilly and Jack?

'She won't even talk to me,' said Jack.

'You're on different sides of the fence right now,' said Miriam.

Jack shook his head. 'It shouldn't be like this. We've always worked together.'

Miriam bit her lip. Apart from a couple of uninspiring and guilt-inducing flings, Lilly had been on her own since the divorce. Jack was just the sort of honest and decent man she'd want for her friend, so why wasn't she happy for her? Why instead did Miriam want to turn this situation to her advantage? She could dress it up as commitment to her cause, but she accepted that calling it manipulation was closer to the mark.

'Lilly doesn't believe Kelsey killed her mother. Maybe you should take her seriously and look into this Max thing. He and Grace had a history you know.'

'Does Lilly have any evidence about this? Has Kelsey said anything?' asked Jack.

'That's a matter for Lilly and her client, Jack, you know that, but maybe he's the one you're looking for,' Miriam answered.

Jack got up to leave. 'I can't chase maybes.'

Miriam nodded, but could see she'd steered him in the right direction. Lilly was his Achilles heel and she had just touched the spot.

Jack left the unit and got into his car. Miriam had a point. Recalling Kelsey's tiny frame, bent over so he couldn't see her eyes, wasn't it more likely that Max had murdered Grace? He was a pimp, a user, a lowlife. Checking him out made perfect sense; at the very least he could find out where he was on the night in question. And it would surely cheer Lilly up. Not that that would be a priority in the murder case, more a happy by-product.

'You, Jack McNally,' said Becca, 'can make anything right in your own mind.'

Becca was Jack's last serious girlfriend. His only serious girlfriend, if truth be told, although he'd had a few short-lived flings. She had imparted this piece of wisdom whenever he blamed hangovers on bad pints and dodgy curries. And she'd repeated it, more vociferously, when he told her she was better off without him on the morning he'd left Belfast for good.

He pulled out his mobile to tell Lilly of his plan when he noticed he'd had a message. He was shocked to hear the voice of the Chief Superintendent in person.

* * *

The drive from The Bushes to Sam's school took less than twenty minutes, but Ring Farm and Manor Park existed in parallel universes. Within five miles Lilly had left behind the grey tombs of the sink estates and arrived in the countryside. She avoided Harpenden and took the winding lanes through the villages which danced round it.

She always felt Harpenden and Ring Farm were both soulless in their own way, but the villages were alive. Cottages and houses jumbled around a post office, a newsagent and a couple of pubs. Each dwelling was incongruous and bubbled with its own personality.

Not for Lilly an estate of any variety, even those where every home had five bedrooms and a double garage.

Lilly's mother had hated uniformity. When the council had painted every door on the estate brown she had got up an hour early and sprayed it silver before heading off for work.

'The joy of life is its twists and turns,' her mother had always said, and Lilly couldn't agree more.

As she neared the school, the trees that flanked each side of the lane stretched over to meet, their branches entwined like limbs. Only dappled light fell through the canopy. Lilly enjoyed the calm of this living tunnel before she pulled into the school gates.

She parked and then stood in the bright sunshine and waved at Sam. He giggled and chatted with a friend as he made his way towards her.

'Can Toby come to tea?' he asked.

Oh God. Lilly had hoped to throw a pizza in the

oven and let Sam eat in front of *Star Wars* while she got on with some research.

'I'll ask his mum,' she said.

She wandered over to the shiny 4x4, where Penny was feeding apple segments to her other children.

'Sam wondered if Toby could come to tea.'

Penny pushed her hair behind tiny ears.

'I'm sure it's too little notice for you,' said Lilly.

'Not at all. I'm sure he'd love it. I was just wondering what day it was,' said Penny.

Lilly was puzzled. 'It's Friday.'

'I mean is it a ballet, tennis or piano day,' said Penny with a musical laugh.

Lilly held strong views on the middle-class obsession with extracurricular activities. 'Ah,' she said.

'But it's not. So by all means take him with you.'

Lilly got Toby safely belted into the car. He looked disconcerted by the muddy seats and the debris in the footwells.

'Are you hungry?' asked Lilly.

'We usually have some fruit on the way home,' the boy whispered.

Sam brandished two bags of Hula Hoops. 'We always eat these.'

A smile broke across Toby's face like a wave. 'Awesome.'

The boys wolfed down their tea and headed off to play football in the garden. Lilly could hear their laughter through the open door as she logged onto the internet. If she were to help Kelsey she would have to give the police something on Max. Something concrete. Jack had confirmed he was a pimp and a pornographer and Lilly wondered if there would be anything about him on the net.

She entered 'Max Harding' and 'sex' into the search engine. Nothing exact came up, but the nearest hit was a site called 'Maximum Hard On'. She checked the boys were still outside and entered the site.

The pixels began to coagulate to reveal a voluptuous blonde sucking a green lollipop. She gave a wave of welcome. Lilly waved back and travelled through the site. Further in, it became more explicit, but there was nothing to link it with her suspect. In any event it was both pedestrian and legal, bog-standard fucking and sucking.

'Hello there.'

Lilly looked up and was shocked to see Luella next to her desk, looking over her shoulder at the large breasts that filled the screen.

'You left your key in the door,' said Luella.

Lilly had been so horrified to see her she hadn't given a thought to how she had got in.

'Penny's stuck at the doctor's with the baby so I said I'd collect Toby,' Luella told her.

Lilly looked from Luella to her computer. The blonde was now on all fours, lollipop still in place, while another woman inserted an unfeasibly large dildo into her arse.

Lilly scrabbled to exit the site. 'Research.'

Luella's terse smile said it all.

* * *

William Barrows felt his sap rising. The girl – *his girl*, as he was already thinking of her – was taking over. He imagined how she would feel and how she would smell. He could concentrate on nothing else, and it was painfully exquisite.

Then the black man had left a message. The idiot had '*experienced some difficulties*' so the meeting with the girl was postponed.

It infuriated Barrows that he was reliant upon such an imbecile, but he had no choice. It was too dangerous to do the grooming himself. He had done it in the past and enjoyed the process, but he no longer had the access or the patience and sought instead only the thrill of action.

He bit the inside of his cheek until he tasted the iron tang of blood. These days, if he encountered any impediment to his ultimate satisfaction he was no longer able to steer himself to a safer path, but instead felt overcome with rage. A rage he needed to satiate.

When the woman answered the door her smell almost knocked him off balance. The foul stench of a thousand fucks and used condoms, drowning in perfume. Oddly, the woman used the old-fashioned kind that came in a glass bottle, which his grandmother had called 'scent'. Violets and sugar. Barrows gagged.

'Put it in the usual place, darling,' she said, and pointed to the dusty bedside table covered in bangles, rings and a snakes' nest of cheap gold chains.

He opened the heart-shaped box, inlaid with small white shells, and placed eighty pounds inside. The woman was leaning against a chair to remove her baggy leggings, the legs beneath as flabby and shapeless as the trousers. She saw that he was watching, grinned, and ran a hand over her vast backside, as white and pitted as the surface of the moon.

The contents of Barrows' stomach, a goat's cheese and vine-ripened-tomato salad, rose in his throat at the thought of even touching this monster.

He inhaled deeply, fingered the damp cloth in his pocket, and reminded himself that he had not come for sex.

CHAPTER SIX

Saturday, 12 September

The glare through the windscreen was painful. Lilly pulled at the broken sun-shield and admonished herself yet again for failing to have her prescription put in some sunglasses. It was not yet 10 a.m. but the temperature was already past seventy degrees. Lilly felt the prickle of sweat in her armpits as she pulled into a parking space, and wondered if autumn was ever going to arrive.

She turned to her passengers. 'Everyone okay?'

Miriam nodded, Kelsey hid her face under a sheet of lank hair, and the three of them made their way into the police station.

The air-conditioning in the custody suite was broken and the desk sergeant was trying to keep the area cool with three rotating fans. As the one on his right swivelled towards him a raft of papers blew to the floor. Cursing, he picked them up and secured them with a cup of cold coffee, which sloshed gently over the rim.

'What have you got for me, McNally?' the sergeant asked as Jack came in.

Jack motioned to Kelsey, who was flanked by Lilly and Miriam, and sat on a wooden bench to the left.

'CID want to interview the girl on an SAO.'

The sergeant sighed. A Serious Arrestable Offence always meant extra bloody paperwork. 'Nobody bothered to tell me. Will you need the video room?'

Jack nodded.

'God help you, it's like an oven in there,' said the sergeant.

Lilly glared at Jack as he arrested and searched Kelsey. 'Got you doing the dirty work, have they?'

He ignored her and completed the paperwork.

'I'll need your details, Miss Valentine,' said the desk sergeant. He pointed to the relevant space on the custody sheet and offered her a chewed biro.

Lilly ignored the pen and slapped her card into his hand so he could copy out the necessary information himself. It was a petty gesture that she instantly regretted.

'I'm sorry if I seem curt, but I object most strongly to this course of action.'

The sergeant turned to Jack for enlightenment.

'Li— Miss Valentine is of the opinion that Kelsey isn't fit to be interviewed, given that she recently tried to harm herself.'

'Given that she swallowed a bottle of bleach only two weeks ago,' Lilly interjected, 'and shortly afterwards found out her mother was brutally murdered, it is my professional opinion that dragging her here for questioning is

83

entirely wrong, and Miriam Zander, the appropriate adult, is of exactly the same opinion.'

The sergeant looked close to sixty and was probably only months from retirement. Lilly guessed he would have no desire to be cited in a case for wrongful imprisonment of a minor.

He turned to Jack. 'What do you say, mate?'

'Interesting though it might be to hear what McNally has to say,' announced a voice from behind, 'it's not his case.'

They turned as one to see a formidable figure striding towards the desk. In one deft movement he collected up all the papers.

'This case is mine, and I say Ms Brand is fit to answer some questions.'

Lilly scowled at the man sitting opposite, pristine in an expensive suit and antique silver cufflinks. She hated these fast-track police officers with their public-school accents and degrees in philosophy. How old was he? Thirty at most, and in charge of a murder rap.

He angled the camera towards Kelsey, who sat next to Lilly, her chin tucked into her chest, her arms crossed tightly around her stomach.

'I assume you've advised your client that interviews for serious offences such as this are sometimes recorded visually as well as orally.'

Lilly's tone was polite. 'Of course.'

'And she understands the procedure?' he asked.

'I've no idea, Officer, I'm not a psychiatrist, nor am I a clairvoyant,' Lilly replied.

Out of the corner of her eye she saw Jack biting his lip.

The younger man took off his jacket and hung it on the back of his chair, releasing the smell of his freshly laundered shirt. Lilly wished that she could do the same but knew there were dark circles under each of her arms.

'Kelsey, I'm going to begin recording, so please look up,' he said.

Kelsey buried her head even further into her collarbone. The camera picked up only the crown of her head.

The policeman's smile didn't slip. 'First, let me explain, for the sake of the tape, who everyone is. My name is DI Bradbury; the officer in the corner is Jack McNally. Also present is your solicitor.' He smiled at Lilly. 'Could you give your name please?'

'I'm Lilly Valentine and should say, at this stage, for the sake of the tape, that this interview should not, in my view, take place.'

Bradbury opened his mouth to speak but Lilly wasn't finished, not by a long way. She put up her hand as if to shush a small child.

'You stated in the custody suite, Detective, that you believe Kelsey is fit to be interviewed, and I'd be grateful if you could expand on that position, given you've never met her before today.'

His smile remained intact. 'This isn't a forum for you to question me, Miss Valentine, this is simply the preliminary stage of the interview where we all introduce ourselves. If you're unsure of the procedure I'm happy to help you as we go along.'

Lilly could feel her colour rising but kept her face serene in case she was in shot.

Bradbury, clearly pleased to have scored a point, pressed on. 'Also present is Kelsey's appropriate adult. Could you state your name please?'

Miriam said nothing.

'Could you . . . ?'

'Oh, you mean me. I thought you said the appropriate adult should state their name, and I wondered who you meant,' said Miriam.

DI Bradbury looked puzzled. Lilly knew she could rely on Miriam. The women had done this many times before and were a class double-act. Jack had been on the receiving end of their treatment enough times to know what was coming, and Lilly half-expected him to intervene. She risked a glance in his direction and saw him chewing his lip even harder. Bradbury was on his own.

'Since this interview is entirely inappropriate I can't really call myself an appropriate adult,' said Miriam. Then she snapped her fingers as if something had just occurred to her.

'How about this? My name is Miriam Zander and I'm the inappropriate adult.'

Bradbury smoothed his tie. 'This is ridiculous.'

Miriam nodded. 'Yes, it is. It's my job, you see, to make sure a vulnerable person receives the extra protection afforded to them by the Police and Criminal Evidence Act 1984, and in order to protect this particular vulnerable person I am asking that this interview doesn't take place.'

86

'If you're unsure of the implications of the Police and Criminal Evidence Act 1984,' added Lilly, 'I'm happy to help as we go along.'

If Bradbury was ruffled he didn't show it. He was good, very good.

'You've had your say, ladies, and made your views abundantly clear, but on this occasion I'm going to overrule you and proceed with the interview.'

'It's open to you to ignore us,' Lilly interrupted, 'but it's for a judge to adjudicate if we're wrong and ultimately to overrule us. Still, I'm sure he'll be glad to learn you decided for him in advance which pieces of evidence were admissible and which were not.'

Bradbury ignored her. 'Kelsey, as you know you have been arrested on suspicion of murdering Grace Brand. You do not have to say anything when questioned but it may harm your defence if you do not mention something now which you later wish to rely upon in court. Do you understand?'

All four adults watched her, but she remained motionless except for the soft rise and fall of her shoulders as she breathed.

The silence was broken by Bradbury. 'I know how hard this must be for you, Kelsey,' his voice was a study in calm and reason, 'but you need to answer some questions.'

'Not so, Detective. That thing we mentioned earlier, the Police and Criminal Evidence Act, provides for a person's right to remain silent. Kelsey is under no duty to answer your questions,' said Lilly.

'You're quite right, Miss Valentine, but, as you also

know, a person's decision not to answer relevant questions can be the subject of comment at a later stage,' he answered.

Lilly smiled benignly as she handed Bradbury a spade. 'You mean a jury may infer her guilt because she chooses not to speak now.'

'Exactly,' he said, and leaned towards his suspect. 'You see, Kelsey, a jury might find it pretty strange that you don't want to set the record straight.'

'True enough, Detective, but I shall be more than happy to explain to any court why it was not the right time to speak today,' said Lilly.

'Me too,' added Miriam.

Lilly could sense the DI's discomfort but it was still thickly masked.

'Once again, ladies, your position is very clear, but once again I intend to continue. Kelsey, where were you on the night your mother was killed?'

Kelsey was curled so tightly he was speaking to her shoulder blades.

'When people see this video they're going to think it very strange that you wouldn't even answer that.'

Lilly sighed as if exasperated. 'No they're not, Detective.'

Bradbury, cut off at every avenue, snapped. He banged his fist on the table, making Lilly and Miriam jump.

'Don't tell me. You'll explain to the jury how terrible the police were. How they shouldn't have even dreamed of investigating the murder of a woman beaten to death with a hammer in her own home.'

Lilly eyed him coolly. 'On the contrary, I think you *should* be investigating who did this, rather than looking to my client. There are plenty of alternative suspects and I've already suggested one name to Officer McNally.'

'And no doubt he's looking into that. In the meantime, I want to ask Kelsey some questions and, frankly, if my mother had been murdered I'd want to set the record straight, wouldn't you?' Bradbury shouted.

She had him on the run. 'What I would or wouldn't do is irrelevant. The point that I was trying to make to the custody sergeant before you burst in like Batman, and the point I've been trying to make since the start of this interview, is Kelsey *cannot* answer your questions today.'

Bradbury was on his feet, towering over Lilly and her client. 'Why the hell not?'

Lilly grabbed Kelsey's chin and brutally displayed her damaged face.

'Because she can't fucking speak.'

The Hart of the County FM may not be *Question Time*, but it has 12,000 listeners, most of whom care nothing for politics but are happy to hear the sad saga of Grace Brand. The weekly current-affairs magazine usually draws a smaller audience than *Gardeners' Half Hour*, but today is different. Today they expect numbers to rival *Drive Time Love In*, when members of the public share their tales of eyes meeting across dance floors dripping in cheap lager and puke.

Cashing in on a story run in the local *Standard*,

which compared, inaccurately but salaciously, the current murder investigation to that of the Yorkshire Ripper, The Hart of the County is using the entire slot to discuss the subject.

Had Grace's life of prostitution led her to such a tragic end?

Was an international drug ring involved?

Are the good citizens of the Clayhill Estate safe in their beds?

Hermione is waiting to be interviewed. She wonders whether the pathetic creature Grace had been in life would have approved of all this publicity. No doubt she would have relished her fifteen minutes of fame.

The presenter's young assistant signals that Hermione will be needed in three minutes. Hermione avoids looking at the huge bulge of her stomach, the breasts rounded and ripened by pregnancy. She takes a deep breath in preparation but her mobile rings.

'Mrs Barrows?'

'Yes.'

'This is the Chief Superintendent, do you have a moment?'

'Literally that, Officer, I'm at the radio station for an interview.'

'Then you'll be glad to have up-to-date information. I wouldn't want you to make a fool of yourself,' he says.

She is tempted towards a clever retort, something William might say, but nothing comes to mind.

'I'm listening,' she says.

'Kelsey Brand has been arrested and is being questioned about her mother's death as we speak.'

As Hermione walks towards the studio, the 'on air' sign lights up in fluorescent green, and she can't contain a smile. Is it this easy to take control, to make things happen? If power begets power she'd be in the cabinet by the end of the year, and everything she'd gone through, everything she'd done, would be justified.

'Look, John – may I call you John?' Hermione asks, her voice just above a whisper, more like a purr but as resonant as glass.

'Of course,' he answers.

'I'm not saying this girl should be hung. I'm not on a witch hunt. I simply want justice to be done and to be seen to be done.'

'But you're pleased that she's been arrested?' says the presenter.

Hermione pauses for just the right length of time. Enough to denote serious consideration of the question without any suggestion of indecision.

'No, John, I'm not happy that the police have found it necessary to arrest a child for such a terrible crime. I wish our children played hopscotch and ate penny chews on their way home from school. I wish they read Enid Blyton and respected their elders, but this is a very different world to the one in which you and I grew up.'

'Kids run pretty wild these days,' he says.

'Yes, they do, John, and we as a community must put a stop to it.'

'Rumour has it the kid is pretty deranged,' he says.

'A source at the local hospital tells us she was admitted for drinking bleach. Is that true?'

Hermione clucks. 'Now, John, you know I can't discuss the details of this case.'

She doesn't dispute it, of course.

'Not the sort of kid you'd want running around the place, wouldn't you agree?' he says.

'The case is very worrying,' she replies.

The assistant rolls her hands. It is time to wrap up and cut to the break. The presenter nods and holds up a finger to Hermione. One minute left.

'Our listeners want to help, Hermione, what can they do?' he asks.

This is her last chance to make an impression. She pictures her mother and goes for it. 'Take responsibility, not just for your own lives but for those of our fellow citizens. Don't bury your head in the sand, be watchful of what goes on around you. Take action to protect your neighbourhood and start today. If anyone has any information about this brutal murder they should contact the police.'

'Because Grace deserved better.'

'Yes, she did.' Only those listening very closely would be able to detect the hint of a wobble in her voice. 'We all do.'

Hermione allows a smile. She knows she did well. She is her mother's daughter after all.

Mrs Mitchell turned off her radio and nodded. 'That politician makes a lot of sense.'

Her husband mumbled something to himself but

she didn't so much as look at him. Instead, she picked up her telephone.

The Chief Superintendent pressed the pause button and froze the scene in the interview room. Kelsey's face filled the screen, her eyes wide in terror, her chin held tight in Lilly's fingers, her mouth, an uneven crust, moving through red, brown and yellow.

Jack and Bradbury looked anywhere but at the screen.

'Jesus Christ, she made mincemeat of you,' said the Chief Superintendent.

'Yes, Sir, she did,' said Bradbury, his calm entirely returned.

'Can we get rid of the lawyer and have another crack?' the Chief Superintendent said.

'On what basis?' asked Jack.

The Chief Superintendent glared at him. Obviously there were ways and means Jack didn't know of.

Bradbury smoothed his tie, something Jack had seen him do throughout the interview. Perhaps it was his way of keeping control. Not a bad tactic, thought Jack, it stopped the man from fidgeting, gave him a second to think and looked thoroughly smooth. Jack resolved to give it a try in his next difficult interview, then remembered he never wore ties except to attend funerals and court hearings – two places he avoided like salad.

'Even if we were able to do that, Sir, we wouldn't be able to use a confession. It would simply prove that Valentine was right, and without the right protection the girl's vulnerable,' Bradbury said.

'Can we charge her without a confession?' the Chief Superintendent asked.

Bradbury nodded. 'There's nothing to stop us, but we don't have enough evidence to secure a conviction.'

'Does that matter?'

'We don't want to be seen to be pushing this because we're bowing to political pressure.'

The Chief Superintendent wagged a cautionary finger. 'But we do want to be seen to be taking it seriously.'

Jack kept his silence as the other men considered the problem. Clearly, there were issues here from which he was excluded not only by rank.

Bradbury spoke first. 'We could send the case papers to the CPS for advice, and make that public.'

Jack was surprised. 'Can't we just run it past the rep here at the station? They'll give us an answer on the spot.'

Bradbury shook his head. Clearly, a speedy response was not what they were looking for.

'I think someone senior should deal with a case of this importance. Maybe the DPP herself.'

The Chief Superintendent clapped his hands. 'Excellent. We'd still be taking action, but the ultimate decision not to do anything wouldn't be ours.'

'In the meantime we could look into the other suspect Valentine mentioned, so we've got legitimate ongoing inquiries,' said Bradbury.

'And we can't be accused of backing one horse.'

The two minds working together mesmerised Jack, and he wondered what it would be like to be included in the plan. He was about to find out.

'Jack, you investigate the other body,' ordered the Chief Superintendent.

'Yes, Sir.'

Jack found Lilly by the vending machine banging the side with full force.

'You'll break that.'

'Don't you start.'

He pressed a couple of buttons and out came a can of Diet Coke. She held the can against the side of her face for a second, opened it and took a grateful drink. The condensation had left a silver film on her cheek.

'What's the score, Jack?'

'We're asking for advice,' he said.

'Can I speak to the rep?'

Jack shook his head gingerly. 'This is too big for that. We're sending the papers to the DPP.'

Lilly threw up her arms in exasperation, showering herself with Coke. 'The DPP? What for? You know what she'll say. Without a confession you've no evidence.' She licked the spilled Coke from her forearm. 'I suppose Bradbury didn't want to let it go. These fast-track wankers love the big ones.'

Lilly rummaged inside her bag for a tissue and Jack took the can before she could spill any more.

'He's a good copper, Lilly. He doesn't want to hound Kelsey but he understands how things work.'

'His type are ambitious,' she said, dabbing her shirt-front.

'What's wrong with that? He doesn't want to spend

the rest of his life nicking fourteen-year-olds for joyriding, and I can't say I blame him.'

He took a swallow himself and handed the can back to Lilly. She put it straight to her lips. The gesture seemed intimate, almost sexual, but Jack was sure he was reading too much into it.

'Don't underestimate what it is you do, Jack. Small things matter to people's lives. We can't all change the world.'

'No, but we can try.'

Back in the custody suite the sergeant had given up on the fans. Sweat poured down his face and pooled under his chin before falling in fat drops onto his paperwork. He ran a damp fist across the soggy sheet and smeared Lilly's name into a blur.

Kelsey stood before him and he spoke to the crown of her head. 'You're not being charged at this time, love, and you'll remain on police bail until the CPS have looked at your case. Do you understand?'

For the first time that day Kelsey reached for the pen and pad Lilly had given her and scribbled a few words. She tore off the sheet and handed it to her solicitor. Tears welled in Lilly's eyes as she read it. Finally, she placed it on the desk.

AM I GOING TO JAIL NOW?

The faded sofa was deliciously comfortable. Miriam leaned back and sipped her wine. She loved Lilly's cottage, with its bowed ceilings and scuffed wood floors. Every inch of it ran amok, bursting with books, toys and photographs, the very antithesis of her own place, which was pared down to the brittleness of its bone.

When Lewis had died she'd wanted to rid herself of everything frivolous or futile, but the clearout became a purge until she could no longer allow herself any comforts.

Looking at the warm chaos around her she knew she was denying herself the most basic of things – a home. It was the ultimate punishment, which she inflicted on herself and gladly suffered.

Lilly stumbled from the kitchen with a tray piled high with food. Miriam helped herself to the dips and salads her friend had rustled up in less than ten minutes. Damn, that girl could cook.

'You did good at the station,' said Miriam. 'We both did.'

Lilly slavered purple putty onto some flatbread and spoke through a mouthful. 'Not good enough, girlfriend. The CPS will hang on to it for at least a month, and in the meantime there'll be a media frenzy. Whatever the outcome, no one will foster this kid.'

Miriam was ever the optimist. 'You don't know that for sure. There are some great people out there.'

'Which is the next problem. If Kelsey is guilty then other people need to be protected, particularly saintly foster mothers with four kids of their own,' said Lilly.

Miriam licked her fingers. The tang of yoghurt and fresh coriander was exhilarating in an evening still crushed by the heat. 'She says she didn't do it and that's enough for me.'

Lilly gave a half-smile. Evidently she couldn't agree.

One last piece of tomato sat in the empty bowl. Lilly stuffed it in her mouth and sighed.

'I've been through all the files and there's nothing to incriminate Max. I can't even find his website.'

Miriam pulled a buff folder from her rucksack. 'That's because you're looking in the wrong place.'

Lilly took the papers from her friend. They were dog-eared and dirty. 'Where'd you get them?'

Miriam shrugged that it was better not to ask, so Lilly began reading the social services file for Maxwell Hardy, dated 1989.

Lilly offered a finger of Twix to Miriam, who took it and went back to her half of the paperwork.

'Anything?'

'Nah. Quiet kid,' said Lilly. 'No background of violence, just a couple of cautions for TDA.'

Miriam shook her head. 'Taking and Driving Away? He's not exactly a master criminal, is he?'

Lilly nodded at Miriam's pile. 'What about that lot?'

'No social problems beyond what you'd expect of a kid in care,' said Miriam. 'School describes him as a persistent truant and an underachiever. Blah, blah. Good at music and art. Actually, he won a prize for a film he made in Media Studies.'

She handed the certificate to Lilly, who took one look at it and walked over to her computer.

'Sorry to bore you,' Miriam called after her.

Lilly tapped the name of the film into her search engine. 'Let's see if this thing is on the net.'

'A school music video? I don't think so,' said Miriam.

'Maybe he still uses the name.'

'After all these years?'

'In a life full of crap maybe it's the only thing he's ever had to be proud of.'

Bingo. Up came the site: www.maximum exposure.co.uk.

Lilly and Miriam huddled together in front of the screen, which had been catapulted into inky black. They looked at each other expectantly and then back to the blank screen. At last, red banners began to emerge.

Check out our live webcam girls. Uncensored xxx action.
see the ladies play in the pool
get hot hot hot in the sauna
or get down to some dirty action in the bedroom.

'On a night like tonight it's got to be the pool,' said Lilly, and clicked the mouse.

Two buttocks separated by a sliver of leather thong appeared in the left-hand corner, their owner unprepared to show herself until she saw the colour of her viewer's money.

Hi, I'm Randy Mandy and I'm dying to talk to you live on my webcam. Sometimes it makes me so HOT I have to take off all my clothes.

'So turn down the central heating, girl,' said Miriam.

Lilly trudged through the security and confirmed that, yes, she was over eighteen, yes, she understood that the site contained nudity and items of a sexual nature which some may find offensive, and, most importantly, yes, she would agree to the call being charged to her at a whopping £1.87 per minute.

Hurry, caller, Randy Mandy is getting uncomfortable and is dying to get naked with you.

'A pair of knickers that fit might help,' said Miriam.

Finally Lilly confirmed she was the person who paid the phone bill and access was granted. 'Shut up, now, Miriam.' Lilly adjusted the microphone on her own computer. Randy Mandy would be able to hear them but not see them. 'If she susses us too soon she'll lock us out.'

A few more minutes at premium rate were wasted with banners proclaiming this to be the wildest live site in the UK with the most beautiful babes on the net.

Our action will not disappoint.

'What action?' said Miriam.

Lilly shushed her as the painfully divided cheeks began to swell until they filled the screen.

'Hi there. What's your name?' came a detached voice.

Lilly guessed the woman was from Russia or somewhere in Eastern Europe.

'Miriam,' said Lilly, and winced as her friend elbowed her in the side.

The bottom retreated from the camera and a slender woman came into view. She stood in front of a cloth backdrop on which was painted a crude approximation of a beach and a swimming pool. Her flat stomach and smooth thighs were almost girlish but her bleached hair, cut in a poor imitation of Marilyn Monroe, and sallow complexion made her seem much older. She looked directly into her camera, and in the half-reality that is live webcam Lilly saw that she had startlingly green eyes.

'Well hello, Miriam, I am having to tell you I am just loving some girl-on-girl action.'

She ran her hands over her baby-pink shirt, so tight the buttons strained to keep the woman contained.

'Tell me, baby, what do you like me to do?'

Lilly turned to her friend in horror and mouthed 'What shall I say?', but Miriam could only bite her hand to suppress laughter.

'Come on, baby, don't be shy. Do you like me to unbutton my top?'

Lilly coughed. Her voice was dry and small. 'Er . . . yes.'

Randy Mandy's laugh tinkled as she ripped open her shirt and let it fall out of shot. A huge pair of gravity-defying breasts, utterly incongruous on such a small frame, were revealed.

'What do you think, Miriam? Do you like my body?'

As the woman fondled herself Lilly caught sight of the telltale half-moon scars. She shuddered.

'How about my pussy, do you like to see that? I am shaving especially for you.'

Lilly spluttered into her microphone.

'You haven't done this before, have you, sweetie?' said Randy Mandy.

'No,' Lilly admitted.

'Don't worry, there's a first time for everything.' Mandy's voice was honey. 'Why do you decide to come to this site?'

The sex worker's question may have been posed to put her nervous client at ease, or perhaps to waste a few premium-rate moments, but Lilly seized her opportunity.

'I knew a working girl called Grace Brand, she told me about Maximum Exposure.'

A shadow of recognition fell over the woman's face but she quickly plastered her smile back in place.

'Did you know her?' asked Lilly.

'That's enough talk now, baby,' said Mandy. 'Let's get hot, yes?'

Lilly wasn't about to give up. 'She got killed last week. It was in all the papers, you must have heard about it?'

Randy Mandy shook her head and tossed her lifeless hair over her shoulders. The breasts remained static.

'What about Max Hardy? You must have heard of him?'

Mandy's smile vanished. She seemed to age ten years.

'Doesn't he run this site?' asked Lilly.

'Not any more. He move on.' Mandy frowned and picked up her shirt. 'If that is type stuff you want you don't find here.'

'What type of stuff?' asked Lilly.

Mandy covered her breasts with her shirt and leaned towards her camera. 'I go now.'

The screen went dead. She had locked them out.

'Well, that's it, she's not going to talk to you again,' said Miriam.

Lilly smiled at her friend, a twinkle in her eye. 'If the mountain won't come to Mohammed . . .'

Barrows watched his wife work the crowd. She shook hands with the party faithful and accepted their support and congratulations with aplomb. Hermione was the hero of the hour and she sparkled with a new sense of purpose, her smile broader, her step lighter.

He waved to her and mouthed 'well done'. She waved back, but when their eyes met he didn't find warmth. Instead he saw something colder and darker.

He reaches for a glass of water and gulps it down together with his fear. He's being ridiculous, of course. She doesn't know. How can she? In all the years he's known her she hasn't been able to work out how to programme the video recorder let alone the blackest recesses of his mind.

Hermione curses herself as she walks towards the car. She had been taken over by the adulation and let her guard down. She had let her husband see beyond her façade, and he would now know that she saw beyond his. After twenty years of pretence they would have to confront the truth.

Barrows drove his wife home in silence. The woman beside him, who he thought he knew, who he thought he controlled, was beyond his reach. Does she know?

And if she did—what would she do now? Would she hand him over to the police? And ruin her newly ascendant star? He thought not. Even when he'd met her at Oxford she had lived life as if she were being watched. While the other students danced and drank with abandon, Hermione felt that what she wore, what she read, what she ate were matters of grave importance. She had waited her whole life to be somebody, she wouldn't blow it now. Instead she would insist it stop, insist he give up the hobby.

He pictured his life without it and rage began to swell in his temples.

He sped faster and faster through the streets of Luton, his hands gripping the steering wheel so tightly they hurt. He considered unlocking her seatbelt and slamming on the brakes so she would hurtle through the windscreen. He'd seen it done in a film and knew he had the guts. He had never allowed anything to stand in his way before.

He glanced at the locking mechanism. Hermione's hand rested on top and held her belt in place. A coincidence, or could she now anticipate his every move? He imagined she could read his thoughts, then berated his paranoia.

Eventually he swung the car onto their drive, a crunch of gravel beneath the tyres. He killed the engine and they sat for a few seconds, side by side, both staring straight ahead. His heart was pounding so loudly he was sure she could hear it.

'Do you have something to say, darling?' he asked, his voice stagey.

Hermione took a deep breath. 'I don't think so, William.'

Barrows was shaking but he had to know. 'I disagree.'

She spoke looking away from him, so that her voice sounded distant although they were only inches apart. 'I have known for some time now about your other life.'

He tried to sound surprised. 'Whatever do you mean?'

He wondered how she would put it. Would she use careful, deliberate language or the gutter expressions of the tabloids she loved to court? If she called him a child molester he would punch her until she could speak no more. He balled his fist, ready.

'Cut the crap, William, we both know you're gay.'

Barrows didn't speak, didn't dare to breathe.

Finally Hermione got out and turned to face him. 'We'll have to find some way to work it out.'

As she closed the door behind her he let out an audible sigh of relief.

'This is beyond stupid,' said Miriam.

'Way beyond,' Lilly agreed.

She wrote down her mobile number for the babysitter and felt a pang of guilt that if Sam woke up he wouldn't find his mother at home, but she needed to act quickly. If Max had sold his site it would be to someone local – Lilly doubted the man had ever even left Luton. That meant Mandy was probably still working in the area, but in a week's time, or even a couple of days, that could change. Girls moved parlours and brothels with ferocious speed, trading with whoever would pay the most. Websites opened and closed on an almost daily basis. Loyalty was in short supply for women in the oldest job in the world.

'Have you considered how we're actually going to do this?' Miriam asked.

Lilly picked up her car keys and ushered Miriam out of the cottage into the humid night. 'We'll head for Tye Cross. Someone will know her.'

'We can't just go to the nearest brothel and say, "Excuse me, we're looking for Randy Mandy. Do you know her? Blonde hair? Big boobs?!"'

'Why not?' said Lilly.

'Because they'll want to know who we are and why we're asking.'

Lilly put the car into gear and set off. 'We'll say we want you-know-what.'

Miriam looked at them both, a black dreadlocked woman in her early fifties with half-moon glasses and Birkenstocks and her colleague still in her now-dishevelled work suit and trainers.

She sounded unconvinced. 'A pair of lesbian sex tourists.'

Lilly gave her friend a wink. 'Just say you're after some girl-on-girl action.'

Tye Cross was synonymous with sex. Everyone in the area knew that this was the place to find a prostitute. Lilly had seen the name appear in numerous court papers, as many of her young clients had mothers working there. Some of them went there themselves, particularly if the lure of drugs had already sucked them into a black hole. Lilly, however, had never actually been to Tye Cross and was surprised to discover what amounted to little more than a few dingy streets dotted with sex shops and strip-clubs. In between were flats where customers prepared to pay a bit extra could satisfy themselves in the comfort of a bed rather than the back seat of a car. A couple of pawnbrokers, an Indian takeaway and an all-night café were the only other signs of life.

Several prostitutes lingered in doorways or wandered along the kerbside and peered into passing cars.

'Looking for business, love?'

Taking a deep breath, Lilly approached a prostitute standing alone outside a disused sari shop.

Everything must go. 50% discount, declared the peeling posters above the girl's head. Up close she seemed impossibly thin, and even tonight, when the temperature had not dropped below 65, her legs were mottled with purple honeycomb and she wrapped an oversized cardigan tightly around her tiny frame.

'I'm looking for a girl,' said Lilly.

The woman didn't respond but blew smoke in Lilly's direction.

'Her name is Mandy,' Lilly added.

The girl shivered, flicked her cigarette at Lilly and walked away.

Another woman, older and almost plump, called to them from her spot further up the road.

'Don't mind her, darling, she's waiting on a fix.'

She smiled at Lilly's blank expression. 'He's late tonight, the man that sells them young ones the drugs.'

Lilly nodded her comprehension. 'I'm looking for a girl called Mandy.'

'Oh aye.'

'Blonde, early twenties, I think she's foreign.'

The woman became distracted as a car pulled to a halt only a few feet away. 'They're all foreign these days, honey.'

Lilly realised that in one night she'd been called baby, darling, sweetie and honey by women she'd never met before in her life. It was intimacy at its most fake, and the women used these names without thinking.

The woman spoke over her shoulder as she moved towards a potential client. 'Try the girl on the counter in Sizzle, she knows most of them. Me, I keep my distance.'

Lilly watched her lean into the driver's window then crossed the road to Miriam, who was embroiled in conversation with two women who seemed to find the whole thing hilarious.

'Honestly, I'm not from any church,' said Miriam.

The taller of the two tugged absently at her hold-up stockings whose elastic had clearly seen much service and better days. 'Sure you are, sweetheart, you lot are always round here. Come to save our souls.'

Miriam persisted. 'No, really.'

'Never mind our souls, try our bloody arses,' roared the smaller woman, 'cos mine's as raw as a frigging bullet wound tonight.'

The women collapsed into laughter and careered across the road, arm in arm.

Miriam sighed. 'Any luck?'

Lilly was about to mention Sizzle when she spotted a familiar face. She gestured towards a group of young boys working the other side of the street. When they realised they were being scrutinised all but one scarpered.

The boy pulled down his baseball cap. 'Fuck it.'

'Hello Jermaine,' said Miriam.

'I ain't doing what you think, Miriam,' he said.

Miriam cocked her head to the left. 'No?'

'I'm clipping. You know, I'm pretending to work and then taking off with the money.'

Miriam kissed her teeth. 'I know what clipping is, and I know it's a stupid boy who thinks he can get away with it before someone gives him a kicking or worse.'

'Take him home in a cab, I'll stay a bit longer,' said Lilly.

'You going to be all right on your own?' asked Miriam.

'Course. I've got a lead I need to follow up.'

Sizzle was clean, bright and spacious inside. Lilly had never been in a sex shop and was amused to find neat racks of magazines and ordered rows of videotapes. The assistant eyed her solitary customer without interest and went back to pricing up outfits from a box marked, 'Fantasy Wear'.

Eventually Lilly made her way to the counter and peered in the glass cabinet displaying a forest of vibrators and dildos, the largest of which was over twenty centimetres and tartan.

The girl spoke through a wad of bubble gum, its saccharine smell filling the air. 'You want one of those?'

Lilly shook her head. 'I'm looking for someone.'

The girl's jaws moved up and down like a piston. 'This ain't a dating agency.'

'She's foreign. Russian, I think,' said Lilly. 'Calls herself Randy Mandy.'

The girl shrugged.

'Come on,' Lilly smiled, 'you must know all the regulars round here.'

The girl wasn't disarmed. 'I come in, do my job and go home. End of story.'

'But you must hear what's going on? Who's working which patch?'

'I make four quid an hour. It ain't enough for chit-chat.'

Lilly took out her purse and pulled out a twenty-pound note. 'She does a chat room called Maximum Exposure.'

The girl took the money. 'Most of the Russians work out of Fat Eric's. I think he's got a Mandy over there.'

Lilly smiled her thanks and turned to leave.

'He won't let you near her,' said the girl, sliding the banknote into her back pocket, her gum pushed into her cheek like a hamster.

'Why not?' asked Lilly.

'It's regulars only, so the girls don't get ideas.'

'What sort of ideas?'

The girl went back to her uniforms and her chewing.

Outside, the air seemed heavier, and Lilly's feet stuck to the pavement as she made her way to the small strip-club called Eric's. The windows were blackened and an enormous man with a strangely small and shaven head sat on a stool in the entrance, one buttock hanging in midair. European disco music filtered through a velvet drape behind him. He was eating an equally colossal sandwich, and Lilly was transfixed by the white film of mayonnaise that covered his entire top lip in an oily moustache. A girl in hot pants and bra pushed aside the drape. She whispered something into the man's ear and he nodded without taking his mouth from his food. She was just about to disappear inside when she glanced at Lilly. It was the eyes, they were unmistakable.

'Mandy,' shouted Lilly.

The girl looked surprised.

'We spoke on the net, Mandy,' said Lilly. 'About Max Hardy.'

The man jerked back his head and Mandy scuttled back inside.

'Can I come in?' asked Lilly.

She heard the too-breezy manner and knew it wouldn't wash.

The man swallowed a mouthful and shook his head. 'Members only.'

'I have plenty of money to spend,' she said.

The man, who had already taken another bite, spoke through a mouthful of lettuce and chicken. 'Spend it somewhere else.'

Lilly stood firm. 'I just want to talk to Mandy.'

The man wiped his mouth with the back of his meaty fist.

'Please,' said Lilly.

'Nobody by that name here,' he answered and turned back to his supper.

'Could I at least leave her a message?' asked Lilly.

'Listen, love, sling your hook before the boss turns up.'

'Are you threatening me?'

He sighed and gave her a small push backwards with one slippery hand. Given the difference in their sizes Lilly hurtled across the pavement and landed flat on her back. The man gave her a pitying look and went inside, no doubt to eat his sandwich in peace.

'You okay, honey?'

Lilly gratefully received a hand to help her to her feet from the doughy prostitute she had met earlier.

'Something tells me I'm not on his Christmas-card list.'

'I doubt that bastard's even got his granny on it.'

Lilly smiled, but as the other woman let go her knees buckled.

'Where I'm from they'd say you need a stiff drink.'

'A cup of tea would do.' Lilly leaned on the other woman's arm. 'I'm buying.'

Lilly sipped her tea. It was so strong and sweet she was filled with a longing for her home in Yorkshire. Or perhaps it was the incident outside Eric's. Vulnerability had always sent her scurrying back up the M1. She'd packed her bags a dozen times since she found out about Cara, only to pour herself a glass of wine and empty them again.

112

How had she ended up here, away from her friends and family? Where she felt out of step with the zeitgeist and often, too often, out of her depth. It was a question she regularly posed, and she knew all the answers, but at times like this they didn't seem good enough.

The other woman squeezed behind the seat opposite. In the harsh, fluorescent lights of the all-night café Lilly saw the skin of the woman's stomach peep through the gaping spaces between her buttons. Around her neck hung a necklace with gold letters that spelled out the word 'ANGIE'.

'I feel a bit of a fraud,' said Lilly. 'I mean, he hardly touched me.'

Angie lit a cigarette and blew the smoke above her head. 'You're just shook up.'

She took another long drag and eyed her companion. 'Can I ask what you're doing here?'

Lilly knew better than to dive in. If she was to get anything useful from Angie she'd need to strengthen their connection.

'I could ask the same of you. Is that a Scottish accent?'

'Aye. Still haven't lost it in twenty years.' Was it pride in her voice or nostalgia?

'What brought you down south?' asked Lilly.

Angie eyed her suspiciously through the smoke. Eventually she shrugged, perhaps acknowledging that she may as well tell the truth.

'A fella. I was sixteen and I followed him to London.'

A man. Always a man. Hadn't Lilly done the same thing herself?

'What did your parents think to that?'

113

'I've no idea, but I'm pretty sure they wouldn't have given a shit as they put me in care at twelve.'

Lilly wasn't surprised.

'Once we got to the city we'd no money for rent or nothing so we slept in a shop doorway.' Angie didn't court sympathy. These were the plain facts of her story. 'After a couple of nights a man offered me a fiver for a blowjob and the rest, as they say, is history.'

'What brought you to Luton?' asked Lilly, her interest genuine.

'My man ended up in prison over this way and I got sick of the train ride. Anyways, the brothels were full of foreign girls in London and there was still plenty of work over here.'

They watched two younger women enter the café and order coffee at the counter to take away. Both spoke with heavy accents and their dark complexions set them apart.

'But it's the bloody same here now. Russians, Turks, Albanians. It's the United Nations out there.'

'The girl I was looking for is from Eastern Europe. Russia, perhaps. She works for Fat Eric,' said Lilly.

'They're all from over there in his place. He brings them here himself, or gets his brothers to do it for him. Not one of them girls is legal.'

'Is that why the man on the door wouldn't let me in?'

Angie nodded. 'They don't talk to outsiders. Poor cows, they work that club sixteen hours a day. If it's quiet they do the chat rooms and the porn sites.'

'Where do they sleep?' Lilly asked.

'He's got some flats just outside the Cross. They get taken there after work.'

'You make it sound like they're prisoners.'

Angie's over-plucked eyebrows shot up like speech marks around her forehead and accentuated the thick layer of foundation that had sunk into every crevice. 'What else can you call it when they're watched twenty-four seven?'

'Why don't they run away? Even without passports they could disappear. London's so close.'

'These girls are from small places, villages and that, Eric knows their families. One tried to leg it and her uncle's throat got cut in front of his kiddies. She soon came back.' Angie pointed a stubby finger at Lilly, its tip stained an unhealthy yellow, not unlike the colour of Kelsey's hair. 'So if you're here to help Mandy, or whatever she's called, I'd think twice if I were you.'

'I've never met her, I just wanted to ask her some questions about a website called Maximum Exposure.'

Angie nodded to a silver Volvo that had pulled up outside. It was clean, brand-new, its owner obviously well-heeled.

'Punter,' she said, and made for the door.

As Lilly drank the dregs of her tea, Angie turned back.

'I've never heard of that site, but I bet it's got something to do with Max Hardy.'

Before Lilly could open her mouth, Angie had sprinted to the car with an astounding fleetness of foot and jumped inside.

Jack was working late at the station. He'd pulled out all the old files on Max Hardy, going right back to when he was a kid in care. The man had a sheet as long as the Dead Sea Scrolls.

Lilly was right, he was a nasty piece of work.

Jack remembered the first time he'd nicked him. Max must have been about fourteen, but he was small for his age, and Jack had seen more meat on a spare rib. Jack had let him off with a warning, like he always did, but it was only a matter of months before he was in again for possession, then for thieving cars.

Over the years his name came up time and time again, running girls and drugs. And yet Jack had never had him down as a killer.

During his years in the RUC, Jack had come across heavyweights on both sides of the divide. Hard men who knew what they wanted and how to get it. Shootings, kneecappings, Jack had seen it all, and Max Hardy didn't fit the mould.

Maybe things had changed.

Jack sighed. Bradbury and the Chief Super had been in a huddle for hours now and he was itching to know what was going on. He'd love to be the one to tell Lilly the case against Kelsey had been dropped.

He tried not to imagine her smile and opened his emails.

To: Sergeant Jack McNally
From: Detective Inspector Marcus Bradbury
Subject: Grace Brand
Here's the extra piece of evidence we were looking for. Have sent it to CPS today. Technically we don't

need to disclose it to the defence at this stage, but feel free to give a copy to Valentine.

I wish I could be there to see her face.

'Shit,' said Jack when he received another message.

> To: Jack McNally
> From: The desk of the Chief Superintendent
> Subject: Grace Brand
> By now you should have received the new information in the Brand case. Clearly this casts the situation in a new light, and although we do not wish to be seen to be putting all our eggs in one basket, you should keep resources to an absolute minimum in pursuing the second suspect.

'Double shit.'

He decided on a text. Yes it was cowardly, but what could he do?

> MEET ME AT THE STATION SUN 5 P.M.
> YES, LILLY, IT IS IMPORTANT.

CHAPTER SEVEN

Sunday, 13 September

Sundays spent in the office were anathema to Lilly, but Rupinder had made it clear that the other partners were placing her under pressure to 'do something about the northerner'. Guilt about her boss's position rather than fear for her own made Lilly agree to spend the day at her desk. Miriam had taken Sam to the cinema so there was no excuse not to put in a full one.

By three thirty Lilly poked her head around the door to Rupinder's office.

'I'm going to meet McNally.'

'You have other cases,' Rupinder grumbled.

Lilly waved her mobile phone as if Rupinder could read the text from her position at her desk. 'He said it was important.'

'I'm sure he did, but you must put time aside to catch up on paperwork,' said Rupinder.

'Yes, boss.'

'I mean it, Lilly, even if I have to tie you to your desk.'

'Easy, tiger.'

Rupinder went back to her work. 'I'm ignoring you now.'

Lilly was too preoccupied to worry about the mountain of forms and memos screaming for her attention. She just hoped Jack needed to see her about something he'd got on Max, something that would help Kelsey's case. After she'd caught up with Jack she would head straight back to Tye Cross to track down Angie, who also knew something about Max.

Things were looking up, and Lilly felt excited and buoyant.

Jack was waiting for her at the entrance to the station.

'Are you arresting me, McNally?' Lilly teased. 'I'm not coming quietly.' She held out her hands to him. 'You'll need to cuff me for starters.'

Jack said nothing but steered her through the security door to one of the evidence rooms inside the station.

'As for the strip search . . . ' she continued.

'Shut up and sit down, woman.'

Lilly moved a box of trainers from a plastic chair. Each shoe was separately bagged in clear cellophane and labelled. Maybe one held a vital piece of information, a clue as to who had committed a burglary, a rape or some other crime. It occurred to her that investigations were like jigsaws, sometimes one piece would reveal the whole picture. Again she thought of the letter and how pivotal it might be if she revealed it to Jack. Although she felt bound by her client's right to confidentiality, it did nothing to make her feel less disingenuous.

She moderated her tone. 'What's up, Jack?'

He pushed a sheet of paper across the desk to Lilly.

I, Millicent Mitchell, of 62 Meadow Hawk Way, Clayhill Estate, Ring Farm, make this statement further to my statement of 8 September in which I stated that on the previous night I saw Kelsey Brand go to the door of number 58 on two separate occasions.

I have thought about that night long and hard and I now wish to add that about five minutes after the second occasion when Kelsey went to number 58 I heard voices and so I went to my window again.

I saw Grace Brand answer the door to Kelsey, who followed her mother inside. I then saw them both in their kitchen and they looked as if they were arguing.

I went to turn down the television so I could hear what they were saying, but when I got back to the window they were no longer in their kitchen.

I confirm that the contents of this statement are true and that they may be used as evidence in a court of law.

'This is crap,' said Lilly, and pushed the statement away in disgust. 'I've been in her flat and I'm pretty sure you can't even see into Grace's kitchen from there. Max is the man you want.'

Jack steeled himself to tell her he could no longer pursue that line of inquiry when Lilly looked at her watch.

'Shit, I have to collect Sam, but I'll meet you on the Clayhill later.'

'I can't do it, Lilly.'

'Of course you can.'

'The Gov is on my back,' he said.

'I'll prove to you that Mitchell has got it wrong,' she retaliated.

Before Jack could mention expenditure and resources Lilly had dashed out of the station.

Lilly was damn sure guilt had played a part in David's agreement to look after Sam, but whatever the reason, as soon as he arrived Lilly pulled on her shoes.

'Where are you off to in such a hurry?' he asked.

'You wouldn't believe me if I told you.'

He walked with her to the door and crumbled the rotten wood of the frame in his fingers.

'This is dangerous. You need a new one.'

'Can't afford it, David.'

He opened his mouth but didn't press it. She was glad as she could spare neither the time nor the energy on an argument.

Money was always an issue between them, or, more precisely, the lack of it. David made a generous payment to Lilly each month, but over half was swallowed by Sam's school fees. Lilly, who had never wanted a private education for her son, would have happily let him take a place at the local village school, but David wouldn't hear of it. He had attended an all-boys boarding school and attributed much of his tenacious personality to his time there.

By the time Lilly had paid the mortgage and other household bills on the cottage there was hardly anything left for luxuries, like a car with a fully operational gearbox or a front door that actually locked.

At first she'd tried to reason with David and pointed out that there were only ten children in each class at the local primary, which was a better teacher–child ratio than Eton or Harrow. David remained unmoved, so Lilly changed tack, arguing that Sam would always be the poor kid at Manor Park, which she knew from her own experience was not a comfortable position.

When that failed she threatened David with court action, but they both knew that most judges would have shared David's background and would be hard to convince that school fees were not money well spent.

She had been furious for months and seized every opportunity to voice her complaint. Now she was resigned to her situation, worn down by it.

'You should ask Rupinder for a pay rise,' said David.

'I already have.'

Max was vexed. Things were not going the way he'd planned. First that stupid girl had got herself nicked by McNally, and now this. He hated the lack of control.

Grace used to call him The Captain because he needed to be in charge, whereas she didn't care, in fact she preferred not to make decisions.

'I go with the flow, me,' she used to say.

Max tried to put her out of his mind. Although things were simpler now she was gone, the thought of her still burnt him. Alone in the world they had found sanctuary in each other. Or that's how it had seemed to Max at the time.

'You watch my back and I'll watch yours,' she'd said again and again.

As a boy, Max had been overwhelmed by the idea of having someone on his side, someone who cared. He dreamed of running away with Grace, of marrying her. Instead, she fell in love with a wanker, went on the game and fell pregnant.

Kelsey had been a sweet baby. Hardly ever cried and always had a big smile for Max. He'd have married Grace and looked after them both if only she'd asked. But she never did. She stayed on the game, and then came the drugs.

Max hadn't touched anything but weed in those days and had watched Gracie's nosedive into addiction with horror. She'd lost weight and all her sparkle. She never went anywhere or did anything else, her life revolved around getting drugs, taking them, then getting some more.

Even so, she'd continued to watch his back, he had to give her that.

As the years progressed she'd often spoken of getting clean, and each time she fell pregnant he thought she might. It was weird how she finally did it at the end. How she finally tried to change her life.

Silly cow, she knew Max couldn't let anyone get in his way.

He cleared his mind and walked towards the club. The man at the door greeted him with a nod.

'The man's expecting me,' said Max.

'You're late.'

Max shrugged. 'I had things to do.'

It wasn't true. Max had waited around the corner for ten minutes. He didn't like being summoned by Fat Eric and refused to behave like an underling. Instead he strolled through the door as if he were passing by and had decided to stop for a drink with an old mate.

He ordered a bottle of tepid beer from the bar and, propped against one elbow, casually surveyed the scene. The girl on the stage wrapped herself around a metal pole and snaked her way to the floor. The spotlights reflected in her hair, which undulated past her shoulders. A looker, right enough.

About twenty men sat at the tables in front of the stage. Some were alone, others sat in groups, drinking and laughing. Most were accompanied by one or more of the girls working the club, who encouraged money out of wallets with their white smiles and black underwear. Occasionally, a girl would lead her client to the VIP room in the back, where hard cash bought hard sex.

'You're impressed by my girls?'

Max had not noticed Fat Eric's approach. He shook his hand warmly.

'What's not to like?'

'No junkies, no drinkers, no thieves. This is the best way to make money, no?' Fat Eric nodded gravely to emphasise his point. 'Anyway, my friend, come to the office. We have things to discuss.'

Fat Eric's office was no more than a dirty, windowless room used to store crates of beer and spirits. A small desk was placed to the side, its surface littered with papers, ashtrays and empty glasses. The air was thick with smoke.

'Drink?' asked Fat Eric, already reaching for clean glasses behind him.

Max noticed that the other man was not fat at all, and although his frame was large he had good muscle definition. He probably spent hours at the gym parading like a peacock.

Fat Eric opened a drawer and took out a bottle of vodka. Not the commercial kind found in bars and supermarkets, but imported from Sweden at over £30 a time.

He held up his glass to Max.

'Prost.'

Both men emptied their glasses in one easy swallow.

'We go back quite a few years, you and I,' said Fat Eric, pouring more vodka.

It was true. Max remembered when the Russian had first arrived in Luton with only two girls in tow. His name had been Gregor in those days, but somewhere along the line he had acquired his new title along with several clubs and over 100 girls.

When Max first started his porn business he had sometimes used Eric's girls, but Eric charged too much and it had eaten into Max's profit margin. Later he used some women Gracie knew. They expected little but their habits made them unreliable and in close-ups they looked like shit.

These days he expended nothing on his stars except TLC and the odd £10 bag.

'We've both diversified, Max, and I cannot say I

appreciate the way in which your line of work has gone. But business is business, I don't judge,' said Fat Eric.

I should think not, man. Your girls are no better than slaves, so don't get ideas that you're higher up the food chain.

Max flashed a smile. 'So what can I do for you, Gregor?'

'A woman has been round here asking questions about you. She spoke to Mandy on the net and then tracked her down to the club.'

'Police?'

Fat Eric shrugged. 'I doubt it. Social services maybe.'

Max forced himself to remain calm but a prickle of fear was spiking the base of his spine. 'What did she want?'

'I don't know and I don't care, except that maybe she come back and next time not on her own,' said Eric.

Yes, you bastard, you wouldn't want immigration turning up here, would you?

'I'll look into it,' said Max.

'Sort it out, my friend. Make sure no one comes here again or I will take my own action.'

Max tried to sound indignant. 'Like what?'

Fat Eric smiled. Despite Max's machismo they both knew who was in charge. 'Like asking you, very politely, to shut down your business.'

'I need a pay rise,' said Lilly.

Rupinder sighed.

126

'I don't want to be a pain. You know me, Rupes, I just want to get on with my cases, but I can't manage on what I'm getting.'

Rupinder sighed again. Publicly funded cases brought little revenue to the firm. The hourly rate paid by the government was less than most plumbers charged. The other partners felt they were loss-makers and that the firm should concentrate its resources on private matters and get rid of the foul-mouthed Yorkshire pudding, but Rupinder had argued that to keep both Lilly and her small number of public cases was a way of providing a service to the vulnerable. Lilly teased Rupinder and called her a 'do-gooder' but she knew that her boss had always put her money where her mouth was.

'You earn more than most childcare lawyers, Lilly. I can't justify more.'

Lilly slumped into one of the chairs. 'I know, but you can't blame me for trying.'

Rupinder pushed a tiny wisp of midnight hair back into her plait. 'There is a way round this, Lilly.'

'A paper round?'

'You'd never get up in time,' Rupinder laughed, 'but you could change your case load and take on some private work.'

Lilly scowled. 'Divorces.'

'And other things. Custody cases, adoptions, and so on. Don't look at me that way, Lilly, the charge-out rates are good and I could pay you more.'

Lilly knew she couldn't do it. 'Rich couples arguing over the contents of the hoover bag. I'd top myself within a week.'

'You could still do your care work, just split your time fifty-fifty. Think about it at least,' said Rupinder.

Half an hour later, on her way to Tye Cross with £1.27 in her current account, Lilly was indeed thinking about it. She knew it made sense but still balked at the idea.

When David had left she'd drowned in misery and antidepressants. The divorce and subsequent arguments over the house and maintenance had left her unable to breathe. To come to work each day, not to escape, but to jump into other people's oceans of despair, filled her with horror. She didn't think she would be able to bear the gloom.

'Whereas this case is just such fun!' she said aloud.

She pulled her car over and got out. Was it her imagination or was it getting hotter as the night wore on?

It was past ten when Lilly entered the all-night café and ordered a can of Coke. She had walked half the length of Tye Cross in search of Angie, but the sticky night air was intolerable. She hoped Angie would head inside for a cool drink at some stage.

Lilly sat at the same table as last night, which afforded her a view of the street. Everything was still. Without a breeze the rubbish lay motionless on the pavement and in doorways. The girls leaned against walls or sat on the kerbs waiting for the few men who could be bothered to buy sex in the heat.

Lilly wondered what her own life would have been like had it not been for her mother's determination that her only daughter would succeed. When her father walked out, leaving only his dirty washing and a mountain of debts, they had lost their home and moved to a council estate in Leeds city centre.

Why had he done that? Why had he left his daughter to live in a shit-hole? How could he sleep at night? He had put it and her out of his mind, that's how. No wonder she had never seen him again.

Elsa, Lilly's mother, was made of sterner stuff. She had taken one look at the decaying comprehensive only four minutes from the end of their new street and determined that Lilly would continue to attend St Mary's, a small all-girls Catholic school run by the formidable Sister Joan. An eight o'clock start to catch two separate buses across town and the incidental fares did not discourage Elsa, who worked as a machinist in a textile factory and as an office cleaner in the evenings.

Lilly had raged against her mother's decision and longed to mix with the local girls who smoked Embassy Regal and scrawled the names of their boyfriends on their bags. They didn't care about trips to museums and ballet lessons on Saturday mornings. They didn't have to do their homework, and if anyone had called them 'council house scum' they would have punched them in the mouth.

Immune to Lilly's pleas, Elsa would not give in.

'You're a bright girl and I won't give up on you.'

At the time, Lilly had not understood what motivated her mother to expose her to the uncharitable opinions of her classmates and their parents, but later she saw that Elsa had wanted more for her daughter than a life in the factories and worse. If Lilly was ridiculed for her shabby coat then so be it. A small price to pay for a better future.

On the morning Lilly left home to take up her place at Cambridge University, Elsa had pecked her daughter on the cheek as if she were going no further than the corner shop, but as Lilly climbed onto the train with her huge rucksack Elsa had let the tears come and shouted,

'This is your chance, Lilly.'

Three days after Lilly graduated her mother died. Elsa's work was finished and she needed to rest.

Lilly sighed. Elsa would have made a fantastic granny for Sam, with all the time in the world for stories and jigsaws. Lord knows what she would make of Lilly leaving him with every Tom, Dick and Harry so that she could sit in this Godforsaken place waiting for a prostitute. Maybe she would have understood what Lilly was trying to do. Maybe not.

'I suppose you're waiting on me.'

Lilly looked up and smiled at Angie.

Angie winced as she sat down and her tea sloshed into the saucer. 'Shite.'

'You okay?' asked Lilly.

'Got a rough one earlier,' said Angie.

Lilly nodded but could only guess at the injuries suffered by the other woman.

'Yesterday you said you knew Max Hardy.'

Angie lit a cigarette. 'Aye. A waste of space if ever there was one.'

Lilly didn't respond, letting Angie fill in the details.

'A drug dealer and a pimp, making money from misery. The lowest of the low.'

Lilly showed her the photograph of Grace. 'Did you know this woman?'

Angie nodded and shifted uncomfortably in her seat. Again, Lilly waited.

'I worked with her in a massage parlour a while back, but the owner hiked up his cut so I left. Greedy bastard.'

'Did you know she'd been killed?' asked Lilly.

'Aye. It's a terrible shame,' said Angie.

'Were you surprised?'

Angie poured the spilled tea from the dirty saucer back into her cup. 'It happens. Sometimes you get a headcase.' She slurped a mouthful and continued. 'She'd a habit as well so maybe she owed money to one of the dealers.'

'She was clean when she died,' said Lilly.

Angie raised her threadbare eyebrows. 'Aye? She talked about it a lot, giving up the drugs. That's why I liked her, I suppose, not like the others who're only happy if they get a hit. She wanted to get away, make a new life.'

'I should tell you, Angie, that I'm a solicitor. I have nothing to do with the police or social services. I represent one of Grace's daughters,' said Lilly.

Angie nodded as if she'd thought as much. 'The one that drank the bleach? God love her, she was like a second mother to the little ones. I mean Grace was no angel, she talked about a new start but she was out of it a lot of the time. Sometimes the eldest would meet her to get some money for the kids' tea before Grace blew the lot.'

Angie had confirmed what Lilly suspected from the start, that Kelsey had been integral in keeping the family together, but that simply strengthened her motive for killing Grace when she dismantled what Kelsey had fought to preserve.

'Was Max Grace's pimp?' asked Lilly.

'She said not, but there was something between them.'

'Was he violent to her?'

Angie stretched for the ashtray, the movement making her scowl. She left it out of her reach and tapped her ash on the floor.

'Only once as far as I know, and that was recent. She came to work black and blue after a real beating. I asked her who'd done it and she said Max, but that it was her fault. He found out she was trying to move away and got nasty, started smashing up her flat.'

'Why?' Lilly asked.

'Didn't want her to leave, I suppose. Grace told him she didn't care what he thought about it and if he tried to stop her she'd shop him.'

'For what?'

Angie shrugged and ground out her dog-end under her toe.

'I just bloody well swept up,' the owner shouted from behind his greasy counter.

With her back still to him, Angie gave him the finger. 'Whatever it was must have been pretty serious cos Grace said he lost the plot and cleaned the floor with her face.'

'Did she go to the police?' Lilly asked.

'Nah. The next I heard she'd put the kids in care.'

That dirty Russian motherfucker. What gave him the right to make threats?

Max felt as if his body were on fire as the fury coursed through him. He reached into his pocket for his knife. The blade felt smooth and cool in his palm. He'd show Eric what happened to those who crossed him.

He'd cut him like a pig if he ever tried it again.

Max breathed hard and reached into another pocket. The rock was wrapped in cling film and had a slight bluish tinge, like a fresh bruise. He rolled it between his thumb and his forefinger.

A few weeks before she died, Grace had told him to knock it on the head. 'You think you can take it or leave it, but you can't. It takes over.'

Another one who thought she could tell him what to do. But she learned the hard way that nothing and no one controlled Max Hardy.

The pipe was still hot when Max put it back into his pocket. The effects of the crack were already wearing off and he would happily have smoked another but he only ever carried one rock at a time. It was a golden rule, and discipline was easy for the strong-minded. Only the weak were out of control.

Through the windscreen of the BMW he saw one of Fat Eric's girls leave the club and head over the road to the all-night café. She remained in the eye-line of the man on the door at all times. When she flicked her hair out of her eyes he could see it was Mandy.

He waited for a few minutes until she came out, clutching a sandwich half wrapped in a paper bag.

'Hey, Mandy,' he called.

The woman looked up and smiled but she didn't approach the car.

'Come here a second, baby,' he said.

Mandy hesitated and glanced up at the silent observer on the door of the club. He had turned away momentarily to speak to a group of drunken young men trying to gain access to some pliant women.

She moved towards the car and bent her head towards Max. Her breath smelled of salty bacon. It made Max feel sick.

'Someone was asking about me,' he said.

It was a statement, not a question, which Mandy ignored.

'Do you know who she was?' Max asked.

'Maybe,' she said.

Max sighed and opened his glove compartment. Inside was a kilo of heroin measured out into clear plastic bags ready to be sold individually for £10. He pressed one into Mandy's palm and closed her fingers around it.

Although not an addict, Mandy, like most of Eric's girls, couldn't resist an opportunity to numb her brain for just a few hours. Anticipating the small taste of freedom it offered, Mandy tucked the brown into the greasy paper bag.

'I no idea who she is . . . '

Max kissed his teeth and considered breaking one of Mandy's fingers.

'. . . but she sitting right there.'

Max followed Mandy's eye-line to the window of the all-night café, where an attractive redhead was getting up to leave.

She was one of those women who don't try too hard. Who don't need to.

Max was still appreciating the woman's good looks when he followed her to her car.

The air from the open window fanned her face. Lilly held up her hair at the nape of her neck and felt the delicious chill as the wind caressed the dampness at her hairline.

She checked the mirror and tutted at the BMW that had been hanging on to her tailgate all the way from Tye Cross.

'Do you want to sit in my lap?' she muttered, and pressed the brake to force the driver to slow down and keep his distance.

When she arrived at the Clayhill Estate she sent a text to Jack asking him to meet her at number 58, and began the climb up the stairs, her legs heavy in the heat. The walkway up ahead was empty and silent and Lilly wished she'd arranged to meet Jack tomorrow. She'd been so desperate to prove Mrs Mitchell wrong she hadn't considered how foolish it was to parade around the estate in the dark. Not long ago someone had been murdered here. She forced herself to turn her mind to the case.

Angie had confirmed that Grace was desperate to get away, but from what? The obvious answer was Max. She wanted to escape from him enough to make numerous applications for a housing transfer and even to threaten Max with the police when he discovered her plan. What was he doing to Grace that he hadn't done a thousand times before? What was sufficiently bad to stand out in a life already heaped high with crap?

Behind her Lilly heard the sound of breaking glass as if a bottle had been smashed. She turned to the noise and caught sight of a figure darting into the shadows.

'Is anyone there?' Lilly's voice was tight. 'Jack, is that you?'

She peered into the gloom and tried to make sense of the shapes. She could see nothing but was sure she could hear someone panting.

'I'm calling the police,' said Lilly, and waved her mobile as if to prove her intentions.

A dark form inched towards her, the rasping louder. Lilly screamed and dropped her phone as it ran across her path, a tongue lolling in the heat.

A dog. A bloody dog. The estate was full of them, roaming from burger box to bin. Most were left to their own devices but well-loved. Just like the kids.

Lilly laughed at her own stupidity and nervousness. She was from an estate herself and knew that danger didn't lurk in every corner. St George's Estate, where she had grown up, had housed every cliché from burning tyres in the play area to the man at 37 who slid from an upstairs window onto the garage door

136

below to evade the police. So regular was his unorthodox exit that Lilly couldn't remember the door ever being closed.

The locals called the estate 'The Dragon', alluding as much to the heroin that was rife on its streets as to any connection to England's patron saint. Rough it certainly was, yet Lilly had never come to harm aside from the odd wallop for going to the 'posh' school.

Her dad had been right, the south *was* making her soft.

She paused to catch her breath outside Grace's flat and her thoughts returned to Kelsey. 'If I find out what you're up to, Max, I'll find out why Grace had to die,' she said to herself.

'There ain't nothing to find out, lady.'

Lilly spun round at the sound of the voice behind her. Too late she tried to push past the black man blocking her path. Instead he grabbed her shoulders and leaned into her.

'Who are you?' Lilly whispered, her shoulder blades pressed against the door.

As he continued to apply pressure the door gave way and Lilly fell backwards into the flat.

'I'm your worst fucking nightmare.'

Jack reread Lilly's text and deleted it. He was determined not to spend the next two hours analysing the six-word message for hidden meaning.

He'd tried to tell her that he couldn't push this line of inquiry any more but she wouldn't listen. She never did.

And now she wanted him over there. At this hour. Ridiculous. He went back to the cookery channel, where a gremlin of a presenter in strawberry-pink hot pants jumped up and down while 'an internationally renowned' chef called John Something-or-other attempted to make a tasty and nutritious meal for six out of a tin of tomatoes, a bag of frozen peas and a mango.

He switched channels and tried to interest himself in a rerun of *University Challenge*.

'In Euripedes' *Hecuba*, who killed the Trojan Queen's son, Polydorus, and threw his body into the sea?'

Hmmm.

Anyhow, Lilly only wanted to prove the old battle-axe at number 62 was lying, and bang on some more about Max Hardy. Frankly he could do without it. The Chief Super had explicitly said to keep resources to a minimum, which definitely ruled out overtime on a Sunday night.

Jack slapped his forehead repeatedly and picked up his car keys.

'McNally, you are one big eejit.'

Lilly landed on her back and a pain jarred her spine.

'I don't have any money,' she said.

The man leered at her, his mouth pulled back from his teeth. 'You think I'm a mugger? Baby, you're gonna wish that I was.'

Lilly shuffled backwards through the hallway, following the trail of bloodstains left by Grace as her body was dragged from the kitchen to the bedroom. 'So what do you want?'

The man followed her, his large frame blocking the way, blotting out the light. Eventually, Lilly could go no further and was pressed against the door to the bedroom.

'What do you want?' Lilly repeated.

The man leaned over her, the heat of his breath filling her face.

'You should have stayed out of my business,' he said.

Lilly's mind raced. This wasn't some kid desperate for his next fix, he was a man, easily thirty, smart, clean and well-dressed. Was he a dealer? Had she stumbled into something she wasn't supposed to see?

'I don't know who you think I am but you've made a mistake. I don't know you and I don't care about your business,' she said.

'Is that so?' asked the man.

Lilly nodded her head with the vigour of a toddler.

'So tell me,' he said, his mouth so close to her ear she could feel as well as hear his words, 'what were you doing at Tye Cross asking about me?'

Lilly's voice was barely above a whisper. 'Max.'

She froze, but only for a second. This was the man who had killed Grace. She launched herself towards him with a force from deep inside her and toppled Max from his feet. He fell back with a crash that Lilly hoped would stun him for long enough for her to jump over him and head for the door. She rose to her feet and leaped. The door was only feet away and she was sure she could make it. She let out a roar of anticipation that turned to a howl when she felt strong hands grabbing at her legs and bringing her to the ground.

She scrabbled with her hands, reaching towards escape, but her body was held tight.

She tried to struggle free but Max was far too strong and pulled her down the hall. Holding her around the waist he forced them both towards the bedroom, kicked open the door and threw Lilly inside.

She landed on her back again and screamed in pain.

'Keep quiet or I'll kill you,' said Max, and pulled out a flick knife.

Lilly had always considered herself to be one of life's fighters. As a child she'd been bewildered to learn that the band played on as the *Titanic* sank into the black waves of the Atlantic. She would have made a boat out of the string section and paddled to safety on a cello.

If yesterday she'd been asked what she would do when faced with an armed attacker she would have envisaged herself kicking, scratching and biting. Instead she found herself paralysed by fear. She didn't even scream, but held her breath, her eyes locked onto the blade arching towards her.

He was going to kill her. He was going to cut her open and she was going to die here, just like Grace had died.

She heard the pounding of her blood in her head and felt the sharp pain as the knife cut into her throat before everything went black.

Jack lumbered his way up the stairs to number 58 and found the police tape broken, the door wide open. Damn the woman. She shouldn't be in there on her own, it was a crime scene for God's sake. Authorised entry only, she knew that.

'Couldn't you just wait for me to get here?' he called through the door.

He waited for the smart-arse reply but none came. In fact he could hear nothing at all.

'Lilly?'

No answer. She'd been and gone and hadn't even shut the door behind her. Was that bare-faced cheek or ineptitude?

Then he saw it. Lilly's bag lay on the floor in the hallway, its contents escaping onto the carpet. A lipstick ground into the carpet, bright red and oily on top of an inky stain of Grace's blood.

At the bottom of the hall the bedroom door was open. Jack crept towards it and peered through. Everything was dark. He waited until his eyes adjusted and he could make out a shape on the base of Grace's bed.

He moved closer, his heart pounding. It was a body. It was Lilly.

'No, no, no,' he howled and sprinted forward.

Her neck and chest were sticky with warm blood. He held her head in both hands to find the wound but he couldn't see a thing. The heavy velvet drapes obscured the daylight and Jack did not dare move to open them.

'Oh my God, oh my God,' he chanted as he searched his pockets for his mobile, his hands locating his wallet, his warrant card, a packet of chewing gum, anything but his phone.

At last he felt it deep in an inside pocket. He grabbed for it but his hands were slick and it fell from his fingers and landed on the side of Lilly's face.

'Ouch,' she muttered, and passed out again.

Disoriented by the brightness of the neon strip directly above her and the violent way in which her aching body was being thrown from side to side, Lilly realised she was no longer at the Clayhill Estate.

She uttered the immortal lines. 'Where am I?'

'Could you not think of anything more original than that?'

Lilly turned towards the voice and focused on the face to her left. Soft lines and dark hair. It was Jack.

She shook her head, still confused.

'You're in an ambulance on the way to Luton General.' His voice was gentle now. 'I found you in Grace's flat.'

Suddenly the mist lifted and Lilly could see the equipment all around her and could hear the wail of the siren outside.

She wasn't dead, she was in an ambulance. Max had tried to kill her but somehow she wasn't dead. Her system flooded with adrenalin, making her heart quicken and her skin prickle. It felt good.

She struggled to sit up. 'Did you go to Mrs Mitchell's flat?'

'What?'

Lilly tried to clear the rasp in her throat. 'Did you check out what she's saying? I'm telling you she's lying about seeing Kelsey with Grace.'

'Jesus, woman, I was a bit busy to worry about that,' said Jack.

'You've got to arrest Max.'

Jack rubbed his head; he looked confused, frightened even. 'Lie down, Lilly, you've lost a lot of blood.'

She instinctively felt the wad of bandages that had been taped over the wound under her chin.

'He tried to kill me, Jack. It was him. He followed me to the flat and attacked me.'

'We'll discuss it when you've been seen by a doctor,' Jack said.

'He cut me open, Jack, just like Grace.' Lilly's voice began to fade. 'He killed her, ask him.'

'I will.'

The momentary high was gone and Lilly felt hot and sick. She let her head flop back down. As she looked up into Jack's face she tried to smile but her facial muscles seemed frozen.

He lifted his hand and reached over to her face. She thought he was going to touch her cheek and longed for the contact but instead he patted her head.

'I'm glad you're all right.'

Yes, yes, yes. Lilly noted her doctor's concern at her intention to discharge herself. Yes, she understood that she had suffered a serious injury. Yes, she realised that they would rather observe her progress through the night. Yes, she appreciated that she needed to rest.

She signed the forms precluding her from blaming anyone if she died in the next twenty-two years, collected her prescription of antibiotics and a flyer for a 'victims of violent crime' support group and called a taxi to collect her. More than anything in the world she wanted to see her son.

Jack poured himself a large glass of Jim Beam. He hardly ever drank spirits. Christmas and New Year perhaps, but his hands were still shaking and, despite three attempts to scrub them with a wire brush that had scraped skin away, his fingernails were still encrusted with dried blood. Each cuticle was outlined like a perfect black rainbow. He held the glass with both hands and swallowed its contents in one gulp.

The sight of Lilly slumped on Grace's bed played in his mind again and again.

He'd seen many dead bodies before. During his police training, at home, in Belfast, he'd come across worse, much worse. But this time it was different. This time he'd been terrified.

When he'd realised she was still alive he'd held her unconscious body in his arms until the ambulance had arrived, not wanting to let her go even then. As the medics stemmed the bleeding and inserted a drip he had continued to stroke her hair.

'Leave her to us now, mate,' said a paramedic, gently but firmly removing Jack's hands.

But on the way to the hospital his tenderness had failed him and he couldn't even bring himself to touch her.

What was that about? he wondered. He really was an eejit.

'I'm glad you're all right.'

What sort of a thing was that to say? He might as well have shaken her hand.

'He's a cold fish, our Jackie,' his father used to say.

But it wasn't true. His feelings were the same as anyone's, he just couldn't let them out.

Later, when he'd spoken to the doctors and gathered himself, he had so many things to tell Lilly, but she'd already discharged herself. To be honest, he was relieved.

Jack topped up his glass and picked up the phone. He wanted to call her now but what would he say? 'I'm sorry I was such a tosser but I really am glad you're all right.'

He was so bad at this stuff. For him actions always spoke louder than words.

But what exactly did he intend to do? It had better be good, because no actions and no words were all Lilly was getting right now.

He abandoned the glass and swigged straight from the bottle. Max Hardy was what he would do. He'd arrange for uniform to drop Lilly's car back at her home, pick the bastard up first thing in the morning and nail him before lunch.

Lilly opened the cottage door and wondered if the doctors hadn't been right. She felt like a deflated balloon, devoid of energy.

David opened his mouth in shock at the sight of her. 'What happened?'

'Don't ask.'

'That's ridiculous, tell me,' he said.

Lilly looked up at him, and her eyes pleaded with him to leave it. 'I can't, I just need to sleep.'

She crawled to the sofa and lay down. The worn linen of the cushion felt like home beneath her cheek. It smelled of moss, berries, wine and wood. Most of all, it smelled of Sam. David nodded that he wouldn't pursue it tonight, but his eyes told her it wasn't over and he would want an explanation in the morning. It was the look her mother had worn when Lilly came home from parties too drunk to stand, her shoes covered in vomit.

David fetched the duvet from her bed, placed it around her and smoothed it over her back. Then he tucked something into her hand. It was a Kit-Kat. The gesture brought a sob to Lilly's throat.

'I can't stay, Lil, Cara's been ringing. She's under the weather herself,' he said.

Lilly nodded and turned over. When she heard the door shut behind him she let the tears come.

Tonight someone had actually attempted to murder her, and here she was alone. David couldn't wait to get away, and Jack – well, 'I'm glad you're all right.' That spoke volumes.

Lilly wiped her eyes and nose on the end of the quilt.

She was a sad woman. She had alienated everyone and the result was that she had no one.

'Mum?'

Sam stood in the doorway to the hall, his hair askew and eyes full of sleep. Lilly lifted the duvet and her son jumped in beside her. He looked puzzled by the dressing.

146

'I had an accident but I'm fine,' she said.

They shared the chocolate under the covers.

'We should brush our teeth, Mum,' said Sam.

'I suppose we should.'

Neither made any attempt to get up, instead they snuggled their sugary faces into the sofa cushions. Lilly shushed her son back to sleep and lay stroking his hair and kissing his head until her misery subsided.

Things would work out. They always did. Whenever there had been no money in her mum's purse and no food in the fridge they had looked down the back of the comfy chair and in every pocket in the house until they gathered enough for a tin of chicken soup. Elsa never gave up and they had never starved. Tomorrow was a new day and Lilly would go back to work, all guns blazing, and Jack would arrest Max and this mess would be sorted out.

Lilly let her heavy eyelids close, and for the third time that night gave herself up to the darkness.

William Barrows smiled as his last patient left. These weekend appointments were excruciating, but many of his clients had to work in order to pay his fees. Inconvenient, really.

As he turned off his computer he caught himself humming a silly tune he had heard this morning on the radio. Even the leaden density of the night air didn't dampen his spirits.

At the conference he had thought his wife knew about the hobby and that catastrophe was close, but he had given Hermione too much credit. She lacked both the wit and the imagination to understand him. Just when Barrows thought his most dissolute secret had been discovered she announced that she had known all along that he was gay. He laughed at the memory.

To be fair, it was an intelligent guess on her part. He and his wife rarely had sex, and when they did succumb he could hardly be described as an enthusiastic participant. No amount of lacy underwear and spicy pillow talk could produce an erection and Barrows usually resorted to spending twenty minutes in the bathroom beforehand for him to emerge with a penis hard enough to make intercourse possible. He recalled one occasion when Hermione had begged him to kiss her 'down there' and he'd been physically sick afterwards.

It was a testament to the woman's ego that she didn't blame herself for her husband's lack of virility. Many women would have questioned their allure and vowed to lose half a stone.

Since Barrows made no attempt to hide the fact that he found other women, of his own age at least, even more repulsive than his wife, it had been safe for her to assume he wasn't having affairs. In the circumstances his being a closet homosexual was not at all far-fetched. She must have suspected for years. Presumably she didn't care as long as no one else knew.

Over supper the previous evening Hermione had spoken of her desire to keep the marriage alive.

'Surely we can continue as we have always done?'

Barrows had nodded vigorously. 'Most definitely.'

He speared a piece of salmon and held the coral flesh in front of his mouth, its smell reminding him of that singular and monstrous attempt at cunnilingus.

'In fact,' he added, 'things will be better.'

'How so?' Hermione asked.

'There will be no deceit between us.'

He blocked off his nose, swallowed the salty fish and looked deeply into his wife's eyes.

'I love you dearly, Hermione, and it has been unbearable to have this huge dishonesty between us.'

'Why did you never tell me? Homosexuality is hardly a crime.'

I never thought of it, you stupid bat. In fact it's such a good idea it's really quite shocking that you thought of it before me.

'For fear that you would leave me, of course.' He put down his knife and his eyes filled with tears. 'That was something I could never have lived with.'

She put her hand over his, and her palm felt cool, almost cold. 'We are a good team, you and I, and I don't see why we shouldn't remain that way.'

His eyes filled again with what Barrows hoped looked like something akin to gratitude. Hermione coughed as if embarrassed by the emotion of the moment and turned her mind to practicalities.

'Our situation isn't uncommon and we should be able to manage it with some delicacy.'

'I agree,' he said.

'The onus will be on you to behave with absolute discretion. I want to know nothing.'

'I would never want to hurt you, my dear.'

Hermione pushed away her plate, her appetite clearly gone. 'Sod that, William, if this comes out I'm in the clear and you're on your own.'

As he remembered her parting shot he was once again surprised by how calculating she could be, but he was too elated by his good fortune to dwell on matters further. He was free to lead a double life and he would never have to have sex with his wife again.

CHAPTER EIGHT

Monday, 14 September

White light, hard and sharp, filled the room. Lilly felt feverish but staggered from the sofa.

Under orders to keep her throat dry for at least a week she abandoned a shower and made do with a strip wash with a damp flannel. Her mother had called it top-and-tailing and they had often resorted to it when Lilly was a child and there was no money for the immersion heater. Sniffing her armpits, Lilly acknowledged today what she had always suspected. It didn't get you clean.

Sam brought a glass of orange juice to the bathroom. He looked pale with concern. Lilly ruffled his hair and took the glass.

'I'm okay, big man.'

'Should I call Dad?' he asked.

Lilly spoke too quickly. 'No, no, no.'

'Why not? He could come over.'

'He's busy with Cara.' Lilly swallowed the juice. The acid burnt her mouth. 'She's not very well.'

Sam sniffed. 'No one's tried to chop her head off.'

'And no one's tried to chop off mine. Now go and get ready for school, we're late as it is,' said Lilly.

Unconvinced, Sam sloped off to his room.

Lilly got dressed without looking in the mirror, afraid of what she might see.

When Lilly arrived at Manor Park she checked in the boot for her 'safety bag', an old plastic carrier that contained an emergency stash of stationery, a spare pair of shoes and an umbrella. It was gone, yet she couldn't remember taking it out. Since none of the doors locked properly it was more than likely someone on the Clayhill had helped themselves.

Suddenly, she realised she had left the car outside Grace's block. So how on earth had it appeared outside the cottage this morning? Jack must have got someone to collect it for her. She smiled to herself, saw she had a full pad of paper on the back seat, looked into the cloudless sky and decided everything would be fine.

She dropped Sam into his classroom and avoided the enquiring looks from the other mothers. She wished she'd worn a scarf, too tired for explanations today. She almost sprinted to her car but was dismayed to see a gaggle of women congregating around the car next to hers.

Snakelike, she slunk past them and opened the driver's door.

'I think that MP's got it right,' said Luella. 'We can't let people do what they want just because they're poor. If someone commits a crime they should be made to pay, whatever their circumstances.'

'I agree,' said another. 'The girl shouldn't be let off the hook just because she's had it a bit tough.'

Penny's tone was soft. 'I think she had it more than a bit tough.'

'Whatever,' dismissed Luella. 'These days people think being underprivileged excludes them from all social responsibility.'

To Lilly's surprise Penny held her ground. 'No one's saying that, but there seems to be little evidence that the girl actually did anything. The police have only pursued it because of the pressure from Hermione Barrows.'

'There's no smoke without fire,' said Luella.

Lilly had hoped to sidle into her car unnoticed during the exchange, but had somehow managed to drop her car keys under the passenger seat. She leaned over the gear stick, arm outstretched, and felt a stab of pain in her neck.

'Shit!'

The neighbouring group turned as one towards Lilly, who gave them a weak smile. The women exchanged embarrassed glances and dispersed. Only Penny was left. She opened the passenger door, picked up the keys and handed them to Lilly.

'Don't mind them, they wouldn't understand the concept of justice if it dressed up as Brad Pitt and bit them on the bum.'

Lilly pushed her hair out of her eyes and tried to laugh, but she was too exhausted.

'Frankly there's more chance of Brad Pitt biting them on the arse than Kelsey seeing any British justice,' she said.

'Things not looking good?' asked Penny.

Who could say? Lilly thought. Maybe Jack had already charged Max, and Kelsey would get a foster family to love her by the end of the week. There again, maybe not.

'I'm on my way to the station to try to persuade the police to see sense,' said Lilly.

'If anyone can do it, you can,' said Penny.

'I wish I shared your confidence in my abilities.'

Penny shrugged and smiled shyly. 'You care about this girl, and people who care always make a difference.'

'Not always,' Lilly murmured.

Penny waited for Lilly to continue but she didn't have the energy.

'Anyway,' she said, 'I'm having a little gathering at my house and you must come.'

Right now Lilly couldn't think of anything worse. 'Thanks.'

'Nothing fancy.' Penny's tone was bright. 'A few glasses of fizz and some nibbles.'

Lilly could just imagine the banquet that would be laid out on a pristine linen cloth.

'Oh, and a lady's coming over to do our colours.'

Lilly frowned. 'Colours?'

'You know,' said Penny. 'She'll advise on our skin tones and what suits us.'

Instinctively, Lilly checked her reflection in the mirror. Her mood darkened when she saw the pallor of her skin. Even her lips were white. Worse still, the wound on her neck had torn and a few drops of blood had trickled down to her breastbone, its path a violent scarlet against her translucent flesh. There was no other way to describe it: Lilly looked like hell.

Penny's laugh tinkled like wind chimes and she offered Lilly a tissue for her throat. 'I think we could all use a little help.'

The place was a mess, the air thick as syrup. Max kicked the takeaway containers across the floor. Days-old jerk chicken and rice scattered around the room and landed among the discarded Coke cans full of cigarette butts. It was disgusting. Like some lowlife junkie lived there.

Everything was getting out of control. Last night had been a disaster. Max had only intended to warn off the redhead but she'd put up a fight. When she'd tried to escape he'd lost his head and had been ready to finish her off. Then out of nowhere McNally arrived. Man, that was some fucked-up scene. Max had hidden under the bed and listened to Jack whispering into the woman's ear,

'Please don't die, please don't die.'

When the paramedics arrived, Max had been sure someone would search the place, but the electricity was off so everything was in darkness – and McNally, well, he was away with the fairies.

Max had slipped away as they were getting the woman into the ambulance, but it would only be a matter of time before she identified him to the police.

Should he run? He needed to think straight, and reached for his pipe.

* * *

Max ground his teeth as he exhaled the last of his third rock. Everything was clear now and he knew exactly what he had to do.

He smiled at his pipe like an old and trusted friend. People like Grace who let the drugs take over were losers. LOSERS. The creative ones, like himself, those with vision, knew that narcotics were a tool to set the mind free. Think John Lennon, Jimi Hendrix. And what about those old poets, Shelley and Byron, weren't they all dope fiends?

When he heard the police ram the door, Max merely smiled.

Jack led Lilly through the bowels of the station to the canteen, where a styrofoam cup of coffee awaited her.

'You look okay,' Jack lied. 'Considering.'

'I look like an extra from *Night of the Living Dead*,' she answered, and fell upon the coffee.

He smiled to himself. Actions could speak louder than words.

'But it's under control,' she said. 'I'm having my colours done.'

What was she talking about? Maybe the loss of blood had affected her brain.

He changed the subject. 'You'll be glad to know we nicked Hardy this morning and he's in custody.'

Her eyes widened. 'Here?'

He could see that the thought of Max in the same building unnerved her.

'In the cells.' He swept his arm to the side to emphasise the distance and nodded in the direction of a smiley twenty-two-year-old with shiny hair and a healthy smattering of freckles. 'WPC Spicer will take your statement.'

Lilly rubbed at the dried blood on her throat with the now disintegrating tissue. 'Can't you do it, Jack?'

'I'm a witness myself, so I'd better not. I don't want any smart-arse lawyer pulling it apart later,' he said.

If Lilly had understood the joke she didn't react.

Jack softened his voice. 'You were attacked, Lilly. It's nothing to be ashamed of.'

He saw the surprise in Lilly's eyes when she registered he understood, so he topped his rendition of all-round good guy by pulling from his pocket not flowers but a king-size Twix. This emotional empathy thing wasn't so hard after all.

'You on a promise?' asked the custody sergeant, picking the wax out of his ear.

'Behave yourself,' answered Jack.

'Well, something's put a smile on your face, cos let's face it, you're usually a miserable bugger.'

Jack shook his head and wrote his suspect's details on the whiteboard.

NAME	CELL	TOA	OFFENCE	COMMENTS
Max Hardy	4	9.22 hrs	Attempted murder	Interviewing in video suite

He ignored the sarge, who was whistling 'Always look on the bright side of life', and collected the paperwork.

He opened the door to the video suite and beamed

157

at Max, who was straddling a chair like a cowboy in an old film, all swagger and attitude. To his left sat Ben Dunwoody, the young duty solicitor who was evidently intimidated by both his client and the gravitas of the crime with which he had been accused. Jack estimated he was around twenty-four and had never been on the sharp end of anything more serious than an ABH.

'Good morning, gentlemen,' said Jack.

'Top o' the morning to ya, Paddy,' answered Max in a poor imitation of Jack's accent.

Jack chuckled. 'I'm from Northern Ireland, Max, but well tried anyway.'

Max smirked in return but Jack knew he had expected a greater reaction. He turned on the video recorder and explained the procedure for the interview.

'What camera is that, man?' asked Max.

'I forgot you were into films, Max.' Jack turned to the solicitor. 'You may not be aware, Mr Dunwoody, that your client is involved in the film industry.'

'No, I wasn't,' the young man stammered.

'Pornography, mostly,' said Jack.

Dunwoody's eyes were as round as saucers.

'Ain't no crime in that,' shouted Max.

'Maybe we should get on,' suggested Dunwoody. The poor kid was desperate to get this over with.

Jack shrugged as if he didn't care one way or the other. 'Tell me about last night, Max.'

It was Max's turn to shrug.

Dunwoody coughed. 'Perhaps it would help if you were a little more specific.'

Jack nodded thoughtfully, as if it was an excellent idea and he was carefully weighing his words. 'Tell me about the attempted murder of Lilliana Valentine.'

'I didn't attempt to murder no one,' spat Max.

'You might know her, Mr Dunwoody, she's a solicitor with Fulton, Carter and Singh. She represents children in care, very worthwhile stuff,' said Jack.

Dunwoody blushed. 'I think I've heard of her.'

'She's an excellent lawyer, one of the best,' Jack added needlessly.

Max, as Jack anticipated, couldn't bear the lack of attention and exploded.

'I don't care who or what she is. I didn't try to kill no one.'

Jack remained calm, his voice low in stark contrast to his suspect. 'You cut her throat and left her to bleed to death, what was that, a birthday present?'

Max smiled and wagged his finger at Jack. 'You're good, McNally, you always were.'

'So let's stop pissing about and tell me what happened last night,' Jack said.

'I was round Gracie's flat,' Max replied.

'Why?'

'I'm keeping an eye on it.'

'Very public-spirited of you,' said Jack.

'Yeah, well. There's a lot of junkies on that estate and I don't want them nicking her stuff.'

'She's dead, so I can't see it matters.'

'The girls might want something. It's their right.'

It always irked Jack when people like Max talked about their rights, but he refused to bite and folded his arms across his chest. 'You're the guardian of Gracie's children now? Quite the hero.'

Max jabbed his thumb in his chest. 'Those kids are like family to me, I just want to see they get what's theirs.'

Jack motioned for Max to continue.

'Like I said, I was keeping an eye on the flat when I sees someone breaking in.'

'Why didn't you call the police?' asked Jack.

'It would have taken them half an hour to get there. The estate's very low on their priority list, according to Hermione Barrows.'

'I wouldn't have thought you were into politics, Max.'

'The woman chats sense,' he said. 'You must have heard what she's been saying about you lot.'

The two men stared at each other across the table in an uncomfortable silence. It was Max who broke first.

'I went up there myself to take a look. I went into the hall and shouted that whoever was in there had better get out.'

'Did anyone answer?'

'Not a word, which gave me a bad vibe. I'm thinking a junkie would have just legged it. So I opened the bedroom door and I saw a shape.'

'A shape?'

'The electricity were cut off and the curtains were shut so it's like pitch black in there, and all I could see was this shape coming at me.' Max slapped the side of his head. 'Then it hit me.'

'The shape?'

'Nah, the idea of who it was. Just like a light bulb going on, I think to myself it's Gracie's killer.'

Jack could see where the story was going but tried to sound incredulous. 'And why would you think that?'

'You're a copper, man, you're supposed to know what murderers do.'

'Enlighten me.'

Max spoke slowly as if explaining a difficult concept to a child. 'They go back to the scene of the crime. It gives 'em a buzz to, you know, relive it. Some of 'em, serial killers and that, take whatsits, hair or fingers.'

'Souvenirs.'

'Yeah, that's it, souvenirs. So they can remind themselves whenever they like.' Max dropped his voice to a stage whisper. 'So they can relive the moment again and again and again.'

Max paused to emphasise his point then burst into laughter. 'It's sick but I don't make the rules.'

Jack shook his head at the theatrics. 'But it wasn't a serial killer, was it, Max? It was a perfectly innocent woman.'

'I didn't know that. I mean, what's a perfectly innocent woman doing breaking into a flat? And not just any flat, but one where someone's just been topped. If you had been there you'd have thought exactly the same as me.'

'I doubt that.'

Max ignored the remark. 'I'm not ashamed to say I were shitting it, man.'

'Really?'

'Serious. I'm thinking: Maxi, you gotta do something or this crazy motherfucker is gonna carve you up.'

'And what "something" did you decide upon?'

'I pulled out my knife, which I know I shouldn't have, but a lot of shit happens on that estate, and a man's got to protect himself. I shouts, "Stay away from me, I've got a knife" – well, maybe not those exact words but you get my meaning.'

'And?'

'He's still coming at me, man, as if he ain't heard me or he don't care. I'm thinking it's my time and sure as shit I ain't ready, so I waves the blade in front of me.'

Max stood and swiped an imaginary knife in front of him from left to right. Dunwoody looked ready to faint.

'I wasn't even sure if I'd caught him until he falls backwards onto the bed, but that's enough for me, man, I'm gone.'

'Why didn't you check whether Miss Valentine was alive?' asked Jack.

'I didn't know it was her, I'm still thinking it's the one that carved up Gracie. I ain't getting close enough to check his pulse, you fool.'

'So you left?'

'Too right. I ran all the way to my wheels. Then I starts to get vexed, I'm thinking this serial nutter needs to be banged up. I mean, I don't like to involve the police in my business, the Feds bring nothing but trouble for my kind, but I figure I ain't got no choice

162

so I picks up my mobile and I'm about to dial 999 when you arrive. I see you going into the flat like a gift from God.'

'Why didn't you stick around?'

'I don't trust the police. I'm thinking you ain't never gonna believe I did what I did in self-defence, thought you'd try to pin it on me and – surprise, surprise – I was right.'

'It's an interesting story, Max.'

'It's the truth.'

'Tell me, then, why does Miss Valentine say in her statement that you followed her, forced her into the flat and attacked her?'

Max paused, his eyes glittering. Both he and Jack knew this was the crux of it. 'She's probably in shock, maybe she's confused.'

'Her statement's very clear. She says you tried to kill her. Why would she lie?'

'You should ask her that, McNally, and while you're at it ask her why she's been snooping round my business. It seems to me that this wifey has got it in for me.'

Lilly needed some fresh air and asked WPC Spicer to let her out of the station. She agreed to stay within a ten-minute radius and keep her mobile on.

'Just in case Jack needs to check something,' said the policewoman.

Lilly was surprised to find the sky had darkened. Since the station canteen was in the basement she hadn't seen the banks of cloud roll in. For the first

time in days the sun's glare was diluted to a comfortable beige. The relief was like being spoon-fed apple
crumble. Lilly felt her shoulders relax until her mobile
let out its high-pitched yelp to tell her she had a text.
It was from Spicer.

GET BACK 2 STATION. NOW.

Jack sat with his arms crossed. He wore an expression
that he hoped conveyed a mixture of contempt and
boredom. Max's story had hung well, too well, but
Jack's body language conceded nothing.

'You want to know what I think?' asked Max.

'I'm all ears,' said Jack.

'You ain't been using the grey matter, McNally.' Max
pointed to his crotch. 'You been listening to the little
man downstairs.'

'Is that right?'

Max laughed lasciviously. 'I expect you're having a
little t'ing with the redhead.'

He paused and cocked his head to one side. 'Nah,
not even that. You just want her, man, and she knows
it, so when she comes to you saying I tried to kill her,
you accept it, no questions asked. She's played you good.'

Jack kept his expression intact but he could feel a
tiny muscle near his eye beginning to pulsate. 'Nobody
plays me.'

'Don't feel bad about it, man, it happens to the best
of us,' said Max.

'Who played you, Max? Grace Brand?'

Max snorted in derision. 'That junkie whore!'

164

Jack flicked a glance at Dunwoody. A seasoned brief would smell what was coming and deflect the blow, but he wasn't Lilly and the young man concentrated on his notes, too nervous to look up let alone join the fray.

'She wanted to get away from you, didn't she? She got clean and was planning a new life. The junkie whore was going to leave you behind and you couldn't stand it.'

Max kissed his teeth but Jack continued.

'You beat her up real bad but that didn't stop her. So, come on, what did you do next? A big man like you had to do something.'

Max shook his head, his breath quickening.

'Come on, Max, you needed to teach her a lesson, had to make sure no one else got out of line, so what did you do?'

Max began to bang his head on the table. Dunwoody looked frightened, but Jack pressed on.

'I think you went round there to make sure she stopped her nonsense for good.'

Max jumped up, kicking the chair behind him. 'You don't know what you're talking about.'

Jack stood up and placed his face a few inches from Max. 'So tell me how it was? Did you plan to kill her or did you just lose your temper?'

The two men remained motionless, glaring into each other's eyes, mouths close enough to touch.

'What I don't understand is why you cut her up,' said Jack. 'Was it just for the hell of it?'

Max balled his fist and drew back his arm.

'Sit down, Mr Hardy,' Dunwoody squealed.

'Shut up,' Max screamed at the solicitor, spit flying in his face.

Jack had him now. Out of control and unable to measure his words or actions. 'And if he doesn't shut up, Max, what will you do? Take out your knife and carve your name on his back?'

Max roared and leaped over the table towards Jack, who fell back.

'I didn't kill Gracie. I didn't kill her.'

Jack backed away. He was probably the stronger of the two, but he knew that when men lost their minds they could tear another man apart. He looked at Dunwoody; the poor kid looked terrified.

'Hit the button,' Jack shouted.

Dunwoody didn't move. He looked from Jack to the panic strip and back to Jack again.

Jack felt Max's strong hands around his throat. 'Hit the fucking button.'

Dunwoody began to cry and Jack knew he was in trouble. The solicitor was paralysed with fear.

Jack prised the fingers from around his throat sufficiently to take a rasping breath.

'You're going down,' he said to Max.

Max smiled and shook his head, his fingers still wrapped around Jack's windpipe. 'Riddell, 46329,' he whispered.

'What?' said Jack.

'PC John Riddell, shoulder number 46329, arrested me at 2.25 p.m. on the seventh of September and brought me in for questioning.' Max roared with laughter. 'When Grace was meeting her maker I was banged up in here.'

Jack knocked on the Chief Superintendent's door with trepidation. He had been ordered to keep expenditure on the Brand case to a minimum but had somehow managed to use 103 extra man hours, not to mention a whole morning in the video suite. He'd been assaulted for his trouble but suspected the dressing down he was about to receive would be more painful. His heart sank further when he saw DI Bradbury sitting in one of the easy chairs, casually sipping coffee. The prospect of a bollocking in front of a younger, albeit more senior, officer was buttock-clenchingly humiliating.

'Come in, Jack, take a seat.'

The Chief's tone was breezy and Jack felt backfooted.

'We need to make a move on Brand. *The Times* are planning a retrospective of the Brixton riots including a three-page piece on sink estates in Britain twenty-five years later.'

Jack wondered how the Chief Super could possibly know that, or why a newspaper article aimed at the chattering classes should impact upon the investigation, but he took his lead from Bradbury and simply nodded.

'The Clayhill Estate is bound to feature heavily,' the Chief continued, 'and I do not want the words "no go area" to appear. We must make it absolutely clear that this force will deal with violent crime firmly.'

'Zero tolerance,' said Bradbury.

'Then let's reassess.' The Chief Super turned to Jack. 'Is the second suspect a runner?'

Jack rubbed his neck. 'No, Sir, he has an alibi.'

'Is it kosher?' asked Bradbury.

'As Passover,' said Jack.

The Chief Super rubbed his hands as if they were discussing Christmas and not the murder of a prostitute. 'Excellent. And this second statement from the neighbour?'

'It tightens things up,' said Bradbury.

Jack was momentarily tempted to point out Lilly's assertion that Mrs Mitchell could not have seen into Grace's kitchen from her window but thought better of it. Why remind the Chief that he had been spending good money, unauthorised money, trying to help the suspect's solicitor?

'Then we're agreed that Kelsey Brand should be charged.'

'Yes,' said Bradbury.

Jack just coughed.

'You let him go?' yelled Lilly.

'On police bail,' answered Jack. 'I needed some time to decide what I'm charging him with.'

'The bastard nearly killed me! Try attempted murder.'

She was astounded by this turn of events and wondered why Jack wouldn't look her in the eye. 'Talk to me, Jack, tell me what on earth's going on.'

Jack looked around to check no one could overhear. 'He came up with a bloody good story.'

He passed a videotape to Lilly. 'I want you to see what he's saying before you commit yourself to a trial.'

168

Lilly took the tape and pushed it into her bag. 'Are you allowed to do that?'

'What do you think?'

Lilly ran her hands through her hair and sighed. She knew Jack was taking a massive risk to do her a favour, that he was thinking of her, but she had never felt so drained. 'I need to go home and get my head straight.'

'Sorry, but you have to stay,' said Jack.

Couldn't he see her mind was about to explode? 'Jesus, surely the paperwork can wait,' she shouted.

At last he looked at her properly. 'You need to be here to represent Kelsey, she's on her way over.'

Lilly didn't understand. 'Why?'

'She's being charged with murder.'

The next hour passed in a blur. Lilly caught herself viewing it all from a position of dispassionate objectivity. Kelsey arrived with Miriam and was led to the custody suite. She stood at the high desk with her face buried deep into her chest and listened as the sergeant charged her with the brutal murder of her own mother. Kelsey made no reply.

Lilly watched as they searched the girl, patting her pockets and unravelling her turn-ups. She felt nothing. It was as if she were a spectator in her own life. Unattached. Apart. The events of the last twenty-four hours had been too much and her emotions had shut down. Frankly it felt better that way.

When WPC Spicer led Kelsey into a side room and scraped the inside of her cheek with a white plastic swab Lilly didn't experience her usual horror at another child being swallowed into the DNA database. Instead she was numb, and it felt good.

Whether through pity for the young accused or fear that her solicitor had suffered some sort of breakdown, the sergeant led Kelsey not to a cell but to an empty interview room.

'Don't leave her,' he said to Miriam. 'Not for a second.'

It wasn't clear whether he was referring to Kelsey or Lilly.

They sat in silence, Kelsey staring at the floor, Lilly staring at the wall, and Miriam staring at them both.

At last, Miriam clicked her fingers. 'Snap out of it, you two.'

Neither Kelsey nor Lilly moved.

Miriam's voice rose. 'Look at me, Lilly.'

Lilly tried to focus on her friend's face. It seemed so distant. Out of focus.

'I know you've had an ordeal.' Miriam's voice was firm but not harsh. 'But this girl needs you firing on all cylinders.'

It was Kelsey that moved first to pick up paper and pen.

I'm sorry he hurt you.

Lilly reread the words three times and felt herself being sucked from her place of safety back to the interview room. She tumbled into reality, gagging at the sickly smell of the bin at her feet, deafened by the noise of everyone breathing and shielding her eyes from the onslaught of light and colour all around her. She gasped in pain and held on to the side of her chair to steady herself.

Miriam smiled. 'Welcome back, girlfriend.'

Lilly grabbed Kelsey's hand and held it against her chest. 'I think I know why your mum was killed. I think she was trying to get away from Max and either he or someone working for him wouldn't let her do that.'

Kelsey nodded. Was it in agreement? Or was she simply acknowledging Lilly's opinion?

Lilly kept a tight grip on Kelsey's hand. 'I won't let you down. I'm going to find all the answers so don't be frightened.'

The look on Kelsey's face confirmed she wasn't frightened. She was terrified.

There was a tap on the door and Jack poked his head into the room. 'We'll take Kelsey to court now.'

Lilly nodded but Miriam was incredulous. 'This minute?'

Lilly's tone was resigned. 'They can't release her, Miriam.'

'Why the hell not? They can bail her till next week and I'll take her to court myself,' said Miriam.

'This is a murder rap, not a speeding ticket. I expect Jack has arranged for a late sitting over at the court so the poor kid doesn't have to stay here in a cell overnight,' said Lilly.

Jack shrugged a confirmation and Lilly took Miriam's hand as well, so they all three sat as if at a séance waiting for a sign.

'Like I said, there's no reason to be frightened.'

Nancy Donaldson checked her watch and was surprised to note she had forgotten to eat lunch. Many of her peers often missed their breaks and worked well into the evenings, but being Hermione Barrows' assistant brought little in the way of stress or constraints upon her time. Until now. The last few days had seen Hermione catapulted into the public eye, and Nancy had been fielding a nonstop stream of requests for comments, interviews and meetings.

Nancy, who had been considering an escape from politics into journalism, found herself enjoyably busy. The other PAs made way for her at the front of the queue to the photocopier, acknowledging that the frisson her boss was creating propelled Nancy along with it.

She relished her advancement up the parliamentary pecking order and wondered if she would get a pay rise should Hermione ever make the cabinet.

'I'm whacked,' declared the MP from the other side of the room.

'I'll get someone to fetch coffee,' answered Nancy. Her new status must, she assumed, preclude her from wasting time in the cafeteria.

Hermione yawned. 'Don't bother. I think I'll go home.'

Nancy hid her disappointment. Surely they had to keep the momentum going or Grace Brand would become yesterday's news. She toyed with the idea of airing her concerns, but instead answered the phone.

She listened intently, making copious notes, to the information she was being given, then turned to Hermione and smiled.

'Never mind the coffee, let's crack open the bubbly.'

'Good news?' Hermione asked.

'They've charged the girl. She's being taken to court right now.'

'Have the press got hold of it?'

At that moment, Nancy's phone, Hermione's mobile, the fax machine and the email sprang into life.

'I'd say they just heard.'

DI Bradbury took Kelsey to the Youth Court himself. Jack and Miriam went with them. Lilly elected to drive over alone on the pretext that she needed some thinking time. In fact she wanted to search her handbag and briefcase for stray cosmetics in the hope of painting some semblance of life onto her now ashen face.

She found an old lipstick, which she smeared on her cheeks and mouth, and a black kohl pencil that produced a thick ring around each eye. The look was more panda than Biba.

Lilly had started the short journey across Luton when spots of rain began to hit the windscreen. Fat and oily, they soon covered the glass. She berated herself for not changing the wipers, which had worn too thin and never fully cleared the left-hand side. As the water came faster and heavier she perched on the end of her seat, trying to peer through the torrents that would not be pushed aside. She pulled alongside the court and parked entirely by memory since she could no longer see anything beyond two feet. She heard the distinctive crunch of metal against concrete. She hoped she had driven over a can but feared she had hit the bollard that had been erected to stop court users from parking so close to the entrance, and was intended to force them to use the new car park to the rear that had cost the taxpayer £100,000 and was consistently empty.

The first clap of thunder boomed as Lilly opened her door. She reached behind her for an umbrella and winced as she remembered the stolen safety bag.

She'd settle back and wait for it to stop, these summer storms never lasted long. Then the voice of the newsreader crackled from the radio:

Information has just reached us that the police have now charged a teenage girl with the murder of Grace Brand. While the police are unable to confirm whether the girl in question is Kelsey Brand, Grace's eldest daughter, they have confirmed that they are pleased with how the investigation has proceeded and are very hopeful of a conviction.

The MP for Luton West, Hermione Barrows, who has campaigned tirelessly for Grace's death to be taken seriously by the authorities, had this to say:

'I hope that it was clear I took no pleasure from the knowledge that the police suspected a young girl of this brutal crime; similarly, I see no cause for celebration when that young person has been brought to justice. It cannot bring Grace Brand back. However, it can and does send out the plain message that the people of this country will

no longer tolerate the way in which young people have been literally allowed to get away with murder.'

Lilly could listen no more. She snapped off the radio and struggled out into the deluge. A dirty river lapped her feet; unable to find its way through a heap of rubbish into the drain it was happy to seep into Lilly's shoes.

She tried to make a run for it but her path was blocked by a group of reporters, clutching cameras and sound booms. Unlike Lilly they were armed with golf umbrellas and hooded jackets.

'Are you here for Kelsey Brand?'

How could they know that? But it was late in the afternoon and the court was being opened especially for this case, it stood to reason Lilly must be involved.

'Can you give us a comment?'

'Is she guilty?'

Lilly tried to push her way through but her access was barred.

'Have you heard what Hermione Barrows had to say?'

It was the proverbial red rag to this particular bull. Lilly stood stock-still and looked directly into the camera, the rain soaking her hair and face.

'It is very easy to take things at face value and score political points without consideration of the effect a court case will have on Kelsey, now and for the rest of her life.'

'Do you think the police bowed to pressure from Westminster?'

'The police have almost no evidence and, in my opinion, would not have pursued Kelsey under ordinary circumstances, but the constant barrage of attacks from the press left them with little option but to build a case around her.'

'If you're right then she'll be found not guilty, so what's the big deal?'

Lilly's eyes widened. 'This whole process will take months, and in the meantime we won't be able to plan for Kelsey's future, we won't be able to find her a new family, and we won't be able to get her the help she needs to deal with the trauma of being dumped in care and having her mother murdered. I don't know about you lot but I would call that a big deal.'

In no mood for further debate, Lilly put her head down and strong-armed her way inside.

The courthouse was deserted. The various preliminary hearings, applications for bail and pleas in mitigation on the cases of over a hundred children had been efficiently dispensed with by 1 p.m. Trials took place during the afternoons but Mondays were kept free, ostensibly for the magistrates and court staff to catch up with box work, the dull task of processing written applications, letters, statements and reports. In reality, anyone who could got away as early as possible and left the building free for the monumental clear-up that a half-day's occupation by teenagers necessitated.

Lilly's work usually took her to the County Court,

where judges rather than magistrates decided the fate of her clients in care, but enough got themselves nicked along the way to ensure Lilly often spent an unwelcome amount of time in the Criminal Court.

She entered the advocates' room, a dingy cupboard of a place where lawyers hid from their clients' endless questions and requests for cigarettes. She pulled a tissue from a box on the central table that took up most of the available space and wiped her face dry.

At the far end sat a small man in his late fifties, picking his way through an egg and cress sandwich from a Tupperware box. He didn't look up.

'Hey, John,' said Lilly, and pulled strings of wet hair through a rubber band.

She didn't expect the man to answer. John Lockhart wasted nothing in life, not food, not money, certainly not words. He had worked as a prosecutor since 1973 and pursued each case with neither humour nor imagination. It was rumoured that in all his years of service he had never been promoted and still lived with his elderly mother. Watching him collect every stray crumb between thumb and forefinger, Lilly could well believe it.

'The evidence is very weak, John,' Lilly ventured. The little man looked up from his lunch but didn't respond.

'Don't you think?' Lilly said.

Lockhart appeared to weigh his response before stating, 'It's not my case.'

'So who –' Lilly stopped mid-sentence at the sight of an impeccably dressed barrister arriving at the court.

As soon as she saw him Lilly knew he was Queen's Counsel, the most senior of barristers.

'They've got a bloody silk,' she said to herself. 'You can't get one this quickly, even in a case like this.'

'Not usually,' said Lockhart.

Lilly tried to fight off her fury. 'They must have had him lined up for weeks. Which means they planned to charge Kelsey all along.'

'Yes,' sighed Lockhart, 'I suppose they must.'

'This is Brian Marshall, QC, he'll be prosecuting for us,' said DI Bradbury.

Jack felt his heart sink. He had known a barrister would be in the pipeline but how had things been organised so quickly? The word 'stitch-up' formed on the roof of his mouth. Lilly would be furious, and he just hoped she'd believe that he had known nothing about it.

'The CPS rep is around somewhere,' offered Jack.

Marshall clapped Jack firmly on the back. 'Let's not worry about him.'

Jack was uncomfortable with the camaraderie, it felt like the boys' brigade banter he had so detested back home.

'Jack here knows the case inside out,' explained Bradbury. 'He's spent a lot of time with the defendant and her brief.'

Another clap almost knocked Jack off his feet. 'Always good to have insider knowledge.'

Jack squirmed at the thought of helping this man against Lilly. And yet this wasn't about her, it was about

Kelsey and whether she had committed a horrible crime. He needed to put aside his personal feelings, and fast.

The air-conditioning in Court 10 had been turned off at the end of the morning's session and the room was now hot, every window rendered opaque by condensation. Lilly felt a growl of nausea low in her stomach.

Being designed for children, the room was less austere than those used for adult cases. The magistrate sat at a large desk at the front with no elevated position from which to shout at defendants and advocates alike. His clerk sat to his left, leafing through her papers.

In the middle of the room were two further desks, side by side but not adjoined. Brian Marshall sat at one; at the other sat Lilly and Kelsey. At the back on mismatched chairs were Jack, Bradbury, Lockhart and Miriam. The hierarchy was well-established even in these deliberately relaxed conditions.

Marshall got to his feet. 'May it please you, Sir.'

The magistrate gestured with annoyance for Marshall to sit down. 'This is the Youth Court, Mr Marshall. No need for ceremonial nonsense here.'

Marshall bowed deeply and sat. 'My apologies, Sir, but you'll appreciate that I am not often called upon to appear in the lower courts.'

Touché.

'Perhaps everyone should introduce themselves,' suggested the clerk, who had confided in Lilly earlier that she was excited to be involved in such a high-profile murder case, but did not want matters to extend beyond 5 p.m. when she had booked an Ashtanga yoga class. A spat between an arrogant QC and her already annoyed colleague was to be avoided if at all possible.

Marshall spread his arms as if the answer to who he might be was obvious. 'I am Brian Marshall, Queen's Counsel, and I appear for the Crown. I am accompanied today by Mr Lockhart of the CPS and the officers in the case, DI Bradbury and his assistant Sergeant McNally.'

Lilly could imagine the grimace on Jack's face at his description. She bit her lip.

'I am Lilly Valentine, Sir, and I represent the defendant, Kelsey Brand. Also present is Miriam Zander, who is the manager of The Bushes Residential Unit where Kelsey is currently staying.'

The magistrate nodded. 'Perhaps, Mr Marshall, you would outline briefly what the Crown have to say.' He peered over his glasses. 'Very briefly.'

The barrister, who was clearly more at home with a jury before whom he could prevaricate at length and gesticulate dramatically, drew himself up as far as the constraints of remaining seated would allow.

'Put simply, the Crown say that on the seventh of September this year, Kelsey Brand murdered her mother, Grace Brand, by a fatal blow to the back of her head. A crime of this magnitude must naturally be transferred to the Crown Court for the case to be listed for a Preliminary Hearing at the earliest opportunity.'

'That's fair, wouldn't you say, Miss Valentine?' asked the magistrate.

Lilly nodded, she could scarcely argue that the matter was trivial.

'And what about bail?' The magistrate's question was directed to Marshall.

'I can't pretend it's not a difficult issue, Sir,' he answered. 'While Ms Brand is, of course, a juvenile, she is charged with an offence that almost never attracts bail.'

The magistrate snapped off his glasses. 'I am well aware of what is and what is not usual, Mr Marshall. What I wish to know is what the Crown has to say in this particular case.'

Marshall paused as if weighing the issues. When he spoke it was with a pantomime gravitas that reminded Lilly why she hated using barristers.

'If Ms Brand did commit this offence, as the Crown believes, then not only did she kill her own mother but she mutilated the body in a manner so meticulous and macabre that it is most certainly not safe to allow her to wander the streets unchecked.'

Lilly dived in. 'My friend has hit the nail on the head, Sir. If she is guilty then she should be incarcerated, but that is a big "if". Kelsey Brand adamantly denies her guilt in this matter and the evidence the Crown have produced so far is flimsy to say the least. I'm no QC but I know this case won't get past first base.'

'That may be so, Miss Valentine, but the papers are not available to me to evaluate,' said the magistrate.

Marshall cleared his throat. 'The second point I was going to make before my friend interrupted was that this offence carries a mandatory life sentence, which must make the defendant at risk of absconding.'

Lilly shook her head in exasperation. 'If my friend knew the first thing about the law involving children he would know that life sentences do not apply.'

'That's true,' said the magistrate, 'but this crime would carry a lengthy term of imprisonment so the point remains valid, if clumsily made.'

'A fair point, but the reality here is that Kelsey has nowhere to go. Nowhere to run.' Lilly took her client's hand, she was not above a few theatrics of her own. 'She has lived on the same estate all her life and has left the area only once on a daytrip to the seaside. Her mother is dead and her sisters are in care; sadly, she has no one else.'

'She could take to the streets, she wouldn't be the first,' spluttered Marshall.

'Yes, I'm sure a life alone in a shop doorway sounds enticing to Kelsey,' Lilly answered, 'but the proof of the pudding is in the eating. Kelsey has known about these charges for some time but has made no attempt to evade the police.'

Kelsey gripped Lilly's hand, her nails digging into the fleshy palm, while the magistrate thought about his decision.

'I am in a very difficult position today as I do not have all the facts. The police and the Crown appear to have rushed over here without due preparation. I feel that the issue of bail should be brought before a Crown Court at the earliest opportunity.'

Lilly allowed her shoulders to relax.

'However, in the meantime I must err on the side of caution and remand Miss Brand into custody.'

Lilly and Miriam watched in silence as Kelsey was bundled into the back of a white prison van. It would be full of women chained to the bar behind their seat. Kelsey would be squeezed in among them then chained herself. The journey onwards would take about an hour in the rush-hour traffic. The windows were placed deliberately high so Kelsey would have no idea where she was being taken.

This is not Rochene. This is not Rochene. Lilly whispered the mantra under her breath, her heart thudding.

Lilly felt the heat of Jack's presence behind her before he spoke. She drank in the smell of damp leather. He must have got caught in the downpour too.

'You'll get a priority hearing at the Crown Court,' he said.

'Not today, Jack,' Lilly sighed.

'She'll be all right.'

He didn't sound convinced.

'She's being taken to jail, Jack. A child has no business being locked up with addicts and thieves and Christ knows what,' said Lilly.

'She's seen it all before,' he said.

'She's still a child,' admonished Miriam, but her tone wasn't stern. She knew what he was trying to say. 'And a child has no business being locked up twenty-four seven with adult criminals.'

'You'll get no argument from me,' he replied. 'But remember, this isn't Rochene.'

Lilly smiled to herself. The man had ESP. The rain had stopped, the temperature had dropped. Jack was one of the good guys, and this wasn't Rochene.

Max checked his watch. As soon as the police had let him go he had sent a text to the girl telling her to come to his place tonight. Then he had raced home to clear up. He knew from experience that the right accessories were everything. A surround-sound TV, an expensive music system, Gucci aftershave in the bathroom. These were things that would impress her, never mind that he lived on the fourteenth floor of one of the most ugly tower blocks in the country.

He watched her now as she fingered the latest iPod he'd left casually but conspicuously on the sofa. A kid from round the estate had robbed it the day before and offered it to Max to clear off the debt from his ever-increasing habit. Normally Max accepted nothing but cash, but he'd fancied the iPod and made an exception. It stored thirty hours of music, which would come in handy on the long flight to LA. He smiled to himself at the thought of his forthcoming trip.

Time to get to work.

'You have a very pretty face, Charlene,' he said.

She blushed and tugged at the frayed edge of her boob tube. 'Nobody's ever said that before.'

Max waved his arm to the side in derision. 'Trust me, you have just what I'm looking for.' He moved towards her. 'I am gonna make you a star.'

He took her face in his hands and turned it to the side. 'Take it off.'

Charlene looked startled and shrank away.

'Your makeup, take it off.' He held out a bottle of cheap lotion. 'I need to get a shot of you totally natural. All the top agencies will want one.'

Relieved at her mistake, she took the bottle from him.

'You're real cute, baby, but I'm a professional, I don't take advantage of my position,' he assured her.

Predictably, he caught the fleeting look of disappointment in her eyes and whispered, 'But you can always take advantage of yours.'

Charlene beamed and removed her makeup to reveal a pasty and pimply complexion.

'Peaches and cream,' Max purred, and pulled her hair into two pigtails held high and tight on each side of her head. He chose glittery hair-bands to keep them in place.

Charlene checked her reflection and pouted. 'I thought I was supposed to be a model. I look bleeding twelve.'

Max rubbed the top of her arm and smiled in reassurance. 'You look perfect. You're just nervous, everyone is the first time.'

'Really?' she said.

He pulled out a small plastic bag containing four pills. 'All my girls need something to relax them before a shoot.'

'I ain't no junkie,' said Charlene.

Max pretended to be hurt. 'Of course not, baby. These are just for fun, to get you in the mood. Kate Moss and all those supermodels take them.'

Charlene held out her hand. 'Kate Moss!'

Half an hour later the girl was sprawled on the sofa giggling as Max took some Polaroids.

'I thought you'd have a proper camera with a tripod and that,' she slurred.

'We use those for studio sessions,' said Max. 'These are just shots for your portfolio. To get people interested.'

'Do you think anyone will be interested?' she asked.

He flashed a smile. 'Definitely. I know one man who'll be chomping at the bit.'

Pleased with this information, Charlene allowed Max to rearrange her arms above her head and didn't even notice that her pants and one breast were exposed.

When the girl had passed out Max sat beside her on the sofa. The photographs were good but Max didn't feel pleased. Disgust was beginning to well in the pit of his stomach, threatening to make him retch. He reached for his pipe. He'd have just a few toots to settle himself. Wouldn't anyone need it in these circumstances?

He nodded to himself as he took the first deep breath and finished the whole rock in seconds.

Now he could look at the last Polaroid and smile.

'Yeah, baby, I know someone who will love this. And when he pays what I ask you're gonna be in the movies.' He turned to Charlene. 'You'd like that, wouldn't you?'

He shook her hard. 'I said you'd like that, right?'

She was comatose.

'Jesus,' he muttered, and pushed her off the sofa.

186

The fall woke her momentarily but she curled foetus like on the dirty carpet and went straight back to sleep.

Lilly parked outside her house. She staggered to her door and noticed the dent in the left-hand wing of her car. Then she saw that the bumper was hanging off and the headlight was smashed. Clearly she had more than tapped the bollard outside court.

Part of her divorce settlement was that David would give her a car and keep up the insurance payments, so she would have to call him with the details to make a claim. It was the last thing she needed, far behind having a bath and a bottle of red wine. Thank God that Sam was at karate club and wouldn't be home for a few hours.

She poured a generous amount of lavender oil into the stream of the hot tap, its heady yet soothing aroma immediately filling the tatty little bathroom. The doctor had told her to ensure her wound stayed dry, but given her earlier soaking Lilly declared his advice null and void.

She slipped beneath the unctuous film into the gloriously hot water below. It was enough to make her skin pink and her mind quiet. She closed her eyes and sighed.

Too soon Lilly's sanctuary was invaded by an annoying but persistent prickle in her throat. She instinctively rubbed the offending spot and immediately it stung. Whether the problem was the water or the oil was a moot point, but it caused Lilly to leap out of the bath like a scalded cat. In the mirror she could see the wound was red and angry; a steady trickle of blood dribbled down and pooled between her breasts. Even dabbing it with a towel was agony.

As Lilly searched for cotton wool the phone rang. It was David.

'I'm glad it's you,' she said.

'It's nice to speak to you too.'

'No, no, I'm not glad because it's you per se,' she said, 'but I'm glad because I need to speak to you.'

'Whatever, Lilly, I'm just glad you're glad.'

There was an awkward silence which David eventually filled. 'So what did you need to speak to me about?'

Lilly swallowed her pride. 'I pranged the car.'

'Ah.'

Lilly stepped outside and surveyed the damage. 'It's quite bad, well, not really bad, but bad enough.'

'Ah.'

'I'll need to make a claim.'

'Who are your insurers?' he asked.

'I don't know, you've got the paperwork.'

'Why would I have it?'

Lilly wondered if he was being deliberately obtuse but his tone sounded genuinely baffled.

'You sort out the insurance, so everything comes to you. I probably have a copy somewhere but I can't put my hand on it,' she said.

'We talked about this a couple of months ago, Lilly. I can't afford to keep up the insurance payments.'

Lilly nodded, she remembered the conversation, one of a million they had every week about money or the lack of it. 'You said you'd ask Cara to shop around for something cheaper but I guess she was too busy having her toes waxed.'

David sighed. 'She called umpteen other companies but they were all as expensive. Perhaps if you didn't have quite so many accidents . . . '

'Well, she didn't call me,' Lilly interrupted, in no mood to discuss her checkered motoring history.

'Ah.'

Lilly pulled the towel around her. The air felt cool on her wet skin.

'What the fuck does that mean, David?'

'You don't need to swear.'

'Yes, actually, I do.'

Another maddening silence; again it was David who cracked. 'Since we couldn't find anything more economical, I reverted to the premise of the original conversation.'

'Which was what?'

'That you would have to pay it yourself.'

He coughed in embarrassment and Lilly finally understood what he had done.

'You bastard! You total, utter bastard! You cancelled my insurance.'

'I couldn't afford it, Lil,' he said.

Lilly raised her voice to a roar. 'I've been driving around in an uninsured car.'

'Cara was supposed to tell you.'

'I don't suppose she cares that I'm ferrying around my son, *your son*, in an illegal vehicle. That, I imagine, is low on her list of priorities.'

'That's not fair, she hasn't been feeling a hundred per cent.'

'Nothing too trivial, I hope.'

'Actually, she's pregnant.'

This time the silence was broken by Lilly hanging up.

The doorstep was hard and cold. It was almost five and Lilly was still sitting motionless, gazing at the state of her car. She adjusted the damp towel that was wrapped round her and took a sip of wine from the glass in her right hand and a bite from the Snickers bar in her left. She tried to ignore the throbbing in her throat and concentrated on the damage. Even on the cheap it would cost more than a month's salary to repair.

Tears stung Lilly's eyes but she didn't swallow them, she let them roll down her cheeks and drip off her chin. Soon, her shoulders heaved.

'Whatever's the matter?'

Lilly looked up and saw Penny at the gate.

She swiped at her cheeks with the back of her hand. 'What are you doing here?'

'Thanks for the welcome,' Penny laughed. 'You seemed in a bit of a state this morning so I thought I'd just check everything was okay.'

'If the mothers have been twittering behind my back you can tell them not to worry. I'm not having a breakdown.'

Penny laughed again. 'Don't be so suspicious, Lilly. This isn't a delegation. *I* just wanted to know you were okay.'

Lilly instinctively felt uncomfortable that someone saw her as anything other than tough. She fought for something funny to say to deflect Penny's concern but nothing came to mind.

'Everyone needs a friend from time to time,' said Penny.

Lilly's eyes welled again. She had friends, didn't she? She wasn't lonely, was she?

Lilly gasped between sobs, 'I crashed my car.'

Penny surveyed the damage and prodded the wing with the toe of a pristine tennis shoe. She sat down next to Lilly and put her hand on Lilly's knee. 'Now why don't you tell me what's really wrong?'

For nearly an hour Lilly set out Kelsey's case. How she had been adamant that Max had killed Grace, but now couldn't even be sure that Kelsey hadn't killed her mother. She admitted that the uncertainty was tormenting her and the responsibility weighed too heavily on her shoulders. She mentioned Jack and her feelings for him. She doubted he would ever forgive her if he found out about the letter. Indeed, Lilly would never forgive herself if Kelsey went on to hurt other innocent people.

Finally, she admitted how shocked she had been on hearing of Cara's pregnancy.

'It's not that I want him back but I still feel hurt. For all the crap that went on between us we still had this special bond because of Sam, and now he'll have that bond with someone else as well.'

Lilly hung her head, embarrassed to have said so much. 'God, I am so pathetic.'

'Don't be ridiculous, everyone thinks you're dynamite,' said Penny.

'Do they?'

'A single mum holding down a hugely demanding job, I should say so,' she laughed. 'In fact I'm quite relieved to see you in this state and know you're human after all. No one likes a Percy Perfect, do they?'

Penny delved into her handbag and pulled out a packet of Marlboro Lights. She lit one and blew smoke contentedly into the air.

The two women sat in companionable silence, one drinking, one smoking. Eventually Penny took her last drag and ground out the end under her heel.

'Look, Lilly, I'm no expert in the law – or anything else for that matter – but from what you've told me it's pretty obvious that Grace was killed by a mad client and not her daughter.'

Lilly nodded without conviction.

'And you can't hand the letter over even if you wanted to,' said Penny.

'It's protected by client confidentiality,' said Lilly.

Penny smiled. 'There you are then.'

'I could breach it.'

'That's not an option, you'd be struck off and you have to think beyond this case.'

'Do I?' asked Lilly.

'Absolutely. You can't jeopardise your livelihood on the basis of what may or may not have happened to one prostitute.'

Lilly winced.

'I'm sorry to sound harsh,' Penny said, 'but it's a

fact. As for this Jack, he's a professional so he'll understand. Business, as they say, is business. He wouldn't really expect you to hand over information to the police, would he?'

Lilly shook her head. Of course he wouldn't.

'So that just leaves the ex and his new tart. Again, I'm going to be harsh and tell you to get on with your own life. You're divorced and you shouldn't be relying on him for anything. Obviously he has a responsibility to his son, but you should cut yourself off from him entirely, lead your own life.'

Lilly knew she was right. What the hell had she been doing allowing David and his silly girlfriend to sort out her car insurance?

Finally, Lilly walked Penny to her car, which was parked in the lane beyond Lilly's gate.

'Thank you so much.'

Penny shrugged, as if giving advice on murder cases was commonplace. 'You can do me a favour.'

'Name it,' said Lilly.

'Get me some information on how to become a foster carer.'

'You want to apply?'

Penny shrugged again. 'I'm thinking about it. Getting to know you has made me think about how privileged we all are and I'd like to spread a little good fortune if I can.'

Lilly was both shocked and impressed.

'So wash your face,' said Penny, 'and be at my house for eight.'

'Actually, you can do me another favour,' added Penny.

'Go on.'

'For God's sake don't tell Luella that I smoke.'

William Barrows looked around the table and drank in the faces of his wife's dinner guests. He hated each one of them, with their delusional self-importance. One of them made a joke and the braying of the others hurt his ears. He supposed he should pity their mundane lives, filled only with ego. Not one of them would ever know the beauty and the joy of the hobby.

The photograph was burning a hole in his pocket so he excused himself and made for the bathroom. The horrid black man had posted it through his letterbox earlier today with a letter demanding twice the usual amount, but written in his usual poorly educated slang '. . . *as things is tricky, what with the police and that.*'

Barrows' first reaction had been to laugh in the other man's face and tell him to keep his little bitch, but then he had seen the girl giggling into the camera in the way only children did and he knew he had to have her.

He locked the door and pulled out the Polaroid. Though unprofessional, the image was crisp and clear, the girl's skin white and hairless against the grubby leather of the sofa on which she lay. He brought the photograph to his face and kissed the girl's breast, which she clearly did not know was exposed.

He sighed, the soft hiss of a grass snake, and stroked his erection. How would she smell, this woodland elf? Would her laugh be the sea lapping pebbles? Would she smile as he penetrated her or would she cry like the rest?

'Bill, have you fallen asleep in there?' came a voice from outside.

Barrows cursed the interruption. 'Just a second,' he laughed through gritted teeth.

'Hermione's on the telly, you don't want to miss it.'

Barrows placed the photograph safely in his wallet and rearranged his penis. When he opened the door he was surprised to see the woman who'd spoken was still there. Her name was Margaret and she was something or other to do with PR for the party. Her husband was a High Court judge, which made them a heavy-hitting couple, in Hermione's eyes at least.

'She's been very clever to manoeuvre herself into this position.' Margaret's eyes glittered seductively and she took his arm. 'I suspect your sticky fingers in it.'

Barrows thought for a moment. Apart from the initial introduction, he'd had no part to play. As strange as it seemed, Hermione had grasped the wheel in both hands and steered the ship exactly where she wanted it to go.

'No,' he said. 'She's her own woman.'

'Then you're a very lucky man, Bill. You don't mind me calling you Bill, do you?'

Barrows loathed it. 'Of course not.'

When he and Margaret entered the room, arm in arm, deep in private conversation, Hermione gave the beatific smile of a wife with nothing to fear.

Margaret feigned embarrassment. 'We were just saying how clever you are, Hermione, weren't we, Bill?'

Hermione raised an amused eyebrow.

Barrows knew the woman's flirtations meant

nothing to his wife. How could they? He opened his arms magnanimously. 'My wife knows everything about everything.'

They had excluded Margaret so perfectly that Barrows could see she now felt genuine unease. He enjoyed her discomfort and imagined his wife did too.

'Oh Hermione, you look wonderful,' exclaimed Margaret, rescued by the sight of the politician on the television.

'The television does make one look so fat,' said Hermione.

'You do not look fat,' Margaret replied.

Next was a shot of Valentine, the daughter's lawyer, standing in the torrential rain and sounding off at the police as her makeup slid down her face.

Margaret shrieked in delight. 'My God, it's the exorcist.'

'Poor thing,' said Hermione, but giggled all the same.

Barrows' attention was brought back to the table by Margaret's husband helping himself to his seventh glass of Burgundy. Glasses clanged and wine spilled onto the cream table linen.

'Bloody hell,' roared the man, and dabbed ineffectually at the stain.

'Not a problem, Hugh,' said Barrows. 'This case has unnerved everyone.'

'I'm sure it's confidential,' said the judge, 'but I've been given the nod that this blasted affair is going to make it onto my list.'

Margaret wagged a chiding finger as if he were a child telling tales out of school. 'Hugh.'

He waved a dismissive hand. 'I'm sure Hermione knows more about this damned nonsense than I do.'

'I owe it to those involved to be well-versed,' she said.

'Do you really believe that?' asked the judge.

'Passionately,' she lied.

The judge slurped his wine. 'I'm not sure I want to know anything about it.'

'It's good to have these high-profile cases,' said Margaret.

'Humph.'

'Perhaps Hugh feels their responsibility too gravely,' suggested Barrows.

The judge burped. 'Not really, old boy, I just hate the press sniffing around, watching my every move. The case is bound to come up soon for a prelim and the defence are bound to make an application for bail. Lord knows what I'm going to do. I can release the girl and take the heat from the justice lobby or keep her inside and get it in the neck from the liberals. Can't bloody win.'

He drained his glass and pointed unsteadily towards his host. 'You're a shrink, what would you do?'

Barrows looked thoughtful and uncorked a bottle of port. 'Since I haven't even met the girl I can't give a reasoned view, only my own opinion.'

'Of course,' said the judge, and reached for his digestif.

Barrows dug a hole and planted the seed. 'She's damaged goods, a danger to herself and maybe to others. Either way, she can't be unleashed on an unsuspecting public. You need to hear from a properly qualified person before you can be expected to make any decisions.'

The judge gratefully accepted his life-raft. 'She needs a psychiatric assessment.'

'Nice gaff,' said the taxi driver.

'Yes,' said Lilly.

'North of a mill, I'd say.'

Lilly shoved a ten-pound note into his hand and got out.

She'd forgotten all about the party at Penny's house and had been deeply engrossed in Grace's autopsy report when Penny rang to say the cab was on its way.

'Just getting ready,' said Lilly, and flung her work bag over her shoulder.

Now, standing at the electric gates, hurricane lamps lighting a winding drive in the dusk, Lilly wished to God she was a better liar.

'Come in, come in,' said Penny, relaxed and gorgeous in pristine white yoga pants and vest, and ushered Lilly through an entrance hall so vast Lilly's cottage would have fitted inside it.

'Pimms okay?' Penny brandished a jug.

Lilly hadn't drunk it since university when it was unleashed every summer, brown and herby, strawberries bobbing about or, worse still, cucumber.

'Lovely,' she said.

The sitting room was ablaze with more lamps and at least a dozen church candles burned in the fireplace. If anyone farted the place would go up like Pudding Lane.

'You know everyone, of course,' said Penny.

Lilly nodded and smiled at the women she had studiously avoided for four years.

There was Luella and her sidekick, Tanya, whose son Daniel had a nose that ran constantly and who attended learning support for his maths.

'He's really very bright,' she'd once told Lilly. 'Gifted, in fact. It's just that he's a kinsthetic learner and you know how they are.'

At the far side of the room, scrolling down her BlackBerry, was Christina. She managed hedge funds and drove a Porsche. Lilly only ever caught sight of her on sports day when she spent the day trying to get a signal in the playing fields. Her kids, two beautiful girls with honey-coloured hair, were looked after by a rather sullen nanny from Azerbaijan who picked her teeth with a match.

The other women were a blur. Abbey, or Annie someone, husband in banking. Oh, and Lauren, her house was on the common and she was extending it.

'Don't you already have seven bedrooms?' asked Lilly and gulped down her drink.

When Penny finally stopped fussing and settled into a chair each woman reached into her handbag and produced a gift.

'Just a little token,' said Luella, and placed a Diptyque candle in her lap.

Just what the place needed, more candles.

The others showered Penny with a selection of essential oils, perfumed drawer liners and soaps shaped like roses. There was even a small gardening fork and trowel decorated with tiny white hearts.

Lilly was mortified. How was she to know that she had to bring something? She rummaged in the dark recess of her bag. Among the case notes and autopsy papers she found a Dairy Milk and a Creme Egg, which she placed with great ceremony among the other goodies.

Tanya and Luella exchanged a look.

'I prefer truffles, myself,' said Tanya.

'Organic for preference,' said Luella.

Lilly opened her mouth in mock horror. 'But what about your carbon footprint?'

The two women exchanged a nervous glance. These were the sort of women who went through their trash like Peruvian litter pickers.

'Imagine how many miles chocolate from Belgium has travelled. The CO_2 emissions must be catastrophic. Whereas this', Lilly opened the bar, 'was made in the UK.'

She broke off a large chunk and handed it to Luella. 'Think of it as an act of eco activism.'

She watched with pure joy as the thinnest woman she had ever met was forced to put at least four hundred calories into her mouth and swallow.

At last a thickly-set Australian with a train-track brace arrived and set down a vanity case full of swathes of coloured polyester.

Lilly poured herself another Pimms. 'I'll go first.'

The woman smiled and sat Lilly in front of a huge mirror, a pile of Mongolian shaggy cushions crowding round her like a herd of sheep.

'Now, let's pull back your hair,' she said, and dragged Lilly's curls into a band.

'Instant face-lift,' said Lilly.

The woman didn't smile. 'And we need to lose the scarf.'

There was a collective gasp as Lilly's wound was revealed.

'Cut myself shaving,' said Lilly, and emptied her glass.

The Australian draped swathes of material around Lilly's shoulders, the static crackling like popcorn.

'Definitely not a winter,' said the woman.

Several women shook their heads in sympathy.

'I'm sensing a problem,' said Lilly dryly.

'No jewel colours,' said Luella.

'And worse,' said Tanya, her eyes wide in horror. 'No black.'

At last the Australian was ready.

'Spring,' she declared.

The women nodded their assent. Clearly they had suspected as much from the start.

'So what happens now?' asked Lilly, hoping she could go home.

The Australian looked grave. 'You buy clothes only in your palette.'

Lilly laughed. It was obviously a joke.

'In fact,' said the colour-fascist, 'I recommend going further and throwing away everything that is wrong for your season.'

'Throw away perfectly good clothes?' asked Lilly.

The woman picked up Lilly's scarf. 'This has to go.'

Lilly snatched it back like a small child. 'I love that. My friend gave it to me.'

The Australian smiled at her audience. 'I see this one needs the full treatment.'

Lilly held the scarf against her chest. 'What do you mean?'

'This lady will come to your house,' said Penny, 'and turf out all the stuff that doesn't suit you.'

'For a fee, of course,' said the Australian.

Lilly picked up a cushion and rubbed the fur against her cheek. 'Toto, I don't think we're in Kansas any more.'

The next hour passed slowly. Lilly tried to make her escape, but whenever she thought the coast was clear someone engaged her in conversation about property prices and collagen injections. She drank another three glasses of Pimms and ate an entire bowl of designer crisps.

She was starting to feel queasy and desperate.

If she could just reach her bag and back out of the room perhaps no one would notice.

'Not leaving us, are you?' the Australian boomed.

'I've got a bit of work to do,' said Lilly.

'Haven't you always,' said Luella.

Lilly reddened. 'Whatever do you mean?'

'I just think it's a little rude to rush off when Penny's gone to so much trouble,' she said. 'After all, it's not as if you do something like Christina.'

Lilly glanced at the hedge-fund manager now glued to her mobile and felt anger swelling. 'I may not earn a fortune but I think what I do is pretty important. Certainly more important than having Ten Ton Tessa there tell me I can't wear blue.'

'If that's how you feel I think you *should* go.' Luella thrust Lilly's bag towards her, and the momentum, coupled with an unhappy amount of alcohol, sent her off her feet. The contents flew into the air. Pens, pencils, chocolate wrappers and loose change showered down onto the crudités. Lilly scrabbled to collect them before stopping in her tracks. The autopsy report and pictures were strewn among the polyester, and Penny's guests were rooted to the spot, each eye wide at the sight of Grace's dead body on the mortuary slab.

With as much dignity as she could muster Lilly pushed past the Australian and picked up the photo. 'I don't know about you but I'd say she was an autumn.'

CHAPTER NINE

Tuesday, 15 September

Lilly woke early. Sam had crept into bed beside her at some point during the night and was still fast asleep. Lilly pushed his hair from his face and kissed his warm cheek, breathing in the delicious smell of her son.

She crept downstairs to fill the kettle and gazed out of the kitchen window while she waited for it to boil. The temperature had risen overnight but the air was still fresh at this early hour.

She sipped her coffee and watched the garden come to life.

Manor Park had an assessment day and Lilly had booked the day off work to spend with her son. There was nothing she could do for Kelsey since the prison would not let her visit without twenty-four hours' notice and the Crown Court's lists were full. All in all, she was reassuringly impotent.

Sam appeared silently in the doorway and rubbed his eyes. 'Can I have hot chocolate?'

'Yep,' said Lilly.

'With squirty cream?'

'Yep.'

'And coco sprinkles?'

'With M&Ms, extra fudge sauce and a bag of crisps if you like, big man.'

The pair spent the morning playing football in their pyjamas, and when it got too hot they made strawberry ice cream and ate the lot straight from the freezer box.

Sam pointed to the fresh dressing on Lilly's throat. 'Does it hurt?'

'Only a bit,' she said.

'You won't do anything like that again, will you, Mum?'

'I'll try not to.'

'I mean, if you died I'd have to go into care, wouldn't I?'

Lilly was shocked. 'Of course not! Your dad would look after you.'

'I don't think Cara would want me.'

It stung Lilly to hear Sam articulate her own greatest fear. For whatever David said and however much he defended her, it was obvious that Cara did not love their son.

Lilly chose diversion tactics and the rest of the afternoon was spent discussing Christmas, a perfectly legitimate activity in mid-September.

When Sam was tucked up in bed Lilly checked her emails. She knew she shouldn't but the urge was too strong.

To: Lilly Valentine
From: Rupinder Singh
Subject: Kelsey Brand

I did as you asked and faxed an application for bail. When I rang the court to check they'd received it I chatted up the man who answered the phone and *voila*, he listed it tomorrow at 2 p.m.

You should try being a bit more charming.

I've booked a barrister and said you'll meet him at court at about 1 p.m.

To: Lilly Valentine
From: Rupinder Singh
Subject: Kelsey Brand

Forgot to say it's been listed at CCC.

Lilly groaned. She should have known that a case this big would be listed at the Central Criminal Court but she didn't relish the prospect. Of all the courts diametrically opposed to the cosiness of Luton Youth Court, the Old Bailey was the worst.

Barrows had sent three text messages to Max, all demanding a meeting with Charlene.

Max smirked as he reread them. As if that pervert was in any position to give orders. Max would make him pay double and make him beg.

He put his phone away and looked up at the window of Barrows' clinic. When he'd first seen it he'd been impressed by the tinted windows and the embossed sign, but now he knew it was just an office where Barrows listened to the whining of well-dressed women.

What problems could they have? They didn't know they were born compared to the likes of him and Grace. Max doubted that any one of Barrows' patients could have survived life in a children's home. The bullying, the negligence, the abuse.

These people needed to learn to put the past behind them or make it work for them. Max had embraced this as a concept even if it meant he had to mix with filth.

He had thought Barrows was evil and that made the man strong. Now Max could see that in fact it made Barrows weak. His depravity ruled him and Max had turned it to his own advantage. Their roles had reversed and it felt good.

What the hell was he playing at? The stupid little black man must have seen the last patient leave so why was he still hanging about outside?

Barrows breathed deeply and tried to contain the rage. It was always like this just before, his anxiety rising, his impatience bubbling. During the act itself he could barely register what was happening, let alone enjoy it, so overwhelmed was he by his need. But afterwards came sweet release and relief and the endless hours of joy reliving the moment on film.

He knew the latter feeling would soon be his, but for now he was locked into the anticipation that bordered on desperation, and anyone who stood in his way at this time would have to suffer the consequences.

At last Max appeared.

'You took your time,' snapped Barrows.

Max shrugged. 'I'm a busy man.'

Barrows gritted his teeth. He would not allow this idiot to see the storm inside him.

'I won't pay double.'

'Sure you will,' said Max.

'There are plenty more girls.'

Max nodded nonchalantly. 'And there are plenty more freaks like you. I'll take her to one of them. Ain't no skin off my nose, man.'

The men stared at each other, their mutual hatred plain.

Suddenly Barrows smiled. 'What the hell, you can have your money, I'm a rich man.'

He threw an envelope at Max, ensuring it fell short so he would have to pick it up from the floor. 'Set it up,' he ordered.

'We'll have to be careful.' Max scooped up the envelope. 'The Bushes is bound to be buzzing with the filth cos of Kelsey.'

Barrows saw his chance to re-establish the hierarchy. 'She's not there any more.'

'Where's she gone?' asked Max, too quickly.

'Didn't you know? She's in prison, and not likely to get out any time soon.'

Max cursed himself for letting the other man steal the advantage, but he had been so shocked to learn that Kelsey was banged up he couldn't hide it.

Poor, poor baby. Jail was no place for a kid like her. Still, shit happened.

208

He fingered the envelope, reassuringly fat with notes. This was it. One last job, his ticket to a better place. The US of A and a career in real films beckoned. He could smell success, women and chilli dogs. What the hell were they anyway? Hot dogs with chilli sauce, he supposed. Maybe he'd stick to McDonald's.

He was heading for the good life, the sweet life. And nothing was sweeter than making that pervert pay for it.

Yes, he would spend some of the money on a plane ticket and live off the rest when he got there until he got himself sorted. In the meantime he'd celebrate with a couple of high-quality stones and half an ounce of skunk. After all, he had plenty to spare.

CHAPTER TEN

Wednesday, 16 September

Rush hour had long since passed and Lilly was left with a choice of seats on the train from Harpenden to Blackfriars.

She watched the landscape change from green to grey as the train raced towards London and felt a nostalgic well of excitement as the city approached.

She and David had spent three happy years in a small flat on Ladbroke Grove watching Polish films at the NFT and eating salt-and-pepper squid in Chinatown. When Lilly fell pregnant they had felt superior to those prudish couples who moved out to the suburbs to give their children bigger gardens. Theirs would be an urban child, immersed in the multi-culture of the most exciting city in the world.

But Sam had not liked his nursery above the bus depot at the end of Notting Hill High Road and screamed during Saturday trips to the Tate. He was frightened of the underground and soon developed asthma.

A decision needed to be taken and was accelerated

by a shooting in the local park. A country village near a direct train line beckoned.

Lilly had loved her new life from the outset. She relished the peace of their shabby cottage and her heart soared at the sight of Sam poking snails with a stick in the lovely meadow garden. She planted herbs outside her kitchen window, their scent pungent and earthy, and taught her son how to cook. She had found a job with a small local firm run by a patient woman who seemed happy to leave her staff to their own devices and found vicarious fulfilment in Lilly's work with children. Rupinder was equally as grateful to have Lilly on her payroll. Her work colleagues and neighbours alike seemed so sure of their right to comfort that it made her feel, dare she say it, greedy. Lilly's work with the disadvantaged children was a necessary antidote to the affluence of Harpenden, a way to give something back, and she treated Lilly as a friend as well as a colleague.

All in all, Lilly was content.

David, however, was restless. He hated the commute to work and railed against late trains and road works. He stayed in London overnight whenever he could, claiming to find it less stressful. He grumbled that life in the country was tedious and that he needed more stimulation.

A year later Lilly discovered what exactly was stimulating her husband. Her name was Cara.

Lilly didn't regret her move away from the city but still loved the buzz it gave her when she occasionally dived back in.

She got off the train and benignly handed a fifty-pence coin to a beggar sitting cross-legged at the bottom of the escalator nursing a can of Tennants.

'Tight fucker,' he said.

Indeed, Lilly did not regret her move to the country.

As she came out onto street level the glare seemed impossibly bright and Lilly scrambled for her sunglasses. This Indian summer must end soon.

The road in front was bumper to bumper as the stream of traffic inched towards Fleet Street on the left and St Paul's on the right. The air was thick with the choking stench of pollution. Couriers on bicycles wove in and out of impossibly tight gaps, clad in impossibly tight shorts. The pavement was a seething mass of men and women in dark suits shouting into their phones and hurrying to collect their lunchtime sandwich. The frenetic activity made Lilly dizzy.

The walk to Old Bailey, the unimposing street that housed the Central Criminal Courts, would only take five minutes, so Lilly sauntered. She was early and had no intention of breaking into a sweat. After her television debacle she was determined to look collected and stylish.

When she turned from the narrow street towards the court she felt a stab of disappointment at the relative quiet, despite herself. The press pack clearly had bigger fish to fry elsewhere.

A middle-aged couple with peaked caps and money-belts squinted up at the building and shook their heads.

'This can't be it,' said one.

Lilly smiled. The façade of the Old Bailey was singularly unimpressive and gave little indication as to its identity. Built in the 1970s as a mere annexe to its majestic yet ancient neighbour, the main courtrooms were housed in a flat box of grey breeze blocks. No ornamentation or ceremonial architecture, the only colour a small plaque bearing the cross of St George that declared the building the property of the London Corporation. The famous domes and Justice herself, gold, blindfolded, scales aloft, were only feet away, but could only be seen at a distance from the other side of the road.

Lilly left them to check their guidebooks. They'd find the small door to the public gallery in the end.

She went inside and wasn't surprised to find extra layers of security. Each visit, it seemed, saw some new round of technology. She passed through the glass pod and placed her bags on the conveyor belt.

When Lilly had started out in the law, back in the days when she wore shoulder-pads bigger than those of an American footballer, she had found herself on her first case at the Old Bailey. The fat guard at reception had merely looked her up and down, no doubt overcome by the smell of Impulse, and had waved her through.

Five years later an IRA bomb had sneaked itself into Court Five disguised as a flask of soup, and so an x-ray machine had been installed.

The latest innovation was a man with a clipboard who asked each person their business in the court. Lilly wondered whether your average terrorist would fall at this final hurdle, unable to think up a plausible explanation.

'Lilly Valentine, I'm here for the Kelsey Brand case.'
The guard checked his list. 'Court number three.'

Lilly smiled, keen to get things underway and get Kelsey out of jail before any real harm could befall her.

'Has anyone else arrived yet?' she asked.

'A Mr Stafford of counsel, Miss.'

Lilly's stomach clenched. Jez Stafford. Surely Rupes hadn't booked Jez Stafford. He was one of the best criminal barristers around and tipped to take silk in the next few years. With a reputation for tenacity and superb attention to detail he was always fully booked. Goodness knows how he was available at such short notice.

Lilly saw him hovering at the list board, double-checking which court he needed to find, and recalled their last meeting at a chambers party, when copious amounts of champagne and no food at all had led to a paralytic and energetic session of tonsil tennis in a coat cupboard, curtailed only by Lilly vomiting down a rather beautiful faux-fur jacket from Prada whose owner had cried when Lilly tried to apologise.

'Jez,' she called.

He smiled warmly and shook her hand. 'Good to see you again, Lilly.'

To her relief he seemed to remember nothing of their pathetic fumble. And why would he? A man as clever and handsome as Jez probably spent half his life fighting off drunken divorcées.

'Walk with me to the robing room, Miss Valentine,' he said in mock grandeur and they climbed the stone stairs to the second floor.

Jez was already dressed in his black gown. A wing-collar shirt and bands were stark white against his olive skin. He spun his battered grey wig around on the tip of his finger.

The robing room was more than a place to get changed, it was a place for gossip, banter and, more importantly, pre-match discussions with the opposition.

'We need to go in hard. Impress upon the court how vital it is that this girl be released,' said Lilly.

Jez didn't reply.

'There's no good reason to keep a child locked up,' she continued. 'Don't you agree?'

He knotted his brows. 'Who's for the other side?'

'Brian Marshall,' Lilly answered.

Jez, unlike most of those called to the bar, was not a man to criticise fellow advocates, but his raised eyebrow told Lilly he shared her opinion of the QC.

Jez waved at a bench. 'You'd better wait, you know, here.'

At least he had the decency to look embarrassed that Lilly, as a mere solicitor, was not even allowed inside. She also appreciated the subtle way he left the door of the robing room ajar.

'Jeremiah,' boomed the voice of Brian Marshall from inside. 'Glad to have you on board.'

'I'm for the defence, Brian,' Jez replied.

'Poor you, not a leg to stand on.'

'We'll see,' said Jez evenly.

'Twenty says you don't get bail today.'

'As I said, we'll see.'

'Don't like the odds, eh? Can't say I blame you in front of this judge.'

'Who've we got?'

'Hugh Blechard-Smith. Nice old duffer, went to school with him. Not the brightest, to be honest.'

'I thought he was at the High Court,' said Jez.

'He was. Drafted him in especially. I expect he had kittens when he heard he'd got this one.'

Lilly looked around her at one of the oldest criminal courts in England. These walls had heard thousands of trials. The cumulative weight of the Krays, Derek Bentley and Peter Sutcliffe hung in the air. Gravitas and solemnity were etched in every archway, yet the fate of a teenage girl now lay with one man of low intelligence who was, by all accounts, shitting a brick.

Jez came out and opened his mouth.

'Don't bother. Let's find a space and talk,' said Lilly.

Their footsteps echoed as they made their way to the old part of the building and settled into the farthest corner of a grand atrium. The marble underfoot was hard but exquisitely cool. Lilly was tempted to take off her shoes.

'I saw you on the telly,' said Jez with a furtive smile.

Lilly groaned.

'No more soundbites please. If we need to issue a statement we'll draft it properly,' said Jez.

'You'll get no argument from me.'

Jez smiled. 'Now, tell me about Kelsey.'

Defendants in custody were rarely produced for preliminary hearings, when often nothing more complex than a timetable was discussed, and never for bail applications. The logistics were far too expensive. If the lawyers made an attempt at bail and were successful the prison would be informed by telephone and the prisoner released. If not, the defendant would work it out for themselves if they weren't asked to pack their bags by teatime.

Preliminaries sometimes merited a video link from the jail to the court, but there wouldn't have been time to make the necessary arrangements for Kelsey. Jez would have to get all his information from Lilly.

She didn't mince her words. 'She's all alone and terrified. We have to get her out.'

Jez rubbed his chin. Lilly thought he'd had a neatly trimmed goatee the last time they met. It had left her with a rash that had subsided before her embarrassment.

'We have to get her bail.'

'The thing is, I don't think we should apply today,' he said.

'What?' Her sudden shout echoed around the empty spaces.

'We can't possibly succeed.'

'Of course we can,' said Lilly. 'We have to.'

Jez smiled with enough patience to spill, as far as Lilly was concerned, into patronage.

'I know it's difficult, but if we make the application today we'll fail.'

Lilly was incredulous. 'So we leave Rochene to rot?'

'Who's Rochene?'

Lilly shook her head. 'I mean Kelsey. Are you saying we won't even bother trying to get her out?'

'It's not a question of being bothered, but one of realism.'

'What are you afraid of? That you'll damage your reputation so close to promotion?'

Jez didn't miss a beat. 'Don't be ridiculous. I'm afraid of starting off on the wrong foot with this judge. If we make foolish applications now he won't listen properly when we need to make a good one.'

'She's a kid, she shouldn't be in jail,' Lilly shouted. 'Some of them can't take the pressure. Some of them don't make it.'

As Lilly's voice rose, Jez seemed to lower his own so that he spoke in barely a whisper. Whether deliberate or not, it made Jez seem the more mature of the two.

'No judge will release her without a psychiatric report,' he said.

'Says who?'

'You do, Lilly. I had the CPS bike over the interview tapes and you make it very plain that you don't consider Kelsey fit for interview. When Bradbury asks whether Kelsey understands the procedure, you say, and I quote, "*I'm not a psychiatrist, nor am I a clairvoyant.*"'

Lilly slumped against a wall. 'It could take weeks to get an assessment.'

Jez pulled out a card from his wallet. 'This shrink owes me a favour.'

Judge Blechard-Smith entered court with a face like thunder. As a member of the High Court he would usually wear red, but the Old Bailey had a uniform of its own. Like fashionistas the judges who sat there wore nothing but black. By the looks of things it suited Blechard-Smith's mood. Before the clerk could introduce the parties the judge launched an attack.

'Mr Stafford, I'm surprised at you. This application is ill-conceived.'

Jez rose slowly to his feet, but the judge was in full flow.

'No court in the land will grant bail to this girl without a proper medical assessment.'

'I agree, My Lord.'

'What?' barked the judge.

'The defence is in full agreement, My Lord.'

Blechard-Smith exploded. 'So what are we doing here? You should know I take a very dim view of wasting court time.'

Jez opened his arms, his stance compliant. 'The defence have no intention of applying for bail at this stage.' He smiled, a picture of reason. 'This is a preliminary hearing, by definition to deal with preliminary matters such as the filing of reports. Our defendant is a child so any psychiatric assessment must be ordered by the court. I am here simply to ask for that and I am pleased Your Lordship has already given the issue consideration.'

'Quite so,' said the judge.

Ten minutes later Lilly and Jez were walking back towards Fleet Street. Lilly had to admit that Jez had been impeccable in court. Maybe working with him would be okay.

The bars were already filling up, drinkers spilling out into the sunshine.

'Fancy a quick one?' Jez asked.

Lilly was taken aback.

Jez laughed, a sexy gurgle in his throat. 'If memory serves you're partial to a glass of bubbly.'

Lilly leaned over Rupinder's desk.

'The prodigal daughter returns, no doubt to do her paperwork.'

'Jez Stafford,' said Lilly.

'I hear he's very good,' answered Rupinder.

'I will never tell you anything again.'

Rupinder batted her eyelids.

'Judas,' said Lilly, and made for the door.

The paperwork was indeed piled high on Lilly's desk. And on the table in the corner. And on top of all three filing cabinets. She picked up the nearest form crying out for completion. It was an APP8, an application to extend the public funding limit on a contact case she had been ignoring for weeks. A plea for more money.

Lilly read aloud. 'What are Mr Stewart's chances of success? A: Excellent. B: Good. C: Satisfactory.'

She laughed. 'Where's the box for "haven't a clue"?'

She swept all the papers off her desk in an untidy bundle and placed them on the precarious pile on the cabinet. The tower teetered dangerously.

'Miriam's been calling.'

Lilly looked up and saw the firm's long-suffering receptionist-cum-secretary, Sheila, in the doorway. 'Thanks.'

The paper edifice collapsed on top of Lilly.

'Couldn't you have gone through some of this for me?' she asked.

'I did,' said Sheila.

Lilly grimaced. 'So this lot . . . '

'Is all urgent,' finished Sheila, and fixed Lilly with a hard stare.

'What?' said Lilly.

'Just get on with it.'

The phone rang and Lilly gratefully snatched it up.

'Lilly Valentine, at your service.' She waved Sheila and her sanctimonious looks away.

'Hi,' came the honeyed reply. 'I'm Sheba Lorenson.'

Lilly couldn't place the name. 'What can I do for you, Miss Lawrence?'

'It's Lorenson, and it's more a question of what I can do for you.'

'Aha.'

There was a gravelly slurp of laughter. 'I'm a shrink. Jez asked me to call you. I understand you want me to see the girl charged with killing her mother.'

Lilly pulled the card Jez had given her from her breast pocket and saw Sheba Lorenson's name embossed on the front. 'Sorry, I wasn't expecting to hear from you so soon.'

Another seductive chuckle. 'Jez can be very persuasive.'

What was the story here? Lilly wondered.

'I can start tomorrow.'

'Wow, I am impressed. You must owe him one,' said Lilly.

'Several, actually. So tell me, where's the girl at the moment?'

Lilly checked herself and realised that she hadn't taken the time to find out.

Miriam put down the phone with a frown. Lilly had refused to discuss what had happened at court and insisted on coming over to talk in person and then going on to Tye Cross together. It could only mean bad news.

At this moment, like much of the time, Miriam felt a surge of guilt towards Lilly. It was unfair to expect her friend to shoulder the burden of Kelsey's letter, whatever the rules might be on client confidentiality. When Miriam had found the letter she should have handed it straight to Jack instead of sneaking it among the other papers to be sent to Kelsey's lawyer. This case and Lilly were always headed for heartache, with the spectre of Rochene ever present. Of course, Miriam hadn't known then that Lilly would be nominated to take the case, but it wouldn't have mattered. Could Miriam say with any honesty that she would have acted differently if she had known her friend and not an anonymous suit was to become involved? Lilly was the closest Miriam would allow herself to a friend, and although she wouldn't set out to deliberately hurt her it wouldn't stop Miriam from doing just that if Kelsey's case required it.

Why Miriam was unable to put anything before the children she worked with was a source of unending discussion among colleagues. It was a question Miriam asked herself so often that even she was bored with rehearsing the answer.

If only someone had been committed to Lewis then maybe he wouldn't be dead. If someone had taken the time to talk to him maybe he would have seen things differently. If someone had sat with him in the early hours when his demons beckoned, maybe he wouldn't have taken the night bus to London Bridge and thrown himself from platform eleven under the 5.25 to Forest Hill. If that someone had been his mother, maybe, just maybe, Miriam could have saved her son and she would not be so obsessed.

Shouts came from upstairs, followed by the tell-tale thud and hiss of a fire extinguisher being let off. Miriam sighed and went back to work.

'This is a bloody stupid idea,' David said.

Lilly crammed the remnants of Sam's supper into her mouth.

'You know I'm right,' he said.

Lilly tried to swallow the congealed crumpet.

'You need a sense of perspective, these children are not yours. Sam should be your priority,' he said.

Incensed, Lilly pushed the outsized ball of food towards her epiglottis. 'I don't see why it's a problem for you to babysit your own son, and don't you dare talk to me about priorities. I'm not the one living ten miles away.'

Since they were back on old turf, David produced his standard retort. 'You kicked me out.'

Lilly also knew her lines. 'Because you were shagging Botox Belle.'

Suddenly worn down by the relentlessness of these exchanges, Lilly walked to the door. 'Thanks for coming over, I won't be late.'

'I never mind helping out, you know that. But what will you do when I can't come, when Cara's nearly due?'

'I'll win the lottery.'

David smiled sadly. 'You don't do this for the money.'

They heard a shuffle at the top of the stairs and saw Sam peering down.

'Why is Cara nearly a Jew?' he asked.

Lilly couldn't suppress a snigger in David's direction. 'Good luck.'

Though it irked her, Lilly had to accept that David was probably right. After her previous experiences in Tye Cross she shouldn't be heading over there again. What was she trying to achieve?

She wasn't, of course, trying to achieve anything in particular. She simply felt the need to act. She had tried to follow Penny's advice and 'go with the flow', but inertia was as unnatural to Lilly as it had been to her mother.

'Time on your hands, mind on yourself,' said Elsa, who, like most northern women, had little time for navel-gazing.

Like her mother before her, Lilly read on the loo and made phone calls while she ironed. Lilly even sent texts while she sat at traffic lights.

Another reason for Lilly's urge to act was that she was dreading having to tell Miriam about the nonexistent application for bail, and hoped her plan to unearth evidence to help Kelsey would sweeten the pill.

Given that Max was no longer a suspect, Lilly was reverting to her original contention that a client had killed Grace. She would track down Angie and ask if she had heard anything on the streets. If someone was cutting girls the word would spread quickly. Getting Miriam to help would make them both feel useful.

When she arrived at The Bushes, Lilly was surprised to see Jack standing at the door talking to Miriam.

'Haven't you got a home to go to?' she called.

He ignored her attempt at humour and rounded on her. 'This is bloody ridiculous.'

She laughed. 'You're the second person to tell me that tonight.'

'I'm not kidding, Lilly, you're putting yourself in danger,' he said.

Playfully, she pinched his cheek. 'I didn't know you cared.'

'Of course I bloody care,' he said.

Miriam grinned and made her way to Lilly's car. She took one look at the dislodged bumper. 'We'll take mine.'

'At least let me come,' called Jack.

'No one will speak to us with you there,' answered Lilly.

Miriam waved a rape alarm and a bottle of mace. 'Don't worry, we're well-prepared.'

Jack looked exasperated. 'I'm a copper investigating a murder and I'm spending most of my time watching out for the main suspect's bloody brief.'

Lilly laughed.

'What's funny?' he asked.

'You admit you're still investigating. You're not convinced she did it.'

'I didn't say that. I just don't like loose ends.'

Both women got into the car and left Jack standing alone. Lilly wound down her window and leaned out to give him a thumbs-up as Miriam drove away.

'Why are you doing this?' shouted Jack.

Lilly leaned out of the window and shouted back, 'To tie up those loose ends.'

The streets of Tye Cross were busy. Cars crawled to a halt and girls jumped in as if at a taxi rank. A steady stream of men were buzzed into the flats. Now the weather had cooled the clients had evidently recovered their appetites.

The all-night café was quiet, with the girls too busy working to sit around and chat. Only a few men sat in one corner, playing cards and smoking as they waited for their meal tickets to return with some hard-earned cash.

The man behind the counter was friendly enough. 'What can I get you?'

'Two teas please,' answered Lilly.

He jerked his head towards the table furthest away from the pimps. 'I'll bring them over.'

'Nice,' said Miriam, and pushed an ashtray full of bloodstained tissues to the other side of the table.

Two cups of dark brown liquid were dropped without ceremony before them.

'Thanks,' muttered Miriam.

The man nodded and turned back to his counter.

'Excuse me,' said Lilly. 'I'm looking for my friend and I wondered if she'd been in tonight.'

The man raised a quizzical eyebrow.

'We're not police,' said Lilly.

He laughed. 'I can see that.'

'She's blonde, in her thirties and wears her name on a necklace. It says Angie.'

'I ain't seen her in a week,' he answered.

'Will you give her this?' said Lilly, and handed over her card. 'I need to speak to her.'

He read the card and slipped it into his greasy apron pocket. 'I wouldn't normally but she's never tried to rip me off.'

Lilly and Miriam left their tea and made their way outside. As Miriam stopped to double-check her bag was closed a girl pushed past them, her head down. Lilly watched her approach the table in the corner and whisper something into the ear of one of the gamblers. He nodded without looking at her and dismissed her with a perfunctory wave.

Lilly saw the woman's face was a mass of purple bruises. One eye was closed and her bottom lip was split in two.

As she came towards them Lilly instinctively caught the girl's arm. 'Mandy.'

The girl looked into Lilly's face and then at Miriam, who gasped at the injuries.

'I know about the women in Fat Eric's, that he keeps your passports and you can't go home.'

Mandy's eyes flicked towards the men in the café.

'Go away,' she whispered.

'I'm a solicitor, I could help.'

Mandy pulled her arm away, fear filled her damaged face. 'I said go away.'

'I know about a place for girls like you. You'd be safe there and I could take you myself.'

Mandy looked deep into Lilly's eyes before she turned away and walked back to her prison. Lilly stared after her and held her breath.

'Let's go,' said Miriam, and they fled to the car.

Miriam drove in silence and Lilly stared out of her window into the night. Neither wanted to voice what they had just seen. They didn't want to make it real.

As they pulled up outside The Bushes, Lilly finally spoke. 'They're slaves.'

'Yes,' said Miriam.

The enormity swallowed them both.

'We can't help everyone,' said Miriam.

'No.'

'So we should use all our energy on the ones we can.'

It was a simple statement, obvious really, but it filled Lilly with optimism. She straightened her spine and lifted her chin. 'I can make a difference to Kelsey.'

'Yes.'

Lilly was woken at 2 a.m., not by demons from the past but by the sound of sobbing. She went into Sam's untidy room and found him with his head buried into his pillow.

228

She picked her way through the debris, stubbing her toe on a re-enactment of the Battle of Trafalgar. 'What's wrong, big man?'

'Cara's having a baby,' came the muffled wail.

Lilly stroked the back of his head.

'Dad won't love me any more,' said Sam.

Lilly pulled her son into her arms and kissed his damp cheeks. 'Of course he will. He'll always love you.'

'But what if he doesn't?'

'Then I will love you twice as much,' said Lilly.

She rocked him back to sleep and worried that poor Sam might be right. No doubt the new baby would have to come first in David's life.

CHAPTER ELEVEN

Thursday, 17 September

Lilly arrived at the prison ten minutes late. She had nagged the appointments office for an early slot and had planned to meet with Kelsey before the psychiatrist arrived. She wanted to assure herself that the girl was holding up. Any sign of meltdown and Lilly would break down the governor's door herself. But Sam had wanted a dozen hugs before settling into his class and Lilly could not bear to deny him. Kelsey had failed to make the priority list again.

The conflict for Lilly as both a lawyer and a mother had yet again bubbled to the surface. It must surely be right to put Sam first, but it didn't stop Lilly from feeling guilty.

HMP Parkgate had been built in the early Nineties to house the overspill of women increasingly receiving custodial sentences, in response to Michael Howard's draconian policies at the time. Ultra-modern at its conception, it already looked dated and housed three times as many prisoners than had been originally planned.

Unlike the old jails in London – such as Brixton

and Highgate – that were situated only feet from the local community, Parkgate was constructed on some wasteland well out of town. Apart from those visiting at designated times there was no reason for anyone to go there and the site seemed to stand almost in a vacuum. The only positive aspect for Lilly was the acres of empty car park.

Lilly approached the entrance and saw a woman outside taking the unmistakable deep pulls on her last cigarette. Her face seemed familiar although Lilly was sure they had never met. The woman caught her staring.

Lilly was flustered. 'I'm sorry, you look like someone I know. Well, I think I know, or . . . '

'You must be Lilly,' said the woman. 'I'm Sheba Lorenson.'

Lilly had expected a petite blonde with a creamy complexion, the sort of professional woman an alpha male like Jez would go for, but Sheba was gorgeously buxom, with midnight hair and a radiant smile. A Fifties starlet with scarlet lips.

'You seem so familiar,' said Lilly.

Sheba threw back her head and laughed, the sound full of sensuality. 'It's Jez, I'm his sister. Didn't he tell you?'

Lilly shook her head.

'Figures,' said Sheba.

Lilly wondered why Jez had failed to mention it, and why Sheba would assume that he hadn't. She also wondered why they didn't share a surname. Lilly noted the absence of a wedding ring, but didn't feel like she could pry into Sheba's romantic history five minutes

231

after meeting her. Besides, Sheba didn't look the sort of woman to countenance cross examination, and as Lilly watched her bottom sashaying through the doors she simply trotted along in her wake.

Together with the usual throng of shoplifters and council-tax evaders the prison housed Category A prisoners, so security was tight. A woman serving twenty-eight days was not likely to organise a breakout, but a lifer might.

Photographs, palm prints and retinal scans were taken of everyone trying to get in, while three male officers took brief written descriptions.

'What colour are your eyes, madam?' the youngest asked Sheba.

'Some say they're green but others say they're hazel,' she gurgled. 'What do you think?'

He peered into them wistfully and smiled.

'Definitely hazel,' he said, and turned to Lilly. 'Yours?'

'Grey,' she said flatly.

Having established that they were not about to help Kelsey escape it was time to ensure that no contraband was to be passed. Since all prisons were awash with drugs, and attacks among inmates regularly took place with weapons assembled from prison detritus, Lilly considered the whole process futile. If she knew that packages of heroin were passed by mouth to the inmates by their visitors' kisses then the authorities must be aware. Lilly suspected the women were easier to handle out of their heads and it was in no one's interest to be too vigilant.

Sheba passed through the framed metal detector

and engaged the guards in banter as they patted her down. Lilly set the machine off four times and ended up removing her shoes, watch, belt and earrings. By the time she made it through she was sweating.

There were no designated rooms for official visits at Parkgate, as the overcrowding meant the space had long since been turned into extra cells. The exceptions were those set aside for closed visits with Cat X prisoners, the mad and the bad. Lilly would not countenance speaking with Kelsey through a Perspex shield à la death row, so their meeting would have to take place in the optimistically named 'Friends and Family Centre', which was in fact a poorly ventilated room with worn carpet tiles, and empty aside from row upon row of tables. It reminded Lilly of the school hall in which she had taken her O-levels.

A guard showed them to a table and asked them to wait while the other tables filled around them. The noise level was deafening and the room soon filled with a dense cloud of smoke. Children jumped around excitedly as they waited to see their mothers, fuelled by the sweets and crisps provided by their dads and grandmas who had dragged them along.

The prisoners began to arrive, waving and shouting at their guests. Only Kelsey shuffled in, eyes downcast, her shoulders hanging. She was wearing the prison uniform, which was not obligatory for an unconvicted prisoner. There was, of course, no one to bring in her own things and Lilly cursed herself for not doing so.

The adult-sized sweatshirt dwarfed Kelsey and to

Lilly she looked even paler and thinner, if that were possible.

'You look well, Kelsey,' said Lilly, her voice unnaturally bright.

She didn't receive a reaction. She didn't expect to.

Kelsey sat down and pressed her white hands on the table, the fingers splayed. Lilly was about to place her own on top when Sheba did it first.

'I'm Sheba Lorenson, Kelsey. I want to help you.'

Her tone was soothing and Kelsey looked up.

Sheba gave an irresistible smile. 'Hello.'

Kelsey kept eye contact and nodded.

Lilly was gobsmacked. The woman was a hypnotist.

'The judge, quite rightly, won't let you out of here until he knows it's safe,' Sheba continued. 'So that's what I'm here to find out.'

She deftly took out paper and pen with one hand, not letting go of Kelsey's fingers with the other.

'I think the best way to find out about a person is just to ask them.' Sheba placed the pad in front of Kelsey in a gentle but deliberate motion that courted no argument. 'So describe yourself to me, Kelsey. Tell me what you're really like.'

Kelsey picked up the pencil and began to write. Sheba caught Lilly's eye and gave a sly wink. Lilly was impressed and couldn't hide it.

Half an hour passed, and Lilly, finding herself redundant, went in search of tea. A small counter was set up in an annexe at the end of the room and sold drinks, biscuits and sweets. It was run by the red bands, inmates sufficiently trusted to deal in hot water and plastic

234

spoons without starting a riot. They were named for their red sashes, which distinguished them from the masses. The prisoners, especially the regulars, vied for the privilege that at least got them out of cells that would otherwise house them for up to twenty-three hours a day.

Lilly surveyed the bars of chocolate and hoped she could get away with two.

'I thought it was you,' said the red band on duty.

The woman was chalky and plain in her prison outfit of sludge brown. Her hair was tied back off her face with a rubber band, her dark roots an unpleasant halo, but the accent was unmistakable.

'Angie. What on earth are you doing here?' said Lilly.

Angie laughed. 'I like the peace and quiet and the food's just great.'

'How long are you in for?' asked Lilly.

'Six weeks. I told them I'd pay the bloody fines if only they'd let me work instead of arresting me all the while,' said Angie.

'You need to work from a flat instead of the streets, then the police would leave you alone.'

'Aye, but the first three tricks would go for the rent and these days I'm lucky to do six or seven a night.'

The plight of the aging pro, out-priced and out-spiced by girls literally half her age. Lilly couldn't even guess at what Angie would do when she and the work dried up altogether.

'How did you land this job on such a short sentence?' she asked.

Pouring tea might not seem such a great little

number but in jail such positions were hotly contested. Women had died for less.

'Better not to ask,' said Angie with a smile and changed the subject. 'Did you ever find Max Hardy?'

Lilly rubbed her throat. 'Afraid so, but he didn't kill Grace.'

Lilly looked over at Kelsey. She was shaking her head and writing furiously on her sheet of paper.

'Can't you get the wee girl out of here?' asked Angie, without any trace of recrimination or criticism.

'We're doing our damnedest.'

'Some of us keep an eye out but we can't be everywhere,' Angie confided.

'How's she doing?' asked Lilly, afraid of the answer.

'Hard to say. Most think she's batty and steer well clear, but there's always one wanting to dish out the aggro. This is no place for a kiddie, especially that one.'

'I need to find out who killed Grace,' whispered Lilly. 'I thought it was Max, but it's not. It could be a punter, someone who likes knives. Did you hear of anyone like that?'

Angie thought for a moment. 'There's a girl just started a six stretch for robbery. She's got terrible scars down her back where a punter cut her up.'

'Do you think she'd talk to me?' asked Lilly.

Angie seesawed her hand. 'I'll ask.'

Lilly finally bought three bars of chocolate, one for each of them. She rubbed her finger along the smooth contour of her Breakaway. She could scoff it down in one bite and half-hoped Kelsey's mouth would be too sore to eat or Sheba would be on a diet so that she could also set upon the other two.

Angie took the money and pocketed half of it with a wink. 'It's a shame about Max, I'd love to see that bastard put away. He'd not last five minutes in a place like this.'

'Did you ever work for him?' asked Lilly.

'I told you, I don't have a pimp.'

'What about his films, were you ever in one?'

Angie gave a derisive snort through her nose. 'I'm too long out of nappies for his stuff, if you get my drift.'

Lilly's brain began to tick and she raced back to Kelsey. 'Could you give me a second, Sheba?'

Sheba made it clear that she didn't take kindly to the interruption, but she didn't resist and moved away.

Lilly stared hard at her client. 'Tell me about the videos.'

Kelsey shrugged.

'Don't give me any crap, Kelsey. Was your mum in them?'

Kelsey shook her head.

'Was that because she was far too old?'

Kelsey nodded her head once and returned her chin to her chest.

I kept my mouth shut when I shouldn't have.

Kelsey retreated so far into herself that Sheba abandoned the rest of the interview and the two women made their way out.

Sheba's pursed lips and straight back told Lilly she was furious.

'I'm sorry,' said Lilly, 'but I had to ask her something.'

'Can you tell me what?' asked Sheba, her tone clipped.

'Not today, but I do think it's important, that's why it couldn't wait.'

'If it pertains in any way to Kelsey's emotional state then I'm going to need to know. I can't present the court with half a picture.' Sheba fixed Lilly with a glare. The girl with soft eyes and a luscious mouth was gone. 'I won't do this with one hand tied behind my back.'

Lilly nodded her assent. 'I wouldn't expect you to.'

The hint of a scarlet smile returned. 'I need to make some calls, then I'll give you my first impressions this afternoon.'

She turned towards her car and Lilly watched Sheba's bottom undulate with a mixture of envy and admiration.

Lilly had been back in her office guiltily shuffling her paperwork for half an hour when Sheba called.

'So tell me, did Kelsey kill her mother?'

Lilly was only half joking. Angie's news had sent her into freefall as she tried to assess whether it made Kelsey more or less likely to have committed the murder. Kelsey knew about the films and had covered for her mum. When that still wasn't enough and Grace put her into care how angry would that have made Kelsey? Angry enough to kill? Lilly needed some evidence to point away from her client. Something positive from a shrink would be as welcome as Christmas.

'It'll be some time before I can give you my opinion on that one,' laughed Sheba, 'and we'll never know for sure.'

'I suppose the mind isn't black and white,' said Lilly.

'Most of the time it's not even grey. Unlike the body, which is much less difficult to assess, which is why I checked whether Kelsey had had a medical upon her arrival at Parkgate.'

'And did she?'

'Yes. Given her age and the gravity of the situation the prison doctor was very thorough and found that Kelsey's larynx and trachea were discoloured but no longer excoriated.'

'In English please.'

'Kelsey's throat is better. She can speak.'

Lilly, however, found that she had been struck dumb, her mind racing ahead to the possible implications.

'How long has she been able to?' she asked at last.

'The doc reckons about a week.'

A week!

Lilly went over the events of the last week. The interview with Bradbury. The hearing in court. And all the time Kelsey could speak.

'There are, of course, two possible explanations as to why she hasn't yet spoken,' said Sheba. 'The first is that she's still in shock. Her body may be ready but her mind may not be willing. The second – well, you know what I'm about to say.'

'That Kelsey's been taking the piss.'

Lilly relived every exchange she had had with Kelsey during the last week – the scribbled notes, the bowed head. Could it all be bullshit? And if Kelsey could be that manipulative, what else might she be capable of?

* * *

239

Max leaned against the window of Pizza Hut. He was far too hot in the Armani jacket he'd purchased this morning in the Arndale Centre but he couldn't resist. He had seen it in the window of a gloomy little boutique that specialised in overpriced tat with the odd designer label thrown in to raise its game.

Max had again broken into the money given to him by Barrows, and justified it on the grounds that he would need to look smart to make it in the States. In a country where image was everything such a jacket wouldn't be an asset but a necessity. When the money started to roll in he might even be able to write it off against tax.

He saw her walking towards him through the town centre, checking her reflection in the window of British Home Stores. Her face was drawn into a scowl. She looked small and vulnerable, despite the tough-girl glower.

'Charlene, baby,' said Max.

She nodded hello. Apparently she had not taken kindly to being drugged during their last encounter, but Max had been doing this for long enough to turn the situation around.

'Listen, baby, I know you're probably embarrassed about what went down at mine, but it happens. You got a little crazy but that's cool.'

He saw her mouth soften to a pout, unsure now as to who was mad at whom.

'The shoot wasn't the best,' he persisted, 'but I ain't vexed.'

'No?'

'Of course not. Anyway, I'm a pro and I still got a couple of good shots.'

Charlene's face flushed with pleasure, as he knew it would. 'Let me see them.'

'I've put them in your portfolio, you can take a look the next time you're round at mine.'

He eased her into the restaurant, his hand in the small of her back. 'In fact, an associate of mine has suggested a film might be just the right vehicle for you.'

Her eyes opened saucer-wide. She seemed nearer to ten than thirteen. 'A film.'

They ate their doughy meal (three slices of margarita and unlimited visits to the salad bar for £3.99 before 5 p.m.) and Max chatted about production companies and distribution rights.

He mentioned his views on agents. Charlene should seriously consider getting one, and indeed he did know at least two with a good reputation, although she might think fifteen per cent a bit steep.

He spoke of trips abroad. Personally, he hated flying, but what could you do, it came with the territory.

All the while Charlene listened and nodded, her mouth crammed with oily cheese, her head filled with previously unimagined plans.

Max was good at this bit: the flannel, the flirting, the fairytale. One night last year when he'd been too strung out to sleep he'd watched a documentary about how some priest had talked a bunch of altar boys into sucking his cock and what have you. Grooming, they'd

241

called it. Max thought that was a stupid word. Like something you'd do to a dog for a show. Whatever it was he had it in spades. After all, he'd learned from a master.

When his mother had finally given up even the pretence of caring for her son and handed him in to the social so she could pursue her favoured pastimes of drinking, smoking and being beaten by whatever lowlife she had most recently taken up with, Max found himself in care at The Bushberry Home for Disturbed Children. One of the men who worked there was not like the others and listened closely to his charges, smiling his wide, warm smile, telling them not to worry. He turned a blind eye to the odd cigarette and gave out little treats of chocolate and fizzy drinks. He wiped away tears and kissed sad cheeks, and if you were one of his special ones you could sit on his knee. Grace had been very special indeed. She'd driven him wild, but it was her fault for being so beautiful. He loved her with all his heart and they'd be together as soon as she was sixteen, but she mustn't tell anyone. They wouldn't understand.

Grace was so happy she thought she might burst, and had to, just had to, tell her best friend. She scrubbed the stains out of her knickers and confided in Max that she was going to get married as soon as she turned sixteen.

And Grace was no chump. She'd lived with her dad long enough to spot a scam when she heard one, but she still took it all in.

God how he had hated that man for breaking Grace's heart; still hated him for what he did.

And yet, Max had to hand it to him, the man could sell sand to Arabs. Yes, the man was a genius.

Lilly arrived home frazzled and starving. A carbo-hydrate frenzy beckoned. She fancied chips, the way her mother had made them. The potatoes dried in a tea towel on the draining board and submerged in a pan of dangerously hot oil. Delicious, but a cursory glance in the kitchen confirmed the absence of pota-toes, clean tea towel or sunflower oil.

Lilly put pasta in a pan and ran a bath for Sam. She wondered what the director of social services would say as she undressed herself and dived into the water with her six-year-old son.

They scrubbed away their days at work and school then dried each other off. For fun, Sam painted Lilly's toes, each one a different colour.

When Sam, pink and squeaky, lay on his bed with a *Scooby Doo* comic, Lilly padded downstairs in an extra-large T-shirt that had come free with a six-pack of Boddingtons, and a pair of orange slipper-socks that Miriam had given to her as a joke.

She opened the fridge and pulled out bacon, cream and cheese. She cracked a free-range egg and separated it in her hand, allowing the white to slip through her fingers into the sink. When she had three oily yolks she added a thick dollop of cream.

The phone rang. Lilly swore under her breath, picked up the receiver with her clean hand and held it with her chin.

'It's me,' said David.

'Aha.'

'I've been thinking about your car.'

'That must have been thrilling.'

'I want to pay for the repairs.'

'I thought you were broke.'

'I am, we are, but Cara should have told you about the insurance.'

'Yes, she should.'

'So you should send the bill to me. But you'll have to take over the premiums.'

'Okay.'

'Okay?'

'Okay.'

'Right, well, I'll be off. Things to do. What about you?'

'Cooking.'

Lilly could almost hear his ears pricking.

'Anything nice?'

'Carbonara,' she deadpanned. It was David's favourite.

'Heavy on the parmesan?'

Lilly reached for the grater. 'I'm shaving that baby now.'

She smiled to herself. Cara wouldn't eat cheese. She was lactose-intolerant. She knew what he was implying but Lilly wasn't going to make it easy for him. 'Where's the salad-muncher?'

'She's out,' he said.

'Having a seaweed body wrap, no doubt.'

He didn't rise to the bait, such was the power of Lilly's food. 'Something like that.'

Lilly relented. 'Want to eat?'

'Give me twenty minutes.'

The doorbell went in ten.

Lilly pulled at the door. 'Did you take the Harrier jump jet?'

It wasn't her ex-husband. 'Jack!'

He looked embarrassed. 'You're expecting someone else.'

'No. Yes. Sort of. Come in.'

Lilly became instantly aware of her appearance. A downmarket Bridget Jones.

'Let me get you a drink. Beer or wine?'

'Whatever's cold. It's bloody roasting out there.'

'I know. It's ridiculous for September. An Indian summer, I suppose.' Lilly could hear herself gabbling about the weather. 'My nan used to predict one every year, and when it rained on the first or the second of September she'd say it was good for the roses and would then predict the coldest winter on record.'

Jack laughed politely.

Lilly went for the drinks and pulled off the day-glo socks, although Sam's pedicure was hardly an improvement. She bolted down half a glass of Sauvignon blanc in the kitchen and filled another for Jack.

Back in the sitting room, Sam was perched at the end of the sofa appraising Jack with studied cool.

'What are you doing up?' asked Lilly.

Sam kept steely eyes on the intruder. 'I heard a man's voice. I thought it was Dad.'

'Afraid not, wee man. I'm Jack and I work with your mum.'

'He's a policeman,' added Lilly, who knew how Sam would react.

'Wow,' Sam shouted, 'have you got a gun?'

'Not with me,' said Jack.

'Did you ever kill anyone?' asked Sam.

Lilly saw a strange look creep into Jack's features, a flicker of something dark. Not more than a shadow, but definitely something.

'Of course not, love, he looks after children,' she said.

Sam made no effort to hide his disappointment.

'I once caught a bank robber,' countered Jack.

The child's enthusiasm returned. 'How?'

'Let's go back up those stairs and I'll tell you all about it.'

Lilly watched in amazement as Jack led Sam back to bed and wondered what Jack would think if she changed into something less shapeless. Jeans and a vest top might set the right note, casually sexy but not obvious. Hmm. Maybe obvious would be better.

She was weighing up the option of a short satin robe she had optimistically bought on sale at Agent Provocateur but had never worn, when David walked in.

'Tell me it's massive,' he said.

'What?' asked Lilly.

'The bowl of pasta.'

'Pasta?'

David shook his head and laughed. 'You can't have forgotten already.'

Jack entered the room.

David looked him up and down in much the same way as Sam had done. 'But I see you have other things on your mind.'

'I'm just leaving,' said Jack.

246

'You don't have to,' said Lilly.

They looked at each other for an excruciating moment.

'I'm just leaving,' Jack repeated and drained his glass.

As he left, Lilly shut the door behind him.

'What was that about?' asked David.

'I have absolutely no idea.'

Jack continued to cringe until he had put a good mile between himself and Lilly. What was he thinking turning up on her doorstep? It had served him right when the husband arrived. They were obviously still involved or he wouldn't still have a key, and she wouldn't have been dressed like that, in only a T-shirt, her legs long and bare and smooth.

Stop it, man.

But she had been pleased to see him. She'd invited him in for a drink, introduced him to her son. Maybe there was something there.

He played bat and ball with the idea all the way home and decided to find some spurious reason to call her first thing in the morning and ask her outright if she liked him. Back home he ate a piece of unbuttered toast and drank three cans of warm lager knowing full well he would do no such thing.

CHAPTER TWELVE

Friday, 18 September

Lilly had a busy day ahead of her. First a showdown with Kelsey at the prison, then a meeting with Jez.

'We need to talk turkey,' he'd said. Whatever that meant.

Sheba was waiting for Lilly in the same place. Defying the heat, she was dressed in a black wrap dress, its jersey skimming her curves. Her only concession to the warm weather was a pair of open-toe shoes with vertiginous heels under which she ground out the remains of a scarlet-tipped cigarette.

'You do the talking, I need to observe her closely,' Sheba said.

'Will you be able to tell if she's lying?' asked Lilly.

Sheba shrugged. 'Maybe. Everyone has a tell. A little gesture they make when under pressure.'

'What's mine?' said Lilly, laughing.

'You push your hair off your face,' Sheba answered seriously. 'I don't know what Kelsey's is yet.'

'But you'll suss it?'

'I hope so, but some people are so good they control them.'

They made it through security without incident until a bored group of officers asked to check in their mouths. Lilly watched the other visitors, their cheeks bulging like hamsters with drugs, saunter past while she and Sheba waited for someone to find the appropriate implement with which to undertake the search. At last one of the guards brandished what looked suspiciously like the handle of a white plastic spoon.

Sheba gave the dirtiest of giggles and opened wide. The guard pushed in his stick and looked as if he'd love to follow.

Lilly took her turn and the guard wrinkled his nose. She regretted the packet of cheese and onion crisps she had eaten on the way. Her humiliation was complete when he offered her a mint.

Kelsey slunk into her seat and took up her usual position.

Lilly was unimpressed. She needed to know if it was all just an act.

'The prison doctor says you can talk.'

Kelsey's head snapped up. It was the fastest movement Lilly had ever seen her make.

'He says your mouth has healed.'

Kelsey's hand hovered around her lips as if to check whether it could be true.

Lilly couldn't tell if the surprise was genuine. She hoped Sheba could judge more accurately.

'Is he right, can you talk?' asked Lilly.

Kelsey picked up a pencil and wrote.

I don't think so.

'What the hell does that mean? Either you can or you can't!'

Her own harsh tone shocked Lilly but she was desperate for answers. She was doing everything she could to help this kid and the prospect that Kelsey was playing some evil little game was too much. Christ, Lilly had tortured herself over the letter and spent her evenings touring Tye Cross to get to the bottom of this mess rather than at home with her son. She'd put her life in danger chasing a pornographer to prove Kelsey's innocence. These kids always told lies. It was second nature and Lilly generally shrugged it off, but she needed to know the truth about Kelsey, too much was at stake to let it go.

Kelsey opened her mouth as if she might speak but nothing came out. Her eyes filled with tears and she wrote,

I'm sorry.

It was so pitiful that Lilly was immediately filled with remorse. This was a damaged child, not a sociopath. She deserved better than the life she had led and she deserved better than prison. She certainly deserved better than Lilly's suspicions.

Lilly glanced at Sheba for acknowledgement that she felt the same but the psychiatrist's reaction was sanguine.

Lilly spoke gently this time. 'I'm sorry too. Now let's concentrate on getting you out of here.'

But Kelsey wouldn't or couldn't look up, she just wept into her chest, hot tears splashing onto the table.

250

Lilly watched them fall until a guard called a halt to the meeting and took Kelsey back to her cell.

Lilly and Sheba passed through the prison back to the outside world. The endless metal doors that opened and then closed behind them only served to remind Lilly of the distance she had put between herself and Kelsey. She should be Kelsey's closest ally yet the wall between them was impenetrable. If the child did anything stupid Lilly had no one to blame but herself.

The acidic smell of vomit filled the air, and up ahead a group of prisoners mopped the corridor. One of them looked up from her work and waved at Lilly.

'Hello, Angie,' said Lilly.

'Who pissed on your chips?'

Lilly laughed in spite of herself. 'Things are, how shall I say, difficult.'

Angie looked at the film of regurgitated food floating on top of her bucket. 'Things are, how shall I say, fantastic in here.'

Lilly laughed again. 'I'm sorry, Angie.'

'Don't be, it's better than bang-up. At least I get a blather with some of the girls.'

Angie pulled out a roll-up from her pocket and lit it without removing her rubber gloves. 'Anyway, I'm glad I caught you, it'll save me using my phone card. I spoke to the girl who got cut and she says she'll talk to you but only cos I told her you were sound, so don't go fucking it up.'

'I won't,' said Lilly.

The guards gestured to Angie to get back to work and moved Lilly along.

'What was that about?' asked Sheba.

'Good news, I hope.'

Generally barristers liked to do business in their chambers. Old-fashioned, book-lined apartments set in airy squares around Temple, the area in the city between the Embankment and Fleet Street.

Lilly resented going there. She hated being met at reception by the teenaged clerks straight out of central casting for *EastEnders* and their endless yet fruitless offers of coffee. She loathed being made to wait while the barristers finished their oh-so-important case in the High Court. Always, it seemed, far more complex than her own.

She wanted to run amok down the dark corridors shouting, 'I'm the bloody client here.'

But no, she would sit and fidget and check her watch until someone would sweep her into their room with more offers of nonexistent coffee.

Happily, Lilly undertook most of her own advocacy in court and so had precious little need of barristers. She had never understood solicitors who did all the hard work – the paperwork, the interviews, the endless conversations with clients – only to hand over the case to a barrister at the fun part: the trial. Lilly would go to any length to avoid such a scenario. Occasionally, when two trials fell on the same day she had no option but to pass one on. Even Lilly couldn't be in two places at once.

But Kelsey's case was different. Lilly couldn't do it alone. She might have years of experience but even she wouldn't attempt a murder case at the Old Bailey.

Jez, however, was not one to stand on ceremony and had proved amenable to Lilly's suggestion that their meeting take place in her office. He arrived early and was shown to Lilly's room by a sullen-faced Sheila.

He looked at the mountainous paperwork dumped on every surface in the small room. 'Let's do this in the pub.'

They ordered their drinks and took a table in a smart and almost empty bar called Lancasters. It seemed to change hands every six months and its current re-incarnation was a New York loft conversion with grey walls and blond wood. The wine list was extensive and the staff predominantly Australian. Quite a change from its former life as a tapas bar with live flamenco dancing on Thursdays and Saturdays. Lilly noted that the only thing that never changed was the lack of customers.

Jez put his file on the table but didn't open it. 'This is a difficult one, Lilly.' He tapped the folder. 'There's not much evidence against Kelsey and I'm tempted to treat it with the contempt it deserves and ask the judge to kick it out before arraignment.'

'Absolutely,' said Lilly.

'I doubt that this one will go for it, of course.'

'But the case is so weak,' said Lilly.

Jez waved a dismissive arm. 'Politics.'

Lilly opened her mouth to argue but was loath to

appear the silly ingénue. Instead she voiced her other concerns.

'But you know what trials are like. There's always the risk that the jury go off-piste.'

Jez nodded. 'Too unpredictable. The problem is the general public like to feel these things are resolved. Someone's dead and someone must be to blame.'

'Then we give them someone else,' said Lilly.

'Like who? It needs to be credible.'

Lilly thought about Max. 'I thought I knew who did it. A dealer, pimp, all-round scumbag. He knew Grace, and when I tried to ask questions he attacked me.'

'Sounds perfect.'

'Just one problem,' she said. 'He didn't do it.'

Jez shrugged. 'Doesn't really matter. He's not on trial so we'll just give him to the jury as a possible alternative. Rake enough muck to cast doubt on Kelsey's guilt.'

The waitress came over with their bottle of wine. Both Lilly and Jez fell silent until she left.

'Normally I'd agree, but the police know for sure it's not him,' Lilly said. 'They're his alibi.'

'Then we're back to square one.'

A group of young men at the next table, flushed by the heat and lunchtime beer, began to whistle and shout. Lilly realised that Sheba was the focus of their attention. She graced them with a wink before sitting next to her brother.

'Such a tart,' he chided.

Sheba drank from his glass. 'Hello, little brother.'

He wrinkled his nose at the lipstick she left on the rim and gestured to the waitress to fetch another glass.

'How did you find us?' asked Lilly.

'Your secretary told me your room was a pigsty so you'd hit the nearest pub.'

Lilly blushed. Neither Jez nor Sheba seemed like the messy types. She had never seen them dressed anything less than immaculately and both were loaded with cool.

'So what have you decided?' asked Sheba.

'We're going to run a soddi,' said Jez.

'Sod what?' she said.

The clean glass arrived and he poured himself more wine. 'A soddi. SODDI. Some other dude did it.'

Sheba opened her palms, none the wiser.

'It's a defence. We can't just say Kelsey didn't do it. If it comes to a trial we'll have to give the jury another explanation of who did,' said Jez.

'Why?' she asked.

'I thought you were the shrink,' he said.

'And when you say something remotely sensible I'll analyse it.'

They were quite a double act.

Lilly came to the rescue. 'Nature abhors a vacuum. If we take Kelsey out of the frame we have to put someone else in.'

Sheba nodded that she understood. 'So which poor sod is it going to be?'

'We had the perfect candidate but it turns out he's not guilty,' said Jez.

Sheba patted his head in mock sympathy. 'What a shame.'

'Grace was on the game so it could just be a punter,' said Lilly.

'Would a jury buy that?' asked Sheba.

'I don't see why not,' said Jez. 'It's an alien lifestyle and most people are prepared to accept it has its inherent dangers. We can certainly wheel out the statistics about how many prostitutes met violent deaths in the last three years.'

Lilly looked at Sheba. 'You don't seem sure.'

'The pathology's wrong. Most prostitutes are killed in very violent circumstances.'

'Grace didn't exactly die in her sleep,' said Jez.

Sheba furrowed her gorgeous brow, the nearest she came to wrinkles. 'Let me finish. The statistics you want to offer up in evidence will tell you that most die as a consequence of unplanned attacks. They're often beaten to death or stabbed by assailants who didn't necessarily want to kill them but clearly didn't care less at the time. Sometimes a client will lash out and then fail to curb the aggression.'

'I think we can safely say Grace's killer failed to curb his,' said Jez.

Sheba shook her head. 'I disagree. Grace received two clean blows to the back of the head. There were no signs of a struggle, nor defensive wounds. I'd say there was no fight at all, no attempt to overpower her, no aggression. He simply waited until she turned around and then *wham*.'

'Grace never knew what hit her,' said Lilly.

'Literally,' said Sheba.

'But what about the mutilation?' asked Jez.

'It's difficult to say what would motivate a person to do that,' said Sheba.

'Dr Cheney, who did the autopsy, thought there might be a bond between the killer and victim,' said Lilly.

'That's probably true,' said Sheba.

'So our killer wasn't a stranger,' said Jez. 'Which would explain why she let him in.'

Sheba's lips glistened with wine. 'But the bond needn't be real. It doesn't have to be familial, which is no doubt what the prosecution will say, it needn't even be mutual. It just needs to exist in our killer's mind.'

'Could a punter feel that sort of bond with a girl he used regularly?' asked Lilly.

'Oh yes. Lots of men, with poor or nonexistent relationships with other women, form deep attachments with a prostitute. It's one-way traffic, of course,' Sheba looked sideways at her brother, 'but self-delusion is a powerful thing.'

Jez lifted his glass in triumph. 'A regular punter it is. I shall be famous for being the first barrister to use the *Pretty Woman* defence. It'll become legendary.'

Sheba put her hand on his wrist and lowered the glass to the table. 'As I said, the pathology's wrong. There's no sign of sexual activity whatsoever.'

'Maybe he killed Grace before it got to that,' Jez offered.

'It's possible, but why go on to cut her?'

'Because he likes it,' said Lilly.

Jez laughed.

'It's not as daft as it sounds,' said Sheba. 'There are three main reasons why assailants inflict post-mortem mutilation of this kind. The first is to disguise the identity of the victim, which doesn't apply here because facially she was left intact. The second is where the assailant is so caught up in his actions he (a) doesn't realise the victim is dead or (b) realises they're dead but can't stop the flood.'

'Doctor Cheney said Grace would have died in the kitchen almost instantly so the killer must have dragged the body to the bedroom to start the cutting,' said Lilly.

'Exactly, not the actions of someone caught in an adrenalin rush,' said Sheba.

'And the third reason?' asked Jez.

Sheba took a long drink. 'Much more interesting. The mutilation is actually more important to the killer than the killing. The post-mortem ritual provides a release which may be psychosexual, particularly if he's impotent, which would explain the lack of semen at the scene. It's as Lilly says, he does it because he likes it.'

'Would someone like that visit prostitutes?' asked Lilly.

Sheba nodded vigorously. 'Almost definitely.'

'Then we have our other poor sod,' said Jez, triumphant again.

'Perhaps,' said Sheba.

'You still have doubts?' Lilly queried.

Sheba circled the rim of her glass with a wet finger, an impossibly sensual gesture of which she seemed oblivious. 'It's so extreme yet so meticulous. Almost textbook.'

'So our man's tidy,' said Jez.

'It's much more than that,' she said. 'For anyone to

go this far he's been fantasising for years. He will probably watch lots of porn, not vanilla flavour, and visit lots of prostitutes. It's all so perfect I would doubt this is his first attack.'

Jez's eyes opened wide. 'He's done it before?'

'Very possibly, although perhaps to a lesser extent,' she answered.

Jez tapped his nose. Lilly could almost hear his mind whirring. 'Something like that would have hit the press. Or at the very least the police would know about it.'

'Maybe they do know,' said Lilly, 'and maybe it's been swept under the carpet.'

Her audience waited, breath held, for more information.

'There's a woman in Parkgate who was cut to ribbons by a punter. She was working the same patch as Grace.'

'We need to find out who she is and see if she'll talk to us,' said Jez.

Lilly gave a half-smile. 'I know who she is and she's already agreed to see me.'

Normally vocal in her complaints, Charlene sat at the kitchen table quietly with the other residents. She didn't comment on the wrinkled potatoes, singed and black like dirty stones. Instead she pushed them around her plate in contented silence and even nibbled at the accompanying carrots which squatted in a cold, accusing pile.

'You on a promise?' asked the boy across the table.

Charlene refused to look at him. Max had told her

there were two types of people in the world: those who made something of themselves, and those destined for the bottom of the bin. Winners and losers, take your pick. Charlene knew what she was and wouldn't waste another second on the sad idiots in The Bushes. Really, she should feel sorry for them.

The boy balled up a piece of kitchen roll and threw it at Charlene. 'Chaz is on a promise.'

'That's right,' shouted Jermaine, joining his friend in the torture. 'He's promised her a facelift.'

Charlene itched to flick him with the nearest dish-cloth but reminded herself that contact was futile and dangerous. These lowlifes were infectious, ready to drag you down.

Knowing that all eyes were on her, she smiled to herself and dissected the dry food on her plate. Miriam, who had no doubt anticipated a battle of insults and low-level assaults, looked particularly wary of Charlene's newfound pacifism.

When the table, floor, walls and cupboards had been wiped down to Miriam's satisfaction, the children sloped off to the television room, but Charlene was held back by the firm hand and insistent look that Miriam could employ with ease.

'Anything you want to tell me?' she asked.

Charlene shook her head and turned to go. Miriam was all right, but she chose to work here and breathe the same air as the others so that must make her a loser too. Charlene would check with Max but was sure he'd agree.

Miriam kept her hand on Charlene's arm. Not tight,

but with enough pressure to convey who was in charge. 'Will you do a drugs test for me?'

Charlene snorted. Miriam regularly tested her charges. Everyone knew she couldn't force them to take the test but everyone also knew a refusal would be taken as a sign of guilt, which more often than not would result in a swift transfer to another unit. Miriam would deal with truancy, swearing, fighting and even stealing with the lightest of touch, but she would not tolerate drugs in the unit.

The Bushes was no palace, but for most of the residents it was the nearest they'd ever come, with warm beds, three meals a day and the grudging acceptance that Miriam did, in fact, give a shit. For most it wasn't a risk worth taking.

'Why should I?' asked Charlene, her return to petulance instantly familiar.

Miriam kept her gaze as steady as her voice. 'Because I'm worried about you.'

'Don't be,' snapped Charlene.

There was a brief hiatus as Charlene tried to push past the much taller woman, who stood oak firm and blocked the escape route.

'You know what will happen if you refuse,' said Miriam.

Charlene began to panic. If she was kicked out of The Bushes where would she go? Her dad wouldn't have her back, not now the bitch from hell and her four dirty kids had moved in, and her mum was still in the nut house after she threatened to throw herself off the flyover.

They might send her to a unit miles away. The last boy went to some place near Dover, wherever that was. Worse still, they could put her in a secure unit, which might as well be prison because you weren't allowed out on your own. Either way, she wouldn't be able to see Max, and although she was special and had star quality she wasn't naive enough to think she was the only girl he was helping. If Charlene didn't grab every opportunity on offer she was sure that some other stupid tart would.

'I ain't on drugs,' said Charlene, but she opened her mouth and allowed Miriam to scrape the inside of her cheek with a swab. After all, the test would take ages to come back, and it was only a week before her new life began.

'And I'll expect an apology.'

Lilly left Jez and Sheba drinking happily and copiously in Lancasters. Their bond was so strong Lilly wished, not for the first time, that she had a sibling.

As a child she had always imagined having a sister, someone with whom to discuss the stories in *Cathy* and pierce one another's ears with a kilt pin. All her life she had been an outsider, always on the outside looking in. Wouldn't it be great to fit in with someone like connecting pieces in a puzzle?

She hoped Jez and Sheba had at least been impressed that she had already managed to track down another victim, that if not part of their gang they at least saw her as an equal.

She went to collect Sam, and planned to call in at

the baker's on the way home to choose a chocolate-covered treat, but as soon as she saw her son she could see he was in no mood for sugar.

Usually, Sam shook his teacher's hand like a fireman at a pump, and bounded out of his classroom, full of enthusiasm for the day's next chapter. Today he mumbled good afternoon and offered a limp wrist, which Miss Lewis mechanically moved up and down, then dragged his feet all the way to the car.

'Good day, big man?' Lilly asked.

Sam didn't answer, but Lilly knew she would find out what was bothering him soon enough. Sam was not a boy to keep any grievance to himself. Lilly wondered if Cara's pregnancy was still playing on his mind.

Sure enough, after a silent journey home, Sam sat at the kitchen table and gave a deep and weary sigh. Lilly would have laughed at the melodrama but knew Sam was in no mood for humour.

Apropos of nothing, Sam demanded to know if his mother knew what Austria was like and had she ever been skiing. Lilly understood where the conversation was going and knew her answer would affect its development. Relieved that his mood wasn't about the baby, Lilly considered how best to deal with her son. Sam, like Lilly, hated diversion tactics, particularly the transparent kind that insulted the intelligence, so talk of cakes or confectionery would only start an incendiary. Pretence by Lilly that she didn't know what he was getting at would simply allow Sam to spell things out at length and in excruciating detail.

Lilly chose the well-worn path of factual accuracy and explained that, although she herself had never had the pleasure of a trip to Austria, Sam's dad had been on business and reported it to be cold but rather pretty. She resisted the temptation to tell him that on the estate where she grew up ski-masks were worn by those robbing petrol stations, and stuck to the bare truth. She herself had never skied but she'd always thought it looked fun.

Sam digested these facts along with his sausage and mash, an unseasonal choice hastily put together because it was his favourite. He held his cutlery vertically, while a slow river of onion gravy ran down his fork and pooled in a rich brown puddle on his fist.

'There's a school trip in January. Everyone's going, but I know we haven't got enough money,' he said.

Lilly recalled how it had hurt when she was a child and Elsa couldn't stretch to the trip to Hadrian's Wall. She'd spent a whole term compiling a project on a place she'd never been to.

She removed the fork and wiped Sam's hand with a dishcloth. 'Maybe we could ask Dad.'

Sam shook his head sadly. 'He won't have it. New babies cost a fortune.'

'That's true,' said Lilly, 'but we could go half each.'

Sam's eyes opened wide and he raced to retrieve a letter from his book bag.

'This tells you all about it,' he gabbled, and thrust the paper at Lilly. 'Do you really think I can go?'

She thought of the insurance premium on her car, the warped front door to the cottage which barely fitted

264

into the rotten frame, the carpet in her bedroom so threadbare that only the stains held it together.

'Yes, you can go.'

Lilly left Sam checking an atlas and collected her emails.

To: Lilly Valentine
From: Rupinder Singh
Subject: Who the hell is Candy Grigson?
Have had a fax from Parkgate saying the above named wants a visit. There's no client by this name on the database and Sheila has never heard of her.

Your paperwork has now reached crisis point and you cannot afford to waste your time and my money on more waifs and strays.

Rupes

PS I've made an appointment for you to see her tomorrow morning.

PPS This had better be good.

PPPS Jez doesn't get any more ugly, does he?

To: Lilly Valentine
From: Bathsheba Lorenson
Subject: Our other poor sod
Further to our discussion today I must stress that I remain unconvinced about the likelihood of our murderer being one of Grace's customers. However, as I thought the internet was a flash in the pan I'll let you run with it as a possible theory.

When you see the inmate who is allegedly another victim of our man you will need to ascertain the exact circumstances of the attack, whether she knew the client, where it took place, and in particular whether she was unconscious at the time of the mutilation – and if so was that as a result of a blow to the head.

A fight with an enraged punter is not what we're after.

With regard to Kelsey, I have been giving more thought as to how we can get her out of Parkgate, but first I need to speak to you about any possible sexual abuse she may have suffered.

Hasta mañana,
Sheba

To: Lilly Valentine
From: Jack McNally
Subject: Not sure really
Just wanted to know how you're doing.
Jack x

Lilly reread all three, not knowing which was causing her the most consternation. She was glad Candy had got in touch but worried she might be just another red herring. Sheba clearly thought so.

Jack's email was the shortest but each word seemed loaded. Lilly wanted to respond but wasn't sure how. Could she start a relationship with someone she was effectively lying to? Kelsey's letter lay like a chasm between them. And what on earth made her think that Jack wanted a relationship with her? She was hardly a catch. His message was, after all, a simple enquiry as to her health. Given she'd been stabbed a few days ago he was probably just being polite. Yet Lilly couldn't help but focus on the last digit.

Finally she decided to call his mobile and ask him over for supper. But she was almost relieved when she heard the beep, followed by Jack's mellifluous Irish accent.

'*This is Jack McNally, 'fraid I can't pick up but leave a message and I'll get back to you.*'

Lilly hung up immediately. It was surely a sign that she should put this thing on ice until after the case was finished.

CHAPTER THIRTEEN

Saturday, 19 September

Hermione Barrows is drawn again to the videotape. She has watched it three times already this morning but its pull is magnetic. She cannot quite believe what she has seen. She is shaken to her core.

She hears her husband enter the room but doesn't turn to him. She is transfixed by what she sees on the screen.

'What are you watching?' he asks, a tremor in his voice.

'I think you can see for yourself.'

She presses the mute button on the remote control and all is silent, the images somehow more potent.

She drags her eyes from the picture and forces herself to look at her husband. She can feel tears pricking her eyes.

'Hermione,' he says, but lets the sentence fall away.

The quiet between them roars like a river.

'It's not as bad as it looks,' he says at last, without conviction.

Hermione turns back to the television, the tears running freely. It is every bit as bad as it looks.

For there she is, in close-up, each contorted expression magnified, every imperfection in her skin on display.

Hermione points at her own flawed face filling the screen, in stark comparison to the tight creamy skin of the woman thrusting a microphone in her face, and howls as if wounded.

'I am old.'

Lilly arrived at Parkgate for the third time in three days but the guards remained cold and unhelpful. Only the youngest spoke to her, and that was to ask after Sheba.

She handed over her identification and was escorted to a table in the Friends and Family Centre.

Candy Grigson ambled into the room with all the swagger of a serious offender. Prison food had made no impact on her bulk, which Lilly estimated to be well over fourteen stone. Nor had it helped her teeth, which covered most of the hues between brown, grey and black.

Candy parked her impressive backside opposite Lilly. 'Got any fags?'

Lilly pushed across a packet of Benson and Hedges.

Candy ripped open the packet, lit up and began to bark like a seal. She hawked up a mouthful of phlegm and swallowed it down. 'Get us a cuppa.'

Lilly sighed and reminded herself that this woman could still be the victim they were looking for.

Candy drained her cup, burped warm tea breath into

Lilly's face and lit another cigarette with the end of her last one. 'Angie tells me you're all right.'

'That was good of her, and it's very good of you to agree to see me. I realise you must be very busy,' said Lilly.

Candy nodded as if her days were a nonstop schedule of activities and commitments. 'I told Angie if it were important I'd make the time.'

Lilly watched the smoke stream out of Candy's nostrils and wondered if she had ever seen such an unattractive woman. 'I'll try to keep this as short as possible.'

Candy shrugged magnanimously. 'I'm here now.'

'Angie told me you'd been hurt by one of your clients,' said Lilly. 'I'm sure it's very difficult to talk about.'

'He carved me up good and proper,' said Candy.

'What happened?'

Candy sat back in her chair. 'He were a right bastard,' she said, gearing up to tell her story. 'Used to come to the flat every couple of weeks. I told Jon I didn't like him.'

'Jon?' asked Lilly.

'My fella. I said he were weird and we should just get rid, but Jon wouldn't have it.' She took another long drag. 'He said we needed the regulars for cash flow and that.'

Lilly nodded as if the half-baked economics of a pimp made perfect sense. Now was not the time to challenge Candy's life choices.

'He said he'd keep a close eye on that bastard, make sure it didn't get out of hand.'

'Make sure what didn't get out of hand?' asked Lilly.

Candy stubbed out the remains of her cigarette and passed the packet from one hand to the other. 'The stuff he liked. The rough stuff, you know.'

Lilly pretended to have no clue, she needed Candy to be more specific. 'Sex games, you mean?'

Candy laughed but there was little mirth in her voice. 'It weren't no bloody game with him. I told Jon he were a wrong-un.'

'In what way?'

'Always the same every time. He wanted me to lie still, like I were asleep or something, then he'd do stuff to me,' said Candy.

Lilly swallowed her impatience. 'What stuff?'

Candy lit another cigarette without taking her eyes off Lilly. She smirked, clearly mistaking Lilly's excitement for voyeurism. 'Not what you think. No sex at all. He didn't even want a hand job. That's why I didn't want to do him – I mean, it's not as if I like shagging 'em but at least you know where you are.'

'So what *did* he do?'

Lilly knew she was pushing too hard, making Candy suspicious, but this sounded like their man.

'Are you getting off on this or what?' said Candy.

Lilly opened her mouth to protest, but Candy just shrugged as if she couldn't care less.

'It started off all right. He just prodded and poked me a bit. Then he started running things over me, a pen or some keys, and he started pressing harder, leaving marks. Jon says, "He ain't hurting you so what you moaning about?" But it weren't what he did so much as what he said.'

'Like what?' asked Lilly.

'Weird stuff. I mean, I'm used to the dirty talk, ain't I? The "ooh, baby, ahh, baby", well, it's just part of the job.'

Candy scratched her massive thighs and Lilly tried not to imagine her in the throes of her work.

'I don't even worry about the nasty stuff as long as it's just verbals,' Candy continued. 'They can call me a bitch and a slut if they're paying. I mean, I ain't too fond of them neither and if it speeds 'em up it's all right by me.'

'But this went further,' said Lilly.

Candy nodded. 'He said I were vile, that the sight of me made him sick. I said, "You don't have to keep coming here, mate, there's plenty of other girls working the Cross," but he just laughed. He said we were all the same. That we were all –' Candy paused, trying to remember his exact words. 'He said we were all damaged goods.'

'Did you suspect he was dangerous?' asked Lilly.

'Too right I did. I kept telling Jon but he said it were only chat, which were true, but I still had a bad feeling about him,' said Candy.

Lilly wondered how she could steer the conversation to the night Candy was stabbed without confirming Candy's view that she was some sort of snuff merchant. She needn't have worried, Candy was in full flow, smoke pouring from every orifice.

'One night he comes over and asks for extra time, says he'll pay double. I wasn't happy but Jon had already taken the money so I start to get undressed – and *bang*.'

Candy smacked her right fist into her left palm. 'He hit me hard. I mean, I can look after myself but he caught me by surprise from behind. I tried to shout but he put something over my mouth, like this.'

Candy yanked her head back by a handful of hair and placed her other hand over her mouth. Though just a re-enactment, Candy's eyes were wide with terror and Lilly felt her own chest tighten.

'He had a piece of cloth in his hand and I could smell the chemicals on it. It made me dizzy and I fell over. I knew what he were going to do but I couldn't move.'

Lilly's chest had started to burn and she realised she was holding her breath. When she finally exhaled, Candy continued.

'He put me on the bed face down and I can't even speak let alone scream. I could hear Jon outside. He were arguing with some mate about some match on the phone so I knew he weren't coming in any time soon. You know how men get when they're on one about footie?'

Lilly nodded, but in truth David had never shown any passion for sport.

'All I could do was lie there and let it happen.'

'You were still conscious?' asked Lilly, her voice strangled by fear.

Candy nodded. Some of her bravado had deserted her and her hand shook as she stubbed out the dog-end.

'It were weird, like being in a coma or something. I could hear everything as if it were all a long way away but I couldn't even lift my head. Then I felt him over me, sat like normal with his legs on either side of me, and I saw a glint of something out of the corner of my eye. I told myself it were a key but I knew it weren't.'

Lilly felt bile fill her throat, its acid sting rising towards her mouth. She forced herself to swallow and looked into Candy's eyes, urging her to continue.

'When he started to cut me I heard it more than felt it, like paper tearing. And I could smell blood, like iron filings, but it didn't really hurt.'

For the first time Candy looked away, as if it were she that should feel ashamed.

'He were so calm. I closed my eyes, thinking that at least he weren't going to kill me. I counted in my head so I'd know when he'd be finished. That's how I know he left fifteen minutes early, so as he'd be gone before Jon got off the phone, I suppose. I expect you want to see what he did.'

Lilly felt the prick of colour rise in her cheeks. 'Oh no, I wouldn't dream . . . '

Before Lilly could finish Candy unhooked her over-alls and lifted her prison sweatshirt to reveal several rolls of white flesh. She swivelled around in her chair to show the exposed skin of her back and Lilly gasped. The scars that crisscrossed under the straps of Candy's bra were too numerous to count. They radiated from the centre like the close-up of a snowflake, beautiful yet terrible.

Candy rearranged her clothes and turned back to Lilly. She jerked her head over her shoulder. 'I'm just glad he only had time to do my back. You wouldn't want that mess on your face, would you?'

Lilly was grateful when the guard informed her that visiting was finished. She had no idea what to say to Candy. Every response would have been inadequate. As Candy pocketed the remaining cigarettes and scraped back her chair, Lilly touched her arm.

'Did you go to the police?'

Candy snorted in disgust. 'Didn't have a choice. The hospital rang 'em when they were stitching me up but it were a waste of time. I had no idea who he were and they had no intention of finding out.'

Lilly was incredulous. 'But you were so badly injured.'

Candy laughed, her bravado returned. 'I'm just a tart, love.'

'So he's still out there,' said Lilly.

Candy shrugged, turned away and swaggered back to her cell.

The buttons on her silk shirt are exquisite, each one a tiny cluster of seed pearls. Barely noticeable, perhaps, worn under a suit jacket, but to Hermione detail is everything. She takes a deep breath and focuses on the buttons rather than the shaking of her hands as she dresses herself.

She had tried not to think about the video and had nearly succeeded until she redirected her cab from Westminster to Harley Street. It can't be just the passage of time that has ravaged her face, she's not that old. She must be ill. If she thinks about it

275

she hasn't been herself for months, her temperature soaring, especially at night.

'So,' says Dr Emmanuel when Hermione emerges from behind the curtain. 'When did you last have a period?'

She pretends to give the matter some thought. 'Three, maybe four months ago.'

The doctor nods and leans back in his chair. 'There doesn't seem to be anything wrong and you're certainly not pregnant.'

Hermione gives a tinny laugh. 'Certainly not.'

'So this is more likely to be the start of the menopause.'

The room tilts violently and Hermione grabs the back of the chair. 'Not a virus?'

He shakes his head and smiles. 'A little early, but there we are.'

Hermione feels her way into the chair as if blinded. Her breathing comes very fast.

The doctor's smile slips a fraction. 'Are you all right, Mrs Barrows?'

She must pull herself together. 'Yes, of course.' Her tone is breezy. 'It's the heat.'

He nods again. At £250 per visit, Dr Emmanuel can do discretion.

'We can manage any symptoms so that your career is not affected in any way.'

'My career', Hermione has found her ballast, 'is what is important here.'

'Absolutely,' he says, and nods once more.

* * *

Sam was spending the day with his dad. Weeks ago David had suggested he stay overnight too, that they might go to the cinema or to Pizza Express, but when it came to it Cara had tickets for the ballet.

'A last treat before she gets too big,' said David.

Whatever. Lilly was too knackered to argue and would make it up to Sam with home-made beef burgers and a DVD.

With a few free hours left, Lilly called Sheba and they agreed to meet in Lancasters. She drove too fast but she was desperate to share Candy's story. She parked outside the bar and slammed the car door behind her.

'You can't leave it like that,' said an elderly man in a navy blazer.

Lilly followed his eye-line and saw that she had not only mounted the kerb, she was taking up most of the pavement.

The man tutted. 'A wheelchair will never get through.'

Lilly had an urge to tell him to get lost and mind his own, but he had a point, however pompously made.

'And I dread to think how a guide dog would manage,' he said.

Lilly got back in. 'I didn't know we were expecting the Para-Olympics.'

'Young lady, sarcasm is the lowest form of wit.'

Lilly pretended not to hear. 'I'd move back if I were you, I'm a terrible driver.'

She gunned the engine, shot towards him and sent him scuttling away.

The first thing she saw when she parked again was Jez's arched eyebrows. Evidently he'd seen the whole incident.

'Terrorising OAPs. I think someone needs a drink.'

Lilly had been expecting only Sheba but wasn't surprised to see her brother as well. The pair seemed incredibly close and Lilly could only hope that Jez hadn't divulged her slatternly behaviour to Sheba. She consoled herself that a drunken fumble with a scruffy single mother wasn't likely to be something he'd brag about.

Inside the bar, Jez ordered a bottle of wine and sat with Sheba, who was already halfway through what looked like a stiff gin and tonic and fending off offers of a second from the man at the next table.

'So tell us,' said Jez, filling everyone's glass, 'do we have our first victim?'

Lilly took a mouthful of wine. Off her feet, the adrenalin of earlier was seeping away and she felt drained.

'I'll type up a full note of what she said, but basically she was drugged and mutilated while semi-conscious.'

'Bingo,' said Jez.

Sheba placed an olive finger on his arm. 'Hold on, little brother.' She turned to Lilly. 'Did the rest of the pathology fit?'

'You're the expert, but I'd say so,' said Lilly. 'He'd been visiting regularly, gearing up to the attack. Practising, really.'

'What about orgasm, did she say he ejaculated? Remember, we have no semen at the scene,' said Sheba.

Lilly took another sip of wine and tried to remember. 'She said there was no sex of any sort so I'd assume not.'

Sheba shook her head. 'I don't like assumptions.'

'Oh come on, sis, this sounds pretty good, you've got to admit,' said Jez.

'It sounds like a start,' she conceded.

Jez leaned towards Lilly in mock conspiracy. 'You'll learn that with Sheba the glass is always half-empty.'

She wiggled her glass under his nose. 'That's because some mean bastard forgets to top it up.'

Jez took the hint and ordered another gin for Sheba and a second bottle of wine for himself and Lilly. She would have to get a taxi home.

'At least it's something plausible I can use at the trial,' said Jez.

'Which is great,' said Lilly, 'but that's at least six months away. Even a challenge of the evidence wouldn't be listed for a few weeks. I wish there was something we could do for Kelsey now.'

'There might be something,' said Sheba.

The others looked at her expectantly.

'It's nothing definite and there are still a few glitches to iron out.'

'For God's sake, sis,' said Jez.

Sheba pursed her lips and turned to Lilly. 'I need some more sessions with Kelsey, naturally, but from what I've read and what I've seen, she's suffering from some type of psychiatric incapacity.'

Jez opened his mouth but Sheba silenced him with the palm of her hand.

'I can't yet confirm the nature of the incapacity. It may be an illness, it may be a disorder – either way I can confirm to a court that she needs specialist care.'

'What type of care?' asked Lilly.

'Assessment and therapeutic input by professionals trained specifically to treat adolescents in a secure environment,' said Sheba mechanically.

Lilly beamed. She had read those same words only days ago on a brochure for a new unit opened in London. 'Leyland House.'

'Would someone mind telling me what's going on?' asked Jez.

Lilly drained her glass. 'We need to make an application for bail.'

Lilly left Lancasters on a high. She'd tasked Jez to set up a hearing as soon as possible and Sheba was to liaise with her contact at Leyland House. All Lilly had to do was get herself home.

She hailed a passing cab and poured herself in.

'You okay, lady?' asked the driver, his tone well short of sympathetic.

Lilly rubbed her temples. 'Just hot. Could you open the windows?'

The driver muttered an expletive, opened all four windows and set off at speed.

Lilly took deep breaths and pushed her face into the stream of cool air. Her hair danced in all directions. Ten more minutes and she'd be home.

The driver eyed her through his mirror. 'You don't look so good.'

'Just a headache,' said Lilly with a plastic smile.

'I'll stop if you're gonna be sick.'

Lilly shook her head, the movement sending her already spinning mind totally out of kilter.

'I'm not going to be . . . '

Lilly sat by the side of the road, the contents of her bag scattered around her. At this time of day and this far from the train station she didn't expect to see any more taxis and doubted one would pick her up even if she did. It would take only twenty minutes to walk home from here, but her legs had lost their solidity and even standing had proved beyond their current capabilities. Crawling was an option she was seriously considering.

Her phone rang.

'Hello?'

'Jesus, girl, you sound like shit,' laughed Miriam. 'Is now a good time?'

Lilly looked at her trousers, shining with fresh vomit, and rummaged through the detritus of her life for a tissue. 'Now's fine.'

'Where are we at with Kelsey?' said Miriam.

'I think we can get her out of jail and into Leyland House,' said Lilly, and rubbed her suit with an old Milky Way wrapper.

'That's fantastic!' Miriam shouted so loudly that Lilly dropped her phone into the road. She reached for it, lost her balance and fell into the path of an oncoming family of cyclists. Although in no danger of hitting her they rang their bells furiously until she made it back onto the pavement and lay flat on her back.

'For all you know I could be dying, you heartless bastards,' Lilly shouted at the sky, unable to turn her head in their direction.

'Are you all right, Lilly?' asked Miriam.

'Uh huh.'

'Where are you?'

At that moment Lilly did not have the mental agility to lie. 'I'm somewhere on the A5.'

'Driving?' asked Miriam.

'No, sitting. Well, actually . . . ' Lilly trailed off.

'You're sitting somewhere on the A5?' said Miriam.

'Uh huh.'

'I suppose I should ask why.'

'The taxi man suggested I leave his thingy.'

Miriam coughed. 'He kicked you out of the cab?'

'Uh huh.'

'Because he didn't like your politics?'

'I think the main reason was because I'm pissed.'

There was a moment of silence in which Lilly imagined her friend checking her watch and wondering what the hell Lilly was doing drinking herself into a stupor at lunchtime when she should be out finding parents for orphans.

'Taxi drivers don't mind people who're a bit merry, Lilly, it's how they make their living,' said Miriam.

Lilly hauled herself upright. 'That's true, but I chucked up on the seat.'

'Right.'

'Twice.'

'Right.'

'He didn't like that.'

Miriam coughed again. Lilly was sure she was swallowing a laugh.

'So I'm just going to walk home now,' she said, and swept her belongings, together with a handful of stones, leaves and an empty snail shell, into her bag.

'Jack's here. He's just finished his shift and I'm sure he'll pick you up,' said Miriam.

'No,' shouted Lilly, sending the phone in a diagonal trajectory that almost knocked out a tooth. 'No,' she repeated, 'it's really not necessary.'

The line was already dead.

It took Jack nearly half an hour to reach Lilly, by which time she was vertical and heading unsteadily towards home, the stench of vomit from her trousers making her want to throw up again. He pulled his car alongside her.

Lilly continued to walk. 'You needn't have come. I'm quite all right.'

'I'm here now,' he said evenly.

She shrugged as if it were no skin off her nose and got in.

'I don't know about you, but I'm melting,' said Jack. 'Do you mind if I put the windows down?'

'It's your car,' she said.

She thought she saw a trace of a smile on his handsome face and inexplicably felt angry. 'I suppose you two think this is funny.'

'If you mean me and Miriam then you're wrong,' he said. 'She's worried about you.'

Lilly pointed a sweaty finger at him. 'But you think it's funny.'

He shook his head. 'No, Lilly, I think it's bloody hilarious.'

She sulked for the rest of the journey and refused to look in his direction. For his part, Jack hummed, which Lilly assumed was done with the sole intention of causing annoyance. It worked. By the time Jack pulled up at Lilly's house she was furious, and pulled open the car door with a force that outweighed her still fragile sense of balance and sent her sideways. Once again Lilly found herself lying on the ground, this time with her right foot still inside the car. She jerked her leg towards her body but the strap of her bag had snaked around her ankle and every yank squeezed it tighter and tighter, like a boa constrictor sapping its prey.

Lilly struggled onto her feet, or at least onto her free left one, and bent back into the car to release its mate. Jack stared ahead in stoic silence and bit his cheek.

The bag, now separated from Lilly, chose to spill most of its contents into the footwell. Lilly let out a guttural moan and pushed the myriad of stationery and makeup back in. When she was finished Jack bent down and picked up a stray item. Lilly held out her open hand like a petulant child and Jack carefully placed a small snail shell into her palm.

She slammed the car door hard enough to knock it off and watched Jack drive away, sure she could see his shoulders lifting and falling, unable to contain his laughter.

As he disappeared Lilly sank onto the step, her anger

completely gone, in its place a dizzying and uncomfortable exhaustion. Why, she wondered, had she been so angry anyway? He wasn't to blame for her ludicrous predicament. It was she, not he, who had drunk enough to fell an elephant but hadn't eaten enough to sustain a mouse on one of the hottest days of the year. She had made a total arse of herself. Again.

She discarded some foliage from her bag, put her key in the lock and decided to send Jack a text to apologise for her unforgivable behaviour.

A moment later, with her phone still in her hand, Lilly was face down on her sofa, snoring softly into the stained sleeve of her suit.

CHAPTER FOURTEEN

Sunday, 20 September

The young fireman stared into Lilly's eyes. He was so close she could smell the intoxicating scent of his skin – something between jasmine and musk. He gave her a knowing look and moved in to kiss her, but before his lips reached hers the sound of a distant bell called him. He shrugged and moved towards the sound as Lilly held her arm out towards him. *Don't go.* He winked, blew her a kiss and descended down a pole.

The bell became more insistent, more irritating, until Lilly could no longer ignore it and woke up.

The phone was ringing.

Her voice was an aquatic croak. 'Hello?'

'I don't know what the hell is going on with you, Lilly, but you can't behave like this,' said David.

A small hammer beat rhythmically over Lilly's left eye. 'I got pissed, what's the big deal?'

His tone told Lilly that it was in fact a very big deal. 'Nothing at all, except the small issue of our son.'

Hell. Sam had been with his dad and Lilly was supposed to collect him at around six yesterday evening. She'd been so exhausted, not to mention drunk, she'd slept right through.

'Is he okay?'

'Of course he's okay, he's with me, but that's not the bloody point,' David said.

The small hammer had been replaced by the type used by builders to break up roads.

'I'm sorry,' she told him.

David sighed. 'Apart from anything else, Lilly, I was worried about you. I eventually called Miriam and she told me what had happened.'

'I'm never drinking again,' said Lilly.

'You and George Best.' His tone softened. 'I know you've got to get to court this morning so I'll keep Sam and take him straight to school tomorrow. Does he need his PE kit?'

Lilly was no longer listening.

'Today is Sunday, why do I have to be at court today?' she shouted.

'Jesus, Lilly, I'm not your bloody secretary. Miriam just mentioned something about bail.'

Lilly recalled a hazy conversation with Jez, sometime between the second and third bottle of red. He'd agreed to get an application listed at the earliest opportunity. But on a Sunday?

She searched for her mobile and found it inside her shirt. A tiny green light flashed ominously announcing an unread text.

BAIL APP. LISTED 10 A.M. TOMORROW. YES, I HAVE MAGIC POWERS. JEZ XXX

'Well, does he need his kit or not?' asked David.

'I've got to go,' said Lilly, and hung up.

She raced to the bathroom, abandoning her clothes en route. The bath looked smooth and cool but she needed to be on a train in fifteen minutes and the Ferrari was in the garage. She made do with a Glasgow shower and squirted toothpaste onto her tongue.

Yesterday's suit was still covered in vomit and the other two were in the dry-cleaner's. Damn. Lilly looked in her closet. An assortment of faded jeans looked back at her. She pulled at a pink linen dress that was hiding in a dusty corner. She had bought it for a friend's wedding four years ago. It needed an iron and one of the buttons was missing. As she pulled it over her head she remembered it had been slightly too tight at the time. As she pulled it over her hips she remembered she'd lost half a stone especially for that wedding.

Like an escapee from Broadmoor in drag, Lilly burst out of her front door then stopped dead in the space where her car should be parked. She had, of course, left it outside Lancasters.

'Nooooo!'

Lilly leaped from the train and charged towards the Old Bailey. Despite the fog of exhaust fumes she could smell herself – a foul mixture of stale red wine and sweat. She was over half an hour late and absolutely starving. Her stomach was unaccustomed to remaining empty for three hours, let alone twenty-four, and it growled for attention.

When she rounded the corner it tightened uncontrollably. Jostling for position in an otherwise empty street were the press pack. They must have got wind of the hearing and, it being a Sunday, worked out that whatever was going down was big.

Shit.

Once again, Lilly would be caught on camera looking less than glamorous. She pulled on her sunglasses and ran into court.

At the top of the stairs Jez stood next to the lists. He was deep in conversation. The other man's face was obscured but Lilly could see the sleeve of a mallow-soft leather jacket. It was Jack. She was pleased the case had not yet been called, but was not ready to face them and instead slipped into the ladies' toilet.

Thus far she had studiously avoided all reflective surfaces, but she now had no alternative but to face herself in the mirror. If asked, Lilly would have been unable to adequately describe how truly awful she looked. Horrible, horrific, horrifying, none of it covered the truth. In short, she looked like a woman who had spent seventeen hours sleeping off twelve units of alcohol on the sofa while fully dressed, followed by only a spray of deodorant.

The toilet in the cubicle behind her flushed and Sheba emerged. She appraised Lilly from head to toe.

'Whatever you've got to say, spit it out,' said Lilly.

'That's an interesting shade for court.'

Lilly ran her hands over the sickly pink. 'Thanks. I've just had my colours done.'

Back at the foot of the stairs Lilly considered turning round and going home. She could easily text Jez to say she was sick and head for the nearest café for a bacon sandwich. But the reporters were there, braying like the hounds of hell. Talk about a rock and a hard place.

'Lilly,' called the handsome barrister.

She waved and dragged her heavy feet up the stairs.

'Got home all right?' he asked.

Lilly nodded, unable to look at Jack.

'I'm just filling everyone in on our plan for this morning and circulating the report,' said Jez.

'Report?' asked Lilly.

'The one I emailed to you last night,' said Jez.

Lilly hadn't been near her computer. 'Oh, that report.'

'You're still half-asleep,' laughed Jez. He turned to Jack, his voice a stage whisper. 'I obviously wore her out yesterday,' he smirked, as he walked out of the room.

Left alone with Jack, Lilly felt acutely embarrassed.

'How are you, Jack?' she said.

'Fine.'

Oh God, he was really going to make her pay. 'I'm very sorry about yesterday, my behaviour was pretty bad.'

Jack merely nodded.

'In fact it was very bad,' Lilly conceded.

'I'd say it was puerile, idiotic and downright rude,' said Jack.

Lilly took it on the chin; frankly, she had it coming.

Jack nodded to the space where Jez had stood. 'Plying you with drink, was he?'

Lilly smiled to herself. Jack was acting cool but he was evidently worried that Jez had taken advantage.

'Sadly I've no one to blame but myself,' she said.

'Why were you drinking anyway?' he asked.

'Celebrating,' she said.

'Jesus. I'd hate to see you drowning your sorrows.'

Lilly pressed one hand to her aching temples and the other to her unhappy stomach.

'I'm never drinking again.'

'Sure you are,' said Jack, proffering a sheaf of paper.

'What's this?' she asked.

'Have a quick look. It's Doctor Lorenson's report.'

Lilly was still skim-reading the report as they entered court. Sheba had done a fine job. The salient issues were covered in enough detail to seem thoughtful and credible while carefully falling short of a final analysis on Kelsey.

When Judge Blechard-Smith made his entrance he too was clutching the document.

While everyone took their seats and shuffled their papers, Jez remained on his feet, eager to state his case.

'I must thank the court at the outset for listing this case with such alacrity,' he said.

'Well, we don't want that lot', the judge waved a hand to the outside wall, 'thinking we're not taking this seriously.'

Lilly sighed. The interest of the press seemed to have more impact on the judge than any sense of justice.

'Quite so, My Lord,' said Jez, 'and you will recall that when this matter was before you last, the defence

291

refrained from making any application for bail as we were in complete agreement with this court that expert evidence was required.'

'Of course,' replied the judge, his tone just shy of poor manners.

Jez flashed a smile. 'I am pleased to confirm that we have been able to obtain the opinion of such an expert and that it is before the court today.'

The judge still had the copy in his fist. 'I must say I'm surprised that you were able to get something so quickly.' His tone betrayed the fact that he was not happy to be revisiting this matter so soon. No doubt he had wanted to keep this particular hot potato in the oven a little longer.

Jez remained unfazed. 'Sadly, I cannot take the credit for that. My instructing solicitor made Herculean efforts to expedite matters.' He made a sweeping gesture towards Lilly. 'Her commitment to the children with whom she works is matched only by her efficiency, and I'm sure that My Lord will join me in thanking her for ensuring that Kelsey Brand's case is not allowed to fester.'

Lilly stared at her hands, her cheeks as pink and as unflattering as her dress. She heard Jack cough down a laugh.

'Yes, I'm sure', said the judge, 'that it's all very admirable, but we must not put speed before quality.'

He seemed to have conveniently forgotten that it was the court that had listed the matter during the weekend.

'Does Doctor Lorenson believe she has had sufficient time to make a judgement?' His frown confirmed that he for one did not concur.

'She says so, My Lord, and you'll see at page five she sets out the number of hours she has spent to date,' said Jez.

Sheba had headed off this line of attack perfectly.

The judge addressed the barrister for the prosecution. 'It doesn't seem very long, Mr Marshall, does it?'

Marshall jumped to his feet. 'Indeed, My Lord, it seems quite paltry.'

'I thought you might say that,' countered Jez. 'Which is why I asked Mr Lockhart to enquire as to the length of time the CPS would normally expect to be taken on a preliminary report. He informed me that Doctor Lorenson's hours are perfectly adequate. In fact they exceed what the CPS would normally expect by thirty per cent.' Jez turned to Marshall. 'If my learned friend wants more time spent I'm afraid he'd have to pay for it himself, as the CPS wouldn't countenance the cost.'

Marshall flushed a deep magenta and spun round to speak to his representative for the Crown, who simply nodded his assent.

Good old Lockhart, thought Lilly. Not the most exciting man in the world, but straight as a mast.

The judge simply nodded, and for a moment Lilly thought he accepted what Sheba had to say.

'Very well, Mr Stafford,' he said, his voice more measured. 'It seems I must accept that this document does fall within the usual boundaries. However, I still have reservations about its scope.'

'My Lord?' Jez sounded puzzled. Lilly sensed trouble.

'In my view it does not deal with everything one would need to know to answer what will undoubtedly be a robust application for bail on your part,' said the judge.

'I see,' replied Jez, and scratched his head.

The judge turned to the prosecution. 'Mr Marshall, are there questions you would wish to be answered by Doctor Lorenson before addressing me on the issue of bail?'

'My Lord, on a mere perfunctory reading I thought of several,' he answered theatrically, holding the report between the tips of his thumb and forefinger as if it were an oily rag.

The judge smiled at Jez, his teeth the ugly grey of a man too fond of the claret bottle. 'You see the problem. I think we have been a little hasty this morning and we need more help from Doctor Lorenson before any decisions can be reached.'

The coward was going to put the whole thing off and blame the defence. He knew full well that by the time Marshall and Lockhart drafted a further set of questions Santa would be baking mince pies. Lilly felt the whole thing unravelling until she saw the suspicion of a smile play on Jez's lips.

'My Lord, I had, of course, assumed that you would want to pursue this matter in the utmost detail. Quite rightly you would not wish to make any decision without sufficient recourse to the facts. To this end I ensured that Doctor Lorenson would be available to the court this morning to offer her expert assistance.'

'She's here?' blurted the judge.

Jez bowed slightly. 'Indeed she is.'

Lilly controlled an urge to clap. It was a memorable performance.

'May I suggest that we adjourn for a moment for you to formulate your outstanding questions, and for Mr Marshall to give the report more than a perfunctory read.'

Sheba glided into court as if on wheels and took her place in the witness box. She smoothed her skirt over her generous hips and licked her lips. There was no sign of a hangover or the slightest fatigue, the woman was superhuman. But Lilly already knew that Sheba was not in fact human at all, she was from a higher plane, a goddess. Right now there was a remote tribe in the Amazon bemoaning the loss of their favourite deity, who had transformed herself from her previous state as a jungle jaguar into a sexy psychiatrist.

'Will you take the oath or affirm?' asked the clerk.

'I'm a Catholic,' Sheba purred and took the bible. 'Lapsed, I'm afraid.'

Sheba swore to tell the truth and introduced herself and her credentials with cool aplomb.

'Is your report a full account of the mental state of Kelsey Brand?' asked Jez.

'Goodness, no,' said Sheba.

Damn, thought Lilly. Sheba's inexperience would give the judge an excuse to delay.

'That might take years.' Sheba gave the judge a sidelong smile. 'But, in my view, it tells us enough to make a reasoned judgement on where Kelsey should be at

295

this moment in time, and what treatment she should be receiving.'

Lilly exhaled.

Marshall got to his feet. 'Doctor Lorenson, you seem very young to be involved in this type of court work,' he said.

'Thank you,' said Sheba. 'I inherited my mother's good skin.'

The barrister had of course meant to undermine Sheba's credentials, but her deliberate misunderstanding deflected the insult to good effect.

The next ten minutes was a veritable tennis match. Marshall aimed high and served each ball with a bovine grunt, Sheba returned them all with style, skill and wit.

'Your analysis seems to focus almost entirely on the defendant's mental state, Doctor Lorenson,' he said.

'Of course,' Sheba replied. 'I'm a psychiatrist. That's what I do.'

'But you don't seem to take into account the seriousness of the crime involved. You do know what the defendant did?' he persisted.

'I'm aware of the offence with which Kelsey has been charged. I thought whether she did it or not was a matter for the jury, not for me, or, for that matter, for you, Mr Marshall.'

He smiled and shook his head. 'You're missing the point, Doctor. Surely even someone charged with such a crime cannot be allowed to roam around freely while assessments are ongoing?'

Sheba smiled back. 'You're absolutely right, which is why I'm recommending Leyland House.'

'Quite so, but it's not a prison,' said Marshall.

'It's a secure accommodation for young people.'

'Which means what exactly? That the staff try to ensure that the inmates don't wander off?'

Lilly thought Sheba would blow up, but instead she just giggled. 'Don't be silly, Mr Marshall, I'm sure you've been to enough of these facilities to know that the *children* can't leave unaccompanied.'

Clever, very clever. Of course the pompous old fool had never been to a children's home of any variety in his life.

'Never mind other facilities, Doctor, let's stick to this one. It's brand-new, hasn't been tried and tested. Let's face it,' he opened his arms to encompass the room 'none of us have seen it.'

Sheba picked up her racket and gently, oh so gently, tapped the ball over the net.

'Actually, I went there last night.'

'Last night!' said Marshall and the judge in unison.

Sheba tossed her head distractedly, her hair shivered like a sigh. 'Mmm. I called Doctor Collins and asked to be shown around before I endorsed Leyland House to the court.'

Dr Paul Collins was one of the most eminent professionals in the field of child psychiatry. Revered by lawyers and judges alike, and hailed by the medics as the new voice in the field. A modern-day Freud. Lilly had seen him give evidence twice, and on both occasions he had blown the court away with a genius that would have grated were it not accompanied so generously with his humility and humour.

'He's always so busy. How on earth did you manage it?' asked the judge, his interest clearly genuine.

'I trained under him,' said Sheba. 'He's remained a close friend, so when I told him I was considering Leyland for a patient he was only too happy to give me the tour.'

'And you were impressed?' asked the judge, who seemed to have taken over from the deflated Marshall.

Sheba nodded vigorously. 'Absolutely. Paul – Doctor Collins – has set up a wonderful place. It takes a maximum of five children at any time. Each child has their own key worker who has been trained specifically for this type of work. Of course, they're all hugely overqualified.' Sheba's tone was conversational, as if only she and the judge were in the room. 'When he put out the word he wanted staff they were queuing round the block. I mean, who wouldn't want to work with the greatest child psych this country has ever seen?'

'Indeed,' said the judge.

Sheba dropped her voice to a whisper. Every ear in the court strained. 'I'd have applied myself but thought it might smack of nepotism.'

'Of course,' said the judge, as if Sheba's integrity elevated her to sainthood.

'Anyhow, there are therapy sessions every day, sometimes twice a day, but they're not standard. Doctor Collins, together with the key workers, devises an individual programme for each child, and the programme is reviewed once a week to see if it's going in the right direction. Even the teachers who come in for academic lessons are also therapists, so the process is seamless. It really would be the right place for Kelsey and', she turned to Marshall, 'there are plenty of bars on the windows.'

Game, set and match.

After a short discussion the prosecution decided not to oppose the application for bail and Judge Blechard-Smith made a secure accommodation order, which although not a passport to freedom did mean that Kelsey could leave the adult prison as soon as a place came up at Leyland House, which Dr Collins had assured Sheba would be in the next day or so.

Jez beamed. 'We did it, Lilly.'

'We certainly did,' she replied. 'Now all we have to do is find out who killed her mum.'

'Don't you ever stop?' he laughed. 'Come on, let's have a drink.'

'No chance,' said Lilly, 'I'm never drinking again.'

'Whatever,' he said, and kissed her on the cheek. Which was pretty brave of him considering she smelled of yesterday's wine and vomit.

Lilly made her way out of the building and headed into the bright day in search of food. The press ignored her as Marshall was giving a statement that attempted to claim the current turn of events as his own idea.

'That barrister of yours is a smooth one,' said a voice from behind her. Lilly turned and saw Jack. 'On kissy-kissy terms already, I see,' he added.

Lilly cocked her head. Jack had been watching her with Jez. Did she detect a note of jealousy or was she flattering herself? She rubbed her hips where the buttons of her ugly dress were digging into a well-defined roll of fat. Definitely flattering herself.

'I'm glad things went well for Kelsey,' he said.

'You're supposed to play for the other team,' she said.

'Doesn't mean I want to see the kid rot in jail,' he answered.

Lilly smiled. 'Where's Bradbury?'

'You don't have a dog and bark yourself.'

Lilly hated it when Jack belittled himself and his job, and was about to launch into a lecture when her stomach wailed. 'Let me buy you breakfast,' she said instead.

'How do you know I haven't already had a bowlful of organic muesli with soya milk?'

Lilly laughed. 'Call it an educated guess.'

William Barrows leafed through the local paper. Why did anyone read this rubbish? All-time highest turnout for the fire station's open day. Local community leaders condemn those breaking the hosepipe ban. Banal wasn't the word. It had been mildly entertaining when Hermione had glared out from the front cover, resplendent in Armani and warning of the dangers of today's 'instant gratification society', but this edition had relegated her finger-wagging to page four and there were no pictures.

It had been an excruciating few days since his meeting with the black man, as Barrows waited for news of his appointment with the girl. Hermione hadn't helped, stomping around the house like a demented teenager, hating the sight of her wizened raisin of a face on the television while simultaneously terrified that the Brand story would die down and her own fifteen minutes would pass.

Then a trip to the doctor's had left her tearful and wobbly. It was familiar territory but Barrows preferred Hermione mark two.

When he received word that things were underway and would be finalised in the next forty-eight hours, Barrows let the relief flood over him before allowing his heart to quicken in anticipation. It had come just in time or he would have been forced to relieve himself, which was always so very unpleasant.

One day he might even get caught. No, he was too clever for that.

Now all he needed was to buy himself some time and space. At the allotted hour there must be no distractions. Like an athlete, he needed total focus on the task in hand, and this strict regime meant daily life must be kept at bay.

In the past he had told his office he was ill and he was not to be disturbed, but there was always the tiniest possibility that his secretary would override these instructions and call him at home. Hermione might ask questions, demand that he leave his mobile on at all times, enquire as to why he was feigning illness. It was a small anxiety, but there nonetheless, spoiling his moment like a dark spot on a white sheet.

He considered how much easier it must have been for his grandfather to remain incommunicado. No phones, faxes, computers. He'd have simply disappeared for the day and then told his wife some nonsense about an accident or a fire. She probably wouldn't even have asked, certainly wouldn't have cross-examined him.

Barrows turned to page sixteen and eyed the community notices. Scouts, Guides and Rainbows (whatever the hell they were), book groups, writing circles, self-help meetings for single parents, the aged, those caring for the aged and anyone in need of finding their inner eye. Then he saw it, like a raft in the open sea.

Are you a gay man happily living a straight life?
If the answer's yes and you want to meet kindred spirits for leisure activities without any hint of pink then join us on the first Monday of each month.
Call Andy on 07728772717.
Absolute discretion guaranteed.

Barrows decided to tell his wife he'd joined the group. Not only would she ask no questions, she would insist on total separation from it. Better still, he wouldn't tell her, he'd just circle the ad and leave it for her to find. Things left unsaid and given room to fester usually took on a life and a truth of their own. As a shrink he knew this all too well.

Thrilled by his own devious genius he drew a deliberate ring in pencil.

'I've just been on the phone to Margaret.'

Barrows hadn't even noticed his wife come into the room and he automatically closed the newspaper. It was a gesture without guile, which was better still. He knew Hermione would check what he'd been reading as soon as he left the room.

'What did she want?' he asked, his voice deliberately small.

'Where shall I start?' she said, and dropped dramatically into a chair. 'Hugh was in court today on the Brand case. The defence had it listed for an urgent bail application or something.'

Barrows felt panic rising but kept his tone even. 'I bet he didn't like that on a Sunday.'

'Not one bit. Margaret said he had to look keen but once he got there he tried every trick in the book not to hear it, but they brought in a doctor who apparently made an unanswerable case to have the girl put in some institution or other.'

'Who was it?' he asked.

'Hugh couldn't remember, said it was a biblical name, but that she was absolutely gorgeous with fantastic boobs.'

'Bathsheba Lorenson.'

Hermione shrugged. 'Could be. Margaret said old Hugh probably took one look at her cleavage and the rest, as they say, is history.'

Barrows managed to squeeze out a conspiratorial laugh. Bathsheba Lorenson was the stuff of most men's dreams. He thought her gross, like an overblown lilo. He'd once had the misfortune of sitting next to her at a conference on transference and her smell was so nauseating he'd actually vomited during the lunch break. He felt a similar feeling creeping into the pit of his stomach now. If the girl was out of jail the black man would panic, he might call everything off.

'Where have they sent the girl?' he asked.

'Some new centre for mad children, run by a hotshot called Collins,' said Hermione.

His stomach muscles relaxed. Collins had set up a new centre called Leyland House. It was a secure unit; the Brand girl was as good as in prison.

Hermione slapped her forehead with her open palm. 'I don't know what to do about it. They'll start asking for a comment any second. If I condemn the courts for letting her out, Hugh and Margaret will never speak to me again.'

'And you'll look as if you're hounding a sick child,' Barrows added.

Hermione's face betrayed the fact that she hadn't thought of that; nor had the idea of hounding a sick child caused her any concern.

'So how shall I deal with this, William?' she pleaded.

'Give a statement to the press saying you know they'll be interested in your views but you really don't want to hound a child who obviously needs help. She's clearly in the best place, blah, blah,' he said.

'But I don't want the story to sink and me with it.'

Barrows smiled. 'You could also point out how the whole saga does raise questions as to why social services allowed a child, with whom they were involved for so long, to remain untreated. Some would say they put both the girl and others at risk.'

'I don't know, William, turning the tables on social

304

services might make me look petulant,' she said, sticking out her bottom lip.

'Not at all, people like to give them a good roasting. They need someone to blame for this mess,' he said.

'But I thought I'd been championing collective responsibility.'

William patted her knee. 'That was last week, darling.'

Lilly left Jack at St Paul's to finish his fifth cup of coffee. He'd clearly forgotten the previous day's debacle and had chatted openly with Lilly about his life in the RUC before he moved to England. That was one of the things Lilly most liked about Jack: he didn't try to evade uncomfortable topics or attempt to reinvent history, he simply acknowledged what was what and moved on. She also liked his laugh. Full and throaty, it filled his whole body and cast an infectious spell on those around him. At least it did on Lilly. She had to admit that there was not very much she didn't like about Jack McNally.

She could have had the day to herself but she decided to see Sam. Lilly never had been able to stomach any bad feeling between them.

'Never go to bed on a row,' her mother used to say.

As she approached David's house, Lilly worried how her abandonment of Sam might have affected him. She needn't have, he'd had a fine old time, he told her. Dad had agreed to go halves on the trip to Austria and Sam had thrashed him three times at Battleships.

'How was Cara?' Lilly asked.

Sam pulled a face. 'Fat. She went to bed at about seven cos her heart was burning.'

Lilly allowed herself a smile. The thought of Cara in maternity clothes and chugging on a bottle of Gaviscon was maliciously satisfying.

When they arrived home, Miriam was sitting on the doorstep.

She waved two carrier-bags groaning with food. 'I come bearing gifts.'

The two women laid out the food in companionable silence while Sam set the table.

'You okay?' Miriam asked at last.

Lilly nodded. They were friends. Miriam didn't need to spell out her worries, the fact that she was here, that she'd brought food said it all. It was enough.

'And what about you, Sam, how're things?' Miriam asked.

'Cool. I'm going skiing after Christmas.'

While Sam was in the kitchen collecting more cutlery Miriam turned to her friend. 'How the hell are you going to pay for that?'

'I'm thinking of selling a kidney.'

They ploughed their way through a feast. Taut black olives glistening with oil, cherry tomatoes and firm avocados sliced onto salty cheeses. Three different types of bread hot from the oven.

'Fantastic,' announced Lilly, and undid a button.

Sam nodded his assent and crammed in a herby slice of focaccia. 'Did you make it yourself, Auntie Miriam?'

306

'She never cooks,' said Lilly.

'Never?' asked Sam in astonishment. 'Mum cooks all the time.'

'I'm much busier than your mum,' said Miriam.

Lilly threw a crust at her friend. A shower of crumbs got stuck in her braids.

'There is one thing I always cook,' said Miriam, and produced a packet of popping corn. Sam whooped with excitement.

She curled her lip at Lilly. 'Bet he doesn't react like that to your home-made pies, girlfriend.'

While Sam settled himself into a battle between a blue plastic mutant-something and a red plastic mutant-something-else, Lilly and Miriam slumped peacefully in front of the television, a bowlful of warm salty popcorn between them.

The local news was awash with stories of the hosepipe ban until the saga of the Brands, heralded by Hermione Barrows, raised its carefully highlighted head.

'What do you have to say to the news that Grace's daughter has been committed to a mental institution?' asked the reporter.

'That's not even true,' shouted Lilly.

'Shhh,' Miriam admonished her friend with a wave.

Hermione Barrows filled the screen. 'Like everyone else I'm shocked and saddened. Shocked that a young person could be so ill under the eyes and ears of the authorities and saddened that nothing was done to help.'

'Do you blame social services?' asked the reporter.

'I'm not one for laying blame, it really doesn't help,

but of course questions must be asked and lessons learned. I've already asked the Director of Luton Social Services to begin an investigation into their involvement with this family, and I will of course be keeping a personal eye on its progress. I for one will not allow this matter to be simply swept under the carpet.'

'Of course you won't, Kelsey's your ticket to fame and fortune,' Lilly yelled.

'Shame on you, Barrows,' muttered Miriam.

Sam was only mildly interested in the sight of his mother and his adopted auntie throwing popcorn at the television. Frankly, he'd seen it all before.

When night fell the two women stepped outside to cool their minds and sip their wine.

'You did very well today,' said Miriam.

Lilly didn't reply.

'You don't think so?' asked Miriam.

Lilly sighed. 'I did. I was over the moon when I knew we could get the kid out of Parkgate.'

'And now?'

'I have doubts about this whole thing.' Lilly looked Miriam in the eye. 'If Kelsey murdered her mother can we really be sure that the other children in Leyland House will be safe?'

Miriam rolled her eyes. 'She didn't kill her mother.'

'We can't be sure of that, at least I can't be. Mrs Mitchell says she saw her the night Grace died, and then there's that bloody letter.'

'You said yourself the neighbour's evidence is poor,

308

and the letter is just a silly threat from an unhappy girl,' said Miriam.

'Or a serious threat from an unhappy girl,' said Lilly.

The slight breeze of earlier had picked up pace and Miriam's T-shirt rustled gently in time with the whispers of the trees. 'She's better off getting proper treatment whether or not she's guilty.'

It was true of course. Nothing would persuade Lilly that Parkgate Prison was right for any child, whatever they had done, least of all one with psychiatric problems.

'And surely', Miriam continued, 'it's far more likely that Grace was killed by a deranged client.'

Lilly finished her wine and enjoyed the sensation of the cool wind on her damp lips.

'I said I wouldn't do this any more.'

'Beat yourself up?' asked her friend.

'Drink alcohol.'

Miriam chuckled and filled both their glasses. 'Tell me about you and Jack.'

'Nothing to tell,' said Lilly. 'Yet.'

'It would be less complicated to wait until after this case,' said Miriam gently.

'Without another suspect the case will go to trial sometime next year,' said Lilly. 'He could be married by then.'

'Better hurry up and solve the mystery, then, Sherlock.'

Lilly nodded. Although Miriam was joking Lilly knew that it was exactly what she had to do.

CHAPTER FIFTEEN

Monday, 21 September

The following morning Jack waited outside HMP Parkgate. Too hot to sit in the car he leaned against the bonnet sipping a cup of tepid coffee that one of the guards had brought out to him earlier. A rare gesture of goodwill.

Eventually Kelsey appeared, squinting into the daylight and carrying an almost-empty clear plastic sack marked 'Her Majesty's Prison Service'. She was handcuffed to a guard at least twice her size.

'Is that necessary?' Jack asked.

The guard scowled. 'Too right. You can do what you like at the next place but we're not losing her on my shift.'

Throughout the journey Kelsey stared out of one window, the guard out of the other. Jack stared straight ahead and drove. He vowed once again to make more effort to get a promotion.

When they arrived at a small parade of shops, Jack turned into Leyland Road and was surprised by the pleasant surroundings. In a leafy part of North London it was a quiet cul-de-sac, with a Victorian mansion house at the very tip flanked on all sides by well-tended gardens.

'This looks nice, Kelsey,' he ventured.

She didn't look in his direction and the guard sniffed his disquiet, no doubt disgruntled that a violent killer was ending up in a house bigger than his own.

Inside, the unit was bright and comfortable, the walls clean and the paintwork fresh. The sound of a piano filtered down the stairs.

'We'll take it from here,' said a member of staff, and indicated the handcuffs which the guard snapped off. Both he and Kelsey automatically rubbed their wrists.

As Jack watched Kelsey being led away he felt a sense of relief. Whatever happened now, the poor kid would get some help. When he got to the door he took a look over his shoulder and was startled to find Kelsey doing the same. It was the first time she had ever looked him in the eyes and he didn't like what he saw.

Once outside, Jack checked his watch. It would take him at least an hour to get back to the station and he was already parched. He'd leave the car here and amble up to the corner shop for a can of Coke.

On his way back down he swirled the liquid around his mouth and wondered how much overtime he'd have to put in to afford a house like the ones on Leyland Road. He sighed. No one went into police work for the money.

As he approached his car the door to Leyland House was thrown open from the inside and the same woman who had led Kelsey away bolted into the garden.

Jack had seen enough panic in people's faces to know something was seriously wrong.

'What's happened?' he shouted.

The woman's eyes were round with fear. 'Kelsey's barricaded herself in. I think she's going to jump.'

Jack followed the woman's eye-line to the windows on the first, second and third floor.

'Which one is she in? How can she open it?'

'She's taken the fire extinguisher.'

Jack was about to ask how that might help when the sound of smashing glass pierced the air and shards rained down.

The woman covered her face with her hands and ran inside with Jack in hot pursuit.

'Are you okay?' he asked.

The woman was breathing hard but managed a nod. It was all Jack needed to sprint past her and up the stairs.

On the first landing were four doors. Shit! Which one? If Kelsey died he would never forgive himself. And as for Lilly . . .

He flung open the first door and found an enormously fat boy sitting on his bed. He was stark-naked, his penis hidden under rolls of flab.

'Can I help you?' he asked, seemingly unperturbed by Jack's wild entrance.

'Sorry, wrong room.'

Jack slammed the door and opened the next.

A small Chinese girl was feeding a goldfish at the far end of the room. Her response to Jack was less relaxed than her neighbour and she screamed.

'I'm looking for Kelsey,' said Jack.

The girl continued to scream.

'The new kid,' said Jack. 'Which room is she in?'

The girl's scream continued at an alarming decibel but she pointed upwards.

'Thanks,' said Jack and ran for the stairs. The wailing reverberated after him like a dog at his heels.

He reached the top and headed to the room directly above the banshee. He tried the door. It wasn't locked but something was blocking the way. Kelsey had put something against it.

He rattled the handle with one hand and slammed the wood with the heel of his other.

'Don't do this, Kelsey,' he roared. 'Please don't do this.'

There was nothing for it but to force the door. He just hoped he was in time.

Jack took two steps back and charged with his shoulder. He felt the pain jolt through him like an electric current but the door didn't give.

Again he took a step back, and this time he kicked with his full force.

'Jesus Christ.' He wished he'd worn his police-issue boots rather than Converse trainers. Both his left arm and leg were numb with pain. Jack felt like he'd had a stroke but he kicked again. This time the door flew open.

'Kelsey!'

She was perched on the ledge, her tiny body framed by jagged glass.

'It's two floors up,' said Jack. 'You might not die but

313

you could spend the rest of your life in a wheelchair.'

A look passed between them and Jack held his breath. Did this poor kid have anything left to lose?

'Sorry,' said Kelsey, and jumped.

Jack crossed the room in a second, his arm outstretched in a desperate attempt to catch her. Too late.

'You poor kid,' he said, and hardly dared look down. When he did he was shocked.

Kelsey had landed on a pile of pillows and duvets and was scrabbling to her feet. She dived across the lawn and headed up Leyland Road.

Kelsey hadn't tried to kill herself. She'd escaped.

The station was like the *Marie Celeste*. A body from uniform had been promoted to the Drug Squad and everyone was down the pub. Jack sat at his desk and waited. He just hoped he could get this done before the hordes returned, noisy and stinking of drink.

At last Bradbury arrived and they headed to the boss's office. Gone was the calm confidence and bonhomie between Bradbury and his superior; instead the Chief was pacing.

'You wanted to see us, Sir,' said Bradbury.

The Chief stopped his march and leered at them from his side of the desk. 'Not really, no. What I actually want is for my officers to run cases efficiently and quietly. I want the minimum of fuss and the minimum of press attention. But what do I get?'

Both Jack and Bradbury knew better than to risk a response. The Chief was in full throttle.

'What I get', he ranted, 'is an almighty cock-up.'

314

'I don't think we're to blame for this, Sir,' said Bradbury.

Jack admired his courage. He himself was saying nothing.

'Our defendant has absconded. So who do you think is to blame?'

Bradbury paused and smoothed his tie. 'I think circumstances were beyond anyone's control.'

It was too much for the Chief, who exploded with a fury Jack had never before seen.

'Do you think the press will give a monkey's left bollock about the circumstances?'

'No, Sir,' said Bradbury.

'No indeed. Together with that bloody politician they'll crucify us.'

The Chief turned his back in disgust. 'I don't care how you do it, just find Kelsey Brand.'

Lilly picked up another form and began to fill it in. Her day had started well. She'd awoken feeling so different from the day before it was as though cold Perrier was skipping through her veins. She'd wolfed down two croissants and arrived at work early to go through Kelsey's case again. Maybe she was missing something.

But as soon as the office opened Rupinder had ushered Lilly down to her office and locked Lilly's door behind her.

'You are not leaving until at least half of that paperwork has been processed,' came the voice from the other side of the door.

'What if I get hungry?' wailed Lilly.

'I'll push a sandwich under the door at lunchtime.'

'What if I need the loo?'

'Use a vase.'

'What if there's a fire?'

'Dial 999.'

Lilly glared at the twin towers on top of her cabinet and threw a pen at them.

Five hours later, Lilly was not even halfway through the first pile.

'Somebody save me,' Lilly said to her desk.

'In hell no one can hear you scream.'

Lilly looked up and saw her boss in the doorway. She hadn't even heard the door being unlocked.

'This is contrary to the Human Rights Act. It's a crime for which you will be punished.'

'Better that than listen to my partners going on about this little lot,' said Rupinder.

'Has anyone called?' asked Lilly.

'Yes.'

'Who?'

'Sheila's taking messages.'

Lilly jumped to her feet.

'Sit,' the boss barked. 'I'll give them to you later.'

'There could be something important,' said Lilly.

'Believe me, there is nothing more important than my sanity, which can only be preserved by you finishing your paperwork.'

Lilly opened her mouth to argue.

'I'm a woman on the edge, Valentine, so don't push me.'

Lilly knew she was beaten and went back to the forms.

An eternity later, Sheila came down with a handful of yellow slips. Each note set out who had called and at what time and had a small space for a comment such as 'will try again after three', but Sheila kept everyone entertained with her own colourful interpretations of what had been said. 'Rude wanker said he'd top himself if he doesn't win his case. Good luck I say,' was not unheard of, so Lilly simply laughed when she read: *Jack somebody – weird Scottish accent – wants a word on the bland case.*'

She dialled his number. 'Jack, it's Lilly, what's up?'

'Jesus, woman, I called you hours ago, where've you been?'

Lilly glanced ruefully around her room. 'Don't ask.'

'Okay, I won't, but you need to know Kelsey's legged it,' he said.

Lilly gasped. 'What?'

'It's a total disaster. She smashed a second-floor window and got through it,' he said.

Lilly had to sit down, she couldn't believe this. 'She jumped from the second floor! She must have broken her neck.'

'You'd think so, but she chucked two duvets out before her to soften the fall.'

Lilly paused for a second to let it sink in. 'Where do you think she's gone?'

'I was going to ask you the same question. Looks like we underestimated wee Kelsey.'

* * *

When Lilly explained what had happened, Rupinder didn't argue as Lilly dashed out of the office. Even she knew not to step into the path of a hurricane.

Lilly drove without caution straight to The Bushes, where Miriam was waiting.

'Has she been in touch?' asked Lilly.

'What makes you think that?' replied Miriam.

'I don't know. These young people tell you things, they trust you,' said Lilly.

Miriam shook her head so wildly her braids danced round like the snakes of Medusa. 'You're wrong. They don't tell me anything. I have no idea when they're feeling desperate or when they're taking drugs.'

Lilly reached out to touch Miriam's arm but she pushed it away.

'They don't trust me at all or I'd be able to stop them doing terrible things to themselves,' Miriam shouted.

'Listen,' whispered Lilly in an attempt to calm her friend and restore the equilibrium, 'not everyone wants to talk about their feelings or their problems, but when these kids do want to talk you're always here for them. Always.'

She reached out to Miriam who, this time, accepted a comforting squeeze.

Miriam's eyes glinted with tears. 'I'm sorry,' she said, 'since Lewis died I always think the worst.'

Lilly said nothing. The tragic death of her friend's son almost never came up, and when it did Lilly felt she should simply listen. What platitudes could she offer anyway? 'Don't worry.' 'It could be worse.' The truth was it could not be worse. Lewis's suicide was shocking, painful and unfathomable. Lilly couldn't imagine how Miriam must feel or how she managed to keep going every day, and she wouldn't patronise her by saying that she could.

When Miriam had gathered herself and wiped her eyes she went straight back to business. 'We've got to find her before the police or they'll revoke her bail without a second thought.'

'They'll probably revoke it anyway,' said Lilly.

'Not when we explain the circumstances.'

Lilly wondered how she was supposed to explain a dive through a second-storey window but could see now was not the time to argue with Miriam.

'You're right,' said Lilly, 'but where on earth could she have gone?'

Things were right on track for Max Hardy. The girl was well under his grubby thumb, pretty much gagging for her starring role. They sometimes got stage-fright at the last minute but a small bag of something usually helped the proceedings along. The trick was to give them just enough to make them sparkle but not so much that things got messy.

Barrows had paid double. Max had known he would, the sick bastard. It was more money than Max had ever seen in one hit, and although Max had to admit he'd dipped into the pot a few times he reckoned he still had enough for a plane ticket to freedom. He'd planned to take a little back-up cash with him but now he'd have to hit the ground running. No sweat, a man with his talent wouldn't let anything get in his way.

He parked his BMW and walked up the stairwell to Gracie's flat. Like always, he checked the nosy bat at number 62 wasn't twitching her curtains, then ripped the police tape from the door of number 58. For a split second he wondered if the council had changed the lock, but no, his old key slid in just fine. By the time they finally got round to it he'd be long gone.

Everything felt so familiar. He could almost see Grace sitting at the kitchen table, smoking fag after fag.

'Get on with it,' she'd say as he traipsed through to the living room, tripod over his shoulder.

He couldn't pinpoint precisely when things between them had changed, when her face had hardened and she began to turn away.

It wasn't the first one. Then she just shook her head. 'It's not right, Maxi, she's the same age as Kelsey.' But the lure of a ton and the promise that it was a one-off arrangement had overcome her barely felt objections, and the film was made.

By the third or fourth time Gracie started whining. 'What if we get caught? It's my place so I'll be the one to go down.'

He'd plied her with plenty of brown, which kept the wheels oiled. Using her place had been perfect. The police could never trace the films back to him and the girls were well-behaved with Gracie there, the family set-up reassuring them that all was well. They'd assumed she wouldn't let things get out of control.

When Barrows got involved she'd got stressed and begged him to stop, literally begged him. On her skinny knees, tears pouring down her cheeks.

'I don't want my babies to get mixed up in this. Not with him. Please, Maxi, please.'

When he still hadn't listened she'd changed, started keeping secrets, making plans to get away. Then she'd got herself clean and he knew he'd have to take serious action. Stupid bitch.

This was the last time. It was over. If only Gracie had waited.

Max was startled from his reverie by his mobile. A text had come through, no doubt from the girl or Barrows, who were both keen to meet up. Max continued to erect his tripod until the bleep began to scratch his brain.

When he pressed the keys and read the message he gasped at what he saw.

I KNOW WOT UR DOING N IM GONNA STOP U. K

He reread it twice, took a deep breath and punched in a number.

'Charlene, baby, I need you to do me a favour.'

'Does she know where her sisters were placed?' asked Lilly.

Miriam shook her head.

'Could she have found out?' said Lilly.

'No chance. Kelsey and her sisters were close so we had to keep it a secret to stop her going round there.

321

The foster carers demanded a closed placement,' said Miriam.

'I don't suppose they wanted a suspected murderer turning up on their doorstep,' said Lilly.

Miriam narrowed her eyes. 'She didn't kill anybody.'

Lilly put her hands up in surrender. 'Let's not argue, let's just try and find her. Get the number and we can at least call the foster family.'

'It's locked in my office,' said Miriam, but then stopped in her tracks when she saw the door clearly ajar.

She pushed it open and both women saw the chaos inside. Drawers were open, files of paper spewed across the floor.

'Shit,' said Lilly.

Charlene was nervous as she waited for Max. She'd mucked the whole thing up and was afraid of his reaction.

She'd sneaked into Miriam's office and jemmied the filing cabinet without a hitch. Christ, her dad had taught her how to do that when she was still in nappies. She did it quickly and quietly and would have left with what Max had asked for undetected if she hadn't panicked. But she'd heard Miriam and the solicitor talking and had been startled not so much by their proximity as by the singularity of Miriam's voice.

She wasn't so much talking as wailing. 'They don't trust me at all or I'd be able to stop them . . . ' Then she mentioned someone called Lewis or Lois and the sound was so guttural, so full of pain, that Charlene had been frightened and had dropped an entire drawer of papers onto the floor. Terrified, she'd rifled through them like a burglar and ran as soon as she found her spoils.

It was only a matter of time before Miriam discovered what had happened.

'Useless, that's what you are,' her mother had always said, and she'd been right.

Charlene's heart hammered in her chest when she saw Max's BMW turn into the lane. He pulled alongside her, his arm outstretched through the open window.

'Why do you want it?' Charlene asked, ignoring his open palm.

Max sighed and killed the engine. 'You haven't got it, have you?'

Charlene puffed out her chest. 'Yes I have. I ain't useless.'

He smiled but Charlene could feel his anger.

'I just wondered why you want it. I mean, I could get into a lot of trouble and everything.'

He got out of the car and towered over her. He was still smiling but for the first time Charlene felt scared of him. Before she had been afraid of disappointing him but now she was just afraid.

'When they find out what I've done I'm in for it,' she gabbled. 'I don't want to be involved in nothing dodgy.'

'How will they find out? I'll just read it and you put it back,' said Max.

Charlene thought back to the mess she had left in the office. She decided it wasn't an image to share with

Max, he seemed pissed off enough as it was. She fished in her bag for the file.

'Good girl,' he said, his eyes darting across the page.

'You wouldn't hurt anybody, would you, Max?' asked Charlene, her voice small.

He didn't answer, didn't have to. Charlene could see very well what he was capable of and was just glad it wasn't her in the firing line.

At last he handed back the file and winked. 'Go home, baby, and put this back before anyone notices. I'll call you when we're ready for the shoot.'

'Is anything missing?' asked Lilly.

Miriam crouched on the floor and swept her hand through the blanket of papers. 'It's impossible to say.'

'The address where Kelsey's sisters are staying?'

'Like I just said, I can't possibly tell,' Miriam snapped as she rummaged through the scattered documents.

Lilly scanned the room. It was a tip but the cabinet had been opened neatly. Someone had been after information.

'We have to assume this is Kelsey's doing and that she has the address,' she said.

Miriam pulled herself to her feet. 'We can't assume any such thing. Anybody could have done this.'

Lilly counted to five and willed herself to remain patient. 'It's too coincidental and I don't believe in coincidence.'

'She couldn't have got into the unit without someone seeing her,' said Miriam.

'Why not? Someone did that only feet from where

324

we were standing and we didn't see anything. For goodness' sake, Miriam, we can debate this for another hour, or get ourselves over there and pick Kelsey up before the police do.'

Miriam nodded and reached for the phone.

'Hi, John, it's Miriam Zander. Could I have the address where the Brand kids are staying? . . . I know, I know, but I can't put my hand to it . . . yes, I'll do the filing tomorrow.'

Miriam scribbled down the address and handed it to Lilly.

Forty minutes later Lilly pulled into the drive of a pleasant but rambling farmhouse just outside Aylesbury. Two red setters bounded towards the car, wagging their tails in furious delight.

A woman in her late forties with cropped hair and flawless skin appeared in the porch. She ushered her dogs back inside with a playful smack on their rumps and smiled at her visitors, but her body language remained guarded.

'Mrs Barton, I'm from social services,' said Miriam, and handed over her identification.

The woman lifted her spectacles, which hung around her neck on a gold chain, and perched them on the end of her nose. 'It's Miss Barton, but do come in.'

Lilly and Miriam followed her through to a stone kitchen hung with photographs, artwork, calendars and timetables. Yellow Post-it notes formed a second frame to the door, providing information on everything from the number of the local vet, a recipe for mushroom soup and the six times table.

The dogs lay in a soft tangle in an oversized basket next to the Aga, and around a solid table that stretched the entire length of the room sat three little girls giggling and playing snap.

Lilly smiled at the girls. Though they still resembled their eldest sister they had evidently spent much of their time with Miss Barton outside and their skin glowed. They had put on weight but their limbs were firmer, their bodies more limber in their shorts and T-shirts. It was shocking how a few paltry weeks of good diet and exercise could transform these children so spectacularly.

'Actually, we haven't come to see the girls,' said Miriam. 'We've come about Kelsey.'

Miss Barton pursed her lips and turned to her charges. 'Run along upstairs, girls.'

The children groaned and Miss Barton chuckled indulgently. 'You can put the telly on for a bit.'

The children ran out of the room cheering and Miss Barton turned to Miriam. 'You'd better tell me what's going on.'

'There's nothing to be concerned about,' said Miriam.

Miss Barton rolled her eyes. 'Don't give me any bullshit.'

Lilly hid a smile. Kelsey's sisters were in good hands. 'Has she been here?'

Miss Barton raised an eyebrow. 'How could she? She's in prison, no?'

'She was transferred to secure accommodation this morning and, unfortunately,' Miriam swallowed, 'she's absconded.'

'But she doesn't have this address,' said Miss Barton.

'There's been a break-in, and it may be nothing –' Miriam's voice tailed off.

'But there's a possibility Kelsey knows where her sisters are,' said Lilly.

'I knew it,' said Miss Barton. 'As soon as that man came here asking about her I knew something was up.'

Lilly and Miriam spoke as one. 'What man?'

'I don't know. He said he was a friend of the family.'

Lilly's heart pounded. 'Young black guy, shaved head?'

Miss Barton nodded. 'Yes. I didn't let him in, of course.'

She looked from Miriam to Lilly, trying to assess what was happening. 'Do I need to worry about this man?'

'Yes,' said Lilly simply.

'I'm sure he means no harm to you or the girls,' said Miriam.

Miss Barton cocked her eye at Lilly, who she seemed to trust. Lilly couldn't abuse that.

'I'm sorry, but he's a violent man,' she said. 'Until we find him and Kelsey, I can't say with any certainty that you're safe.'

Miriam sighed. 'Well done, girl, another placement broken down.'

Lilly spun on her heels to face her. 'He attacked me.'

The two women glared at each other until Miss

Barton broke the silence. 'I'll pack some things and take the girls to my sister's for a few days. That should give the police sufficient time to pick both Kelsey and her friend up.' She gave a pointed look over her glasses. 'You have informed the police about this break-in, I assume.'

Max headed home. Kelsey hadn't gone to her sisters'. In fact, the look on the posh cow's face when she opened the door told him Kelsey had no idea where they were plotted.

He didn't like the sound of her text. Something had changed, the tone was defiant. He needed to find her, to put her back on track, but he couldn't think where she was hiding. She'd never really had any friends, spent her time helping Grace with the babies. Maybe she'd met someone inside who'd steered her to a safe place.

He needed to think, but his best brain-work came at the end of a pipe and all his rocks were at home out of temptation's way. Although he congratulated himself on his iron willpower he regretted having to drive over twenty miles for a fix.

Lilly called Jack.

'This is Jack McNally, 'fraid I can't pick up . . . '

She gulped back her relief. 'Jack, it's Lilly. Someone broke in at The Bushes and took the Brand kids' address. We're over there now and Kelsey hasn't been here but it looks like Max Hardy has. Call me when you get this.'

Miriam was still refusing to look directly at Lilly. 'I can't believe you've called in the police.'

'What else can we do?' Lilly was exasperated. 'Anyhow, I'd rather they find her than Max. If he catches up with her, breaking bail will be the least of her worries.'

Miriam mumbled something that may have been a grudging acceptance. Or maybe not. At that moment Lilly didn't care.

'We know what he's capable of and we know he's gone to a lot of trouble to find her.'

'You don't think he trashed my office, do you?' asked Miriam.

'I doubt he did it himself. Probably got one of the kids to do it for him,' said Lilly.

'Which one would get involved with something like this?' asked Miriam.

They answered as one. 'Charlene.'

'I swear I'll throttle that girl,' said Miriam.

'Never mind that, we need to put our heads together here,' said Lilly. 'Where has Kelsey gone?'

'If you had no one in the world to take you in, what would you do?' asked Miriam.

Lilly thought for a second. 'I'd go home.'

Max fumbled for his key. His need had grown throughout the course of the journey from a craving to a compulsion. His habit was no longer a pleasing vice but a fixation that enslaved him. He sprinted across the room, arm outstretched towards his pipe, knocking a pile of videos to the floor.

'Careful there, Max, don't want to spoil your product.'

Max spun round, his hand automatically retrieving his knife. He gasped at the sight of Gracie's ghost looming above him.

'I don't understand this, you're dead,' he whispered.

A luminous mist swirled around the ghost. 'Don't think so.'

Max shook his head and blinked repeatedly. How could this be happening? He looked again into the woman's face and the incandescence ebbed away. At last he realised it wasn't Grace.

'Kelsey,' he choked.

She stood before him, her features as sharp as her mother's, her skin almost translucent from time in prison. She looked from him to the videos strewn between them.

He noticed pink patches of new skin around her mouth where the scabs from the bleach must have fallen off.

'Baby,' Max whispered.

Her eyes bored into him, challenging, accusing. She wasn't the biddable child he had known. She even stood differently, with her shoulders back. Jail time had obviously toughened her up.

She pointed to a camera left carelessly on the sofa. 'I thought this was finished. You said you'd had enough.'

Max nodded frantically. 'I had. I still have had enough but I need to get out of here, baby, and this is my ticket.'

Kelsey shook her head. 'No more, Max.'

'This is the last one, I swear.'

'How many times did you say that to Mum?' she said.

He put his hands up in acceptance. 'That was different. This time it's for real. One more and I'm out of here.'

'No, Max, this stops right now.' She opened her arms to encompass the videos and equipment. 'Get rid of this lot and leave.'

He nodded vigorously. 'That's my plan, baby, burn everything just as soon as this last one is over.'

They stared at one another, Kelsey's eyes full of anger and hate, Max trying to work out how best to get through to her.

'I'm getting a lot for this,' he said. 'Serious dough.'

'I don't care.'

'And I'm gonna split it with you,' he said. 'Give a share to you and the babies now your mum ain't here to look after you.'

Her eyes didn't waver, not even a flicker. 'I can't let you do it.'

Max cocked his head to one side. 'Meaning?'

'You know exactly what I mean.'

Their eyes locked together, both refusing to look away.

'People like us never grass,' he said.

'Don't push me, Max. I never said a word before cos of Mum, but she ain't here any more.'

'And what do you think she'd say if she was?'

Kelsey didn't answer, so Max answered his own question.

'She'd say let him get this out of the way and it'll be finished for all of us.'

The fire in Kelsey's eyes extinguished and she turned towards the door.

'This will never be finished.'

Faced with the sight of number 58, Lilly felt cold. The drive to the Clayhill Estate had been fuelled by the need to find Kelsey, and Lilly had not even considered how she would feel returning to the place where she'd been attacked. Now that the door was in front of her, she was frightened.

'You okay?' asked Miriam.

'It's just a place,' said Lilly, but she didn't move.

Miriam patted Lilly's arm. 'You stay here. I'll check whether she's inside.'

Miriam passed in front of Lilly and opened the door. The corridor was as empty and dark as it had been on the night Max had forced her inside.

'I'm your worst fucking nightmare.'

It was still too hot for more than a T-shirt but Lilly was freezing, each muscle shaking, sweat pouring down her back.

She saw the knife coming towards her.

'I'm your worst fucking nightmare.'

What if he was there now? Her friend would be chopped to pieces. She tried to warn Miriam but once again she was paralysed by fear, the sound of her heart-beat resounding like thunder in her ears.

Miriam was now at the end of the hall, moving nearer and nearer to danger. Lilly opened her mouth to scream, willing the sound from the pit of her stomach, but nothing came and Lilly was forced to watch Miriam disappear into the bedroom.

A few seconds went by, maybe four, maybe five. Enough time for Miriam to check the room and leave. Enough time to be forced down onto the bed and bled like a halal goat.

'*I'm your worst fucking nightmare.*'

'No, you bastard, I'm yours.'

Lilly hurled herself into the hall and ran towards the bedroom. She threw open the door and looked wildly around the room trying to make out the shapes in the dark. At last she saw two figures on the bed. One was Miriam, who appeared unhurt and had her arm around the other. When her eyes became accustomed to the gloom Lilly could see it was Kelsey.

'It's all right, you're safe now,' whispered Miriam. At first Lilly thought the words of comfort were directed at her, but now she could see Miriam was speaking to Kelsey. 'I know you're frightened and you think you've come to the end of the road, but I'm here.'

Miriam pushed Kelsey's hair off her face and held it in her hands. 'My son was just like you. His name was Lewis and he thought he had no one to turn to, nowhere to go.'

Lilly swallowed a sob at the raw intensity of her friend's grief.

'He thought he couldn't trust me,' said Miriam, 'and I will never forgive myself for that.'

So this was how Miriam felt. When all the jokes and

bravado were pushed aside she was still completely bereft. Lilly would feel the same if it were Sam.

She breathed in a huge lungful of air. 'Miriam, don't.'

Miriam continued to look deep into Kelsey's eyes as if Lilly hadn't spoken.

'Every day of my life I turn it over and over in my mind. What could I have done? How could I have stopped him? And the conclusion I come to is always the same. I could have stopped running around like a headless chicken, doing this and doing that, and taken the time to listen.'

Lilly could bear it no longer. If she couldn't distract Miriam she'd engage with her client. 'What are you doing here, Kelsey?'

It was a rhetorical question. Lilly didn't imagine there was a simple answer, and anyway, she hadn't given Kelsey the means to write anything down.

'I wanted to be with my mum.'

The words hit Lilly like a punch. The voice, calm and clear, was neither Lilly's nor Miriam's. Kelsey had spoken.

Lilly kept her own tone neutral. Now was not the time for accusations. 'When did your voice come back?'

'Tonight. I went to see Max and it just came out,' said Kelsey.

Lilly reeled backwards. 'You went to see Max!'

'I know Kelsey's got to answer a lot of questions but now is not the right time. And here is definitely not the right place.'

It took Lilly a second to register that it was Miriam who had spoken, and she didn't react until Miriam spoke again.

334

'Let's get her back to Leyland House before the police get here.'

When they arrived at the pretty cul-de-sac Lilly was surprised to see Sheba leaving Leyland House.

'Just the woman,' Lilly called. 'I've got Kelsey here, and as soon as we've got her settled back in I need to ask her some questions. It would be fantastic if you could sit in.'

Sheba regarded Lilly coolly, her forehead pinched into a frown. 'She can't go back to Leyland House.'

Lilly felt winded, as much by Sheba's frostiness as what she had actually said.

'She has to, otherwise they'll send her back to prison,' Lilly managed.

Sheba shrugged. 'I'm sorry, but there's nothing I can do about that.'

Lilly felt a flash of anger. These children weren't dolls, you couldn't just put them down when you got fed up of playing with them.

'You have a responsibility to Kelsey.'

Sheba's icy detachment left her as she too became angry. 'Don't you dare lecture me about responsibility. I worked my butt off to get Kelsey out of jail and I pulled a huge favour to get Kelsey a place here. Paul is absolutely furious.'

Paul Collins' feelings were the least of Lilly's concerns. 'It's supposed to be a place for damaged kids, so he needn't get bent out of shape because one of them does something a bit loopy. I think he should expect it from time to time,' she said sharply.

'Correction, Lilly, this is supposed to be a *secure* place for damaged kids, and your bloody client has shown that's not the case,' said Sheba.

'Can't they just sort it out?' asked Lilly, a lot less sure of her ground.

'Yes, I'm sure they can, in time, but until then Leyland House can't be considered secure,' said Sheba.

Lilly gulped. 'So what's happened to the other children?'

'They've been sent elsewhere,' said Sheba with a sigh, her heat dissipating. 'Listen, Lilly, I know none of this is your fault. I know it's not Kelsey's either. I'll stand by my evidence that she needs special care, but until Leyland reopens I'm not sure how far it will get you.'

Lilly heaved herself back into the car. 'She can't go back there, it's had to close.'

'Close?' asked Miriam.

'Don't sound so surprised. One of the patients managed to escape out of a window only minutes after she arrived.'

'I'll take her back to The Bushes,' said Miriam.

'It's not secure, she'd be in breach of Blechard-Smith's order,' said Lilly.

'I don't care about a stupid piece of paper,' said Miriam.

Lilly shook her head. 'Don't be absurd, you'd be sacked, and what would happen to all the other kids?'

Miriam's shoulders sagged. 'So what now?'

Lilly was out of ideas and pulled out her phone. 'I'll call Jack.'

They met him in the police-station car park.

'Thanks for bringing her in,' said Jack.

'Not my idea,' said Miriam with a degree of tetchiness that made Lilly worry that the evening's events were sending her friend over the edge. The way Miriam had bared herself to Kelsey about Lewis had been so out of character that Lilly wasn't sure what to expect next. She wanted to protect her friend but feared there might not be enough of her to go round.

She shook her head almost imperceptibly to warn Jack not to get into it with Miriam.

He ignored the crack and kept his tone casual. 'We'll keep her here tonight and let the judge decide what to do tomorrow morning.' He put his arm around Kelsey. 'Come on you, I expect you're starving.'

'I'll see you in court, Kelsey,' said Lilly.

'Indeed you will,' said Jack, and he led her inside.

Max was seriously spooked. He'd expected to have to track Kelsey down but she'd made the first move. Now his head was toast. What if she went to the police?

He'd always thought Kelsey was solid, that he didn't have to worry about her, but he'd thought that about Gracie once upon a time. He was beginning to question his own judgement. Nah, Kelsey wasn't as flaky as her mum, didn't take drugs for a start, which made her a whole lot more predictable. She was pissed about

337

the films but wouldn't do anything about it. He knew where he was with Kelsey.

Then again, she didn't even look like herself tonight. She'd looked just like Gracie. Maybe she was thinking like Gracie too. After all, he knew what happened to a person's mind in jail.

He lit a joint and put his keys in the ignition. He didn't normally drive and smoke. First, this was good weed that demanded to be enjoyed in comfort, preferably with a chilled soundtrack. Second, the old bill would smell it if he got pulled, even the fat traffic lemmings knew the smell of skunk these days.

But Kelsey had fucked with his karma and he'd had to use three rocks just to even himself out. Now he was jangling, his edges ragged. He never smoked in the car but tonight he made an exception.

By the time he reached the clinic his mind was muddled and his fears had taken hold. Kelsey being on the out was bad news. It would end with them all getting caught, just as Gracie had predicted.

Max had done time before. Short stretches here and there for small stuff, but he'd hated every minute of it, banged up with some psycho or a smackhead doing his rattle, screaming into the darkness. There was no way he could go down for this. Years in Belmarsh would finish him off.

Then, when everyone found out what he was in for – and you could be sure the screws would put it about – he'd have every lowlife robber and arsonist on his back. The only safety would be in the VP wing with the other nonces. No way, man. He couldn't do time for this.

From the outside the place seemed to be in darkness. Only one window glowed with a pale light, which Max assumed came from a lamp. He imagined Barrows alone in the room, like a worm hidden in an apple. His stomach lurched when he realised the light must emanate not from a lamp but from the television. The pervert was watching one of his tapes.

Barrows buzzed him up.

'What's going on?' he shouted as soon as Max opened the door.

To his relief Max saw the television was off, and Barrows was illuminated by the screen of his computer. It cast his face in a sickly green.

Barrows lowered his voice but his tone remained threatening. 'I asked what's going on.'

'I'm calling it off, man,' said Max.

Barrows breathed through his nose as if trying to contain himself but Max saw his fists open and close. 'You can't do that.'

Max shrugged. 'I can and I am.'

Barrows leaped to his feet. 'I've paid.'

Max threw a crumpled envelope onto the other man's desk. 'It's a little bit short. I'll sort the rest out in the next couple of days.'

For a moment both men stared into each other's eyes. Max willed himself not to be the first to lower his gaze and was pleased when Barrows sank back into his chair and dropped his head into his hands.

'Weak, weak, they are all weak,' he said, apparently to himself.

At last he raised his head and levelled Max once again in his eye-line. His eyes seemed to Max to be entirely empty, hypnotically so.

'What do you want more than anything else?' asked Barrows.

Max answered without thinking. 'To escape.'

Barrows closed his eyes again as if contemplating his response, and Max cursed himself for giving anything away.

'And where would you go?' asked Barrows.

'America.' Max wondered again why he was telling this piece of filth anything.

'Very well,' said Barrows. 'If you bring the girl tomorrow, I will bring you a plane ticket to New York.'

'LA,' said Max.

The suspicion of a smile played on Barrows' lips and he put the envelope back into Max's pocket. 'LA it is.'

CHAPTER SIXTEEN

Tuesday, 22 September

The journey to London was very different from the one Lilly had made only two days earlier. She had neither hangover nor headache. She had collected the black trouser suit from the dry-cleaner's, the one that everyone said made her look slim, and had teamed it with her embroidered scarf. It covered the ugly scab that was forming on her throat and it reminded her of Rupes. Who could argue with that?

She found a seat immediately and the train sailed into town, depositing Lilly at Blackfriars with sufficient time to buy a coffee from Starbucks. She sauntered to court sipping hot froth through the plastic spout of the cup. It always made her feel deliciously cosmopolitan. Lilly laughed at herself – so unsophisticated, so easy to please. You could take the girl out of Yorkshire . . .

When she rounded the corner Lilly saw that Jez was waiting for her outside the Old Bailey, dwarfed by the uniformity of the exterior. His gorgeous face was the only point of interest in the vast expanse of grey.

The press pack on the other side of the road chatted

idly, clearly unaware of the tabloid-bolstering events of the previous evening.

'This is a disaster,' he said as they passed together through security. 'Why the hell did she do it?'

'We'll have to ask her that,' answered Lilly, and made her way through the belly of the court towards the cells. 'She should be here by now.'

'They won't produce her,' said Jez. 'They never do.'

Lilly pressed the buzzer to be let through. 'Jack McNally said he'd bring her himself.'

'Isn't he the idiot that lost her in the first place?'

'Hardly,' said Lilly. 'She jumped out of a bloody window.'

'Whatever,' Jez shrugged. 'Do you trust him to bring her?'

They heard the distinctive rattle of iron keys as the doors were opened.

At last the final lock was released with a soft clunk. 'No doubt about it,' said Lilly. 'I'd trust that man with my life.'

The cell area in the Old Bailey was ancient. Although the security had been updated from time to time it was far from modern and the area held its natural gravitas in every stone. An air of apprehension filled the corridor between the cells as those charged with the gravest of offences waited for their fate to be sealed only feet above their heads.

The guard used one of at least twenty keys attached to a jangling hoop wider than his fist, and opened cell three.

Kelsey sat on the floor at the far end. Her skin

seemed as grey as the bricks behind her, her eyes every bit as lifeless.

'This is Jez, your barrister,' said Lilly. 'He's going to ask the judge to give you another chance.'

Kelsey shrugged with an indifference that irked Lilly. This was not the frightened little girl in The Bushes.

'I need you to tell me why you ran away, Kelsey,' said Jez, and held paper and pen in his outstretched hand.

'She won't be needing that,' said Lilly. 'She's redis-covered the power of speech.'

Jez looked stunned. 'She can speak?'

Lilly gave a rueful smile.

'So why isn't she saying anything?' he asked.

Kelsey sighed. 'Because I ain't got nothing to say.'

The voice, like last night, was clear and composed – not, thought Lilly, the painful whisper of one recently recovered. Suspicions were crowding Lilly's mind and she recalled her conversation with Sheba on exactly this point. Kelsey was either still in shock, or . . .

'Cut the crap, sister,' said Lilly. Her tone startled both Jez and Kelsey, who snapped to attention in unison. 'Since I took this case I've been shouted at by coppers, ridiculed on the telly and pushed into a road by the biggest man I ever saw in my life. I've been followed and attacked with a knife by your mother's lunatic pimp. Jesus, even my sex life has nosedived, so don't sit there like a sulky toddler.'

Lilly knew her behaviour was entirely inappropriate but she couldn't keep her anger in check. 'Answer the man's question. Why did you run away from Leyland House?'

Lilly saw indecision register in the girl's features and she didn't wait for Kelsey to process her thoughts but pressed harder.

'If you want to play silly beggars that's fine, but you'll do it with someone else. I'm not wasting another second in this hellhole unless you've got something to tell us.'

It was bully-boy tactics but Lilly had had enough of playing games. She'd had enough of games, period. It was time for everyone to lay their cards on the table.

Kelsey must have realised that this was no bluff. 'I told you I wanted to be with my mum. I wanted to say goodbye.'

Jez lowered his eyes as if genuinely sorry for this poor girl.

Lilly, however, had her bullshit detector turned all the way up. 'Why yesterday? You could have gone to the flat anytime you were in The Bushes and you wouldn't have needed to jump out of a window.'

'It didn't hit me till yesterday,' said Kelsey.

Lilly stood up. 'Come on, Jez, I'm sure you've got innocent people to get out of jail.'

Kelsey jumped up too and shouted, 'I am innocent.'

Lilly shouted right back at her. 'So why are you lying?'

Kelsey's eyes darted from side to side and the muscle at the corner of her mouth twitched. She's wavering, thought Lilly. Time to change tack.

'You don't have to keep quiet any more. Your mum's dead, nothing you say can hurt her or get her into trouble,' said Lilly, lowering her voice.

Kelsey nodded. Obviously this thought was one she'd toyed with before. 'I know, but I don't want them to say bad things about her.'

'Words can't hurt Grace now, but rotting in Parkgate will certainly hurt you,' said Lilly. 'Let us help you, please.' This last plea was said as she looked directly into Kelsey's eyes.

Kelsey slid her back down the wall to the floor. Lilly sat down next to her.

'I thought he'd stop when Mum was killed. I thought he'd see how sick it all was,' said Kelsey.

'Max,' said Lilly.

Kelsey nodded. 'I should have known he was in too deep.'

'He was making films, porno films,' Lilly prompted.

'Yeah, but not like the ones Mum used to make, with a story and that. These were just one man. Doing it with a girl,' said Kelsey.

'How old were the girls?' asked Lilly, who suspected she already knew the answer.

'I'm not sure. Twelve, thirteen maybe.'

Lilly hid her horror and pushed on. 'What did it have to do with your mum?'

Kelsey screwed up her face and shut her eyes tight. She clearly wanted to say it had nothing to do with Grace.

Lilly put her hand on Kelsey's shoulder. 'Sticks and stones may break my bones . . .'

Kelsey spoke without opening her eyes. 'He made them in our flat.'

Lilly swallowed. What in God's name had this kid seen in her short life?

'Max, the man and the girls, they all came to our place and', Kelsey's voice wavered, 'did it in the front room.'

'Your mum let that happen?' said Jez.

No, Jez, don't badmouth Grace, that's what she's afraid of.

'I'm sure she tried to stop Max,' said Lilly, directing her words and a chastising glare at Jez.

Kelsey seized upon this like the gift it was. 'She did try to stop him. She told him again and again but he wouldn't listen.' She aimed her words at Jez, begging him to understand, not to judge. 'She wasn't very strong, cos of the gear. She couldn't do without it, see, but she kept it under control as best she could. We weren't living in a pigsty or nothing.'

Lilly nodded and recalled how neat number 58 had been.

'But Max kept bringing more and more drugs so she wouldn't put up a fight,' said Kelsey.

Jez smiled his understanding and Kelsey's face filled with gratitude. 'One night, after they'd all gone, I found her crying in bed. She kept saying, "I've got to get you away from him, I've got to get you away." I says, "Come on then, Mum, let's go. Let's pack up and take the babies away from here, and I meant it cos I could see where it was all heading. But she says no. Says we can't just take off in the middle of the night, that we've got to do it properly.'

'And she did try,' said Lilly.

'Yeah, she did. At first I thought she'd just forget about it, like everything else she ever said she was going

346

to do, but this time was different. She stopped taking the drugs and sold 'em to Tracey in the next block.'

'The girl who found your mum?'

Kelsey nodded. 'Then she started writing to the council for a transfer but she kept getting knocked back. Then Max found out somehow and beat the crap out of her. Next thing I know the social came for us and put us in care.'

'I think she did it to get you out of there,' said Lilly.

'I think you're right. I didn't get it at first, and then when I did it was too late,' said Kelsey.

Someone thumped loudly on the cell door.

'Five minutes and we're in court,' said Jez. 'You have to tell us why you left Leyland House.'

'I knew he was going to do it again and I couldn't let it happen. Enough people have been hurt. I thought I could give him a shock, make him see sense.'

'What made you think it was going to happen again?' asked Lilly.

Kelsey's reply was emphatic. 'Someone came to see me. I can't tell you who cos I promised, but they said they'd met up with Max and I worked it out from there. I just wanted to warn him off.'

Judge Blechard-Smith made no attempt to hide his fury at the case coming before him again. Having been strong-armed against his better judgement to release the girl, he looked apoplectic to discover she'd escaped. As she was led into the dock he could barely contain himself.

'Stand up,' he yelled at Kelsey, who could barely see over the top of the dock railing.

'She is standing, My Lord,' said Jez. 'I'm afraid these courts were not designed with children in mind. Perhaps you would allow her to sit beside her solicitor.'

'Indeed I shall not,' snarled the judge. 'Child or not, this is a court of law and she is the defendant.'

There was a two-minute commotion while several books were dispatched to the dock and arranged in a pile for Kelsey to stand on.

The judge turned to his clerk. 'At the trial, please arrange for an orange box to be available.'

The clerk nodded, but the height of his eyebrows told Lilly that he too was wondering whether such things still existed. The scene reminded Lilly of another case where her client had been deaf. In the absence of a signer the judge had conducted the hearing by shouting.

'Mr Marshall, can you please tell me why we are here today,' said the judge.

Marshall got to his feet. 'As your Lordship may recall, a secure accommodation order was made in respect of this defendant following an application by the defence . . . '

'Good God, man, it was two days ago,' roared the judge, 'I think I can remember that far back. What I want to know is what has happened since to bring us all back here yet again.'

Marshall bowed. 'The defendant was taken to the institution in question, Leyland House, by Officer McNally, and some moments later she absconded.'

'I thought the building was secure,' said the judge.

'Indeed, that is what we were told, but it seems the defendant was able to smash open a second-floor window and jump to her freedom,' said Marshall.

The judge threw his hands in the air. 'But Doctor Lorenson said it was as safe as a prison, she said she'd been there herself.'

The unfairness of the comment was clearly too much for Jez, who jumped to his feet. 'With all due respect, it is not Doctor Lorenson's job to check every window.'

'But it is her job to recommend a suitable unit,' said Marshall, clearly in no mood to forgive the trouncing he had received at Sheba's hands. 'And the unit in question was certainly not that.'

'So what is the prosecution's position today?' continued the judge.

'We oppose any further applications for bail on the grounds that this defendant is likely to abscond,' said Marshall.

Lilly sneaked a look in Jack's direction. He shrugged helplessly, both palms open. The decision to oppose bail would have come directly from Bradbury, not from him. She understood his position and nodded.

'And what do the defence say, Mr Stafford?' asked the judge. 'Frankly, I'm intrigued.'

Jez shuffled his papers unnecessarily. He was great at his job but the unassailable fact was that Kelsey had escaped.

'My Lord, Kelsey has known that the police suspected her involvement in her mother's death for quite some time, and until last night made no attempt to evade due process. She could easily have run away during her time at The Bushes, but did not.'

'She hadn't been charged at that point,' said Marshall.

Jez sighed. It was a fair point. Since Kelsey had been charged she'd been in custody, and had taken her chance at the very first opportunity that presented itself.

'My Lord, I think we have to ask ourselves how serious this attempt to flee really was,' he said.

'She jumped from a second-floor window. I'd say that was pretty serious,' said Marshall, evidently enjoying himself.

Jez ignored the interruption from his left and continued. 'She went straight back home, the very first place the police would look.'

'And had she not been discovered?' asked the judge.

'I have no doubt she would have handed herself in,' said Jez.

Marshall shook his head and gave a stagey laugh. 'In the famous words of Mandy Rice Davies, "he would say that, wouldn't he". None of us can say what she would or wouldn't have done if Sergeant McNally hadn't found her.'

'If Mr Marshall had bothered to read the policeman's notebook, as I did, he would know that the officer in question not only lost Kelsey, he was not the one to find her either. That task was left to my instructing solicitor.'

Jez let his stinging indictment of Jack settle in everyone's minds before continuing. 'The point is, Kelsey could easily have escaped again but chose instead to go to the station voluntarily to sort this matter out.'

It was a triumph, but a minor one, and Lilly could only watch as the judge revoked bail and sent Kelsey back to Parkgate.

'There was nothing I could do, Lilly,' said Jack.

'To stop her jumping out of a window or getting sent to jail?' asked Jez.

Jack looked for a moment as though he might punch Jez, but instead he turned his back and looked directly at Lilly. 'You look a better sight than in recent days.'

'I'll take that as a compliment, though I'm not sure that's how it was meant,' said Lilly.

'Och, woman,' he said, his accent thick in his laughter, 'you're so suspicious.'

Jez laughed and threaded his arm through Lilly's. 'I thought you said your sex life was in ruins?'

Jack looked from Lilly to Jez and back again. 'I've got to go.'

That night Lilly ran a bath and chose a CD. She turned the volume to its lowest setting so as not to wake Sam. She searched in the bathroom cabinet for some bubble bath but found only four empty cans of deodorant and an unopened tub of foot scrub. Right at the back was a bottle of tea tree oil to see off nits, zits and other unwanted guests in the Valentine household, but no bubble bath. She settled for a squirt of washing-up liquid, something her mother, who rarely had cash for cosmetics or bathroom luxuries, used most of the time. No doubt it contributed to the endless fungal infections that plagued her, but Lilly decided to risk it this once.

She sank into the froth and sang along with Jay Kay. The view from the window was stunning, the field beyond alight as the evening sun gave its last blast of energy to the rapeseed below. David had wanted to frost the bathroom window. Lilly's frequent nakedness would, he insisted, 'attract perverts'. Lilly refused, and since David's departure rarely bothered to pull the blind. If a curious farmer or hiker caught a glimpse of her arse it was a small price to pay for the sense of wellbeing engendered by letting the world beyond into the tub.

On the footpath that snaked between the garden and the fields, Lilly could see two walkers striding towards the village. They stopped to take in the view, the day-glo yellow now settling to buttercup, and for a second she was tempted to wave.

She slid deeper and closed her eyes. The day had not been a great one. In fact, she was in precisely the same position she had been in three days ago. Kelsey was in custody with little prospect of release and her trial would not be listed for many months. The fact that she had tried to abscond only strengthened the prosecution's case against her.

Lilly yawned. For the first time since she had picked up this case she felt relaxed, succumbing to the pleasant idea that at this moment in time there was nothing she could do.

At some stage she would need to start looking at the police files on Candy Grigson's attack and ascertain if there was any clue to the identity of her assailant or a connection with Grace. Lilly would also check if Kelsey knew anything about Candy. In the meantime she would think of something else . . .

And yet Miriam's words still rang true. Find out why Grace put her kids in care and you'll find out why she was killed.

Lilly was sure Grace had given up Kelsey and her sisters in a desperate attempt to remove them from Max. The key was the pornography, but Candy had not mentioned films or anything close. True, Sheba had said he would probably be an obsessive watcher of skin flicks, but if his predilection was for children why keep visiting Candy? Why visit Grace? Lilly was no expert, but the paedophiles with whom she'd come into contact showed little interest in adults, prostitutes or otherwise. It was children that gave these people their buzz, and even the most fertile imagination couldn't mistake Grace or Candy for much under thirty.

Lilly smacked her forehead. She was being stupid. The murderer didn't visit Grace for sex, at least not with *her*. Grace must have known him through Max. He was the man in the films. There was no sign of a struggle because she let him in, she had no reason to suspect he'd come to kill her.

But that was the point, why did he kill her? Was it just for the kicks? Candy would say so but it didn't ring true to Lilly. But what if he had found out that Grace was digging an escape tunnel, or that she'd threatened to reveal the secrets of number 58, wouldn't that be enough to scare someone into violence?

And yet, and yet . . . If he killed Grace to silence her, why mutilate the body?

There were two theories at play here, but they didn't make sense together.

Lilly sank deeper into the bubbles. Her brain was starting to ache.

Nancy Donaldson was working late. She was miffed to be missing *Celebrity Big Brother* but she'd put the overtime towards the new Balenciaga handbag she'd seen in the sweaty paws of at least three footballers' wives in the latest edition of *Heat*.

The office had been busy since the Brand girl had been sent to the loony bin, with endless articles and programmes needing a comment from Hermione. The red-tops couldn't get enough of the story and were happy to print a few anodyne quotes to offset another rehashing of the gruesome details of Grace's death, but a number of the pieces in the broadsheets had not flattered Nancy's boss, accusing her of jumping ship.

'All publicity is good publicity,' Hermione had said, but Nancy wasn't so sure. The PM took the *Guardian*, everyone knew that, but his advisors paid more attention to the *Daily Mail*.

The new MP who'd won the Chichester South by-election needed an assistant. Maybe he and Nancy should have a chat.

The fax machine began to vibrate and a sheet of paper shuffled into the tray. Nancy reached across her desk and pulled it towards her. She ignored the heading marked 'private and confidential'. A good parliamentary secretary didn't heed such nonsense, at least Nancy did not. It was usually a sly ruse by a constituent attempting to land a begging letter directly into the MP's lap, the idea being that she would be more likely to attend a sub-committee meeting on recycling, or a school fete, if she received the request in person. How little they knew Hermione Barrows, thought Nancy.

She read the fax and gave a strangled squeal.

Hermione was at a dinner for a trade delegation from Indonesia and was not to be disturbed. By the time Nancy had reread the fax three times her knickers were slightly damp, and she picked up the phone.

'This had better be urgent,' snapped Hermione.

Nancy could hear the hum of conversation and cutlery scraping on china. Laughter tinkled like wind-chimes.

'Well?' Hermione hissed.

'You've had a fax from the PM's office,' said Nancy.

Hermione's tone changed from angry to hungry in a millisecond. 'Read it.'

'"*Dear Mrs Barrows,*" – blah, blah – "*you may not yet know that Kelsey Brand escaped yesterday from Leyland House . . .*"'

'Christ,' whispered Hermione. 'Go on, go on.'

'"*While Miss Brand is now safely back in custody, the Prime Minister feels that this unfortunate series of events must be investigated at parliamentary level. To this end we intend to set up an official inquiry and should like you to sit as chair . . .*"'

'Bloody hell,' said Hermione.

Bloody hell indeed.

CHAPTER SEVENTEEN

Wednesday, 23 September

The next morning Lilly found herself in the rare position of being early on two consecutive days. It was a dizzying experience and Lilly wasn't sure how best to use her time. She settled into the front seat of her car in the picturesque environs of Parkgate car park and unwrapped a king-sized Mars Bar. It had already begun to melt in the heat and she smeared chocolate on her copy of Jez's notes of their meeting with Kelsey in the cells at the Old Bailey.

She smiled at his handwriting, which danced with elegant loops. He had doodled flags and crowns in the margin. Didn't that mean an inflated ego was at work? She'd ask Sheba – if Sheba ever deigned to speak to Lilly again.

As she reread the conversation, Lilly felt again how forcefully Kelsey had defended her mum. Even a crap mother was still a mother. How ironic that Grace finally came good but died before her children could benefit. Poor Grace, a joyless life and a luckless death.

Then she saw Kelsey's last comment, which hadn't

356

seemed important at the time. Someone had visited Kelsey in prison.

'Sorry love,' said the guard, whose demeanour convinced Lilly he was anything but. 'That stuff's confidential.'

'I'm her solicitor,' said Lilly, her gaze fixed on the guard's fat finger, which had disappeared into the depths of his nostril. 'And you must keep records?'

The guard studied the contents of his nail, eager to see what he had extracted.

'Of course we keep records. Every visitor is logged onto the prisoner's P22.'

'Can I see it?' asked Lilly.

'No,' said the guard, rolling his nasal matter between thumb and forefinger.

Lilly checked her urge to gag. 'It's very important. I need to know who she's spoken to.'

The guard flicked away his mucus ball. 'So why don't you just ask your client?'

Lilly returned to her car, seething at the ridiculousness of her situation. Of course she should just ask Kelsey to identify her mystery visitor, but Lilly knew the answer would not be forthcoming today. Kelsey's life was constructed on secrets and pacts not to reveal the truth. She would cling to what she knew until the alternatives became bearable, and that process would take time – the one luxury none of them had.

Lilly wondered if Jack would have access to prison documentation, but decided she had already stretched his good nature beyond the acceptable boundaries of friendship.

Then it struck her. Leyland House would have been given copies of anything useful. All manner of sundries might have found their way into Kelsey's file. Medical records, social services history, prison documentation.

Lilly punched the number, which rang only twice before being answered with a curt hello.

'Hi there, I wasn't sure if anyone would still be around,' said Lilly.

'We didn't all leave with the rats,' came the reply. 'Can I help you?'

'I hope so. My name is Lilly Valentine and I represent Kelsey Brand. Who am I speaking with please?'

'Doctor Paul Collins.'

Hell. Lilly was hoping for someone in administration or a clueless maintenance guy, not the main man himself.

He sounded every bit as irked as she imagined he would. Perhaps an apology might help. 'I'm sorry for the problems my client has caused.'

'Problems,' said Collins, letting the word roll around his tongue, toying with it as if it were new to him. 'Leyland House has been closed, the patients ripped from their therapy and sent goodness knows where. Yes, I'd say your client has caused us a few *problems*.'

'As I say, I'm very sorry,' said Lilly.

'This is the culmination of my life's work, Miss Valentine,' said Collins.

Lilly disliked his theatrics. As her mum had always said, 'If a bird shits on your head you don't stand under the nest and shout.'

Move on, brother.

She was about to thank him for his time when he sighed. 'Of course, Kelsey's not to blame, it was waiting to happen. I'm just glad she wasn't hurt.'

'Not a scratch,' said Lilly.

'I suppose the authorities will make me jump through a thousand hoops before I reopen,' said Collins.

It hadn't occurred to Lilly that the closure was temporary. 'I didn't realise you intended to reopen.'

Collins laughed. 'You thought this was it! Miss Valentine, I didn't get where I am today by giving up at every little obstacle. And I suppose you want to know if there'll be a place for Kelsey when I've done my penance.'

It hadn't even crossed Lilly's mind but Collins continued regardless. 'I still say Leyland House will give her the best chance of recovery, so yes, we will take her back.'

Lilly was speechless. It wasn't just his court appearances that made this man the best in the business.

'I'd better get on,' said Collins. 'Unless there was anything else?'

Finally Lilly remembered the reason for her call. 'Do you have Kelsey's prison file, Doctor Collins?'

'It's in front of me. I suppose I should send it back,' he answered.

'Before you do, could you tell me if Kelsey had any visitors in Parkgate? The information should be on a document called a P22,' said Lilly.

'I have the form. Not very popular, was she? Visitors

359

include your good self, the lovely Doctor Lorenson and a Miss Tammy Bluebell,' he said.

'Tammy Bluebell?' asked Lilly, stifling the urge to laugh.

'Indeed. Doesn't sound very likely, does it?'

Lilly contemplated her conversation with Collins as she passed into the prison.

'Back so soon?' said a familiar voice.

Lilly saw Angie leaning over her mop on her usual tour of the corridors. She was sporting a black eye. Swollen and purple, it had a cartoonish quality.

'What happened to you?' asked Lilly.

Angie took a drag on her roll-up and found it had gone out.

'Bit of a scrap,' she said, and patted her pockets, presumably for a box of matches. She signalled to Candy who was on shift with her, pointing to the end of her cigarette. Candy hauled herself from her own bucket and struck a match.

'These young girls come in, want to prove themselves, show they're hard,' said Angie.

Candy shook her head. 'I said to the one that did it,' she pointed her thumb towards Angie's injured eye, 'just do your time quietly or else you'll go mad.'

'They won't listen to a bit of friendly advice,' clucked Angie.

The two women could have been standing on any street corner putting the world to rights.

'Always the same,' said Candy. 'They start mouthing off and it ends in tears.'

'Yours, by the look of it,' said Lilly.

The inmates exchanged an amused glance. 'Aye, it's a bit sore,' said Angie.

'But it ain't you in the hospital wing,' added Candy.

They shared a chuckle and Lilly guiltily joined them.

'Have you seen Kelsey?' asked Lilly.

'Oh aye,' said Angie. 'Stupid girl. Gets away on her toes and goes straight home.'

There was ambivalence in Angie's reply. Having managed to escape from a second-floor window, Kelsey, it seemed, was no longer considered a vulnerable child, just another idiot lacking sufficient prison nous.

'She had a visit here from someone calling themselves Tammy Bluebell,' said Lilly.

Candy yawned. 'That's a good one.'

'Did you see who it was? Do you know her real name?' asked Lilly, suspecting she was beginning to bore the women.

'Some kid came to see her, but I'd never seen her before,' said Angie. 'It sounds like she used the old porno chestnut. You know, the name of your first pet and the name of your street.' She wandered back to her chores.

'Thanks,' called Lilly, and hoped Kelsey was not relying on Angie's support or protection to see her through.

Lilly watched Kelsey enter the Friends and Family Centre and began to understand Angie's change of heart. Kelsey walked with her shoulders back and her chin up. She seemed four inches taller and three years older.

'Got any fags?' she asked.

'I didn't know you smoked,' said Lilly.

'I can trade 'em later.'

Lilly regarded Kelsey for a second. 'The men who came with Max to your house, tell me what they looked like.'

'Most of 'em just came the once and I didn't pay no attention,' said Kelsey. 'Only one was round our place a lot. He made so many films his house must have been like Blockbusters.'

'Could you describe him?'

'No,' Kelsey answered quickly. 'Mum never let me see him.'

It was a blow. The suspect possibly narrowed down to one, and Kelsey wouldn't be able to identify him.

'Can you remember anything about him?' asked Lilly.

Kelsey shook her head. 'Mum made me stay upstairs with the babies. She didn't want them wandering down and seeing that lot.'

'Perhaps you heard something?' asked Lilly.

Kelsey nodded. 'I'd say he were posh, not from round our way.'

'Did your mum ever say anything about him? Call him by name?' Lilly persisted.

'Nah,' said Kelsey, 'but I think she might have known him, and not just through Max. She hated him, said he was pure evil.'

'What he did was vile,' said Lilly.

362

'It was more than that. She acted like he'd done something to her, like it were him, not Max, she were scared of.'

The car park outside The Bushes was full and Lilly parked in the neighbouring street, intrigued to know what was going on. The children had very few visitors apart from their social workers and solicitors. They had congregated on the corner, sitting on a road sign, smoking weed, unimpressed, it seemed, by whoever had descended upon their home.

Lilly waved at Charlene, who stood slightly apart from the others. She greeted Lilly with a one-finger salute and turned her back.

Miriam answered the door.

'I came to give you an update on Kelsey, but I see you've got your hands full,' said Lilly.

Miriam checked over her shoulder that no one was listening. 'It's an inspection. All the units are getting one, apparently there's going to be some sort of inquiry.'

'Good,' said Lilly. 'Maybe they'll work out you're underfunded and understaffed.'

'It's more likely they'll spot the float is two pounds short and I'm behind with my paperwork.'

Lilly chuckled. 'I'll leave you to it.'

As she walked back to her car something tickled the edge of her brain like a half-memory. She retraced her steps to the corner, now abandoned by the kids, who were no doubt pestering Mrs Patel in the off-licence for cigarettes and cider. She stood for a while, not knowing what she was trying to see, then it came to her and she read the street name aloud.

'Bluebell Close.'

Kelsey's visitor lived at Bluebell Close – The Bushes. Now which girl there would be stupid enough to get mixed up with the likes of Max? Lilly sighed, she had just discovered her mystery porn star.

Sam packed the dishwasher and Lilly smiled through gritted teeth. The approaching school trip to Austria had mined a rich seam of helpfulness in her son, which was a mixed blessing at best.

Lilly winced as he emptied half a bottle of rinse aid into the salt well and punched the button for a hot wash.

The machine groaned. Sam punched again.

'Not so hard, big man,' pleaded Lilly.

Another groan, accompanied by a dying shudder.

'I didn't break it,' said Sam.

This time it was Lilly who groaned and stuck her head into the belly of the beast. She tugged at a teaspoon that seemed to be lodged in the filter. When it came away it brought with it the filter and a year's worth of sweet corn.

The doorbell rang and Sam jumped to his feet. 'I'll get it.'

Lilly hoped it was Miriam. The woman had a spooky knack for fixing things.

'It's a lady,' said Sam.

'You didn't ask who she was or what she wanted, I suppose?'

Sam shook his head. 'I'll go and tidy my room.'

Lilly walked to the door carrying the sludge-coloured filter. The visitor was Sheba. She looked puzzled by the dripping piece of machinery in Lilly's hand but dived straight into what was obviously a well-rehearsed speech.

'I've spoken with Paul and he's quite right,' she said, her eyes following a small, ancient floret of broccoli as it fell from the filter and landed on Lilly's bare foot. 'We can't give up when things get a bit shitty, we have to see them through, so I'd like to carry on with my work with Kelsey, if that's all right with you?'

Lilly smiled as the words tumbled from Sheba's mouth. It was the first time she had seen her even remotely flustered. 'Are you any good with a wrench?'

Sheba followed Lilly through to the kitchen, tiptoeing over the trail of decaying vegetation.

'Help yourself to some wine,' said Lilly, and gestured with her head to the fridge. Sheba poured them both a glass of white while Lilly tried to refit the filter.

'You'd be better off calling a plumber,' said Sheba.

Lilly sidestepped, too ashamed to admit she was without funds for workmen. 'It looked easy when I started.'

Sheba picked up the Brand file, which Lilly had left on the table. 'Making any progress?'

Lilly decided upon brute force and pushed the filter with both hands. 'Two steps forward and one step back. Kelsey confirmed Max was using their home to make porn films, paedophile stuff. It was mostly the same man having sex with children and Grace was pretty scared of him.'

The filter made a shrill cracking sound before collapsing into two perfect halves. Lilly jettisoned them into the sink and slammed the dishwasher door. The crockery rattled nervously.

'He could be our man. Grace would have let him in without a struggle and he would have a motive to kill her if he found out she was threatening to grass.'

Sheba nodded. The wine had given her cheeks a pink, almost girlish glow. 'But that doesn't tell us why he mutilated the body.'

Lilly picked up her glass, her slimy hands leaving smears around the stem. 'Exactly. Is it possible that he likes children *and* cutting?'

'It's not common,' said Sheba. 'Studies show that most paedophiles aren't violent. When questioned about why they want to have sex with children they describe it as an orientation as opposed to a choice, much like being straight or gay. Those who commit murder generally do so to cover up what they've done, rather than to gain satisfaction.'

'So he's not likely to be our man,' said Lilly.

'It's not likely but it's not impossible. There are plenty of sites on the web dedicated to hurting children and women, and murderers such as Ian Brady certainly gained enjoyment from torturing their victims. Hurting and killing were as important as the sexual act in his pathology.'

They went into the garden for Sheba to smoke. Lilly was fairly liberal on the subject but Sam was a nicotine nazi and called in the SS to deal with anyone found lighting up within the castle walls.

Sheba gazed out into the fields beyond Lilly's garden. 'It's a lovely spot.'

The smell of lemon balm filled the night air.

'It needs a lot of work,' said Lilly, and kicked an old paving stone which immediately crumbled.

'I suppose a legal-aid lawyer's salary doesn't go far,' said Sheba, 'at least not around here. I dare say you could make it stretch back in Yorkshire.'

Lilly smiled. She'd considered moving back a thousand times. Sam would go to school with his half-cousins, Lilly would get a job in Leeds, and they'd live like kings.

'I left home at eighteen and I've never been back except for births, deaths and marriages. I've lived more of my life in the south and Sam has only ever lived here.'

'But you don't fit in,' said Sheba. It was not meant to be hurtful or critical, just a bald statement of the facts as she saw them.

'I can't think where I would,' said Lilly.

Sheba exhaled slowly. 'My father was a Polish Jew who came to England after the war. He married my mother, a good East End girl, and had two strange-looking children. As a child I would wail that I was neither Eastern European nor a cockney. "I don't belong," I'd yell, "I'm not one thing or the other." And my father would always answer in exactly the same way. "Bathsheba, just be yourself." She flicked her cigarette into the hedge. 'Now let's get on with some work.'

They fanned the case papers out and reread every sheet. Sheba made meticulous notes with a silver-ink pen. Lilly chewed the end of a pink felt-tip.

'There's another problem with my theory,' said Lilly.

'Just the one?' asked Sheba.

'If the man in the films did kill Grace to keep her quiet, then how did he know she intended to say anything? I can't believe Max told him. He wouldn't want to admit to a chink in his armour, but who else knew?'

Sheba returned to the papers and pushed one sheet across the table. It was the letter Grace had written to her MP.

CHAPTER EIGHTEEN

Thursday, 24 September

The Winnie Mandela Community Centre shared its time with Tiny Town Tumble Tots, Over-55s First-Aiders and a Thursday morning session of Bums and Tums.

Lilly had never been to an MP's surgery and had expected something grander.

There was no appointment system, just a list on a clipboard to which you added your name on arrival.

Lilly took her place in the queue in a grey corridor. The woman in front leaned heavily against the wall, her wheezing punctuated by short blasts from the inhaler she kept permanently in her hand. She wore a man's shirt pulled tight over her pregnant belly, the sleeves rolled up in thick folds above her elbows.

'This weather ain't doing me any favours,' she said, rubbing her bump.

When her name was called she dragged herself into an upright position and lumbered through the door, her shoulders heaving the beat to some asthmatic dance. Seconds later she emerged with a smile.

Before Lilly could ask what instantaneous magic the politician had spun, her own name was called.

Hermione Barrows spoke without looking up from the note she was finishing.

'Could you tell me your full name?'

'Lilliana Valentine, I'm the solicitor for Kelsey Brand.'

Hermione put down her pen and appraised Lilly quizzically, no doubt comparing her to the rain-drenched swamp monster as seen on TV. She stretched out her hand.

'You look very different in real life.'

Lilly took the hand in her own and noticed that Hermione, although elegantly dressed in oatmeal-coloured trousers and crisp cotton shirt, was less slick without professional makeup. She seemed much older, much more tired. 'So do you, Mrs Barrows.'

Hermione's hand flew to her cheek. Lilly had hit a nerve.

'If you've come to berate me about my campaign, Miss Valentine, then you've wasted your morning. I stand by what I said, though of course I am sorry it transpires your client is ill.'

'It's a shame you don't focus on our shameless system that has mentally ill children locked away,' said Lilly.

'I intend to, Miss Valentine.'

'You mean the inquiry.'

Hermione raised an eyebrow that seemed thin without the brown pencil to give it substance.

'You're very well informed, but I can't talk about that just yet, and something tells me that's not what you're here for.'

Lilly had already considered what would be the most efficient way to approach this. She figured Hermione would offer no information unless cornered, and so went on the offensive.

'Why didn't you tell the police you had had prior dealings with Grace Brand?'

She didn't know for sure that Hermione had not volunteered this information but her suspicion proved correct.

'Whatever makes you think I had any dealings with her?'

'You saw her here on September the third. If you check the list for that day I'm sure you'll find I'm right.'

Hermione opened a ring-binder and found the list. She traced the row of names with her finger, the nail painted the exact same colour as her trousers. 'Grace Brand, yes, she was here. How strange that I never put two and two together.'

Too strange, thought Lilly.

'Let me see what she wanted,' said Hermione and pulled out a notebook. 'I remember now, she'd made a number of applications to transfer her tenancy, which had all been turned down.'

Lilly tried to read Hermione's handwriting upside-down, realised she couldn't and decided to bluff it. 'She told you she was being threatened, that she and her children were in danger.'

'She said a great many things.'

'She told you she needed to escape from a paedophile.'

Hermione smiled. 'Her story was pretty wild.'

'You didn't believe her,' Lilly said.

'I asked her to substantiate her claims, which I think was reasonable in the circumstances.'

'Reasonable?'

'She was a drug addict and a criminal. I see quite a number and, believe me, they will say anything to get what they want. I can't take action without evidence.'

'Did she give you any evidence?'

'She said she would come back and prove to me that everything she was saying was true.'

'But she was dead before she got the chance.'

Lilly wondered if Hermione felt any remorse at having ignored Grace's plea and the chain of events that could have been averted. Probably not.

'I think the story was true,' said Lilly, 'and I think whoever was involved killed Grace. Did you tell anyone about your meeting?' she asked.

Hermione looked away. 'To my shame I did not.'

Lilly couldn't be sure, but for the first time during their meeting the MP seemed genuine.

Max watched the girl sitting next to him out of the corner of his eye. She was nervous but not frightened. That was good, very good.

'There's something for you in the glove compartment,' he said.

Charlene opened it and took out the gift. A fluffy toy dog with a pink diamante collar.

'I know you ain't a kid, but I saw that cute face and straight away I thought about you.'

She hugged it to her, beaming. 'I can put it in my handbag, like Paris Hilton does! Where are we going?'

'I got this flat where I do all my shoots.'

He let it sink in that he had another property. 'It ain't fancy but the light is perfect.'

'Will the man be there? The one who wants to put me in a film?' she asked.

'Definitely, so you have to be nice to him, baby, real nice.'

The Bushes was quiet when Lilly arrived. Most of the kids were watching MTV. Miriam made coffee and they settled in the empty kitchen.

'Did the powers that be pronounce you A1 and ship-shape?'

Miriam scowled. 'They'll send me their report in due course.'

Lilly helped herself to a biscuit. 'I went to see Hermione Barrows.'

Miriam's eyes widened.

'You'll be pleased to know she looks like crap in real life,' said Lilly, her mouth covered in crumbs.

'What did she say?' asked Miriam.

Lilly wagged a half-eaten coconut ring. 'That Grace *did* go to see her and *did* tell her all about what was happening at number 58, but she didn't do anything about it or tell anyone else.'

'Do you believe her?'

'I can't see why she'd lie.'

Miriam kissed her teeth. 'Were her lips moving? She's a politician, girl, it's second nature.'

'I've also worked out who visited Kelsey in prison.'

'You have been busy.'

'It was Charlene.'

'What has that girl got herself mixed up in? Let's go and talk to her.'

They looked in all the bedrooms but Charlene wasn't there, and she wasn't in the television room with the others.

'Has anyone seen Charlene?' asked Miriam above the din.

No one answered so she snapped off the picture with the remote. The ear-ripping hip hop was replaced by a cacophony of protests.

'Has anyone seen Charlene?' Miriam repeated

'I seen her go off in a car with some black geezer,' said Jermaine, and punched the programme back to life.

Earlier that day the man on the news had confirmed that Kelsey was back inside and Max was relieved. He loved Kelsey and that, but he needed her out of the way. He'd been back to the flat first thing and set up his equipment inside. It was not until he pulled up outside the stairwell that he wondered whether the girl would know whose house it was. Maybe she'd seen it on the telly and would recognise it. He watched her anxiously for any reaction and relaxed a little when he saw none.

Barrows' car was parked in his usual spot at the foot

of the stairs, which meant he was already inside. He preferred to get there first, which didn't bother Max, who was glad to spend as little time as possible doing the thing.

In thirty minutes, an hour at the most, he'd have a ticket to LA. He was on his way.

'You seem pleased,' said the girl.

Max hadn't realised he was smiling. 'Of course I am, baby, this is your moment and you're gonna shine like a star.'

He reached for a bottle of Bacardi Breezer lying on the back seat, took what looked like a swig himself and handed it to the girl. 'Dutch courage.'

She giggled and put it to her lips, unaware of the valium he'd slipped inside.

Lilly set off before Miriam had even fastened her seat belt, and they shot across town. It was a busy lunchtime at the Clayhill Estate and women trudged along the dirty pavements, their bags bulging with produce from the market. Young men huddled in packs, many with their hoods up despite the heat.

The sight of an eight-year-old Mondeo with its bumper hanging off, careering along at seventy, caused barely a blink.

Lilly slammed on the brakes next to an equally ancient BMW parked at the bottom of the stairwell. She jumped out without locking the door and vaulted the stairs two at a time. She could hear Miriam breathing heavily close behind. She stopped outside number 62, her view of the Brands' flat obscured by a pillar, and cursed Mrs Mitchell and her half-truths. Then she ran to the end where the walkway bore right. She stopped in her tracks so suddenly that Miriam ran right into her.

There was Max opening the door to number 58, his arm around Charlene's shoulders, steadying her as she swayed.

'Get over here now, Charlene,' Lilly shouted.

Both Max and Charlene looked up. Lilly saw Max recognise her instantly, but Charlene seemed to take a moment to focus.

'You can't tell me what to do,' said Charlene, her voice fuzzy around the edges.

'Do as you're damn well told, the police will be here any minute,' Lilly answered, her voice steely.

Charlene turned to Max, who gave the tiniest nod of his head, and she walked away from him, each step becoming more of an effort.

When Miriam had got Charlene secured around the waist Lilly turned back to Max, who hadn't moved.

'I know what you do.'

He smirked, sending a fearful tingle to the base of her skull. She remembered his face inches from hers, leering at her when he had pulled her into the flat.

'You know nothing,' he said.

Jack McNally stood outside The Bushes with his hands on his hips. His scowl confirmed he was unimpressed with Lilly's behaviour. 'You should have called the police.'

It took both Lilly and Miriam to drag a flaccid Charlene out of the car.

'I did,' said Lilly, 'I called you.'

Jack threw his hands skyward. 'Not until it was over. Jesus, he could have killed you.'

Charlene's head lolled from side to side and her knees buckled.

'Are you going to stand there wagging your finger, or give us a bloody hand?' said Lilly.

He mumbled something Lilly assumed she wasn't supposed to catch and lifted Charlene, fireman-style, over his shoulder. The girl moaned from the very pit of her stomach and vomited down his back.

Having dumped Charlene unceremoniously onto her bed, Jack removed his shirt and swiped at it with a wad of toilet paper.

'Have you been working out?' asked Lilly in her best Californian accent.

'Is that what you say to that barrister fella of yours?'

Lilly reddened. 'He's not *my* anything.'

Jack balled the tissue paper and threw it at the bin. It missed and stuck to the wall with a wet thump.

'Nice,' said Lilly.

Jack tried not to smile but it hovered on the edge of his lips. 'You owe me a drink.'

'Why don't I cook you a meal?'

She'd spoken without thinking and instantly regretted how forward it sounded.

She tried to backtrack. 'I mean if you'd like to, if you're not too busy or whatever.'

He gave up hiding his smile. 'I'll come around after my shift.'

Barrows remained hidden in number 58 for at least an hour. He had heard the shouting from the perfect darkness of the bedroom and expected the police to arrive at any moment. When they hadn't shown up he'd sat in the grotty room ruminating on what had taken place.

As time wore on his fear turned to anger and, later, to cold fury. Someone had found them out and dared to stand in the way. Her voice was familiar but he couldn't place it.

He'd called Max and demanded they meet. True to form, the black man was reluctant, whining about getting away. Barrows had pointed out that he still had Max's means to do just that in his pocket, which had, predictably, changed the other man's mind.

Barrows unlocked the clinic, aware that he was taking risks. His hunger was making him reckless and stupid.

But no, he'd worked this all out. Hermione thought he was playing ten-pin bowls with a bunch of closet poofs, everything was under control.

'I don't know why you want to see me,' said Max. 'It's over.'

Barrows shook his head. 'Nothing is over until I say so.'

'If Charlene talks we're knackered,' said Max.

Barrows put up his hand. 'What will she say? That nice Mr Hardy was going to introduce her to a man who was going to make her a star. No crime has been committed.'

Max looked wildly around the room as if searching for something to allay his fears. Barrows would need to act with care. He patted his empty pocket.

'I have your plane ticket right here. You can call the airline tonight and reserve yourself a seat.'

Barrows assumed correctly that Max had never flown before and had no idea that flights could not be booked on such little information. The stupid man probably didn't have a passport. 'It's business class, of course.'

Life had taught Barrows that no amount of nonsense was too much when selling something that a person already wants. Each exaggerated detail only served to further justify. Reality had no place in the lives of the self-deluded. They wanted – no, needed – the lies, and Max was no exception.

'That woman, the solicitor, is fucking everything up,' Max muttered.

So that's who she was. Barrows remembered seeing her on the television. 'She's nothing,' he said. 'A minor inconvenience. You can't let her stand in the way of your dreams.'

Max nodded and looked at Barrows' pocket. There was a longing in his eyes that Barrows might have found pitiable if he hadn't been so disgusted. The pathetic, like the old and the disabled, had always repulsed him.

Lilly sang at the top of her voice in the shower and

dragged a blunt razor across her armpits. It stung like hell but Brucie's wig had to go. She flung open the curtain and looked at herself in the mirror. Excitement and hot water had flushed her cheeks with a healthy glow.

When two walkers meandered through the field at the back of the house she couldn't resist a cheery wave. They seemed startled by the red-faced mad woman jiggling her breasts in their direction and hastened their pace.

She was still laughing when she headed to the kitchen to check the goat's cheese tart she had thrown in the oven before her shower. The air was full of tangy promise when the bell rang.

'Something smells good,' said Jack, 'and I know it's not me.'

She handed him a cold beer, which he rolled across his forehead before taking a long and grateful swig.

When he spoke it was with his mouth around the bottle, his words whistling down the neck. 'Charlene won't talk, you know.'

'Have you spoken to her?' Lilly asked.

'Don't need to.'

Lilly knew he was right, and piled salad leaves on two plates and placed slices of tart alongside. The dark green against the creamy white of the cheese appealed to Lilly's aesthetic sense of opposites attracting and complementing each other. Christ, she thought, I have gone far too long without sex.

'I expect he's been grooming her for weeks. She's probably pissed off that I spoiled everything by turning up,' Lilly said.

She watched him take a bite of the tart. She knew it was good but she also knew he was wondering if there'd be any seconds. She waited till he'd devoured the plateful.

'That was delicious,' he said.

Lilly whisked away his plate and whispered in his ear. 'Don't worry, that was the starter.'

'Thank Christ for that.'

After two helpings of green curry, which fizzed with lemongrass and fresh ginger, they made their way to the living room. Lilly sat at one end of the sofa and Jack at the other. There was a substantial gap between them but he could easily have chosen another chair.

'There's ice cream,' she said.

'I'm stuffed.'

'It's home-made.'

'I couldn't.'

'It's chocolate.'

Without warning he leaned over to kiss her. The sudden lurch startled Lilly and instinctively she drew her head back.

'I'm sorry,' he said, his voice loaded with embarrassment.

'Don't be,' she replied.

Jack was visibly cringing. 'I misjudged the situation. I'm an idiot.'

Lilly laughed, edged along the sofa and touched the side of his face. 'I don't think so.'

She kissed him on the lips briefly, almost fleetingly, hardly a kiss at all.

'Right then,' he said.

'Right then,' she answered, and kissed him again.

He pushed her back against the sofa, his full weight on top of her. Lilly felt breathless, giddy. Within seconds they were partially undressed.

'I'm going too fast,' said Jack, 'I'm sorry.'

What could she say? Actually, she loved it when a man skipped the small talk and foreplay.

He sat up and smoothed down his T-shirt. 'Chocolate ice cream sounds good.'

He loped to the kitchen, zipping up his flies. Lilly closed her eyes. Dessert had not been part of her immediate plan. She should follow him now and demand uncompromising sex, or at least a return to their previous position.

She peeped around the kitchen door. 'Wanna bring two spoons for that?'

But Jack had not even got to the fridge. He was leaning with both hands against the counter, his head down.

'Jack?' she said, and moved closer.

He didn't move, transfixed by what was in front of him. It was Kelsey's file.

'You shouldn't be looking at that,' Lilly whispered, more afraid than outraged.

He turned slowly and looked at her, his eyes full of incredulity. Slowly he held up the letter from Kelsey to her mum. 'You knew she'd done it all along.'

Lilly shook her head. 'It doesn't say that.'

'It's as good as a bloody confession. When the jury see that . . . '

Lilly interrupted. 'They won't see it.'

Jack was indignant. 'I'll take it to the CPS myself.'

'It's protected by client confidentiality.'

He laughed but it was hollow. 'I suppose you've been having a good giggle about this with your pal, Jez.'

'You'll never know how far from the truth that is.'

He pointed at Lilly, his face contorted. 'You've had me running around, trying to pin this rap on someone else.'

'It's not like that.'

'Yes,' he said sadly. 'Yes, it is.'

He swept past her, knocking both the letter and the ice cream onto the floor.

When Lilly heard the slam of the door she sat next to the sticky puddle and cried.

Lilly drank the rest of the wine and crawled to bed at two. She fell into an uneasy sleep filled with images of Kelsey and, of course, Rochene. The dream stopped when it always did and Lilly awoke with her own tears soaking her pillow.

She tried to resist playing out the terrible scene but tonight it was futile. She didn't have the strength.

Rochene couldn't breathe. The walls around her closed in. She sang the songs her granny had taught her, the old songs passed down for hundreds of years.

'Shut the fuck up,' someone screamed from another cell.

Her solicitor said it would only be for a few days, that she'd have her out as soon as she could. Rochene had believed her. She seemed so nice with her curly red hair, and other travellers she knew had used her before. They trusted her and so had Rochene. But it had been nearly two weeks now.

Rochene sobbed silently until she could cry no more. Finally, when she was drained, she placed each of her belongings in a neat pile, the clothes folded, pencils returned to their case, toiletries wiped clean.

Lilly imagined the girl nodding, a smile of satisfaction tickling her mouth before she took a pair of jeans meticulously cut in two and hung herself.

CHAPTER NINETEEN

Friday, 25 September

The weather broke and autumn arrived. Fresh air ran through the countryside like a blood transfusion. The population breathed a collective sigh of relief and shook their heads in faux dismay.

'*That's the summer gone then.*'

Lilly barely registered the drop in temperature and stood in the kitchen rubbing her bare arms.

'What's up, Mum?' asked Sam.

How could he understand? The only decent man she'd met since David was gone. The relationship was dead before it was born, over some stupid kid who probably murdered her mother.

'Nothing, big man.'

And there it was. The starkness of it frightening, yet crystal in its simplicity. Kelsey probably *had* killed Grace. The letter *was* a confession. The neighbour had seen her. Kelsey had lied about her voice and probably a lot of other things too. How could Lilly have been so stupid? She had been so desperate to evade the demons of a case from the past that she had failed to evaluate the details of the one in the present.

Up at Manor Park, the mothers were ahead of the game. The linen suits had been replaced by fitted trousers and shearling jackets from Boden. Only Lilly had failed to check in with the three-day forecast and still sported a vest top and goose bumps.

Penny waved. 'Hi Lilly.' She was gorgeous in a tan waistcoat, breathless with excitement. 'I've got my first meeting today.'

Lilly was irritated. How was she supposed to know what this woman did from day to day?

'Meeting with who?'

Lilly's tone clearly stung Penny. 'Social services. They're going to take me through the steps to becoming a foster carer. I can't wait to meet my first child.'

Lilly glowered. 'They're not pets, you know. These kids have problems. They set fires, wet themselves and nick anything that's not nailed down. I've one client who likes to masturbate at the dinner table with her chicken nuggets and another who keeps his shit in a shoebox under his bed. A few cuddles and a bedtime story won't make it all go away.'

Penny turned on her heel. 'I didn't for one moment think it would.'

Lilly sighed. She had been grossly unfair and would have gone after Penny to apologise, but she was already late for her next appointment.

Max sat in his car and waited. He was edgy, given what

he was about to do. Who wouldn't be? He scissored his knees and rapped the ring on his middle finger against the window. He had spent the night in a friend's flat on the north side of the estate. Well, not really a friend, just some guy he knew around the Clayhill. They'd clubbed together to buy ten grams of coke and spent the first part of the night washing it into stones, planning to at least double their outlay.

Max had used the rest of Barrows' money but he hadn't been worried, the profit margin on crack was huge. This way he wouldn't need to take the plane ticket. Fuck it, he'd buy one himself.

He couldn't remember when they'd agreed to toot the first one but it had seemed like a good idea. The merchandise needed testing.

By five in the morning the stash was almost gone, and Max was so wired he punched his friend in the mouth. His hand was numb from the drugs and he'd felt nothing when his fist connected, but the sickening squelch and the arc of blood told Max the blow had been a hard one.

He'd taken the remaining rocks and left his friend dribbling obscenities and spitting out teeth.

When dawn arrived Max had an empty wallet and bruised knuckles. With so much stimulant in his system he hadn't a prayer of getting any sleep. Most users took opiates to help with the comedown but Max wouldn't touch brown on account of what it had done to Gracie. Instead, he circled the estate over and over, his mind galloping in time with his step.

Got to get away. Got to get away. Got to get away.

He needed that plane ticket but there was only one way to get it. Barrows. Charlene.

But how could he put them together with the redhead around?

He couldn't let anyone stand in his way.

At nine he'd called the bitch's office and had been told Miss Valentine would be out all morning on a prison visit. It didn't take a genius to work out who she was going to see, so he decided to get there before her.

He thought he'd just scare her. Make sure she saw him following her. After the business in Gracie's flat it might see her off, stop her interfering.

Now, as he watched her car pull into the car park, he wasn't so sure that would be enough.

Lilly had thought about it long and hard. She'd wrestled with her conscience and weighed the options. Eventually she came to the conclusion that she could no longer represent Kelsey. The kid would be gutted and Miriam would probably never speak to her again. Word would spread and Lilly's practice would be decimated, but it was still the right thing to do. She could not do a good job when she had serious doubts about Kelsey's guilt. She deserved to be represented by someone who believed in her, not a doubting Thomas.

As Lilly pulled into Parkgate she rehearsed what she intended to say.

'I'll ensure you get another brief immediately, and of course you'll keep Jez and Sheba. I have a meeting with them this afternoon when I'll sort it all out.'

She walked to the passenger side to collect her papers. Although phones had to be turned off inside she slid her mobile into her jacket pocket where it stood less chance of being stolen.

'I know you're upset and that's understandable, but please believe me that this is for the best,' said Lilly, still practising her spiel.

'Talking to yourself is the first sign of madness.'

Lilly couldn't see the speaker but she felt his presence close behind her and instantly recognised his voice. She looked around the car park for help, but as usual it was desolate.

She forced herself to remain calm. 'What do you want?'

'For you to do what I tell you.'

Lilly felt her throat begin to freeze and swallowed hard, forcing the airway to stay open.

'And if I refuse?'

She heard his breath crackle and felt something hard pressing into the small of her back.

'If you refuse I'll finish what I started that night in Gracie's flat.'

Max guided her to his car with his right arm, his left keeping the pressure of his knife firmly in place. Lilly gauged the distance to the prison entrance. It would take less than a minute if she went at full pelt, but could she outrun Max? One glimpse of her captor told her that if she couldn't he would kill her instantly. His eyes were bloodshot and she had been around enough addicts to recognise the smell of crack on his clothes.

He opened the door of a familiar BMW, pushed her

into the back seat and got in beside her. Her bowels lurched when she saw rope and duct tape on the floor.

'What are you going to do?' she asked.

'Shut up,' he said.

He tied her hands together and ripped off a single piece of tape with his teeth.

'Please don't,' she begged. 'I won't speak, I won't make a sound.'

Max shook his head and placed it over her mouth. 'I'd like to believe you, but you women just can't help yourselves.'

He pushed her sideways so her hands were trapped beneath her and her cheek rested against the old leather of the seat.

Lilly was concentrating so hard on breathing that they had driven a few miles before she realised she had wet herself.

Max rubbed his cheek. His skin felt alive, like ants were moving under the surface. He told himself it was just the comedown from the drugs. After all, he had caned it last night.

And yet it seemed more than that. His dreams were imploding, and without them what had he got? No family. No Gracie. Nothing. Nothing at all.

He shot the solicitor a glimpse. Even now when he had her cornered she was lying there like butter wouldn't melt. Like she was in control.

He could see in her eyes that she thought he was scum, that he was stupid. He saw the same look on Barrows' face every time they met.

Well, they'd both got it wrong and Max would show them just what he was made of.

Lilly caught him looking at her, his eyes sly, furtive. She tried to seem calm, in control, and hoped he couldn't smell the urine that burnt her legs.

In films the victim of a kidnap has to try to remember significant things about their journey so that they can work out where they have been taken, but Lilly couldn't even have guessed how long she'd been on the back seat, her cheek bumping rhythmically against it.

For minutes, maybe hours, Lilly concentrated solely on breathing, terrified that she would pass out, the adrenalin pumping through her and making her dizzy. At last she forced herself to take note of her surroundings. How could she formulate a plan to get out of this if she didn't even know where she was?

She was disorientated both by fear and her position, but she was sure she was still on a main road. She could hear other cars, and Max slowed and quickened as if in traffic. She could only see the top of things, office blocks and lampposts. Where on earth was she? Where was Max taking her?

Lilly tried to ease her head up to get a better view but it was impossible. She pushed down on her hands but they had lost all feeling. She was about to give up when a bus pulled alongside. Inside she could see a man in the window seat reading a paper. Behind him two girls giggled and whispered to one another behind their hands. If Lilly could see them they must be able to see her if only they would look down. She urged the man to turn from the news and look to his right, willed the girls to notice a handsome boy passing on a cycle and at the same time to notice the woman bound and gagged only feet away.

Her instinct was to shout but the tape muffled every sound.

If she kicked hard against the glass might they hear it? Probably not above the sounds of the street with its cars, sirens and road works. Still, she had to try.

She shuffled onto her back and tucked in her knees, preparing to push her feet upwards.

'Don't even think about it,' said Max, and flashed the silver of his knife.

Lilly sank back into the seat. Soon the office blocks became tower blocks and Lilly realised where Max was taking her.

He didn't know where he was going until he pulled up outside the flat. Then it seemed obvious. This was where it had all started to go wrong for Max, and this was where it had to end.

At the top of the stairs Lilly willed Mrs Mitchell to be keeping guard and turned her head to display the tape. Surely she'd realise Lilly was in trouble.

Max emitted another low crackle as if his throat were raw. 'Unlucky. The nosy bitch ain't in.' He opened the door to Grace's flat. 'Her old man snuffed it last night and she's down the morgue.'

Until that moment Lilly had been cold, unable to take in what was happening, but the thought of that tiny old man, whose last years had been spent as a prisoner, a hostage to both his body and his bitter wife, was unbearable. Her shoulders began to heave in silent sobs and soon her eyes began to fill. Not long behind her eyes came her nose, suddenly blocked by thick streams of mucus, and her sadness turned to panic as she realised she couldn't breathe. She snorted hard but this seemed only to push the blockage deeper.

She opened her mouth to scream but her lips were sealed.

When Max pushed her inside the flat she fell to the floor, gyrating, her body racked by convulsions as she tried to fight for air.

'Stop it, woman,' shouted Max, but Lilly couldn't. Like a fish pulled from the sea she lay on the deck fighting only herself.

When her head repeatedly banged against the skirting board Max bent over her and pulled off the tape with a vicious flick of his fingers and stuck it to his sleeve.

'What the fuck are you doing?' he shouted, but Lilly could only gulp in the air in greedy rasping mouthfuls.

He cut the tape around her hands with one vicious swipe of his knife and pinned her arms above her head.

'What the fuck are you doing?' he repeated.

She lay on her back until her breathing became steady, with Max straddled across her. When her chest quietened she looked up into the face of her kidnapper and saw that he was out of his mind.

'Why did you have to stick your nose in, get involved in stuff that ain't got nothing to do with you?' he asked. 'You should have let me alone, let things be.'

His face was inches from hers, in a twisted version of the position she had been in with Jack less than twenty-four hours ago. Horror seeped through her. She literally felt it start in her toes and worm its way upwards, burrowing into every cell, leaving its paralysing poison. Lilly knew that if she didn't do something before it reached her chest she would pass out or lie there immobile while Max cut out her heart.

Lilly's body became rubber, unresponsive, and Max's nostrils began to flare like a wild bull. She sensed herself on the precipice without any idea of what to do next, but commanded herself to stay calm.

They say that in the moment before death your whole life flashes before your eyes, a seamless sequence of events that make perfect sense. Lilly experienced nothing so cerebral. Instead she could smell the soft caramel of her son's head and feel the warmth of his cheek on her lips.

If she'd known she was going to die like this she would have done it all so differently. She would have stayed with David and ignored his affairs. It would have hurt like hell but Sam would have had his father with him instead of competing for attention with a pampered anorexic. She needn't have worked so the poor kid could have had his mum at home like the rest of his friends instead of being shunted from pillar to post like an unwanted parcel. *Oh Sam, if only I'd known. If . . .*

Laughter rang out in another room. It was so familiar. What on earth was Sam doing here? No, not Sam, but Elsa. Lilly could hear her mother laughing.

'Oh my girl,' said the familiar voice in the distance. '*If ifs and buts were apples and nuts we should never go hungry.*'

Lilly almost laughed too.

Elsa's voice was muffled inside Lilly's head. '*Down there for dancing, up here for thinking.*'

'And use your mouth for everything else,' said Lilly.

'What?' said Max, momentarily snapped out of his own private nightmare.

Lilly strained to hear her mother. 'Use your mouth, my girl, keep him talking.'

Lilly understood and looked deep into the eyes of her tormentor. 'Tell me about Grace.'

Max threw back his head and grimaced. Lilly thought he might howl uncontrollably but instead he spoke softly. 'I told her again and again to leave things as they were, but you and her are just the same, you won't listen.'

'Oh my God,' whispered Lilly, 'it was you. You killed her.'

Max laughed. 'Is that what you think?'

'You had the most to lose. She couldn't stomach the paedophile stuff any more and she threatened to report you.'

'She'd never have grassed me to the old bill. Not Kelsey. Not Grace.'

'No, but she did tell her MP.'

Lilly saw he was genuinely surprised. 'What a bitch. She deserved all she got,' he said.

Lilly wondered for a split second why she was discussing what had happened to Grace with this psychopath, but a part of her realised that he was less likely to kill her while he was talking, and part of her still needed to know what really had happened.

'If you didn't know what she'd done, why did you kill her?' she said.

He came close enough to kiss her and she could feel his breath on her mouth.

'I didn't kill Grace.'

Lilly once again looked deep into his eyes, their gaze so intense they could have been lovers. She wanted to believe him, thought she did believe him.

'So who did?'

Max jerked himself from the moment. He let go of her arms, leaned back and the connection was lost. 'I ain't got the faintest idea.'

'Sure you do, Max. You say it wasn't you and I don't think it was Kelsey.'

He sniffed and shrugged his shoulders. 'Could have been anyone.'

'I think you know. It's the other person with most to lose, the other person who wouldn't like Gracie to tell tales.'

Max furrowed his brow as if weighing this information then shook his head. 'Nah, it couldn't be him.'

Lilly assumed they were talking about the man in the films. The man Grace had been scared of. The man who'd hurt Candy. The man bank-rolling the whole thing. She could see by the cheapness of Max's shoes and the level of his addiction that he was not the driving force behind the pornography.

'That person isn't like you, he's sick in the head. You just want to make a few quid but he'll stop at nothing,' she said.

'That's true, but Barrows would never have the bollocks to do something like that.'

Lilly went to speak again but Max put his hand over her mouth, a childlike gesture that reminded her of Sam.

'Did you hear that?' he said.

Lilly shook her head, her chest once again contracting.

They listened together. Something was scratching the door.

'A dog,' said Max.

With a lightness of foot that came from nowhere, Max sprang to his feet and pulled Lilly by the hair from the hallway into the bedroom.

'Lie on the bed and say nothing.'

He pulled out his knife and went to the door. 'One sound out of you and I'll finish this.'

Shut in the bedroom, lying in the same spot that Grace had been butchered, Lilly was trapped. If she opened the window and screamed for help Max would kill her long before anyone on this estate glanced in her direction. Violence and screams were a way of life, part of the white noise of the estate.

She felt the pressure once again in the small of her back and could still feel the shape of the knife. It was a delusion, she knew, but no less terrifying for being all in her mind. Then she half-remembered putting something in her pocket, which was twisted beneath her and digging into her back. Lilly felt for the object hurting her spine. It wasn't a knife but her mobile phone.

Silently, she took it in both hands and brought it to her face, kissing it like a talisman. She couldn't risk even a whispered call, a text was her only option. She lifted her fingers to it but she was shaking so violently she dropped the phone onto the bed. Panicking that Max would return any second she placed the phone on the bed in front of her, then digit by excruciating digit she spelled out a message. When she was finished her hands trembled with such ferocity that she pushed the phone off the bed before she had pressed send.

Lilly almost cried out but bit down hard to silence herself. She could taste the blood from her tongue. She crouched at the side of the bed and patted the floor for the phone. Her fingers felt the scratch of worn nylon carpet. At last she found the familiar solidity of her lifeline and forwarded a text to the one person she knew she could trust with her life.

Jack retched into the toilet bowl. He had downed half a bottle of bourbon before midnight and spent the early hours bringing it back up.

He rinsed his mouth with a handful of tepid water and headed back to bed. Who would believe that he of all people would get himself into such a state, and over a bloody woman.

He turned his pillow and laid his cheek on the cool

cotton, ignoring the beep of his phone. It was a text and it could wait.

Five minutes later, Jack cursed himself for being the sort of man who couldn't ignore his messages even when he was dying.

AT 58 WITH M, PLEASE HELP

Jack groaned and rolled onto his back. Lilly was some piece of work. Even now, after the trauma of last night, she was working on the case with Miriam and expected his assistance. Some people just didn't know when to stop taking the piss.

Max muttered to himself, passing his knife from one hand to the other as he came back into the bedroom. The increase in tension was palpable. A slick of sweat glistened on his top lip.

This time the voice in Lilly's head was Miriam's, her tone calm and lilting, like waves lapping the shore.

'Keep him talking, girlfriend, keep him talking.'

'Was it a dog?' Lilly asked.

Max looked at her as if he had forgotten she was in the room and shrugged. He seemed dazed and distant, madness clouding his face.

'I know you and Grace were friends. That she meant a lot to you,' said Lilly.

He looked at her again as if unsure what she was doing there.

'I think she loved you, and the only reason you had words was because she was afraid for her kids.'

Max laughed. It was high-pitched, almost a giggle, and totally inappropriate. The laugh of a madman. It frightened Lilly more than the knife.

Please hurry, Jack.

Max sat on the end of the bed, his left hand resting the blade inches from Lilly's leg.

'They were good kids. Always did what they was told.'

'Did that include Kelsey?' Lilly asked.

He raised an eyebrow. 'She did what she had to and I loved her for it.'

'But the other man, he didn't love Kelsey or any of the others?'

Max grunted. 'He don't love nobody.'

Lilly's eyes darted to the door, willing Jack to burst through.

'He uses and abuses people, gets them to do what he wants them to do,' said Lilly

'He didn't make me do nothing,' said Max, his pride aglow even now.

Lilly kept her tone soothing as she tried to exonerate the monster before her, show him his way out, that none of this was his fault, that some other dude did it.

'But none of this was your idea, I'm sure of that.'

'He didn't make me do nothing,' Max repeated, as if to himself.

'But he suggested this, didn't he?' Lilly opened her arms. 'That you come and get me. You said yourself he's too much of a coward to do it himself, so he gets someone else to do his dirty work.'

Max whipped round to face her, hatred swelling in his eyes. He grabbed a thick fistful of red hair and pressed the knife against her cheek. Lilly held her breath.

'Nobody controls me. Not him, not Grace, not you,' he shouted.

She felt a sting as the sharp metal pierced the top layer of her skin.

'How do you think I got this far without a mind of my own?'

He was ranting now, the knife digging deeper and deeper into the fleshy mound of Lilly's cheek.

She didn't dare speak or move except to push her head into the bed away from the burn of his weapon. She felt the wet trickle of blood tickling her ear and closed her eyes.

'What's that?' said Max and flailed his arms.

Lilly swallowed hard in relief and followed the arc of the knife, now above her.

'The dog?' she said. 'Someone's bound to come looking for it, you should let me go now.'

It wasn't true, of course. Kids ran wild, unchecked, never mind dogs.

Max let out a sound so guttural he seemed more animal than man.

Lilly began to gabble. 'I won't tell anyone what you do. I'll leave you alone.'

In one deft movement he pulled the tape still attached to his sleeve and pressed it to Lilly's lips.

'You talk too much,' he said.

Again the scratching came at the door.

'I'm gonna cut its throat,' he said, and sprang from the bedroom.

Lilly touched her cheek and felt the skin wet and open. She heard the front door slam as Max stepped outside and knew she had only seconds to take action. Jack had let her down and she was on her own. As always.

Lilly didn't waste time on the tape but moved to the window. Maybe she could jump. It was awkward but she pulled hard at the frame. It was locked, the key hidden goodness knew where. Lilly looked around the room for something to smash the glass but the room was almost bare. She threw open the tiny wardrobe and snatched at a flimsy shirt. If she wound it around her hands she could break the window with her fists. With the lavender cotton acting as little more protection than a lace glove she readied herself to punch the glass, but as she pulled back her fists she looked out of the window. What was she thinking? Even if she smashed it there was a three-storey drop straight onto the concrete pavement below.

She darted instead to the bedroom door and opened it as steadily as possible. From there she could see down the hall to the front door. The dark figure of Max stood in front, visible but distorted through the frosted glass, his arms flailing in agitation over the poor dog that had inadvertently strayed onto the walkway and into this insanity. She heard barking and snarling, which could as easily have come from Max as the dog.

She fell to her knees and crawled on her belly down the hall, away from the bedroom and into the kitchen.

Max was outside, only feet away, so she kept her body pressed tightly to the wall.

Outside the howls turned to whines and Lilly imagined the dog bleeding to death, its life pumping out of it onto the walkway. She wondered how it would feel, that descent into darkness. Would she know she was dying?

When Max rattled a key in the lock Lilly knew she had to act. Using her elbows as leverage, she jumped onto the work surface and made for the window. As she heard Max's footsteps padding down the hall she pushed with all her might.

'Bitch,' he screamed when he saw she was missing, and crashed from Grace's room to the girls' room, then to the sitting room and the bathroom. Glass smashed against tiles, chairs shattered against the wall, and Lilly struggled with years of gloss paint binding the frames of the kitchen window together.

Lilly heard Max approach the kitchen, his fury increasing, and knew the window was not going to open. She took a breath, as deep as a diver's, and kicked at the glass with all her force. It cracked from top to bottom like the San Andreas Fault, like the magic mirror in *Snow White*. The wood splintered in a shower of off-white chippings but the window remained shut, the glass intact.

Lilly pulled back her leg for another kick when the kitchen door flung open, ripping itself from the hinges. Max stood in the gap, howling like a wolf.

A moment passed, no more than a heartbeat, but time seemed to stand still. Max fell silent and stared at Lilly up on the counter. Her leg stopped in mid kick and she stared back.

When he spoke his voice was as clear as water. 'I'm going to kill you.'

He leaped towards her, his arms grasping the air as she scrambled backwards along the counter, falling into the sink.

Then *boom*. Another door flew off its hinges. This time the front door. It landed, together with Jack, in a pile of shards. Max instinctively turned to the noise and Lilly immediately knew what to do. She reached along the windowsill and snatched the nearest hard object. Before Max could look back at her she swung it above her head, and with every bit of strength left in her arms she brought it crashing down on his skull. Max fell to the floor. Lilly looked first at his head, split above his ear, and then to the plant pot in her hand. She wiped off his blood and read the words 'To the world's best Mum'.

Jack helped her down to the floor with one hand and removed the tape from her mouth with his other. Lilly rubbed her torn lips. 'What kept you?'

'Is he dead?' Lilly asked the paramedic who was cleaning her cheek.

'Just resting,' he said. 'You're going to need a stitch in this. Do you want us to take you back with us?'

Lilly shook her head. She didn't think she could move from her spot at the top of the stairwell. 'I'll make my own way, thanks.'

She watched Jack on the street below, moving a handful of onlookers back so that the ambulance could get on its way. He climbed the stairs towards her and she tried to smile but it hurt too much.

When he came closer she noticed his pallor. 'You look like hell.'

'You're none too radiant yourself,' he said.

'I've been kidnapped and held at knifepoint, what's your excuse?'

'I hit the bottle and spent the night wondering what to do with my life.'

'Come to any conclusions?'

'None whatsoever.'

'Ouch.'

A burly nurse pulled the suture tight.

'Nearly finished,' she said, and dug the needle once again into the soft flesh.

Lilly closed her eyes and winced. What sort of train track was being laid?

'My God, it's the bride of Frankenstein.' Miriam poked her head around the cubicle curtain. The nurse tutted at her audience but didn't ask Miriam to leave.

At last she cut the thread and held up a mirror for Lilly to see. Although the skin was slightly raised, Lilly had to admit it was a very neat job. The nurse's sausage fingers had been unexpectedly deft.

'Wow,' said Lilly, 'you should have been around when I gave birth to my son.'

The nurse wrinkled her nose. 'I prefer to stay at the North Pole.'

The three women laughed.

* * *

Lilly confirmed once again that she was up to date with her tetanus jabs, collected one bottle of antibiotics and another of pain relief, and signed herself out of the hospital.

'I wouldn't have thought your job was so dangerous,' said the nurse.

'I'm getting a new one,' Lilly replied. 'Knife-thrower's assistant.'

The nurse gave a half-smile and went back to her needlework. Lilly headed out of the ward but took a right turn before the exit.

Jack was leaning against the vending machine at the hospital entrance, his arms crossed high on his chest. He didn't look at Lilly but fished deep into his pocket and pulled out a handful of coins, which she grabbed like a grateful addict. She fed the machine and a Kit-Kat took its dive to freedom, followed closely by a Mint Aero and some Milky Way Magic Stars.

'For Sam,' she muttered through a mouthful of chocolate, and made her way out.

Lilly was surprised to find it was still broad daylight. Somehow she thought the day had long since passed. Funny how major things can happen in such a short space of time. Earthquakes, plane crashes, murders, they all passed in minutes, less time than it took someone to wash their hair.

A brisk wind was gaining momentum. Lilly let the chill dance around her.

'What happened, Lilly?' asked Miriam.

'We don't need to talk about this now,' said Jack.

His tone was gruff, his body stiff. Clearly, he had not forgotten the letter.

Lilly wanted to speak but found she had nothing to say. She turned away and shivered.

From behind, Lilly felt the weight of Jack's jacket being placed over her shoulders. She pulled it around her, grateful for the comfort of Jack's familiar smell as much as its warmth. 'It's fine. I don't really know what happened. I arrived at Parkgate and he must have been waiting for me there, but I didn't see him until he put a knife in my back.'

'Jesus,' Jack muttered under his breath.

Lilly put her hand on his arm with the lightest of touches. He tried to force a smile and she left her hand there. 'He tied me up and took me to number 58.'

'What did he want?' asked Miriam.

Lilly paused. What *did* he want? 'He'd made a connection in his mind between me and Grace and kept saying we'd both tried to get in his way.'

Miriam opened her eyes wide. 'Do you think he killed Grace, after all?'

'He couldn't have,' said Jack. 'He has an alibi.'

'He could have got someone else to do it,' said Miriam.

Lilly opened the second bar of chocolate and popped half into her mouth. 'I don't think he had anything to do with it. He was genuinely shocked when I told him Grace had been to see her MP.'

She took a last bite and screwed the wrapper into a ball. 'Could you give me a lift to Lancasters?' she asked Jack.

'The pub?'

'Mmm,' Lilly said. 'I've a meeting with counsel and the shrink in there, and I'm late.'

Jack shook his head, but it was in resignation not refusal. 'You should rest.'

'I will.'

Jez and Sheba were settled at what had become their usual table. Unlike Lilly they seemed well at home in the smart surroundings, smoking Marlboro Lights and sharing jokes.

That morning Lilly had planned that this would be their last meeting, on this case at least, but now all thoughts of pulling out of the case were abandoned. For the first time in weeks she felt like her mother's daughter. She had seen off an armed attacker with a strength, both physical and mental, that had surprised her. It had been a glimpse of her inner resources, which she was sure could be further mined to help Kelsey. And there was something else, something tugging in her mind. Something she couldn't put her finger on.

When he saw her in the doorway Jez waved, his eyes cheery, but then looked puzzled at the sight of Miriam and Jack. When she got closer and he could see the fresh dressing on her cheek and her limp, he frowned in what Lilly took to be concern. She couldn't help feeling a little buzz at the thought that he might have feelings for her, however minuscule. All this power had definitely gone to her head.

'Something tells me there's been a development,' he said.

They listened intently as Lilly relayed the morning's

events, Jez shaking his head in disbelief, Sheba nodding hers in encouragement to continue the story.

Jez fixed Jack with a pointed look. 'You'll charge him this time.' It sounded like an imperative, not an enquiry.

Jack bristled at the unfairness of the statement. It hadn't, of course, been his fault that Max had walked last time, but Jez didn't know that.

'He's still in hospital at the moment. Jackie Chan here gave him quite a whack, but as soon as he's fit he'll be taken to the station and he's under police guard till then,' said Jack.

Jez nodded stiffly as if Jack's answer were just about good enough. 'And what about Grace's murder? Surely this points to him as the most likely suspect?'

The others answered as one. 'No.'

'He was in custody at the time,' said Jack.

'He didn't know Grace had spilled the beans,' said Miriam.

'He doesn't fit the profile,' said Sheba.

'Okay, okay,' said Jez, his arms open in surrender.

'I think it was the other man involved,' said Lilly.

'I thought we'd decided that wasn't likely,' said Sheba.

'But not impossible,' said Lilly. 'You said so yourself, and my only alternative is Kelsey and I'm not yet ready to give up on her.'

They all nodded, even Jack.

'But we're no nearer to finding out his identity than before,' said Sheba. 'All we know is that Grace seemed to know this man and, given her line of business, I suspect she knew more than one or two.'

Lilly smiled so broadly she felt her cheek smart. 'I know his name.'

Everyone turned to Lilly open-mouthed.

'Max said his name was Barrows.'

Barrows was silently drowning as the man from MI5 spoke. Hermione had always loathed the security services but conceded they were a necessary part of political life. They were supposed to protect the national interest, but since the days of Thatcher they had been used by each successive prime minister to protect the government from those who would harm it, not just by sarin gas or mortar attack, but also by rumour and scandal.

The man was thin and pale, his hair the colour of dirt, his features instantly forgettable. No wonder Hermione referred to them as spooks.

'What was the man's name again?' asked Hermione.

'Max Hardy, madam.'

Hermione shook her head and turned to her husband. 'It doesn't ring a bell with me. Could he be one of your patients, darling?'

Barrows was unsure what to do and it was a feeling he couldn't stomach. He dare not lie in case they'd already checked the clinic's records.

'I don't recall the name,' he said, 'but I've seen so many people over the years one doesn't remember them all.'

The spook nodded as if this were a perfectly reasonable answer.

Hermione poured some tea. She seemed a picture

of calm but the lid of the china teapot rattled, alerting Barrows that she was anxious. He assumed the other man had seen it too. They were trained for that sort of thing.

'What exactly has this person done?' he asked.

The spook set down his cup without the merest chink as it touched the saucer.

'He attempted to kill the solicitor for Kelsey Brand. Apparently it's not the first time.'

'That's awful,' said Hermione, 'simply awful. Perhaps he's one of these vigilante types.'

'Perhaps,' said the spook, and helped himself to a biscuit. 'But that still doesn't explain why the last call received by his mobile phone was from your husband.'

There was an uncomfortable silence punctuated only by the slight clicking sound of the spook's jaw as he chewed.

'Darling,' said Hermione, her voice shrill, 'didn't you have your mobile stolen last week?'

'Yes,' said Barrows.

'There we are, then,' she sang.

The spook finished his biscuit. As he swallowed Barrows watched his Adam's apple move conspicuously.

'There we are, then,' he repeated, and got to his feet. 'Of course we'll go through Mr Hardy's phone records for the past year or so. If we need anything more we'll be in touch.'

Hermione showed him to the door, but Barrows couldn't even get to his feet. When she came back she no longer looked nervous, her face was grey and stony.

'Hermione,' Barrows stammered, but she held up her hand to stop him.

'I thought I made it very plain that if you did anything to embarrass me, then this', she opened her arms, encompassing their home, their marriage, their life, 'would be over.'

He nodded and pulled himself to his feet. Though his legs felt leaden he forced himself to walk out of the room and out of the house. Hermione didn't even watch him go.

'The problem is,' said Jez, sloshing wine into five glasses, 'it's a pretty common name.'

'Did it come up in the case papers?' asked Miriam.

Lilly sighed. 'Maybe, but there are thousands of documents, it would take us forever to find it if it's there.'

Jez took a gulp of his wine and shook his head. 'Uh uh.' He reached into the slim black attaché case by Sheba's feet and pulled out a pristine ring-binder. Every sheet was hole-punched and aligned precisely, the edges littered with multicoloured tabs.

'My sister cross-references everything, and I'd be shocked if she hadn't a list of names mentioned in alphabetical order.'

Lilly was awe-struck.

'I have issues, okay,' said Sheba, and passed Lilly a long list of names.

Lilly ran her finger down the line. 'Bagshot, Bajari, Ball . . . Here it is, Barrows, page 199.'

Sheba flicked to the page and passed the file to Lilly.

It was a psychiatric report, not on Kelsey but on Grace during her time in care. Lilly checked the author.

'He worked in The Bushes years ago when it was a home for disturbed children,' said Lilly.

'Now it's a home for children with disturbed parents,' said Miriam.

'It was back then, but no one had the balls to say it,' said Jack.

'Let's not get sidetracked,' said Jez. 'Let's get back to the shrink.'

'What's his first name?' asked Sheba.

'William,' said Lilly.

Sheba threw her arms up and her head back. 'I met him once at a conference, he was jittery and smelled of sick. He used to be quite big in behavioural stuff in the early Eighties, but there was a whiff of scandal and he went into private practice.'

'What sort of scandal?' asked Lilly.

Sheba raised her eyebrows. 'They say he got too close to the children in his care, if you get my drift.'

'What happened to him?' asked Lilly.

Sheba shrugged. 'As I said, he went into private practice.'

'The bastard swept it under the carpet,' said Miriam.

'I wonder where he is now?' asked Lilly.

'Living a life of misery, I hope,' said Jez.

Sheba gave a hollow laugh. 'Sadly, men like that always bounce back. He's married to that politician with the cardboard hair.'

Lilly jumped to her feet, sending two glasses of chardonnay onto the floor. 'Sorry,' she called to the waitress as she hopped to the door, aware that Jack was only feet behind her.

Jack stood at the door to the clinic with a skeleton key. Lilly had always imagined a single pick-like implement with mythical powers and was disappointed to see a myriad of keys, from small to huge, but all unimpressively key-like, hooked onto a silver ring.

'This could take hours,' said Lilly.

Jack sifted through the keys and isolated a small brass one. 'Not if you know what to look for,' he said, and opened the door.

Lilly raised her eyebrows at him.

'Misspent youth,' he explained, and they made their way through the reception area.

'Strictly speaking, this is none of your business,' said Jack.

'The hell it's not,' said Lilly.

'I mean it's police business,' he said.

She took hold of his hand. 'Lucky I brought one along.'

From outside the clinic had seemed empty, but they could hear sounds from the room that seemed most likely to be Barrows' office. Jack put his finger to his lips and they crept to the door, then there was an almighty bang as Jack kicked it open.

'That's twice you've done that today,' said Lilly, pleased to find them both full of surprises. Not only was she the sort of woman who could kick some serious ass, the man she fancied beat down doors when the need arose. Who said the South made you soft?

414

Inside the office Barrows was nowhere to be seen, but his wife, Hermione, was behind his desk emptying a bottle of fluid into a bin full of videotapes.

Hermione looks up at the door. 'That was unnecessary.'

'Where is William Barrows?' asks Valentine.

'Such melodrama.'

Hermione's glare is cold, and so is her tone. She knows that everything is at stake. Her career, her marriage, her life.

She turns to the man. 'And who, may I ask, are you?'

'You know who I am,' says the solicitor angrily. 'And you know why I'm here.'

Hermione ignores the solicitor and smiles at the man.

He flashes his badge. 'Sergeant Jack McNally.'

This time the solicitor shouts, 'Where is William Barrows?'

'He's away,' says Hermione.

'Where?'

Hermione shrugs and looks at the videos that are sizzling and smoking in the bin. The acid has worked well and the tapes are all but melted, filling the air with heavy chemicals.

McNally puts out his hand. 'I'll take that, Mrs Barrows.'

She holds the bottle against her chest and hopes nothing leaks onto her beautiful cashmere sweater. 'Under what authority?'

'It's evidence that a crime has been committed,' he says.

'What crime?' asks Hermione.

Valentine becomes furious and snatches the bottle. She waves it in Hermione's face.

'Do you know what those tapes are? They're films of your husband having sex with little girls. He paid someone to find them for him, mostly from care homes, girls without families, girls without anyone to watch out for them, then he raped them.'

Valentine's voice cracks, no longer an angry shout but a strangled cry. 'And, not satisfied with that, he had someone get it all on film so he could enjoy what he'd done again and again and again.'

She stops to catch her breath, and McNally puts his hand on her shoulder. Hermione might almost find them sweet were she not so contemptuous.

'Must you really behave like a fishwife?' she asks.

'I think you need to come with me, Mrs Barrows,' McNally says.

'I think we should call your superior,' says Hermione, and punches the number into the telephone on William's desk.

'Yes.' The familiar voice of Bradbury comes over the squawk box.

'It's Mrs Barrows again,' Hermione purrs. 'I have one of your subordinates here, an Officer McNally. Please confirm to him what we were discussing earlier.'

'Jack, is that you?' asks Bradbury.

'Yeah.'

'Barrows didn't kill Grace,' says Bradbury.

'Of course he did,' Valentine shouts.

'Who the hell is that?' asks Bradbury.

'Never mind,' says Jack. 'How can you be sure?'

Bradbury sighs. 'Mr and Mrs Barrows were at a charity dinner for the NSPCC on the night Grace Brand was killed. Also present were the Chancellor and his wife, and the editor of a national newspaper. I believe Judge Blechard-Smith sat at their table.'

Valentine and McNally are shocked into silence. Hermione stifles a laugh. She is pleased to have taken control of the situation, but crowing is so unseemly.

'What about the tapes?' says McNally, but the edge has gone from his voice. 'She's destroyed the lot.'

'That's being dealt with at a higher level,' says Bradbury.

McNally guides Valentine away. She still hasn't spoken.

Bye bye, silly girl.

Lilly was still aghast when she got home. Jack had tried to impress upon her the futility of a confrontation about the tapes. Hermione Barrows was government, and his experience in Northern Ireland had taught him that what the government wants it usually gets. Justice, morality and the like came a very poor second to the 'bigger picture', whatever that might be at any given time.

'But you came here to escape all that bullshit,' she'd pointed out.

He gave a half-smile and dropped her back at Parkgate to collect her car.

'You okay to drive?' he'd asked.

Lilly had imagined how she must look, wounds at her throat and cheek, her foot swollen to twice its size.

'I'll keep her below ninety.'

Outside the cottage David was helping Sam unload something from the boot of his car. He did a double take when he saw Lilly's cheek.

'What on earth happened this time?'

Lilly evaded the question. 'Thanks for bringing him home from school.'

David looked at the ground. 'Actually,' he said, 'I'm collecting a few bits and taking him back to mine.'

Sam was also studiously avoiding her eyes and kicked at a stone that was lodged between two flagstones.

'Sam?' said Lilly.

'It's just for a few nights, Mum, while you're so busy and everything.'

She looked from David to Sam and back again, but neither could tear their eyes from their feet.

'What does Cara think about this new arrangement?' asked Lilly.

'She'll be fine,' said David.

'So she doesn't know,' said Lilly.

This time David did look up, and when he spoke his words cut through her. 'Sam's unhappy.'

They got in the car and drove away. Lilly stayed on the drive long after they'd gone, and long after she could make out the car in the distance, unable to get David's words out of her head. A bite was circling in the wind and it made Lilly shiver. Her cheek stung and she was tired, so very, very tired, but still she didn't go inside. She wondered if Grace had felt like this when the girls were taken into care. Did she stand on the walkway outside number 58, afraid to go back inside to the place she could no longer call home?

CHAPTER TWENTY

Saturday, 26 September

A navy blue sports holder containing Sam's football kit sat in the passenger seat next to Lilly. They had bought it together during the Easter holidays. It was the make preferred by the England team and Sam was determined to track one down. By the sixth shop Lilly was peckish and losing patience. Weren't these bags much of a muchness? Somewhere to sling your dirty boots and shin pads? Sam had looked at her with such a toxic mixture of disgust and pity that she had felt compelled to continue the dogged search. By three thirty, delirious with hunger, she harangued a young assistant with livid acne to call every shop in the same chain within a fifty-mile radius and had managed to secure the last one in a shopping centre in Watford.

Sam had paraded that bag like Donald Trump with his latest wife, savouring each ooh and ahh like fine champagne. Lilly had to admit that for the amount of kudos that bag had inspired it had been worth each painful minute in its pursuit.

Lilly was surprised that Sam had forgotten it. Maybe

it was a good sign. Maybe Sam hadn't been thinking straight when he'd asked to stay with his dad. Or maybe Sam didn't want it any more and was planning to shed his former life with his mum.

Whatever the truth, Sam would need it for this morning's match so Lilly drove to school.

How many times had Lilly prayed for silence during the morning school run, trying to navigate the country lanes and Sam's conversations, which twisted and turned irrationally.

'Let's listen to music,' she'd beg, but Sam would chatter over it, grinding Lilly's brain to pulp. She had never done mornings well.

'What's the capital of Mexico?'

'Do frogs' legs really taste like chicken?'

'What's the distance between the earth and the moon?'

'Is it better to be clever or kind?'

This morning there was nothing. Lilly could hear the engine, the tyres on the dirt tracks, the squeak of the cup holder when she took a bend. She had never felt so bereft.

She trudged towards the changing rooms, the bag slung over her shoulder, wondering whether she should just leave it on the bench and let it speak for itself or give it to him personally. She didn't want him to think she wasn't speaking to him but she didn't want him to think she was hounding him either.

'Now there's a glum face.'

Penny smiled. Her lips shone with a hint of pink that made her face quite lovely.

'I'm sorry about the other day,' said Lilly.

'Don't be. You were right in a way, I'm not cut out to care full-time for a damaged child, however much I might want to.'

'I didn't mean to put you off.'

'You didn't. We're going to provide respite care for a severely disabled child. Apparently his parents are just about holding up but are desperate for the occasional break.'

'That's fantastic,' said Lilly, and meant it.

'So what's going on with you? I saw Sam coming in with his dad earlier.'

Lilly held up the kitbag by way of explanation. 'He doesn't want to be with me any more.'

Penny let out a tinkle of laughter and hugged Lilly. 'Don't take it to heart. My parents separated when I was six and I spent my life doing the dance of the seven households. For most people the grass is always greener and kids are no different. A week of Dad's classical music and his girlfriend's mung bean curry and he'll be begging to come home.'

Lilly didn't feel as confident.

'Trust me,' said Penny, and hugged her again.

Lilly's mobile beeped to tell her she had a text.

'Oh to be in demand,' said Penny, and waved.

'If only,' said Lilly, and pulled out her phone.

JUDGE HAS LISTED CASE THIS PM. MEET US AT CCC. JEZ

The Old Bailey was cold. Whoever was in charge of maintenance hadn't noticed the change in the weather and the air-conditioning was still belting out.

The guards all wore their nylon security jackets, styled by some corporate guru in a bomber style. The look probably worked on the muscle-bound LAPD, but Group 5 Systems employed retired soldiers and disgraced coppers with healthy bellies and balding pates. Still, they were happy to be called into work at the weekend. 'Double time,' each one informed her.

At least someone's doing well out of this case, thought Lilly.

Sheba stood at the top of the stairs, a pencil skirt hanging low on her hips, Fifties style.

'What's up?' asked Lilly.

'Jez is trying to find out now. His clerk got a call to say we were all needed here, even Kelsey's being produced.'

Lilly let out a low whistle. 'Must be serious.'

Jez emerged from the judge's chambers, still in conversation with Brian Marshall. Jez was shaking his head in disagreement.

'Old Blechard-Smith is beside himself,' said Jez. 'Apparently he's a close personal friend of the Barrows and wonders what effect that might have on the case.'

'He'll have to recuse himself,' said Lilly.

Jez nodded. 'That's what he wants. This business is a total nightmare from his point of view, and he'd like nothing better than to hand it over to some other poor sucker.'

'So let him,' said Sheba.

'I'm not so sure,' said Jez. 'If he stays he'll bend over backwards to give Kelsey a fair crack of the whip.'

It made good sense. Once again Lilly was impressed by the barrister's tactics.

'He wants everyone's views in half an hour,' said Jez.

Lilly didn't need that long. 'He should stay,' she said, 'and he should make Hermione Barrows explain why she destroyed those tapes.'

Jez laughed. 'He's not going to do that, Lilly, but we can submit that Kelsey won't get a fair trial without the jury having the full picture, and ask him to chuck the case out now.'

'Will he go for it?' she asked.

Jez shrugged. 'Depends on what the prosecution say. Marshall's pretty jumpy but at the moment he's peddling the party line that William Barrows was not involved in Grace's murder so the tapes aren't pertinent to this case.'

'That's bullshit,' said Lilly.

At the far end of the atrium, outside courtroom four, Lilly made out the figures of Jack and Bradbury. She set off towards them.

Bradbury smiled. 'Miss Valentine.'

Lilly ignored him. 'Jack, will you tell the judge what happened yesterday and that you suspect William Barrows of Grace's murder?'

'Barrows has an alibi,' said Bradbury.

Lilly didn't take her eyes from Jack. 'If they can sweep what he did to those girls under the carpet they can set up an alibi.'

'That's quite a conspiracy theory,' said Bradbury.

'Why can't *you* tell the judge?' asked Jack.

'Because I'm too biased. But you, you're on the other

side, and if you think she didn't do it, he'll believe you.'

'And what if I think she did?' he asked. 'What if I don't know what to think?'

'Come down to the cells with me and speak to her. Look her in the eye and ask her yourself. If you have any doubts you should say so.'

'And if I don't?'

The spectre of the letter floated in the ether between them.

'Then you must do what you think is right.'

Jack looked at Bradbury. 'We need to know one way or the other.'

Bradbury closed his eyes as if in thought, then gave the slightest of nods.

The cells were even colder than the rest of the court, and Kelsey leaned against the wall, a rough brown prison-issue blanket wrapped around her shoulders. She jerked her head towards Jack and Bradbury. 'What are they doing here?'

'We need to talk about your mum,' said Lilly.

'Not in front of them we don't,' said Kelsey.

Lilly reached out to touch her client. The blanket was stiff and itchy in her hand. 'The whole thing's gone tits-up, love. We found out who the man in the videos is. Your mum met him when she was in care, he might even have abused her when she was a child.'

'Did he kill her?' Kelsey asked.

'We don't know. He's legged it.'

Kelsey pulled the blanket tighter. 'Then he must

have.' She finally looked at Jack. 'You thought I'd done it, didn't you?'

He wasn't in the habit of lying and sucked in a gulp of air. When he spoke his voice was steady. 'Yes, and if I'm honest I'm still not convinced that you didn't.'

The explosion Lilly anticipated turned out to be little more than a spark, with Kelsey banging a fist on the wall.

'Whatever she done, I loved her. She weren't perfect but she was my mum.'

'If you didn't kill her, what were you doing at the flat on the night she died?' he asked.

Kelsey pressed the heels of her hands into her eye sockets. 'It's complicated.'

'Try me,' said Jack.

Kelsey released her hands and blinked to clear her vision. 'I needed to tell her everything was going to be okay, that me and the babies could come home.'

'From where I'm standing, Kelsey, things didn't look okay.'

Kelsey nodded as if she understood his point. 'But I'd got it sorted, see.'

Jack held open his palms for her to continue.

'Mum was desperate to get us moved, but the housing people kept saying no, so she went to see the MP, told her all about what was going on. She said she needed proof, and Mum was just about ready to give up when I says if it's proof they need I'll get some.'

'And how were you going to do that?' asked Jack.

Kelsey shrugged. 'Get a video from Max.'

'Somehow I doubt he would just have given one to you.'

'Course not, and anyway a video of one of them other girls wouldn't have proved anything, would it?'

Lilly's pulse quickened, afraid of where this was leading.

'Who would need to be on the video?' said Jack, his voice shockingly calm.

Kelsey picked at the edge of the blanket and pulled at a thread until it began to unravel. 'Someone who would stand up and say they were underage. Say where it happened and who made them do it.'

Jack took a breath. 'And who would that be?'

When she spoke she didn't look up.

'Me.'

Before anyone else could speak, Kelsey whipped up her head, her eyes defiant. 'It's not as if I were a virgin.'

'What did your mum have to say?' asked Jack.

The defiance melted. 'She wouldn't have it, kept crying and crying, saying there had got to be another way. I told her straight, if you can think of one then let's have it. Next day she puts us all in care.'

'That must have been hard.'

The genuine sympathy in Jack's tone proved too much and tears began to trickle, unchecked, down Kelsey's cheek. 'I'd never been away from home before, not even for a night, and they wouldn't even let me see the babies. I couldn't take it, no way.'

'So what did you do?' he asked.

'I did what I had to do,' she said, her words echoing those of Max.

427

Bradbury handed Kelsey and Lilly a tissue. Until then Lilly hadn't realised that she was crying too.

'Let me get this straight, Kelsey,' said Jack. 'Max arranged for you to have sex with William Barrows and for it to be filmed.'

Kelsey opened out the tissue and hid behind it. 'If that was his name, then yeah.'

Lilly moved towards Kelsey but Jack shook his head. This was clearly something he needed to finish, however hard.

'Tell us what happened next.'

Kelsey lowered the tissue and began to shred it. 'I thought it would be okay, that it was something that needed to be done. I thought I could just put it behind me, but I couldn't.' She sprinkled the pieces of paper like confetti into her lap and ran her finger over her lips. 'No matter how many times I brushed my teeth I could still taste him. I tried the bleach but it didn't make me feel any cleaner. I reckon that's why Mum took the drugs, it was the only way to stop her feeling so bad.'

Kelsey looked up at Lilly. 'Will I always feel like this?'

'You need some help, love,' said Lilly.

Kelsey nodded as if this seemed reasonable. 'I couldn't get a copy of the video anyway. Max wouldn't give me one and I couldn't find one at his place to nick. It was a stupid idea really.'

She gestured to Lilly. 'Then she gave me a better one.'

'A better what?' asked Jack.

'Idea. She told me that evidence can be written

down, like statements and that, so I wrote down every-thing that had happened to us and sent it to that MP.'

When Lilly found her voice it was loud and clear. 'You wrote to Hermione Barrows?'

Kelsey nodded. 'I thought they'd have to re-house us. I thought she'd help us when she saw what I'd written.'

'You thought you'd saved the day,' said Lilly.

Kelsey smiled as though the memory warmed her. 'I was so happy I went to tell Mum.'

'What did she say?' asked Jack.

Kelsey's smile faded and her face crumpled. 'She was mad as hell, said she couldn't believe I'd sell myself like that. Said I'd let that man ruin my life. That was a bloody laugh considering what she'd done over the years. I had to get out so I went for a walk. About half an hour later I'd calmed down but she had someone in there. I thought it must be a punter so I went back to The Bushes. That's when I wrote that letter.'

'What letter?' asked Bradbury.

'Later,' said Jack.

Back at ground level Jack and Bradbury were huddled in discussion, each talking, then listening, shaking their heads then nodding. From her position at the other side of the corridor Lilly couldn't guess which way they would go. Jez and Sheba virtually sat on her to prevent her from intervening further.

'You've heard the term over-egging the pudding,' said Jez.

When they finally moved towards her their pace

was so heavy, their faces so grave, she assumed the worst. Her fears were crystallised when it was Bradbury, not Jack, who spoke.

'This isn't a decision we have taken lightly,' he said.

Lilly nodded. It was a fair decision. They had listened to Kelsey and that was as much as she could ask.

When Bradbury spoke again Lilly barely paid attention. 'But Jack is prepared to speak to the judge.'

Oh my God! Lilly wanted to pirouette across the marbled floor but restrained herself to a formal smile. 'Thank you.'

'Officer McNally,' said Jez, 'could you please summarise the dramatic events of yesterday to the court.'

Jack leaned both hands against the rail of the witness box and addressed the judge directly. 'Miss Valentine, the defendant's solicitor, was kidnapped by a Mr Max Hardy, a man whom Miss Valentine had suspected was involved in the death of Grace Brand.'

'Did you suspect him, Officer?' asked Jez.

'I certainly looked into it. He was known to the deceased and had involved her in some pretty nasty stuff.'

'Could you enlarge on that?' said Jez.

'He was making pornographic films involving children in the deceased's home. During her ordeal Miss Valentine was told by Hardy that the other person involved was a Mr William Barrows, a well-known psychiatrist, who had in fact treated the deceased when she herself was in care.'

The judge squirmed in his chair, no doubt reliving

the dinners he had eaten and jokes he had shared with a paedophile.

'I then went with Miss Valentine to Mr Barrows' clinic,' said Jack.

'For what purpose?' asked Jez.

'To arrest him and search the premises for evidence.'

'And did you find any evidence?'

'We did, or at least we would have, had Mr Barrows' wife not destroyed his entire collection of videos.'

'Then you cannot be sure what was on them,' said the judge.

Jack held his back straight. 'No, but I am convinced they contained child pornography. I doubt Mrs Barrows would have felt the need to scrap hours of nature programmes.'

Lilly recalled Hermione Barrows' reaction throughout their exchange. She had been combative towards them but without any sense of outrage. She had made no attempt to defend her husband. Nor had there been any shock, as if she'd known what sort of man her husband was. And if Hermione had known her husband was the man Kelsey had written to her about, Lilly was sure she would have alerted him to the imminent danger of discovery. In order to keep his secret he had more motive to kill Grace than anyone. The stone in the cherry was his alibi, but had anyone outside government checked it?

Lilly crept out of court as inconspicuously as a person can while simultaneously knocking over a water jug, thankfully empty and thankfully plastic. She bowed to the judge, fell into the corridor and pulled out her phone.

'NSPCC press office.'

'Hi,' said Lilly. 'My name's Jackie McNally, features editor for *Happy Living*, a new lifestyle magazine.'

'Like *OK*?' asked the chirpy press assistant.

'Exactly,' said Lilly. 'We launch in October with the usual stuff. Interviews with the cast of *Footballers' Wives*, beauty tips by Posh Spice and gossip on JLo's latest divorce.'

'JLo's getting divorced again?' The assistant was incredulous.

'Uh huh. Anyway, we've got space for a charity function and we thought we might use the dinner you held at the Grosvenor on the seventh. Was anyone there we might be interested in?'

'Oh yes. The fat one from *Big Brother*, I can't remember her name now, handed over a cheque for ten grand, and the Chancellor gave a very nice speech. We were hoping for the PM but he was busy, what with the war and everything.'

'How about the MP who's in the papers a lot at the moment, Hermione Barrows, were she and her husband there?'

'They were invited, yes, and he certainly came, but if memory serves she had to leave after half an hour, some emergency meeting or other.'

Lilly flew back into court and passed a scribbled note to Jez. He looked at it and went seamlessly back to his witness.

'Officer McNally, what did you make of Mrs Barrows' behaviour?'

Jack paused to marshal his thoughts. 'She seemed intent on not letting me have the videotapes.'

'Covering up her husband's criminal activity?'

'Yes.'

The judge leaned towards him. 'That's a very serious accusation, Mr McNally.'

Jack nodded. 'And not one I make lightly, but she made no effort to help us. When Miss Valentine pointed out what was on the tapes, she seemed to know already.'

'I need you to think very carefully before you answer my next question,' said Jez, and paused to let the gravity of it sink in. 'If I told you that on the night that Grace Brand was killed, Hermione Barrows has no alibi, would you consider her to be a suspect?'

'Yes,' said Jack, 'I would.'

'I'll be glad to get back to my patients,' said Sheba and lit a cigarette. 'At least you know where you are with the insane.'

She, Lilly and Jez waited in the street outside while the judge took counsel on what to do next. Bradbury had sent Jack to arrest Hermione and was ordering searches of her parliamentary office and surgery from his mobile. Someone had tipped off the press, who were out in force and following Bradbury's every move. Lilly smiled to herself – they couldn't possibly guess how exciting tomorrow's headlines were going to be. Bradbury gave Lilly the thumbs-up – he might be losing one high-profile case but he was jumping feet first into another.

'If the judge decides there's no case to answer, what will happen to Kelsey?' asked Jez.

'There'll need to be a Care Order. Someone has to take responsibility for her,' said Lilly.

'Leyland House will be open in a week or so,' said Sheba.

Lilly was surprised. 'That soon?'

'When Paul puts his mind to something it usually happens. He's a bit like you in that regard, Lilly,' said Sheba.

Lilly smiled at the compliment, but her self-satisfaction proved premature.

'There'll be a reopening party, you should come. Just a few drinks, nothing as depraved as Jez's chamber parties.'

She raised an eyebrow, tossed her cigarette in the road and led her brother inside by the arm.

Lilly flushed deepest crimson.

Judge Blechard-Smith took off his glasses and cleaned them thoroughly before returning them to the bridge of his nose. Lilly settled into her seat ready for the Mother of All Speeches.

The judge cleared his throat. When would these men learn to cut to the chase?

'This case has undoubtedly been extraordinarily difficult for all concerned. I myself have swum in uncharted waters from the very start. We have all had to remind ourselves repeatedly not to judge a book by its cover, but to question, challenge and measure the evidence again and again.'

He took a sip of water so tiny it could have barely wet his tongue.

'The prosecution brought this case in good faith, I am sure, and it is to the credit of the police that they have not simply ducked out but have continued to investigate new facts as they have arisen. However, when one of the officers in the case states that someone other than the defendant should be pursued for the crime with which she has been charged, I am forced to act, and to this end I recommend most strongly that the prosecution withdraw their case. What do you say, Mr Marshall?'

The barrister turned to Bradbury, who turned to Jack. It was like a pack of dominos collapsing.

'My Lord,' said Marshall, turning back, 'the prosecution agree.'

Lilly breathed a heavy sigh of relief and tried to catch Kelsey's eye, but she was staring intently at the judge. Lilly wondered if she had understood it was all over.

'As for you, young lady,' said Blechard-Smith to Kelsey. 'You have suffered a terrible ordeal and I will not try to patronise you by pretending I can guess how you feel. I only hope that you leave here knowing British justice did not fail you. Please accept my sincere best wishes for your future endeavours.'

Kelsey stifled a yawn. 'Yeah, yeah, tell it to a judge.'

The house was empty and cold. It seemed to have been not so much left as abandoned. A carton of milk stood open on the kitchen table and had begun its slow descent into cottage cheese. Two slices of bread stood erect in the toaster waiting for the golden tan they had

435

never received. The bedroom and bathroom were a jumble of discarded clothes and cosmetics, jewellery strewn across the unmade bed. The overall scene was of a burglary, but as Jack McNally ran his finger through a trail of ivory face powder he knew the signs of a hasty departure when he saw one.

'Hello,' came a voice from the hallway. 'Hermione, are you there?'

An attractive woman in her mid-twenties appeared in the doorway and let out a gasp when she saw the state of the room.

Jack flashed his badge. 'Police. Do you know where she is?'

The woman's hand went to her throat and she shook her head. 'I'm her assistant, Nancy. She didn't show up for an important meeting today and she's not answering any of her phones. I got worried and came over.'

'Have you any idea where she went?'

The woman shook her head. 'Sorry.'

Jack sighed. Hermione was long gone, probably out of the country by now.

'I told the others we weren't close or anything,' the woman was gabbling.

'Others?' Jack's tone was sharp.

'Secret service. They came this morning and took all Hermione's papers.'

Jack sat down on the edge of the bed, careless of the silk shirts beneath him.

Nancy Donaldson hurried back to the station. As she

436

reached into her bag for her ticket her fingers brushed against the stained brown envelope containing a photo-copy of the girl's handwritten statement. When Nancy first opened it two weeks ago she'd thought it was the ranting of some nut, but when the Brand story broke she'd put two and two together. At the time she'd retrieved it from Hermione's drawer and made a copy, thinking she could sell it to the papers when Kelsey was convicted. She'd never once suspected that her boss was somehow involved. She supposed she should give it to the police now Hermione had run away, but Nancy's job prospects would be a lot better if this whole saga died a death. Better to hang on to it and see what happened.

The next tube to Westminster was in three minutes, just enough time to buy two takeaway lattes, one for herself and one for the Right Honourable Member for Chichester South.

Wise or not, Lilly really needed to see her son. Not to beg him to come home but simply to fold him in her arms for just a moment.

When David answered his door, Lilly gasped. His shirt was stained with blood, all colour drained from his lips, his eyes hollow and dark.

'What's happened?' she screamed. 'Where's Sam, is he hurt?'

David muttered something incoherent, and from inside the house came a shrill cry.

Lilly pushed past her ex-husband. 'Sam? Sam?'

Her son came running to her and threw himself

into her arms. She held him for only a second before pushing him from her to check for injuries. Only when she had spun him round twice did she see his eyes shining and his wide smile.

'What's happened, Sam? Tell me, please.'

'I saw it all,' he said, breathless with excitement. 'I saw Cara having a baby.'

'It just came,' said David, who Lilly could see was in shock. 'No time to get to the hospital, no time to call the midwife. I had to do it all myself.'

'I helped,' sang Sam.

'I'm sure you did,' said Lilly, stroking his head. 'So what have you got, a brother or a sister?'

Sam's mouth opened, and so did David's. Neither spoke. Lilly shook her head in disbelief and headed up the stairs towards the crying.

The sight of Cara, crumpled and sobbing, her hair hanging in strings, should have filled Lilly with glee, but instead she helped her onto the bed and wiped her face with the nearest thing to hand, which happened to be one of David's hand-stitched shirts. She peeped at the baby and kissed Cara's head.

'You have a beautiful little girl.'

Back in the kitchen, Lilly made tea.

'Cara doesn't do carbs,' said David, his hands still trembling. 'She won't drink it with sugar.'

'Trust me, she will today,' said Lilly, and stirred in another heaped spoonful.

David took the cup and staggered out of the room, sloshing a brown trail in his wake.

'Mummy,' said Sam, his bravado vanished.

'Yes, big man.'

'I want to come home.'

Lilly's heart leaped into her mouth. 'Why's that?'

'It's too quiet here and Cara only lets us eat green stuff.'

Lilly stifled a laugh.

'Thing is,' said Sam, one eye on the door, his voice dropping to a stage whisper, 'I don't want Dad to think it's because of the baby.'

Lilly nodded solemnly and answered in hushed tones. 'Why don't you stay tonight so they don't think you legged it at the first sign of trouble, and I'll collect you in the morning.'

'Do you think they'll mind?'

They listened to the sound of the baby screaming.

'To be honest, love, I don't think they'll notice.'

The old sofa had never been so inviting. Lilly stretched out with feline contentment, a bag of Minstrels in her hand, a glass of room-temperature Merlot on the floor beside her. Kelsey had been taken back to The Bushes by Miriam until Paul Collins could take her into his care. Sam would be home tomorrow. Everything had worked out just fine, everything except . . .

When she answered the door and discovered Jack slouching in the brisk evening air she imagined herself as he must see her, dressed in an 'Axe the Poll Tax' T-shirt she'd had since university and a pair of jogging pants that hadn't seen the wash basket in several months.

'Do you want wine or are you still hung over?' she asked.

'I'll force it down.'

She handed him a glass and they settled down, Lilly on the sofa, Jack on a chair.

'Hermione's disappeared,' he said.

Lilly nodded. Tomorrow she might care but tonight she was too tired.

'Your instincts were right,' he added. 'They usually are.'

She patted the cushion next to her and he moved across the room. She put her head on his lap and he stroked her hair.

'You know,' said Jack, 'I think we should go to bed.'

He looked down at Lilly and smiled. She was fast asleep.

Read on for an exclusive extract of Helen Black's
new novel, *A Place of Safety*,
coming in 2009.

Things, as Luke Walker's mum is fond of saying, are getting out of hand.

The voices of his friends jar his ears as they stumble through some song by Lily Allen, clapping out of time urging the girl on. Tom whoops like a small child at Christmas, saliva dribbling down his chin. Charlie digs Luke in the ribs and shouts something in his ear but the words are lost in a fit of giggles. The girl is in the middle of their ramshackle circle, her laughter almost hysterical. She says something none of them can understand and spins round and round so that her skirt flares up and the boys can see her knickers. Tom reaches out to touch her. 'Yeah, baby,' he brays but the momentum makes him lose his balance. He gropes the ground and swears.

Luke feels sick. He wants to go home. He would go home but he's boarding tonight and if the House Master catches him in this state he'll be in detention for a month.

And anyway the field is spinning and he doesn't think he can stand.

'You like?' asks the girl.

Tom and Charlie applaud but Luke can't even nod his head. He doesn't like, not at all.

That night had started like any other. With prep finished and Mr Philips dealing with one of the new boys, homesick and in tears, Luke and his friends sneaked out of school to mooch around the village. They pledged how different their lives could be when they could drive. Charlie's the eldest and is getting lessons for his seventeenth but that's not for over two months. Luke should be next but every time he mentions it his parents exchange the look and talk about how many young men die in road accidents.

As the youngest of the group Tom will probably still be the first to pass his test. His Dad already lets him drive an old jeep across their land.

They wandered down to the off-licence. Luke doesn't know why they bothered because Mrs Singh knows they're all underage. Tom called her a 'fucking paki' and knocked over a rack of crisps. Luke hates it when Tom does stuff like that. They finally dragged him out with Mrs Singh threatening to call the police and there was the girl leaning against the post office window opposite.

She was one of that lot from the hostel. You could tell by the way she dressed, the way she wore her hair. And she stood like they all do, hunched in on themselves as if they trying to disappear. She was smoking what smelled like a spliff.

'Let's have some of that,' Tom shouted.

She looked startled at being spoken to and threw

what was left of her roll up into the gutter. She was about to move on when Tom dashed across the street and caught her arm.

'Do you want to earn some money?' he asked. 'Money,' he repeated and rubbed his thumb and forefinger together as if she were deaf or an imbecile. So they paid her five quid to get them some bottles of cider and headed to the park. It was built for the local kids but they're all at home on their Nintendos. Only the boarders use it when they manage to slip out. It's cold and deserted but at least they can get pissed in peace. Luke doesn't know why the girl came with them. Maybe she liked the look of Charlie who's tall and dark, and all the girls fancy him. Or maybe Tom talked her into it. He's ginger and has a big gap in his front teeth but he has a way of getting people to do what he wants. Leadership qualities his Mum calls it. Either way she came and sat on the swings. She shared their booze and they shared her grass. She said her name was Anna and Luke remembers thinking how pretty she was.

Now things are going pear shaped.

Tom has managed to pull Anna onto the ground. She's still laughing but trying to push him away.

'No, no no,' she says.

Tom mimics her accent. 'Yes, yes, yes.'

She tries to push him away but she's not very strong and Tom's the captain of the first elevens. Luke notices how tiny she is and Tom easily holds the sticks of her arms above her head. Her sweater has ridden up and Luke can see her ribs protruding through her skin.

'Come on, Tom. Leave her alone,' says Luke.

'Fuck off,' says Tom, his breath coming in hard pants. His forehead is greasy with sweat and the unmistakable bulge of his cock pushes against Tom's trouser leg.

Luke feels the acid burn of bile in his throat and tries not to retch.

The girl struggles to free herself.

'Give me a hand, Charlie,' says Tom.

Charlie seems unsure and hovers above them.

'Hold her arms,' Tom grunts. When Charlie still doesn't move Tom snarls at him.

'Hold her fucking arms, you queer.'

Charlie steals a look in Luke's direction. He's terrified of what's about to happen but more terrified of defying Tom. Luke wills him to walk away, make a joke out of the whole thing. He doesn't. He kneels above Anna's head and presses firmly on her wrists.

Luke realises now that she is screaming. Tom clamps one hand over her mouth and uses the other to pull at his flies. Luke tries to get to his feet but falls sideways and ends up flapping like a fish in a net.

Tom laughs. 'Don't worry, you'll get your turn Lukey boy.'

He thrust his hips forward and Anna's eyes shoot open. Luke feels his own sting with tears and wishes for tomorrow morning.

CHAPTER ONE

The sky outside the office window was clear. The pale autumn sun attempted to make its presence felt and Lilly longed to take her lunch time walk. She'd instituted a daily turn around Harpenden Park after a four week kidnapping case that had frazzled her mind. She found the fresh air calmed her mind and it stopped her from wolfing more than a sandwich for her lunch.

She turned her gaze back from the window to her client and sighed. Mr Maxwell was so absorbed in his story he'd failed to notice his solicitor's lack of interest.

'I simply cannot justify another penny,' he said. 'And I cannot see why she should be able to sit at home all day why I am working my socks off.'

Lilly wondered why a man with such a profound lisp would choose so many words beginning with 's' and pretended not to notice the spittle that was accumulating on his tie.

'She has three children to care for,' said Lilly, 'and they are your children.'

'We have an au pair for them.'

He fixed Lilly with eyes that bulged like marbles in

an otherwise flat face. 'You have a child, Miss Valentine, and you seem to manage to work without too much trouble.'

Lilly thought of her ridiculously complicated child-care routine involving her ex husband, friends and anyone prepared to offer a lift to school.

'What do you think she could do to earn some money?' Lilly asked.

Mr Maxwell gave a dismissive shrug. 'She used to be a model.'

Lilly tried to hide her shock. What beautiful woman would go for this unappealing specimen of manhood?

Mr Maxwell gave a tree frog blink. The sort who would be happy to sit on her fat arse all day and count his money was the obvious answer.

'As galling as it seems, Mr Maxwell, the court has ordered you to pay maintenance to your wife,' said Lilly.

'Ex wife.'

Lilly nodded. 'So you will have to pay.'

Mr Maxwell shuffled his whinging backside out of Lilly's office, his eyes pulsating like a dark star.

As he left the building she watched him limp up the road. Lisp, blinking eyes, a limp – maybe she was being too harsh on the poor man. Then a bleached blonde bounced towards him, her breasts fighting to escape. She covered his bald head in tiny kisses and squealed.

Mrs Maxwell mark two was waiting in the wings. Some men never learn.

Lilly checked her watch and groaned, realising that

her next client was due any minute. She tried to leave a gap between them but these private divorce cases always overran. These people paid by the hour so it was their funeral if they blabbed over their allotted appointment. When it came to splitting up the marital assets this lot would argue over the contents of the hoover bag.

Lilly missed her care cases. Stroppy teens who might spare you ten seconds between shop lifting in Tescos and meeting their mates in the arcade. Sometimes they didn't turn up at all but left convoluted messages about ASBOs, social workers and pregnancy tests.

God, she missed it.

She pulled a Kit Kat from her bag. Chocolate and no exercise, a double whammy.

The only thing keeping her sane was the weekly trip to Hounds Place. At least there she could do some good. Some real good.

'Might pop over there after this client,' she mused.

'Don't even think about it.'

Lilly turned to the door where the ever-scowling secretary-cum-receptionist Sheila had appeared.

'You don't even know what I was talking about,' said Lilly.

Sheila crossed her arms. 'You want to go running off to the Dogs Home.'

'It's called Hounds Place,' said Lilly. 'As you bloody well know.'

Sheila scooped up some papers fanning the floor and slid them back into their file.

'Do you keep your house as tidy as this?'

'Have you just come to annoy me or did you get bored with filing your nails and fancy a chat?'

Sheila tried to put the file back in its drawer but the runners were jammed. She pushed and pulled, the metallic groan of the drawer matching her own.

Lilly sighed. 'Do you actually want something, Sheila?'

'The powers-that-be want to take you for a drink after work,' she said, without turning around.

Lilly put her head in her hands. 'Bloody marvellous.'

'Stop whining,' said Sheila and thrust her arm into the cabinet. It disappeared like a vet's arm in a cow. 'They probably want to thank you for hard work and good attitude.'

'In my new role as advisor to the rich, ugly and divorcing, I make them shitloads of money. Good attitude is not part of the package,' said Lilly.

Sheila was now virtually inside the cabinet, her shoulder and chest lost in its recesses, her face pushed against the handle. 'I don't know why you're so miserable. It beats the bunch of no-hopers that used to come here thieving the staplers.'

'Vulnerable kids,' Lilly sniffed.

'Junkies, most of them.' said Sheila, her cheek contorted by the pressure of the metal. 'And as for those scroungers at the Dogs Home, I don't know why you bother.'

'Because it stimulates my intellect,' said Lilly. 'Something you wouldn't understand.'

At last Sheila withdrew her arm, bringing with it a battered book.

'This was stuck at the back,' she said and threw it onto Lilly's desk. *The Art of Positive Thinking*.

'Something to stimulate your intellect.'

Lilly put her head on the desk. 'Do I really have to go for a drink?'

Sheila's laugh was nothing short of cruel. 'Rupinder says it's a three line whip.'

It's been a horrid day. A nightmare. Mr Peters had balled Luke out for not paying attention in Latin. He'd said he was wasting his talents, and that it was nothing short of criminal. Luke had wanted to tell him how close to the mark he was.

During computer studies he'd surfed the net to see how long people got for rape, how old he'd be when he got out of prison. He couldn't breathe when he saw that life was an option. He'd seen a politician on the telly saying the Government were cracking down, that 'life should mean life.'

He'd bitten his lip until it bled, terrified he would burst into tears in front of the entire class.

Worse still, Tom had been acting like nothing was wrong. He'd even boasted in the common room about meeting a 'right little goer.'

The other boys had laughed at him, said he was talking bollocks.

Tom leaned over the snooker table and potted the black. 'Ask Lukey boy. He'll tell you what she was like,' he said. 'Gagging for it wasn't she?'

Luke smiled weakly, but he could still hear the girl screaming and see her wrists being held so tightly they

451

seemed to turn black-blue. A bit like the sky before a storm.

Now the bell is ringing and Luke can finally escape. Thank God he's not boarding tonight. He wants to go home, to throw himself onto his Arsenal duvet and let it all out.

Maybe he should tell his mum. Maybe she could help. Even if she can't, it might stop the whole thing running through his head like some bad film on a loop.

He sees her car parked by the cricket pitch and bolts towards it. Inside smells of clean washing and lavender water.

His mum smiles. 'Had a nice day, love?'

He can't answer and squeezes his eyes shut.

'Is everything alright, love?' asks his mum.

He stirs his pasta with a limp wrist.

'Luke?' her voice is so very gentle.

He feels wrung out like a damp cloth, all the moisture down the sink.

She lifts his chin and looks into his eyes. 'You would tell me if something was wrong?'

He sees in her lined face, a lifetime of wiped noses and birthday teas. This isn't a broken window or a bad school report. How can he tell her what he has been part of, what he has done? She can't make it better. No one can.

He forces some words out. 'I'm just tired.'

'You look peaky,' she says and presses a cool palm against his forehead. 'You're not hot but you're obviously sickening for something.'

He pushes his bowl away. 'Yeah. I feel sick.'

Relief plays at the corners of his mother's mouth. This is her territory.

'Better lie down, love,' she says. 'Will you be alright while I collect your sister?'

The thought of Jessie, a year younger than Luke, fills his mind. What if some boys took her to a park . . . held her down . . .

He runs from the room, his hands over his mouth, acid bile running through his fingers.

His bedroom is spinning and Luke concentrates on a small brown water stain on the ceiling.

'I'll be twenty minutes,' his mum calls from the bottom of the stairs. 'How about I call into Waitrose for Lucozade?'

Luke doesn't answer.

When he hears the front door close he lets the tears spill. He curls into a ball and weeps, snot pooling under his nose, sliding onto his lips, until it becomes clear what he has to do. He wipes his eyes on the back of his hands and packs a bag.